Prais~
Shepher~

"W. L. Dyson's remarkable storytelling ability and knowledge of the treacherous world of bounty hunting pours across every page of *Shepherd's Fall*. Suspense, intrigue, and redemption dominate this exceptional storyline. A highly recommended read!"

>—MARK MYNHEIR, homicide detective and author of *The Night Watchman*

"The story of a family of bounty hunters, *Shepherd's Fall* held me captive way past my bedtime. However, it was worth every sleepless moment to join W. L. Dyson's beautifully flawed characters not only in the recovery of a fugitive, but in finding God in the journey. So this is how all those kids feel while awaiting the next book in a gripping series…"

>—TAMARA LEIGH, author of *Splitting Harriet* and *Faking Grace*

"Gut-tightening, palm-dampening, jaw-dropping suspense as only W. L. Dyson can do. *Shepherd's Fall* delivers. In spades."

>—JOHN ROBINSON, speaker, teacher, and author of *Until the Last Dog Dies, When Skylarks Fall,* and *To Skin a Cat.*

"*Shepherd's Fall* is a great book that leaves its mark after the final page. Tautly written and quickly paced, it offers everything I need for a good read that leaves me thinking about the characters…and about myself."

>—HANNAH ALEXANDER, author of *A Killing Frost*

"Once again, Dyson delivers a powerful tale that gets better with each heart-pounding turn of the page."

>—CRESTON MAPES, author of *Nobody*

"*Shepherd's Fall* is great suspense with wonderful characters. A rip-roaring beginning to a great series."

>—GAYLE ROPER, author of *Fatal Deduction*

"W. L. Dyson has created page-turning suspense in *Shepherd's Fall* that keeps the reader guessing to the final pages. A unique blend of characters enriches this well-woven story. I look forward to more in this series."

—SHARON K. SOUZA, author of *Lying on Sunday* and *Every Good & Perfect Gift*

"If you like the breathless pace of the TV series *24*, you'll love the action, suspense, plot-twists, and family drama of *Shepherd's Fall*. I couldn't put it down, and I can't wait for Dyson's next release!"

—LINDA WINDSOR, award-winning author of The Piper Cove Chronicles series and The Fires of Gleannmara series

"*Shepherd's Fall* captures the reader with vivid characters, a relentless pace, and a heart-pounding conclusion that explodes like an emotional roller coaster."

—TERRY BRENNAN, author of *The Sacred Cipher*

"W. L. Dyson's *Shepherd's Fall* is a fast-paced, suspenseful tale full of twists and turns that will keep readers flipping the pages until the last sentence. Dyson is a master at penning heart-wrenching emotion laced into action, with a strong thread of the Father's redeeming love interwoven into the prose. This is a 'don't miss' series. I've fallen in love with the characters at Prodigal Recovery Agency and anxiously await the next installment."

—ROBIN CAROLL, author of the Bayou Series (*Bayou Justice, Bayou Corruption, Bayou Judgment, Bayou Paradox, Bayou Betrayal,* and *Blackmail*)

"*Shepherd's Fall* will not disappoint anyone looking for action, danger, and suspense. This novel is a true page-turner. *Good news: The book was outstanding. Bad news: We have to wait for more.*"

—GLENN L. RAMBO, twenty-year police veteran in New Jersey, currently holding the rank of lieutenant

Shepherd's Fall

A Novel

W. L. DYSON

WATERBROOK
PRESS

SHEPHERD'S FALL
PUBLISHED BY WATERBROOK PRESS
12265 Oracle Boulevard, Suite 200
Colorado Springs, Colorado 80921

All Scripture quotations, unless otherwise indicated, are taken from the King James Version.

ISBN 978-1-4000-7473-0
ISBN 978-0-30745-810-0 (electronic)

Published in the United States by WaterBrook Multnomah, an imprint of The Doubleday Publishing Group, a division of Random House Inc., New York.

WATERBROOK and its deer colophon are registered trademarks of Random House Inc.

Library of Congress Cataloging-in-Publication Data
Dyson, Wanda L.
    Shepherd's fall / W. L. Dyson.— 1st ed.
      p. cm.— (Prodigal Recovery Agency ; book one)
    ISBN 978-1-4000-7473-0
  1. Bounty hunters—Fiction. 2. Kidnapping—Fiction. I. Title.
    PS3604.Y77S54 2009
    813'.6—dc22

                       2008049857

Printed in the United States of America
2009 — First Edition

10 9 8 7 6 5 4 3 2 1

In memory of Daniel Isaac Byrd
September 2, 1990–December 13, 2008
In our hearts and in the Father's embrace

———✦———

This novel is about siblings, and I want to dedicate it to mine—Buddy Byrd, Jane Warne, Donna Ruel, Lenny Byrd, and Joe Byrd.

And to my brother-in-law Roger Ruel, and sisters-in-law Lois and Liz Byrd.

I love you all and am eternally grateful that, although we were all prodigals, the Lord welcomed us all home.

Last Will and Testament
for Roswell Shepherd

—◁◆▷—

To my firstborn, Nickolas Samuel Shepherd: I leave my
Glock—use it with wisdom and mercy. I leave my grandfather's pocket watch—redeem your time wisely. And I
leave one-third of Prodigal Fugitive Recovery—may you
continue to be the leader you were born to be. I leave in
your care your mother, your younger siblings, and the
family business. I know you'll serve them all to the best
of your ability.

Prologue

*G*ood news—*I have my fugitive cornered. Bad news—I don't have any backup.*

The chase had encompassed forty-three hours with no sleep, very little food, and too many cups of cold coffee to count. It had crossed one state and three county lines and twice as many jurisdictions, only to circle back to within three miles of where it all started. And it looked like it was going to end at an abandoned house near Lisbon, Maryland.

Now fugitive recovery agent Nick Shepherd just had to decide whether to wait until his team arrived, or go in after Richie Carver on his own.

The old house looked as if it hadn't been occupied for years. The whole structure was leaning on its foundation, the roof had holes in it, all the glass in the windows had been broken out, and weeds tangled across the yard nearly waist-high, hiding anything from old tires to snakes and groundhog holes.

He'd have to go in low and slow.

Glancing over at the front porch, he discounted it immediately. Half the boards were gone; the rest didn't look like they were too far behind. One wrong step and he'd be risking a broken leg or worse. His best bet was to enter one of the windows along the side of the house—

the same way Richie had gone in—and to pray that Richie wasn't standing there ready to shoot him as he climbed through.

When a fugitive jumps bail and disappears, fugitive recovery agents suit up and go hunting. They are experts at tracking and pursuing and have powers even local police don't have. Relentless and more than a little fearless, they sometimes have to run a fugitive into the ground. But a cornered animal can be far more dangerous than one on the run.

Richie Carver was as nasty as they came. He and his brother, Jon, were known for drugs, prostitutes, illegal gambling, and who knew what else. If it was illegal and lucrative, they probably had their hands on it. Jon was the brains of the operation, preferring to stay close to the office and the money. Richie, on the other hand, was the brawn. His job was to make sure that no one crossed Jon. The problem was, Richie had gone beyond breaking legs and busting heads to straight-up murder. And after he jumped bail, he became Nick's problem. Nick and the rest of the Prodigal Fugitive Recovery agents.

Nick glanced at his watch again. It had been nearly seven minutes since Richie had disappeared through that window. He knew better than most that the worst thing a bounty hunter could do was run into a situation like this without backup, but sometimes he had to break the rules.

He keyed the radio on his shoulder. "Conner. Come in."

It took a couple of seconds, but he heard his second-in-command's voice crackle through in his earpiece. "Here, Boss. What's going down?"

"Richie's run into an abandoned house. Where are you?"

"Rafe and I are ten, maybe fifteen out, Boss. Hold them horses."

"No can do, Conn."

"Wait for us, Boss. We're close."

"He's been in there almost ten minutes. Can't take a chance on him getting away."

"Don't do it, Boss. I've got my foot to the floor. Hang on."

Nick stared at the house. He figured the best and worst that could happen and then keyed the radio again. "Just make sure you're here before it turns ugly."

He had just pulled the slide on his Glock when his cell phone vibrated. Assuming it was one of the members of his team, he flipped it open. "Yeah?"

"Daddy?"

"Krys? Honey, I'm right in the middle of something. Can I call you back?"

"Sure. I was just calling to say I love you and also to find out if maybe you want to go out for pizza tonight. Mom's working late."

"Sure, baby. I'll give you a call in a couple hours."

"Okay. Love you, bye."

"Love you, bye." He used his thigh to close the phone and then shoved it down inside his shirt pocket, protected inside his Kevlar vest.

He checked his Taser to make sure it was fully charged and put it back in his thigh holster, then eased up to a low crouch and began to make his way from the edge of the woods to the house. He nearly tripped twice but managed to avoid twisting his ankle on the pile of lumber hidden in the weeds and the gopher hole on the other side of it.

He thought he might have seen a black snake slithering off near an old wheelbarrow, but he didn't look too closely. He wasn't exactly fond of snakes, so he resorted to the childhood philosophy that if he didn't see it, maybe it didn't see him.

Easing up along the side of the house, he glanced furtively into the window. Living room. White plaster walls yellowed to beige and cracked with age. Light fixtures pulled from the ceiling. Wires dangling.

Wood floors. And dust thick enough to leave footprints heading toward the back of the house.

Tucking his gun down in the holster, he prayed that Richie was somewhere else in the house and would stay there long enough for Nick to get through the window and pull his gun back out. He was halfway through the window when he saw the other footprints. Two pair, small, sneakers or athletic shoes. Kids. Probably teenagers. Were they here now? Or were they remnants from a previous night? Nick moved a little faster, scrambling through the broken window, snagging his shirt.

Then he heard a scream. Female. Young. And in terror.

Yanking his shirt away from the glass, he pulled his gun, gripping it tightly as he followed the tracks through the house. At the kitchen door, he flattened against the wall before tilting his head to do a quick look into the room. Empty. He stepped into the kitchen, sweeping his gun out in front of him as he noted the bare walls, the missing countertops, the cabinets hanging lopsided on each side of the window. Then he spotted the basement door.

This is as close to Russian roulette as you can get.

Crouching down, he descended the dark stairway. He could smell the dust, decay, and mold mixed with something far more familiar—sweat and fear.

The wood creaked beneath his feet, and he knew then that there would be no element of surprise. Best just to go charging in and hope for the best.

The girl was whimpering now, like a wounded animal. Nick tried to narrow in on the sound of her voice. He reached the bottom of the stairs and took a deep breath before stepping out and turning, gun firmly in both hands and straight out in front him.

There was a small window at ground level, and the sun, low in the sky, was slipping through the window, guiding Nick to Richie and the girl. She was even younger than he had imagined; maybe fourteen, fifteen tops. Her long, dark hair had been pulled back in a ponytail, but now most of it had come loose and was falling across her face. Richie was standing directly behind her, a grin on his face and a knife to her throat.

Bad news—there's a hostage. Good news—Richie doesn't have a gun.

And then he realized that she looked far too familiar. His stomach twisted. Lisa Jewell. His daughter's best friend since first grade. What in heaven's name was Lisa doing *here*?

A flood of memories came over him. He remembered her and Krystal, swinging in the backyard, dressing and undressing their Barbie dolls, running through the house, their pigtails flying. There was one birthday party… He couldn't recall which, but Lisa had cried through most of it. Nick's wife, Jessica, had finally noticed and, after taking Lisa aside and talking to her, found out that Lisa had never experienced the joy of a big party to celebrate her birthday. Jessica then went to great lengths to plan a huge surprise party for Lisa on her next birthday. Lisa's parents hadn't even bothered to show up. From then on, the girl had practically become their second daughter.

Stay focused, man. Stay focused on the moment. Forget it's Lisa. Forget you know her. Just get her out alive the way you would any hostage.

"Knew you'd be coming for me, bounty hunter."

"Managed to get one thing right, Richie. Now drop the knife and make it two in a row."

"Can't do that." Richie pulled the girl up tighter against his body. "Can't go to jail. I'll die there."

"You'll die here if you don't let her go." A quick glance at the floor next to Richie and Nick saw a boy, sprawled in the dust, eyes open and unseeing, blood pooling around his head.

A young life gone. Ended. Why? Because he and his girl were probably just looking for a place to hang out. Maybe to sit and talk about their dreams and their futures. To hold hands and sneak a shy kiss from time to time. Nick clenched his teeth, pointed to the boy's body, and looked Richie in the eye. "That was a mistake, Carver. A big mistake."

"Nah. Just one less problem for me. Drop the gun, bounty hunter, or I'll kill her now."

Lisa emitted a high-pitched wail as Richie dragged her sideways, attempting to skirt around Nick and reach the stairs. "No, please. Don't. Don't let him kill me!"

Without a doubt, if Richie made it to the top of those stairs, that girl was dead.

Nick raised his hands slowly, holding the gun out and away from Richie. "Let her go, Richie. She doesn't have to get hurt in all this. It's between you and me."

Richie shook his head as sweat rolled down his face, putting a sheen on days of beard growth. Nick could smell the man's body odor, pungent, as it soaked his clothes. "Can't do that. You stay back and I'll let her go as soon as I get away."

Nick slowly set his gun down on a bench. "Not alive, you won't. I know you well enough, Richie. We've been through this dance before, haven't we? You're not a man who keeps his word."

Richie licked his lips, his eyes darting from the stairs to Nick and back to the stairs. Nick could almost hear Richie figuring out how many steps, how much time, could he make it? Would Nick reach him first? Weighing the odds. Working the angles.

"You can't make it, Richie."

For two days, Nick and his men had been running Richie into the ground, keeping him moving, never letting him stop to sleep or eat or rest. Nick had learned the technique from his days riding horses. If you had a horse that didn't want to get caught, you ran it until it begged you to catch it. It sometimes worked with fugitives too. And the ones that didn't beg to get caught usually slowed down enough to get cornered, whether they wanted to or not.

Richie tightened the knife against Lisa's throat, and her whimpering stopped as she held her breath. A tiny trickle of blood eased down away from the knife. Nick shifted his stance, widening his arms to distract Richie from noticing that he was also moving his feet a little farther apart.

"Come on, Richie. You're in deep enough without making things worse."

The man choked, but Nick wasn't sure if it was the dust in the air or his frustration with the situation. "Can't get no worse, bounty hunter. If I go down, what's it matter if it's one body or two? Or three? Death row is death row, ain't it?"

"The more bodies, the less chance of life without parole."

"Like I'm interested in that." Richie stepped back. Lisa was up on her toes now, her feet stretching against her little white sneakers, her eyes begging him to save her.

Boom!

The sound of wood on wood crashing upstairs had Richie jumping. The blade sliced against Lisa's throat, and her scream gurgled. Richie realized what he'd done and, in one wild moment of irrational thought, shoved her at Nick and ran for the stairs.

Nick caught Lisa with one arm and pulled her up against his body as he pivoted on his left leg and spun out with his right leg, clipping Richie across the calves, knocking him off his feet. Richie's head hit the concrete with a sickening *thunk*. He groaned and rolled, slowly trying to get up. Nick would have loved to inflict a few more kicks and punches to knock Richie out, but there was no time. He whipped out his Taser and zapped him. Richie jerked and then sprawled, shaking and trembling as the voltage racked through him.

"And don't move."

Slowly, Nick lowered Lisa to the ground. Her eyes locked with his, and he knew time was running out fast. He hit the radio on his shoulder. "Conn? I'm in the basement of the house. Richie is down. Got a girl hurt bad. Knife to the throat. Bring the medical kit and call for an ambulance."

"On it."

Nick quickly unbuttoned his shirt and yanked it off, then folded and pressed it against the girl's wound. "You just hang in there, sweetheart. Help is on the way."

She reached up and touched his hand, her lips quivering. He could see her trying to say his name.

He wrapped his fingers around hers, squeezing lightly, hoping to give her the strength to stay with him until the ambulance arrived. "I'm sorry I didn't get here sooner, Lisa."

Her tears spilled over, and it wrenched his heart. "I'm so sorry. But you're safe now. No one can hurt you anymore. I promise."

She squeezed his hand again, but this time, it was so slight he almost wondered if he'd imagined it.

It couldn't have been more than a few minutes before Nick heard Rafe and Conner's heavy-booted thuds coming down the stairs, but it seemed like an hour.

" 'Bout time," he said.

Conner dropped down next to him and opened the medical kit. Rafe stood over the fugitive. "Richie's stirring."

Nick grabbed the gauze pads from Conner and used them to replace the shirt. "Cuff 'im. And if he complains, stun him again."

By the time the ambulance crew arrived, Nick's hands were covered with the girl's blood, but she was still alive. He saw the gratitude in her eyes. And the sadness. She may have been a sweet, innocent girl an hour ago, but since then, she'd seen her boyfriend murdered, had been assaulted by an escaped convict, and had her throat cut. Nick knew that even if she survived, the sadness in her eyes would deepen into a haunted echo of memories she would never be able to outrun fast enough or bury deep enough.

Richie glared at Nick as two police officers led him, handcuffed, to a squad car. "I'm going to beat this, bounty hunter. I'm going to get out, and the first thing I'm going to do is hurt you. And you know how?"

One of the officers shoved Richie in the center of his back. "Shut up and get in, Richie."

Richie ignored the command. "I'm going to find that sweet little girl of yours, bounty hunter. And I'm going to hurt her real bad. You want me to tell you how?"

The police officer, a friend of Nick's from his days on the force, smacked Richie's head against the top of the vehicle. "I said, shut up!" He shoved Richie into the squad car before Richie could finish his threat.

Rafe held out his hand to Conner. "Got the keys? I'll take the SUV and follow them back to lockup. Make sure we get credit for his capture."

Nick glanced up at his two best employees. Matt Conner was a former bouncer, former professional wrestler, and Nick's right-hand man. Conn was sharp, dedicated, as tough as duct tape, and knew the business inside out. When a takedown went sour, there was no one he'd rather have at his back than Conner.

Then there was Rafe. Half the size of Conner, Rafael Constanza was a thirty-nine-year-old former police officer who Nick lured over to fugitive recovery after a shootout where Rafe had taken a bullet to the face. Even with a jagged scar across his face, he was the kind of guy who could charm any woman of any age at any time.

And once again, they were getting the job done, oblivious to the fact that Nick was fully aware they were trying to give him some time to process what had just happened inside that house. Process and deal. How many times had he done the same for them? And something in Conn's face told him that the news wasn't good.

Conner tossed Rafe the keys. "Meet you back at the office." Then he turned to Nick, who was sitting on the hood of his vehicle, wiping the blood from his hands. "You okay?"

Nick took in a deep breath and held it for a second, gearing up for what he already suspected but had to ask. "How is she?"

Conner shook his head. "I'm sorry. She's gone."

"You drive." Nick slid off the hood as the fatigue dragged at him.

Conner nodded and opened the driver's door. "You should have waited for me, Boss."

"No. I should have gone in sooner. Maybe if I had…"

"But you didn't know about the kids before you went in." Conner started up the engine and snapped his seat belt. "You always tell us—"

"Never go in alone. Always wait for backup. I know." Nick turned and looked out the window. He didn't want to be reminded that things could have come out differently. It would haunt him anyway. His father had warned him a thousand times about his rash, impulsive behavior. He always ignored the warning, and now it had come back to smack him in the face. How was he supposed to look his daughter in the eyes tonight and explain to her that her best friend was dead and that it was his fault?

1

Eight months later
Monday, 1:00 p.m.
Sinai Hospital, Baltimore, Maryland

She was dying. It haunted her like a specter, dogging her every step, her every thought. Okay, everyone was dying, but she could actually see the ticking clock and the sand running through the hourglass. *How long do I have to live?*

For weeks Annie McNamara had been watching the people all around her, thinking how unfair it was that the only thing they were worried about was what to order for lunch. She wondered if she would ever be able to stroll down a street or visit the Inner Harbor with little more on her mind than a casual lunch with friends or a new pair of shoes.

Today, walking through the lobby of the hospital, she looked into the faces of those coming and going and realized that she wasn't the only one suffering in the world. She wasn't the only one who was thinking about death.

Yet even though she was surrounded by others just like her, she was still alone. They were all too wrapped up in their own misery, their own pain, and their own verdicts to see the pain in anyone else. Annie knew that they were just like her, wondering why it was happening to them and feeling as if they had a losing ticket in life's lottery.

"Hi, Annie." Helene was seventy-two and a widow. She volunteered at the hospital and served faithfully behind that reception desk every day, five and sometimes six days a week.

Annie slowed down as she passed the desk, letting one hand trail across the cool surface. "Good morning, Helene. How are you today?"

"Blessed, as always." Helene's smile was as wide as the white wig she wore and as firmly in place. "You have a wonderful day."

"You too." Annie replied as she headed for the elevators.

"Annie! How are you doing?" One of the two nurses bustling by stopped for a second. "We miss not seeing you in here all the time, but we're glad you don't have to be. A final checkup with Dr. Burdine today?"

"Something like that," she replied and punched the Up button even though it was already lit. "How's your little boy?"

"Doing much better, thanks. He finally made a friend at the new school and never asks about the old school at all."

Annie fought to give the nurse a little smile. "That's great. I knew he'd settle in quick enough. He's such a good kid."

"Well, you take care." The nurses moved off.

"You too." Annie stared up at the panel and watched the elevator's progress to the lobby. What did it say when you knew more people at your local hospital than you did in your own apartment building?

The elevator dinged, and the doors opened. Annie waited for everyone to exit and then stepped in and pushed the button for the fifth floor. Oncology.

For three years she had been battling to stay alive. She'd quit her job at the catering business to do data entry at her dad's company just so she could come and go to doctors' appointments, stay on his hospitalization plan, and have the freedom to be as sick as she needed to be without worrying about losing her job.

She had lost weight along with her long red hair. Then came the remission. The family had celebrated. Little by little, she'd regained her strength, her hair, and her hope. She had been about to call the catering company to see if she could get her job back when she started feeling bad again. Another series of tests. Another round of doctors' visits. Another block of sleepless nights.

She stepped up to the counter and waited while the nurse finished her phone call. "Hi, Annie. Dr. Burdine will be back from his rounds in just a few minutes. You can wait in his office."

She wandered around his office for nearly ten minutes before settling in front of his window and staring out at the street below. There was nothing in his office that she hadn't seen more times than she'd wanted to. The degrees on the wall framed in oak to match the desk and file cabinet. The pictures on the floating shelves of his kids, his dog, his boat, his wife, his golfing buddies at some tournament. She knew this office as well as she knew her own bedroom. Maybe even better.

The door finally opened, and Dr. Burdine stepped in, his glasses perched on top of his head, his eyes on the chart in his hands. He was a small man, barely five foot seven, with a thick shock of gray hair and twinkling blue eyes. It was those blue eyes that compelled her to trust him time and time again. When she wanted to give up, he would pin her with those eyes and dare her to make all his efforts a waste of time.

But his eyes weren't twinkling today. They were bright with concern, but heavy with the bad news she knew was coming.

"Hi, Doctor. What's the scoop?"

Dr. Burdine pulled out the chair behind his desk and sat down, setting the chart aside. He folded his hands on top of the desk and nodded toward the visitor chair across from him. "Why don't you have a seat?"

"I'd rather stand, if you don't mind. I have a feeling I won't be doing much standing in the future."

"I'm not going to lie to you, Ann."

Annie. Please call me Annie. Nothing bad ever happens when they call me Annie.

"Tell me."

He reached up and lifted his glasses off his head and folded them gently. "No donor match."

"I see." She turned and stared out the window again. Her worst fears were being realized. It surprised her that she could feel as numb as she did. She was still standing up. Still breathing. Still thinking. Death was knocking at her door, and she was still capable of talking. She would have thought she'd melt into a puddle on the floor.

"Ann, I'm sorry. I was really optimistic this time, but we've checked both your parents and your cousins, and it didn't work out. I've got you on the nationwide donor list, but I've already explained how crucial time is now. We can't count on that. We can pray for it, but we can't count on it."

"I know." There was one last chance for her. Just one. And it was far from a sure thing. Finally she walked away from the window to stand behind the visitor's chair, resting her hands on the back. "What if I had a sister?"

He leaned back in his chair, folding his hands over his stomach and giving her that little half smile that she'd seen so many times over the years. A little bit of amusement, a whole lot of patience. "That would change things dramatically, but I think your parents are a little old to think about having another child this late in life. And honestly, I don't think we have nine months."

"What if she were a twin sister?"

As he stared at her for a long moment, she saw the frown forming, dragging at the corners of his lips. "Ann—"

"Her name is Barbara. She was born three minutes after I was."

He jerked forward, his hands gripping the front of the desk. "What? Why didn't you tell me this?"

"Because I don't exactly know where Barbara is." Annie stepped around and slowly eased down into the chair.

"You have to find her."

Annie reached up and combed her fingers through her hair, fighting back the tears, but they escaped her efforts and slid down her cheeks. Her mind argued vehemently. *It's all a huge mistake! I'm in remission! The cancer is gone. This is all a big misunderstanding. I can't find Barbara. She doesn't want to have anything to do with any of us. It's all too hard. Tell me I'm okay. Please tell me I can go back to my life now.*

"The last time we heard from her, she had been arrested for prostitution and wanted Dad to bail her out of jail. He refused. Told her she had to live with the consequences of her choices."

"But that's your father. We're talking about you, here." He picked up a box of tissues and held them out to her. She pulled a couple out and wiped at her tears.

"Barb called me too. I didn't have the money to help her. I was still in culinary school and working full time and barely had enough to keep my car running. I don't think she believed me." She took a deep, cleansing breath. "But if she's my last hope, I'll try to find her."

Dr. Burdine sat quietly for a few moments before finally reaching for a tissue. Then he started wiping his glasses. "I wish you'd told me this sooner."

"Meaning?"

He slipped his glasses on and tossed the tissue into the wastebasket. "We're down to a matter of a month, Ann. Maybe two. Maybe not even that long. You need to find her fast."

——◦——

Monday, 3:15 p.m.
Annapolis, Maryland, suburb

"Come on out, Alan. You can't escape." Nick Shepherd eased down to look into the little door that led to a crawlspace under the house, ignoring the protest from his knees. Nothing worked as well at forty-two as it had when he was twenty. Or even thirty. "You can't run anymore, Alan. Why make this any harder than it has to be?"

Alan Allerton had been arrested for assault with a deadly weapon, possession with intent to sell, and possession of stolen guns. He'd bailed out with Kline Bail Bonds and then proceeded to run. So Harvey Kline had called Nick and his team in to track down Alan and bring him in.

At the top of a small set of concrete steps with an aluminum overhang, which led to the house above the crawlspace, a screen door opened and a tiny woman in her seventies stuck her head out. "What are you doing in my yard? Scat! Go on! Get out before I call the police!"

Nick held up the badge hanging around his neck. "It's okay, ma'am. There's a fugitive hiding beneath your house. Just go on back in and lock the door."

"Oh, dear." She disappeared, the door slamming.

Conner knelt down in front of the crawlspace door, opposite Nick.

"Alan, listen up. If you make me come in there, I will Taser you and then haul you out by your heels, letting you eat that dirt the whole way."

"I don't want to go to jail!"

"Well then, you should have shown up for court." Conner looked up at Nick and shook his head.

"I didn't know about a court date, I swear."

Nick holstered his gun. "Then come on out. We'll call Harvey, and he can see about getting this straightened out with the courts and get you bailed out again."

"Yeah?"

"Yeah."

A few seconds later, Alan crawled out from under the house, covered in dirt and grime. He was thin and wiry, and while the top of his head barely reached Conner's chin, there was a high-octane energy humming through him strong enough to make him appear larger.

Conner stood up and stepped back, giving Alan room to get all the way out and stand up.

As soon as Alan was on his feet, he took off running again.

"I'm going to hurt this guy," Conner muttered as he headed off in pursuit.

Nick stayed right behind Conner, trying to see how best to cut their fugitive off before he ran them all into the ground. But luck was one step ahead of him. As Alan went to jump another fence, a Doberman came lunging out of his doghouse, barking with that one-more-step-and-I'll-eat-you show of teeth that had Alan flailing backward off the fence and landing on his backside.

Scrambling to his feet, he glanced over his shoulder at them and then sprinted off to the right. He made it about six feet. Nick aimed his

Taser and shot. Alan jumped in place, danced sideways, and then hit the ground.

Alan screamed as he curled up on the ground. "You hurt me!"

Conner, breathing hard from the chase, flipped him on his stomach and handcuffed him. "You'll get over it."

Nick holstered the Taser gun and leaned over Alan. "Now why did you have to go and do that? I thought we had this settled all nice and gentlemanlike."

"That hurts! That hurts!"

"Not as bad as it would have had I used the Glock instead," Nick reminded him as he keyed his mike. "Rafe, where are you?"

The third member of the Prodigal team tapped Nick on the shoulder. "Right behind you."

Rafe stepped up and helped Conner haul Alan to his feet. Alan let his knees buckle, crumbling to the ground to keep from having to walk. With Conner hauling him from under one arm and Rafe under the other, they half-carried, half-walked him back to the truck.

"Thought he was going to run me into the ground," Conner muttered as he finished strapping Alan into their vehicle. "I'm getting too old for this."

Nick just laughed as he slapped Conner on the back. "You love it and you know it."

After processing Alan at the station, Nick dropped Rafe and Conner off and headed home. Knowing there wouldn't be a thing at the house to eat, he swung by Panda Delights and picked up some General Tso's chicken and a couple of egg rolls. After paying for his food, he was on his way back out to his SUV when his cell phone rang. He flipped it open. "Shepherd."

"Mr. Shepherd. This is Paul Overton again. I was just wondering if you had reconsidered my client's offer."

Every once in a while, Nick got calls from a lawyer named Overton offering the same deal: bury the paperwork on a bond recovery and get paid big. All he had to do was comply. End of story. Everyone happy. Money in the bank and all that. Paul Overton's client had been persistently offering Nick a retainer of $125,000 to look the other way.

Nick opened his door and slid in behind the wheel, setting his food on the passenger seat. "I'm going to tell you the same thing I tell you every time you call. No. I don't operate that way."

"You sure? I know that your business is about to go under. Is that what you want? All you have to do is look the other way on a couple of skips and you stay in business. Don't you think it would be worth it?"

"Not to me. Why don't you tell me who your client is?" As if he didn't know. Whenever any of Jon Robinson Carver's people got into trouble, Jon sent in his lawyer, Paul Overton, to handle the legalities. What Nick was more curious about was who Jon wanted to protect. Richie had been sentenced twenty-five to life for murder and was safely behind bars. Sure, Lester and one of Jon's hookers was on Nick's radar, but this was way too much for that. It had to be someone farther up in his operation. But who?

"I'm afraid I'm not at liberty to do that."

Of course not. "Well, I'm not at liberty to accept your offer. You have a nice day, and by the way…lose my phone number."

"But—"

Nick hung up, but Jon Carver's increased pressure to comply continued to nag at him. Something was up. Nick just had to figure out what it was.

Monday, 8:40 p.m.
Baltimore City Correctional Center

The prison's visitor area was as dismal and depressing as the rest of the building. Gray walls, gray floors, gray and black plastic tables, and gray-clad guards with watchful glances. Even the children, on the rare visit to see Daddy, were subdued and nervous.

Cutter Thorne looked over his shoulder to make sure no one was close enough to overhear, then leaned forward, his voice little more than a harsh whisper. "I want it to go down perfect, you understand? No mistakes. Make sure you're in place long before we get there. Just in case they decide to move me any earlier."

The woman reached back and swept her hair up into a ponytail and then let it fall again. "I got it, lover. You don't have to keep going over this a million times."

He frowned, glaring at her. "Don't get cute. I've been planning this for a very long time. I just don't want anything to go wrong. We won't get a second chance at this."

She tilted her head and gave him a long stare. "I got it. We got it. Everything is going to go perfect. Trust me."

A guard walked over, his hand on his club. "Time's up, Cutter. Let's go."

Cutter glanced up at the clock on the wall. "We got twenty more minutes."

"I said time's up. That means you move *now*."

Cutter stood up and glanced back at the woman. "I'll see you later."

"Count on it," she replied softly.

———◦———

Monday, 8:55 p.m.
Towson, Maryland

The house was dark when Nick pulled up into the driveway and killed the engine. Even after three years, it still jarred him to come home to his parents' house instead of his own, and for no one to be there waiting for him when he arrived. His father had died, his mother was in a nursing home with Alzheimer's, and his wife had divorced him. He still wasn't sure which of the three hurt him the most.

In the kitchen he grabbed a Mountain Dew out of the fridge and settled in the guest room to eat.

At one time the room had been the bedroom he and his brother, Steven, had shared growing up. When Nick had married and Steven had gone off to college, Mom turned it into a sitting room where she could watch television, sew, or work on her scrapbooks while Dad watched golf and basketball out in the living room.

Nick hadn't changed a thing when he'd moved back in. His mother's sewing machine was tucked in the corner, covered with dust and stacks of fabrics. Her scrapbook supplies were stored in little plastic bins on top of a short bookcase across from the daybed. There was a small television on a stand in the corner, and he turned it to a news channel but didn't pay much attention to it. It was background noise and nothing more. Something to fill the silence and make him feel less alone.

Pulling the tab on his Dew, he glanced over at the family pictures his mother had hung on the wall above the bookcase. Steven in his cap and gown, grinning; he'd just earned his second degree. Marti, his sister, at sixteen, dressed up in her first formal gown and standing next to

Nick's friend, Michael, who had offered to take her when her boyfriend dumped her three days before the prom. Nick with Jessica in front of their first home, holding two-year-old Krystal in his arms.

Back then, he had believed that his life would end up just like his father's—happily married until death with a loving family and a fulfilling career.

So much for those dreams.

When the phone rang, he pulled it out, tucked it under his chin, and reached down to untie his boots. "Shepherd."

"O'Shea." Michael laughed. "Where are you?"

"Home, why?"

"Color me surprised. You're in early tonight."

Nick looked over at the clock on the wall, the one with the little ducks that he and his siblings had given their mother on some Mother's Day. According to the ducks, it was just after ten. "Well, not everyone can keep banker's hours."

"That's because not everyone was smart enough to become a banker. Hey, the reason I'm calling is that the loan department is meeting in the morning about your business loan. I should know something by nine."

Nick felt relief stir. He toed off his boots and then set them aside. "You'll call me and let me know?"

"You might as well come on in. If it's approved, I'll need you to sign the papers so we can set up the credit line."

"Works for me. I'll be there around nine."

"I'll be waiting. See you in the morning."

Nick closed the phone and set it down on the tray table next to his food. *Wonder what Carver will try next, now that money isn't going to be a problem.*

It was amazing how fast good news could change a mood. He turned up the television and listened to a talking head explain why the president's plan couldn't work, regardless of how good it sounded.

"That's just because your party didn't think of it," Nick muttered as he stabbed a piece of chicken.

When his stomach was full, he turned off the television and headed out through the kitchen and into the garage. Flipping on the lights, he stood and stared at his pet project. It was exactly as he'd left it. Mostly in pieces.

He had first laid eyes on it not long after he had graduated from the police academy, and recognized it about three seconds later. There was a picture on his father's desk of his father and his father's best friend leaning against the hood of a car and grinning like monkeys with a crate of bananas. This was that car.

It was a blue 1958 Impala two-door convertible with a 348 and triple-turbine Turbo-glide and white-walled tires. His father would tell stories about him and his friend, Jack, racing that car and rarely losing against other street racers in the area. They had been a legend in their time. Nick purchased it for next to nothing in hopes of surprising his father with a restoration project they could do together. Ros Shepherd had taken one look at it and asked, "What did you buy that piece of junk for?"

"To restore. It's just like the one you and Jack had.

"Son, it was the good times with Jack that I treasured. Not the car he owned."

As he realized his father wasn't the least bit interested, Nick's hopes fell into as many pieces as the car.

His father had set a hand on Nick's shoulder. "Son, it was the scene I enjoyed. Not the car. I don't know the first thing about putting a car together. You and Steven can work on it together."

Leaving the box of parts in the backseat, Nick had covered the car and let it sit. It was only after the divorce that Nick had ordered a copy of the mechanic's manual for the car and started tinkering with it in his spare time.

Shaking off the bad memory, he walked over to the worktable where he'd been rebuilding the carburetor and perched on the high stool. He reached up and flicked on the overhead light. Within minutes he was lost in the task. *I may never learn to play the guitar, but maybe one of these days I'll make this car sing.*

His cell phone rang, startling him. He dropped his wrench and reached for the phone. "Shepherd."

"Nick, I need to talk to you."

His heart lurched. Every time he thought he was over her, she would call or stop by the office and the pain would hit him hard, reminding him that nothing had changed. She was still a bitter, angry woman, and he was still in love with her. Not a healthy combination. Closing his eyes, he pinched the bridge of his nose. "What is it now, Jess?"

"There's a drip in the master bath faucet. It needs to be fixed."

"Then fix it. It's not my house anymore, remember?"

"And maybe I could afford to do that if you'd send money on time, but you're two months late."

Nick stood up and started pacing, trying to burn off the frustration. And the hurt. "And I explained to you that things have been tight lately. I'm sending you what I can when I can, but I have to try and save the business too."

He heard her snort in disgust. "It's always the business first with you, isn't it? Nothing has changed at all."

"Look, you make good money at your job. Please don't try and tell me that you're not able to put food on the table. This whole money thing is just a way to smack me around. What? You didn't do enough of that during the divorce?"

"I don't know how we stayed married as long as we did. Oh, wait. Yes, I do. You were never there!"

A loud click. He flipped the phone closed and set it on the workbench. When was this going to be over? All he asked for was a little cooperation. Was that so hard for her?

The phone rang again. He snatched it up without glancing at the screen. "Look, Jess. I'll send you more money when I can. In the meantime, if the faucet is driving you that crazy, maybe I can stop by next week and look at it."

"Hey, I appreciate that, Nick, but this isn't Jess."

"Rafe." Nick felt the tension in his muscles ease up. "What's up?"

"You remember that gangbanger from DC that we got a paper on about two weeks ago?"

"Yeah?"

"I got him. But I'm alone and I need backup."

Nick snapped off the workbench light and headed for the house. "Grabbing my coat and on my way. Tell me where you are."

⚬

Monday, 9:30 p.m.
Baltimore

Annie kicked the refrigerator as she snapped on the kitchen light. The rattle immediately stopped. "Thank you," she muttered at it as she opened the door and pulled out the carton of orange juice.

A year after graduating from college, she moved into a sweet little apartment in Columbia, a suburb of Baltimore filled with the up-and-coming. Columbia had been the brainchild of James Rouse, a commercial real estate developer. About forty years ago, he had purchased thousands of acres from many different owners and revealed his overly ambitious plans to build a city. At the center of the project was Columbia Mall, surrounded by a dozen villages. The village streets took their names from famous works of art and literature: streets in the Village of Hobbit's Glen would come from the work of J.R.R. Tolkien, Running Brook from the poetry of Robert Frost, and Clemens Crossing from the work of Mark Twain. For Annie, living in Columbia had been a small way of proving to herself that she was on her way to becoming a success. She loved every inch of the villages—the people, the feel, the convenience.

But after being diagnosed with cancer, she'd given up the apartment and moved to a smaller one in an old brick building just north of Baltimore's downtown, close to both Sinai, where she would be receiving treatment, and her parents' house. They had pressured her to move back home, where they could take care of her. The apartment was a compromise she second-guessed every time she walked into the boring square box she now called home.

As she reached up into the cabinet for a glass, the phone rang. She picked it up. "Hello?"

"Annie McNamara?"

"Yes?" Annie finished pouring the orange juice into a glass. Her medicine was lined up on the counter like a battalion headed off to battle. She scooped up a pill and tossed it in her mouth.

"You called about Barbara?"

As she swallowed the pill, the voice suddenly jogged her memory.

It was Karen Lewis. An old friend of Barbara's. Annie didn't know if Barb had stayed in touch with her or not, but Annie had spent the whole day leaving messages and voice mail with everyone she could think of who might point her in the right direction.

"Karen? I'm so glad you called me back. I wasn't sure you were still at this number."

"I don't know what I can tell you, Annie. I haven't talked to Barb in almost a year."

"Anything that would help me find her would be great. Any friends she might have mentioned? Or a favorite hangout? Or where she is or was living?"

"Oh Annie, I don't know. I think she was living in a rooming-house motel near the interstate, but don't ask me the name of it. She was still working the streets, and she'd taken up with some guy named Richie. He and his brother owned a couple of bars in the area."

Annie wrote it all down in the little notebook on the counter. It wasn't much, but it was a start. "I really appreciate this."

"Oh, you know what I just thought of? She had a friend she talked about. Some street person named Charlie. She said he was a Vietnam vet and not quite all there anymore, but she would hang with him when she needed to hide out. I remember because I asked her why she needed to disappear, and she wouldn't talk about it."

It wasn't hard to figure out. Barb had done the same thing with her family—steal money, jewelry, or anything else of value to buy drugs. Then she'd disappear for a week or two until she figured everyone was over it. Then she'd come dragging back in, crying for help, begging everyone to still love her. And then the cycle would start all over again.

Until Mom and Dad put their foot down and told her either go into rehab or don't come back.

In spite of being twins, they were nothing alike. Barb had been wild, adventurous, full of spark and fire and big dreams. Annie had been the studious one, the quiet one, content to watch life go by before deciding how to proceed.

Until the cancer. Now she couldn't afford to watch life go by. There wasn't enough time. She had to step out and be adventurous, courageous, and aggressive. If she didn't grab what she wanted, she wouldn't have anything.

"Annie?"

"Oh, sorry, Karen. Lost in thought for a minute. Look, I appreciate this. You've been a big help. If you think of anything else, I'd appreciate it if you'd call me. And if you happen to hear from her, please tell her to call."

"I can do that, but I doubt she'll get in touch. I was pretty hard on her the last time we talked."

"I understand. But you never know."

The pause was so long that Annie almost thought that Karen had hung up. But then she heard the heavy sigh. "Annie, listen to me. Be careful. Barbara has gone too far. She's not the same person…that's not right either. She was always selfish and self-centered, but she's way worse now. She cares about only one thing in her life. Drugs. Don't trust her."

"I know she's into drugs."

"No, she's not just into drugs. She is controlled by them. And they're killing her soul. I know that sounds harsh, but it's the truth."

"I'm her sister. She's not going to hurt me, for pete's sake."

"Don't be so sure."

2

Tuesday, 3:15 a.m.
Baltimore City Correctional Center

Richie Carver shuffled along, the jangling of his leg irons echoing down the narrow concrete and metal hallway. He kept his hands clasped in front of him, holding the chains that connected to his feet, trying not to trip as the guards hurried him along.

"*Why* are you transferring me in the middle of the night?" he asked for the third time.

"Safer," one of the guards told him for the third time. "Move."

He knew, after he was sentenced to life in prison—thanks to the good old bounty hunter he'd not soon forget—that he'd eventually be moved from Baltimore out to the Maryland Correctional Institution in Hagerstown, but he didn't expect to be moved so soon, and he needed to let Jon know. How was that supposed to happen? "I thought I'd be here at least another week."

"You thought wrong," the larger of the guards replied, stopping at the door and buzzing to be let through.

Richie was nervous. Something was up. He could smell it.

Outside, he realized that he wasn't the only prisoner being transferred, and his nerves started to calm down. A guard opened the back of the transport van while another stood, shotgun loaded and draped across his arm, watching carefully from a safe distance. The other prisoner was loaded first—the guards shoved him into the van and then secured his chains to a metal bench. Then Richie felt a guard push him forward. He shuffled up to the edge of the van, climbed up, and took his seat. He glanced over at the other prisoner while the guard secured his chains.

His fellow inmate was enough to make him sit up a little straighter, look a little tougher. He was tall, broad, with white-blond hair and ice blue eyes that stared at him as if toying with the idea of breaking his neck.

The transport van pulled out and headed west through the city and then onto I-70 west. Richie kept his eyes on his hands, trying to figure out what to do. He had to let Jon know about the transfer as soon as possible. Twenty minutes into the drive and he started getting antsy. "Whatta you in for?"

The other prisoner glanced over at him, giving him a blatant, appraising look that told Richie he was being weighed and measured but never revealed the verdict. "Murder," the man finally replied in a voice that was as rough and grating as his penetrating stare.

Well, he could hold his own with that. He grinned. "Yeah? How many?"

"What do you care?" The man gave Richie a cold stare.

Dropping his gaze again, Richie gripped the metal bench as the truck hit a pothole.

A few minutes later, Richie tried again. "Any idea why they're taking us in the middle of the night?"

"I didn't get the memo."

The man was clearly not in the mood for conversation. He seemed focused. He remained tense, alert, as if expecting something.

Finally, Richie understood. "What are you planning?"

"None of your business."

Rolling his eyes, Richie looked over at the man, but the amusement died as he stared into the stranger's eyes. Something *was* up. He sat there for a minute and then it gradually made sense. "You're going to try and make a break, aren't you? Are you crazy?" he whispered. "There are two guards, and they're both armed. You'll get us killed."

"Just shut up."

"Listen. If you make it, I'm going with you."

There was a frown, and Richie could almost hear the mental doors closing and locking. "I don't know you, man. And I don't want to."

Richie licked his lips. No way was he going to get left behind or worse…killed. If there was a way off this transport, he was going to take it. "I'll make it worth your while."

The man stared, those ice blue eyes pinning Richie. "Make it worth my while, how?"

Richie swallowed hard. "What do you want?"

The man dismissed Richie, turning his head to listen to the sounds outside the transport—the road, the tires, the guards murmuring up front.

"Look," Richie pressed. "I have access to anything you need. Money, guns, a job, a place to hide, food, clothing. Whatever you want."

"You got a place no one knows about?"

"You serious?"

"As these chains." He lifted his hands, jangling the constraints.

"I can do that. Yeah."

"How private?"

"Doesn't get any more private. Farmhouse, out in the country, back in the woods. Can't be seen from the road. Work for you?"

The man studied Richie, as if trying to determine whether he was telling the truth or just making up something to impress. "Fine. Stick with me and be ready."

"Sure. Okay."

When the time for the escape came, Richie was totally unprepared for it, even though he'd been expecting it. A fake car accident in the middle of the road. The transport forced to stop. Shots fired. The guards going down. The back door opened and someone in a mask jumped in. He held up a key. "Someone call for a breakout?"

The other prisoner laughed. "I knew you'd pull it off." He held out his hands. "Get me out of these."

When his chains fell away, the man nodded toward Richie. "Him too."

"But—"

"Just do it." He jumped out of the transport and looked around. Richie saw him smile as another person came around from the side, carrying a black duffel bag.

It was a woman. The kind of woman that would make a man drop to his knees and beg for mercy. Tight black jeans, a low-cut black sweater, black cowboy boots, and long dark hair that whipped around her face. She angled her face up to the white-haired man with an inviting smile. "Hey, lover. Miss me?"

Richie's companion let out a low and throaty laugh. "Nothing has been the same since the last time I saw you, Leese." She held the duffel bag out to him, but he ignored it, wrapping a hand around her neck and pulling her up for a kiss. "You being a good girl?"

"I'm always good, Cutter. You know that."

Richie felt his heart squeeze in his chest. *Cutter.* He knew that name. Had heard about the man around the exercise yard. He was rumored to be a hired killer out of Atlantic City—ruthless, experienced, and as cold as steel in an ice storm. At the time, he dismissed it all as just talk—like so much in the yard was—but this man had a reputation for getting the job done quickly, quietly, and efficiently. And he'd just proved his reputation wasn't rumor at all.

Richie's chains fell away and he stood up, rubbing at his wrists as he climbed out of the back of the transport.

Cutter continued to ignore him as he spoke to his companions. "You two have a good alibi, right?"

The masked man tossed Cutter a set of keys. "Yeah. When the cops show up, Leese and I will be tangling the sheets at my pad. I mean, dude…you're gone for twenty-five to life. The woman's got to move on. Who better to take care of her than your old partner?"

Cutter shook his head slowly as he jangled the car keys. "Just don't get too tangled in those sheets. I'm coming for my woman, and when I do, I'd hate to have to kill you."

The man threw both hands up in the air. "Chill, dude. It's all alibi and no action. I'd never cross you, Cutter. You know that."

"Disappear," Cutter told his associates. "Make sure your alibis are solid. I'll be in touch." They bumped fists and left.

Richie followed Cutter into the woods, his prison shoes slipping in the wet grass. Just beyond the trees, an old Bronco sat, apparently waiting for them.

Cutter tossed the duffel on the hood and opened it. He glanced over at Richie as he pulled out a plaid shirt. He looked in the duffel, pulled out a sweatshirt, and tossed it to Richie. "That'll have to do. Cover up."

It took Cutter only seconds to strip out of the orange jumpsuit and into the clothes his friends had supplied.

Richie buttoned up the shirt, climbed up into the old Bronco, and reached for his seat belt. "You really pulled it off."

"What's your name?"

"Carver. Richie Carver." Richie buckled his seat belt. "I've heard of you."

"Well, I haven't heard of you, so it's time you put up or I don't need you."

Richie felt a shiver of fear slide down his spine as he stared into those cold eyes. He licked his lips. "Head back to the interstate. Then go west two more exits and get off. Then north. There's a—"

Cutter cranked the engine, revved it, cutting Richie off. He turned the radio up and, tapping his fingers on the steering wheel, pulled out on the pavement. Richie stared at the prison transport sitting there in the middle of the street like road kill. The doors were sitting open. One guard was slumped behind the wheel, shot before he even had a chance to pull out his weapon. The other guard was sprawled in the road, hand still gripping his weapon.

He smiled to himself as Cutter drove around the crash scene. *See ya, suckers*. Then as the vehicle accelerated, jumping from twenty to fifty, Richie settled back in his seat and looked out the window. *I'm coming for you, bounty hunter.*

———※◯※———

Nick stepped into the kitchen, sweeping his gun out in front of him as he noted the bare walls, the missing countertops, the cabinets hanging lopsided on each side of the window. Crouching down, he descended the dark stairway into the basement. He could smell the dust, decay, and mold mixed with something far more familiar—sweat and fear.

He could hear a girl whimpering like a wounded animal and tried to narrow in on the sound of her low cries. As he stepped away from the bottom step, he swung around, gun firmly held in both hands out in front of him. There was a small window at ground level, and the sun, low in the sky, was sending beams of gold light through the window, guiding Nick to the girl.

She stood in front of him, her long dark hair falling across her face as Richie Carver stood behind her, a grin on his face and a knife to her throat.

Richie grabbed a fistful of her hair and yanked her head back so that Nick could see the blade pressed against her soft throat and the blood that was slowly beginning to spread along the edge of the knife. "Been waiting for you, bounty hunter."

Nick's hands began to shake as he recognized the young girl. His stomach twisted. His daughter. Krystal.

"Daddy? Help me. Please. Don't let him kill me!"

Stay focused, man. Stay focused on the moment. Forget it's Krystal. Forget she's your daughter. Just get her out alive the way you would any hostage.

"Put the knife down, Richie."

Richie pulled Krystal up tighter against his body. "Can't do that, Nicky boy. I warned you not to send me to jail."

Krystal emitted a high-pitched wail as Richie dragged her sideways, skirting around Nick. "Daddy! Please. Don't. Don't let him kill me!"

Nick raised his hands slowly, holding the gun out and away from Richie. "Let her go. She doesn't have to get hurt in all this. It's between you and me."

Richie grinned as he tightened the knife against Krystal's throat. Her whimpering stopped as she held her breath.

Slowly, Richie brought the knife across Krystal's throat. Blood pulsed out, hitting Nick across the face. "You should have listened to me, bounty hunter." *Then Richie tossed Krystal's body into Nick's arms before he turned to run.*

Nick caught Krystal with one arm and slowly lowered her to the ground. Her eyes locked with his, and he knew time was running out fast. He reached for his radio, but it was gone. Quickly, he unbuttoned his shirt and whipped it off.

"Daddy..." She closed her eyes.

Nick grabbed her face. "No! Krystal!"

He heard a heavy sigh, and then he felt her body go limp. "No! No!"

"NO!"

⟶⟶✦⟵⟵

Tuesday, 3:45 a.m.
Towson, Maryland

Nick jerked upright, breathing hard, trembling as he scrambled to pull himself out of the dream. He reached over with shaking hands and turned on the light. Swinging his feet to the floor, he bent forward, burying his face in his hands. Just a dream. It was just a dream. Not real. Richie was in jail. Krystal was safe in her bed. It was all just a bad dream.

It took a few minutes, but Nick finally flopped backward across the bed, draping one arm across his eyes. He'd give anything to be able to get up and walk over to Krystal's room and check on her. To lean down and hear her breathing softly as she slept. To brush back her hair from her face and pull her covers up to her chin, tucking her in the way he had when she had been little. Back in the days when he had been her hero.

If there was any consolation at all, it was that he'd put Richie away where he'd never be able to hurt Krystal.

3

Tuesday, 8:00 a.m.
Prodigal Recovery offices, Baltimore

The team at Prodigal Fugitive Recovery met in the conference room as they did several mornings a week. In spite of the mandatory attendance required for all team members, there was an empty chair at the table, and Nick did his best to ignore it, even though it annoyed him. The rest of the team was chatting quietly when Nick spoke up. "All right, guys. Let's get started. First thing on the list: we have less than two weeks to find Tommy Lester and bring him in."

"Dead or alive, at the end of a rope or over a saddle." Rafe mimicked in his best John Wayne voice, which still wasn't all that good, but it made them all laugh.

Shaking his head, Nick turned his attention to Conner. "So where do we stand with Lester?"

"No sign of him at the clubs, his parents' house, or his own apartment. I've been talking to several of his ex-girlfriends, but so far, none of those leads have panned out." Conner shifted his massive body back in his chair and folded his arms across his chest. "I've been pinging his cell phone, but so far, nothing. Either he's picked up a throwaway or he's not using his cell."

"Best guess?" Nick asked as he reached down for his Mountain Dew. Everyone else was drinking coffee.

"I know he isn't all that smart, so I figure Jon Carver has him tucked away somewhere. The Lily is advertising for a new bouncer. I applied for the job. Maybe I can get inside far enough to find him."

"Stay on it." Then Nick turned to Rafe. "What about Zeena Bantham? Any word on her?"

Zeena Bantham was what they called a tweeker—a meth addict— which made her one of those people that could run a bounty hunter into the ground. Hyped for days on end, they would bounce from place to place, from person to person, until they finally crashed out to sleep it off somewhere. When awake, all they thought about was the next high—how to get it, where to get it, who to get it from. Made them difficult to catch.

Rafe set his coffee cup down and flipped open his notebook. "The last anyone can recall, she was on the streets about a month ago, which would have been a couple days before her court date. One of the girls told me that Zeena mentioned having a family in West Virginia somewhere, but so far, I haven't been able to find anyone local." He lifted a finger into the air. "However, I did find out that one of her main sources for drugs is a loser by the name of Danny Sloop. Problem is no one can recall seeing him around for a while either. Could be they scored big and are holed up somewhere going through their stash."

"What do we have on Sloop?" Conner asked.

Rafe leaned forward, clasping his hands on top of his file folder. "Typical street punk. Twenty-five years old. Has a rap sheet as long as a cat's tail, but mostly low-grade stuff. Petty theft, possession, shoplifting, burglary. Last known address was a bust. Landlord tossed him out when he got three months behind on the rent. No one has any idea where he's living now. No car registered to him. His probation officer tells me Sloop is working construction, but that was another dead end. The company told me Sloop stopped showing up for work a couple weeks ago and they have no idea where he is and don't care. The foreman said Sloop was more interested in stealing the company blind than actually working. I let his probation officer know so if he shows up there, he can be picked up for violation of probation. It's not much, but it might give me a chance to have a little chat with him. One of my snitches tells me he's now dealing on a small scale."

"If Zeena's no longer at the address we have for her," Nick said, "it could be she's gone to the streets. Put up wanted posters at the shelters. Say something like she has inherited some money and needs to contact an attorney."

"On it," Rafe replied, leaning back and stretching out his legs.

Half an hour later, the meeting ended. The men gathered in a small circle and bowed their heads, as was their tradition after every team meeting. Fugitive recovery was supposed to mean more to this group than just being tough guys who hunted criminals. The Prodigal team felt called to their work and hoped that with each recovered skip, they were serving justice and maybe even saving lives. These days, to Nick, that seemed like a load of junk, but he faithfully said the prayer anyway.

"Lord, protect us all today as we go out onto the streets," Nick droned. "Guide us to these fugitives and give us the wisdom to deal with them, and we pray that after we do, they might turn to you rather than return to a life of crime and destruction. Amen."

The prayer was taught to him by his father and was repeated after every Prodigal Recovery meeting since the doors had opened in 1977. Today, he ran through it a little more quickly than usual, but he had a lot on his mind, including a meeting he couldn't afford to miss.

As Rafe left the room, Conner eased his hip against the conference table. The table shifted a fraction. "You okay?"

Nick nodded. "I'm fine. Just a little distracted. And if you break that table, you bought it."

Conner laughed as he stood up. "I've never broken a table. Heads yes, tables no." Back in his younger days, Conner had been one of the "bad boys" of the wrestling ring, and breaking heads had been his key to success. That success led to alcohol, drugs, and very nearly divorce. His wife, Ria, had packed her bags and given him the ultimate ultimatum: if he ever wanted to see her or their children again, he had to change his lifestyle. She was gone less than two weeks when Conner made his decision. He left wrestling, saved his marriage, and two years later, ended up at Prodigal.

Nick gathered up his file folders and soda. "I have a meeting across town. Don't break any heads until I get back."

"Nick."

He stopped in the doorway and looked back at Conner.

"I'm sure Steven has a good reason for being late this morning."

Nick bit down on his temper. "He always does, doesn't he?"

It took Nick ten minutes to drive through the rain to his meeting. And it took five minutes to find out it had been a waste of time. Lately, his life had become a run of dead ends and false turns, and the way out was proving to be as elusive as the typical bail jumper.

"I'm sorry, Nick." Michael nudged his coffee mug aside and picked up his gold pen, running it through his fingers. As always, he was dressed in a sharp-looking suit—which today was navy blue with pinstripes—with a light blue button-down shirt and navy blue tie. "I even tried to go to bat for you, but they just decided that they couldn't approve the loan."

Bowing his head, Nick ran his fingers through his hair, squelching the desire to pull it all out. Then he glanced up. "Okay. What if I use Mom's house as collateral?"

He hated to think that it had come to this, but with his mother in a nursing home with Alzheimer's, she wouldn't even know. In fact, most of the time, she didn't even remember the house. Or her children. And that hurt, but Nick set that little twinge of pain aside.

"Same problem as the office." Leaning back in his chair, Michael shook his head as he tossed his pen back to his desk. "Your parents left everything to you, your brother, and your sister. Without both Steven and Marti's signatures, you can't use it."

Nick swallowed the response that rose up to the tip of his tongue. Michael was a banker, but he was also an old friend. "A whopping one-third of everything is mine."

It sounded like whining, and while it bothered him that it had even escaped from his thoughts to run out of his mouth, he knew Michael would understand.

Michael leaned forward, resting his hands on his desk. "Nick, if I had that kind of money to give you, I would. But I don't."

And Nick knew that Michael would. They had been friends for years, sharing a love for the Orioles, old cars, and tall blondes with cool smiles. Michael had season tickets at Camden Yards, two restored Corvettes, three boys, and a petite brunette wife who worshiped the ground he walked on. Nick, on the other hand, had married one of those tall blondes with a cool smile before he'd been smart enough to realize that the cool smile indicated a frigid heart and an icier temper.

"I know. But I'm not asking you for what is yours, Mike. I'm asking for what is mine."

"Then find Marti."

"I've been looking for her. Every time I get close, she disappears again." Nick slowly pushed himself to his feet, wondering if he'd aged ten years in the last few days or if it merely felt that way. If he looked in a mirror right then and saw himself with white hair and the sagging jowls of an octogenarian, it wouldn't have surprised him. Instead of a mirror, though, he looked into the eyes of his friend and tried to ignore the pity he saw there. "In the meantime, Dad entrusted this business to me, and I can't let it die without a fight."

"I understand. Have you tried asking Jessica to let you use the other house as collateral?"

The laugh that rolled off Nick's tongue tasted as bitter as it sounded. "She told me she wouldn't let me put that house at risk even if we were still married."

"I'm sorry."

Nick glanced out at the rain, drizzling down the office window. Then he turned, holding out his hand to Michael. "Don't worry about it. I appreciate you trying to get me the loan."

Michael clasped his hand, shook it firmly. "What now?"

"I don't know. But I can't just let Prodigal close up shop."

Standing in the doorway, Nick shrugged his jacket on, staring at Michael. Finally he squared his shoulders. "Dad expected me to take care of the family. I'll find a way to do that."

Nick pulled the door closed behind him and strode briskly through the bank lobby, his gaze fixed on the double glass doors. He'd always heard that when life tossed you lemons, you made lemonade. But what did you do with *rotten* lemons? There wasn't enough sugar in the world to help him make things any sweeter.

The gray skies had become even gloomier while Nick was in the bank, and the cold rain was coming down as if it were pressed to get as much soaked as possible in the shortest amount of time. As the downpour sent rivulets down his back, Nick strode through the parking lot, fingering the keyless remote as his mind raced.

He stuck his key in the ignition, then picked up a CD and slid it into the player. As Alabama started singing about angels being among us, he turned up the volume and started to back out of the parking space.

As the wipers cleared the windshield, movement caught his eye. He moved the gearshift into park and climbed out of the vehicle. Kneeling down, he stared into the big brown eyes of a small white dog huddled under the car next to him. It was dripping wet, shivering with cold, collarless, and looked as if it hadn't had a decent meal in weeks.

"Hey, little guy. Are you lost?" He held out his hand, gently inviting the dog to accept his presence as nonthreatening. "I won't hurt you."

The dog shivered, then whined. "I can call the pound for you. They'll give you a good meal and a warm place to sleep." Poor guy looked how Nick felt, and he figured at least one of the two would be cared for today.

The little dog inched forward, eyes hovering between wary and grateful for attention. Nick told himself not to fall for it. "Oh, there's no way I can keep you, little guy. You don't understand how much I have on my plate right now."

He rolled his eyes as the pup whined pitifully. "I think I have a cold hamburger somewhere in the backseat. You're welcome to it. And when we get back to my office, I'll call the pound."

Finally the dog sniffed his hand, wagged his tail, and looked up at Nick with something as close to hero worship as a dog can get. Taking that as an invitation, Nick scooped up the muddy little pup and carried him to the rear of the SUV. He popped the rear hatch and pulled a towel from his gym bag. He wrapped it around the dog, closed the rear, and walked around to slide back in behind the wheel. He set the dog on the passenger seat and leaned back to rummage through some trash in the backseat.

"Aha! I knew it." He held up a fast food bag. "Yesterday's lunch."

After giving the pup the rest of the hamburger and cold fries, he turned up the heater and headed to the office.

The dog swallowed the food whole, then tapped his little foot on Nick's thigh. "No, I will not get attached to you. You need to be in a nice home with a couple of kids."

The pup withdrew his paw, curled up in a tight ball, and closed his eyes with a heavy sigh.

Nick's thoughts drifted back to business as he pulled up to a stoplight. Somehow, he had to keep Prodigal from going under.

When his father started Prodigal Fugitive Recovery, the county—just a half hour outside Baltimore—was a rural farming district where the crime was primarily trespassing, drunk and disorderly, and the occasional bounced check.

But in the late seventies, those suburbanites who had once turned their noses up at their grandparents' farms suddenly found themselves nostalgic for the country life. They came in droves, buying up farms, building homes, and opening businesses. With the increases in the population, crime skyrocketed. Drug dealers moved in. As did the prostitutes, strip joints, liquor stores, and pawn shops right behind them. Where there were drugs and drug money to be made, the gangs moved in, pushing out the old residents and taking over large blocks of the city. Then Baltimore became a sanctuary city, and crime jumped up again.

With the increase in crime came more lawyers, more bail bond companies, and with the upsurge in more violent crime, bail bond companies needed someone to bring in the criminals who decided to skip their court dates.

And Prodigal Recovery was there to help out all those small bail bond companies. But now, those little bail bond companies were being overshadowed by the larger ones that tended to employ their own fugitive recovery agents. Like Triple A, one of Prodigal's biggest competitors.

And Prodigal's business began to decline.

The only answer now was to start writing bail bonds. Unfortunately, the surety companies that would guarantee the bail bonds all claimed to have agents in the area, and none were willing to saturate the market with more. Nick was forced into the unfortunate position of needing his own assets to guarantee the bonds. Assets that were tied up until he could find his sister. But after months of searching, researching, and even hiring detectives, finding her was proving as hard as getting a loan.

Tuesday, 10:45 a.m.
Belvedere Ave., Park Heights section, Baltimore

Annie closed her umbrella, took a deep breath, straightened her suit jacket, and pulled open the door to the Stark Lily. She wanted to turn around and run out. It took a minute for her eyes to adjust to the dark, but the smells hit her immediately—sweat, alcohol, smoke, and the not-so-subtle odor of despair. This was the third bar she'd been to so far, and they were all so similar that she wasn't sure if she was just revisiting the same one over and over.

Spotting the bar along the side wall, she wove through a few tables and approached the bartender, a rough-looking man with more muscle than age. "Excuse me?"

"Macy's is down at the mall, sweetheart. You're on the wrong side of town."

Annie licked her lips and tried to ignore a man who was moving down the bar to get closer to her, leering in a way that made her ease farther back. "Um…I'm looking for, uh, Zeena. I understand she frequents—"

"Frequents?" The bartender laughed as he twisted the cap on a bottle and set it on the shelf behind him. "Honey, people don't *frequent* this place. They hang out here, they do business here, they get drunk here. But they don't *frequent.*"

"Okay, she 'works' out of this bar. Have you seen her lately?"

He tipped his head and stared at Annie with nothing but loathing. "Honey, if she works outta this bar, she don't show up for work until dark." He leaned over the bar, his sour breath forcing her to lean away. "Johns don't come in here at ten in the morning looking for a good time, ya git me? 'Course I ain't seen her."

"But you know her?"

He smirked. "You think I know every working girl on the streets of Baltimore? Gimme a break."

"Listen," Annie said, trying to muster a harder attitude. "I'm trying to find my sister. Have. You. Seen. Her?"

He shook his head. "Try missing persons." He picked up a rag and started wiping down the counter, dismissing her.

⟞⟞⟨◦⟩⟝⟝

Tuesday, 10:47 a.m.
En route to Prodigal Offices, Baltimore

As Nick drove, he was distracted by thoughts of his sister. After all his searching for her, he had still not gathered any legitimate clues. *Where are you, Marti?* Just as he had done many times before, he tried to get into her head. Why would she have left? Where would she go?

As he was chasing his sister's mental rabbit, his cell phone chirped. He turned down the music and flipped it over to hands-free. "Shepherd."

"Nick?" It was Jenna, Prodigal's secretary, bookkeeper, and general all-around office manager. She was forty, looked thirty, and had a son in his first year of college. Her husband, Mark, had been killed while in Egypt on business—a terrorist bomb at a hotel that was known for housing American tourists. A widow for several years, she tended to mother the men at Prodigal. She said it helped her keep a line drawn that she didn't want to cross. He had the sense that Rafe was the one she wanted to keep behind the line, but if Rafe ever figured that out, Nick knew he'd have Jenna at the altar before she had time to pick out a wedding cake.

"Yeah, Jenna?"

"We just got a call from Robbins Bail Bonds. They have two skips they need to find like yesterday and want to know if we can give them immediate attention."

The light turned red and Nick hit the brake. "I thought we lost all their business to Triple A."

"Seems Triple A took on more than they could handle and can't guarantee they can get to them for at least two to three weeks. Robbins doesn't have that long."

Grinning, Nick felt the first nudge of hope all day. "Tell him we'll give it priority. Then tell Steven to get right on it."

There was a slight hesitation before she replied, "I'll tell him."

"He's not in yet, is he?" Nick ground his teeth. "Never mind. Give them to Conner and tell him I said highest priority."

"Will do."

Snapping his phone closed, Nick heard a horn honking and then noticed that the light was green. He hit the gas. The dog opened one eye and sighed. "Well, sorry to disturb your sleep."

A few minutes later, he pulled into the parking lot behind Prodigal and cut the engine. He stared at the building for a moment. Prodigal Recovery was housed in a three-story red brick building on the corner of Second Street and Market. It was practically a landmark in the county. It was tucked neatly between the courthouse and the nine-story glass and steel building commonly known as Lawyer's Row. In the late 1800s, a judge found out that property had been acquired to build a new courthouse. He immediately purchased the lot next door and built himself a home so that he could live close to work.

The old courthouse had moved as the area had been taken over and incorporated into Baltimore's city limits. The judge's house remained a private home until Nick's father bought it and turned the first floor into the office for Prodigal Recovery. The second floor of the building was leased out to a defense attorney and an accountant, while the third floor was for storage. Maybe he should think about converting that third floor into offices for rent. He could use the extra income.

Pushing his thoughts aside, he picked up the dog. "Okay, little dude. Let's go see if Jenna has a bowl of water for you."

"Not another lost dog." Jenna pursed her lips as Nick walked toward her desk.

"I couldn't help it." Nick shook the rain from his hair. "Look at him. He's so small, and he was wet and hungry. You think I should have just left him out there in this weather?"

Jenna sighed as she took the dog from him. "I think there's still some kibble in the kitchen from the last stray you found." She took a few steps and then turned around. "They're waiting for you in your office."

"Who?" He picked up the stack of messages on the corner of her desk and started paging through them as he stepped into his office.

Rafe was lounging on the sofa, his feet propped up on the coffee table. Conner was leaning against the wall, arms folded across his chest. They were both looking at the TV. They didn't look happy.

Nick tossed the messages on his desk and unzipped his coat.

"You're going to want to hear this." Rafe picked up the remote to the television and increased the volume.

"…statewide for any information leading to the capture of either of these two escaped fugitives. Back to you, Heather."

The pictures of two men flashed up on the screen. He didn't recognize the one, but he knew the other one better than he wanted to. Richie Carver. "Richie escaped?"

"Yep." Rafe replied.

Nick could feel everything in his body slow down, as if waiting for him to decide whether to breathe, think, or react. The dream came at him, flashing in black and white and color images—the dark basement, the knife, the blood, and Krystal dying in his arms. It brought out a cold sweat across his forehead as he sank down into his chair.

They flipped to other channels, finally hearing the report several times before Nick had the full story. "I can't believe they transferred two dangerous criminals in the middle of the night with only two guards. What were they thinking?"

"They moved them a week before they were scheduled to go, so they probably thought they had their bases covered," Conner explained.

"Then how did Richie plan this escape?"

Jenna strode into the office with a file folder and tossed it on the corner of Nick's desk. Then she pursed her lips with that disapproval that mothers were famous for and turned the television off. "You've watched the same report four times. I think you know all there is to know. I believe we have work to do, boys."

"Boys?" Rafe clutched both hands over his heart. "That hurts, Jenna, my love. That really hurts."

Shooting him a withering glance, she picked up an empty soda can from the corner of Nick's desk and left the office.

Nick reached for his soda, and when he realized it was gone, recalled that Jenna had just picked it up. He stood. "Conference room. Immediately."

Jenna stuck her head in the door. "Nick, someone's on the phone. Wouldn't tell me who he was."

Nick reached for the phone and nodded toward Conner. "I'll be there in a minute. Pull all the active files and have them ready for me." Nick sat down as his men left the room. "Hello?"

"Hey, bounty hunter. Miss me?"

"Where are you, Richie? Let's make this easy." Nick pulled up the caller ID, but the number was blocked.

Richie laughed, obviously far more amused than Nick was. "You always made me laugh, Nicky-boy. Nah, I just wanted to let you know that I didn't forget my promise to you, and I hope you ain't forgotten either."

"I see you haven't grown any smarter, Richie. Stay away from me and mine."

"Yeah, well, I think Jon told you to stay away from us and you didn't listen too good. I'll see you soon, bounty hunter."

Richie hung up before Nick could respond. Slowly, Nick set the phone down. If that man came anywhere near his daughter... He couldn't bring himself to think that far. Still, protecting Krystal had just become his highest priority. He pushed back from the desk and strode briskly to the conference room.

Everyone was sprawled out—feet up on the conference table, talking over coffee, Rafe munching on one of the doughnuts Jenna had brought in. Nick walked straight to the whiteboard and began writing names. "I want the name of anyone we have paper on that is in any way connected to Jon or Richie Carver. I don't care if it's his dog's veterinarian that didn't pay a parking ticket."

Conner's feet swung down and hit the floor. "What's going on, Nick?"

"We need to find Richie Carver. I want him back in custody before he even has a chance to remember what freedom tastes like. Rafe, pull his prison calls. Get the tapes along with log lists. I want to know everyone he's talked to since he's been in. Track every number. Steven can put the plumbing signs on the van and do surveillance at Jon's. I doubt Richie will show up there, but if he does, I want to know before Jon does."

Conner glanced over at Rafe and then back to Nick. "The police are on it, Boss."

"I don't care. We can go places they can't." He placed both hands on the table and leaned forward. "Larry Borden works for Jon. So does Tommy Lester. Zeena works out of Jon's bars. Any of them may have information on Richie, so I want them at the top of our to-do list. Who else do we have?"

Conner didn't bother to hide his concern. "Boss, this isn't our job. He didn't jump bail. He escaped from a prison transport."

"He escaped." Turning, Nick drew lines under the two names. "We know him better than anyone. I want him back in jail." He looked from Conner to Rafe and then tossed the marker down.

"We have no authority," Conner said. "You know that."

"I'm going after him, Conn. I want that piece of slime back behind bars before he can even think my daughter's name. I will kill him if he touches her, and I'm pretty sure we don't want another man in jail for murder. So let's make sure I keep a clean record and find him."

"You don't really think he's going to go after Krystal, do you? We get threats like that all the time, Boss."

"The man hates me. I've turned him in to the authorities more than a few times, and now for a life sentence. Not to mention he's had eight months to plan his vengeance out to the very last detail." Nick looked down for a second. "Look. He *just* called to say he's after her. He's fixated on the idea."

Conner whistled softly, then threw his hands up. "Fine. I'm with you on this."

"Where should we start?" Rafe asked.

"I want his phone log at the prison. Track every number he's called since the day he stepped into that cell. There's no way he could have done this without outside help. If it looks like a dead end, run all the phone codes. He may have traded with another prisoner to make his calls. Run Jon's number too, and make sure it comes up on Richie's phone code. See how fast you can get the recordings for all Richie's calls."

"You don't really think that Richie and Jon would plan a prison escape over the phone, do you?" Conner planted both arms on the table and started fingering through the open files.

"No, but Richie isn't as smart as Jon. He's merely the muscle. He may have slipped up somewhere before Jon had a chance to shut him up."

Rafe picked up the phone to order the phone logs. Conner, on the other hand, was still reluctant. "Boss, we have skips to find. Skips that bring in money we need. Finding Richie isn't going to fill the coffers. And even if the state eventually puts a bounty on his head, you know they are notoriously slow about paying up. *If* they pay up."

"We'll get the skips."

The two sat in silence for a moment while Rafe ended his phone call.

"What's the story on the logs?" Conner asked as Jenna came in and set a message down in front of Nick.

"We'll have them this afternoon." Rafe grinned, wiggling his eyebrows. "Patty is crazy about me. She said she'd have them couriered over."

Jenna sniffed. "Hotshot Rafael does it again."

Rafe laughed as he puffed out his chest. "When ya got it, ya got it."

"Depends on what you've got and if there's a cure for it." She turned on her heel and strode out.

Nick picked up the message. It was from his ex-wife. She could wait. He tucked it in his pocket.

Conner stood. "So where to first?"

"Borden," Nick responded. "He and Richie barely moved without telling the other when and how. Richie might run to him for help."

"Wouldn't he run to Jon first?" Rafe offered.

Nick shook his head. "Too risky. He knows every police officer in the state will already have Jon under surveillance. He'll need someone like Borden to be the go-between and get to Jon for him. Borden's where we look first." Nick stood, reached for the doughnut box, then took a big bite of a chocolate glazed. With his mouth full, he said, "We're done here. Let's get started."

Without another word, they spread out, preparing to go out on the streets. Cans of Mace were strapped on, handcuffs clipped to their belts. Guns were holstered and badges donned. Rafe also had a telescoping baton strapped to his belt, while Conner had a shotgun tucked in his duffel bag and Nick clipped on a Taser.

Together, they walked out of the building and climbed into Nick's SUV.

4

Tuesday, 11:55 a.m.
East Baltimore

With Conner riding shotgun and Rafe in the backseat, Nick eased the black SUV down the trash-littered street, passed the house he was targeting, and then up to the curb. The rain had stopped, but the sky was still as gray as a banker's suit and as heavy as his need for profits.

A long time ago, the brick row homes on Livingston Street had been a thriving community. The women hung their wash while chatting over the small hedges that divided the backyards. Children had run the streets, knowing that every home had an adult who would watch out for them. The men had all arrived home about the same time each day from the factories and shipyards nearby, signaling the dinner hour and driving everyone inside. The homes had been well cared for—lawns trimmed, shutters painted, and windows sparkling.

Now, most of the lawns were dirt, few of the homes had shutters at all, and the majority of the windows were either boarded up or covered by metal bars. Desperation clung in the air, and poverty haunted like a specter. What was once a sanctuary for wholesome living was now a trash dump.

The three men emerged from the SUV, carefully watching the house. Nick assessed every shadow, every noise, every movement.

The men gathered in front of one of the duplexes and split off. While Rafe and Nick moved in a crouch along the front porch, Conner crept through the garbage-littered yard to the back door. Nick figured if anything went wrong and Borden tried running out the back door, he'd hit the brick wall named Conner and find himself flat on his back, wishing he had stayed put.

Nick flexed his hands, encased in fingerless leather gloves, as he climbed the steps to the front door. Tension tightened his muscles, sending little sparks of adrenaline through his bloodstream. He eased his Mace out of his pocket, while Rafe pulled his gun from his holster.

Cautiously, Nick opened the warped screen door, glancing quickly over to his partner. With Rafe's nod, he took a deep breath, counted to three, and then knocked lightly on the door. A few moments later, it opened.

A young woman answered—presumably Borden's latest girlfriend. She was a tiny thing, barely standing five foot, with short black hair streaked with red and purple. She had a bruise forming on her cheek, and the realization that Borden had hit the girl was enough to make Nick's blood boil.

"I need to talk to Borden. Where is he?"

She looked over her shoulder with a mix of reluctance and relief. "He's still passed out. Been down here doing them drugs all night and still at it this morning." Wringing her hands, she glanced up at Nick. "I don't know if I should let you guys in."

"We just need to ask him a few questions. That's all."

After another moment's hesitation, she stepped back, letting Nick and Rafe into the house.

Sure enough, Borden was passed out, sprawled across the sofa as if he didn't have a care in the world. As Rafe pulled out his cuffs and prepared to deal with Borden, Nick turned to the girlfriend. "I have a man at the back door. His name is Conner. Could you let him in for me? And do you have any coffee made?"

"I'll make a pot."

He and his team had no need for the coffee, but it would keep the girl out of the way for a few minutes. As she disappeared into the kitchen, Nick glanced over at Rafe, who had one of Borden's hands cuffed and was standing there staring down at the man who was still passed out, unaware that his world was about to turn upside down.

"Ready?"

Rafe nodded. "Oh yeah. I'm ready."

Nick stepped over, grabbed Borden by the shoulders, and flipped him to the floor. He landed on his face, and by the time he realized something wasn't right, both his hands were cuffed behind him.

"Who are you?" Borden mumbled against the carpet.

Rafe knelt down, his knee pressing into the small of Borden's back. "Prodigal Recovery. How ya doin', Larry?"

Borden cursed as he struggled. "I didn't know nuthin about a court date." Rafe must have dug a little harder with his knee as he stood up, because Borden wailed.

Nick leaned over and grabbed an arm, helping Rafe lift Borden to his feet. "Ya hit your girl, huh?"

Borden glared at Nick. "Ain't none of your business what I do."

"Wrong answer, Larry." Nick's cell phone vibrated. With his free hand, he checked the Caller ID. It was Jessica. Again. Didn't the woman have any patience?

Just then, Borden must have had a brain cell go AWOL, because he lurched forward, jerking out of Rafe's and Nick's grip and lunging for the door.

Nick ran after him, but just as Borden entered the foyer, Conner appeared. Borden tripped over Conner's foot and hit the hardwood floor with a thud and a scream. Conner reached down and hauled Borden up by the collar with one massive hand.

Borden continued to struggle, flailing against Conner's grip.

Nick stepped forward and leaned in close. "I'm going to ask you nicely. Where is Richie Carver?"

"In jail, idiot!"

"Wrong answer. Where is he?"

"Last I heard, he was doing time. I swear. I ain't heard nuthin."

Borden tried to jump to his feet and run, but Nick grabbed him by the shoulder, sending him sprawling across the coffee table. It tipped over and crashed to the floor, Borden flattened by it. Conner reached under the table and lifted Borden to his feet. A small packet fell out of Borden's pocket.

Nick stared down at the packet and then looked at Borden. "Try again. And talk fast before I call the cops and tell them you have drugs on you."

Borden's eyes were darting faster than a Border collie on steroids. "Just a rumor. That's all I got, man."

"Talk."

"Heard he and another prisoner made a break. But they say it wasn't Jon that did the planning. No one knows who he is." He looked up at Nick. "And no one is saying where Richie's hiding. I swear."

Nick stared at him for a long moment. His instincts told him the man was telling the truth. But it didn't make any sense. If Jon didn't plan the escape, then Richie just happened to luck out and stumble on someone else's break? Not likely. Jon was probably putting out the word that he wasn't involved to cover his own backside.

"Heads-up, Larry. If I hear otherwise, I'm coming back for you, and I won't be so polite. You hear anything about Richie, you call me. You see Richie, you call me. You *think* you see Richie, you call me. You understand?"

"I got it. You want Richie." But his eyes kept darting left and right and never meeting Nick's. "I got it, man. Now let me go."

Nick stepped back and nodded at Conner. "Let him go. For now."

As soon as Conner released the handcuffs, Borden rubbed his wrists and glared at Conner and then turned to Nick. "If Richie's out, he'll be looking for you."

"Good. Make it easier for me to find him."

As the three men walked back to their vehicle, Nick dialed a familiar number.

"Linc? Nick. I was just talking to Borden, and a small quantity of cocaine fell out of his pocket. Just letting you know."

"Gotcha. You callin' 'cause you need a favor?"

"No. I was asking him about Carver, and it fell out of his pocket."

"Thanks, Nick. We're on our way."

"Where to now?" Conner asked as they climbed back into the SUV.

"Richie's old girlfriend Angela. I doubt he'll go there, but it's worth checking."

Nick was sitting at a stop sign just two blocks from Borden's when his cell phone rang again. He flipped the phone open. "I'm working, Jessica."

"You know what, Nick? I have a job too. But while you've been ignoring my calls, I've learned that your daughter skipped school three times last week."

Making a right turn, he hit the gas. "I'm sorry to hear that. But I'm in the middle of something here. Can this wait?"

"I know this might be hard for you to grasp, but I'm not the only parent Krystal has. I can't be expected to just drop everything every single time she gets into trouble. You need to pick up some of the slack."

"I do what I can when I can, but I need to work every hour possible, Jess. My finances are a little tight, and you're not helping any."

"I don't care."

Jessica's words ripped at an old wound and drew fresh hurt. "Tell me something I don't already know."

He snapped the phone closed, looked into the rearview at Rafe's sympathetic expression, and pulled into the parking lot. He didn't know whether Jessica was done with her rant or not, but he wasn't going to waste any more time on the same conversation they'd had a million times before. It was the same old story—he was the bad guy, she was the good parent, and their daughter was spinning out of control.

As Nick shut off the engine and climbed out of the SUV, Conner yelled out, "Look out! She's running!"

Nick jumped back into the SUV as Angela's car peeled out of the parking lot and made a right at the main street. "Let's go, let's go!"

Tuesday, 12:10 p.m.
Prodigal offices, Baltimore

Steven took off his coat as he entered the building. He hadn't planned on being so late, but his mother was having one of her rare "good" days and actually knew who he was through most of the visit. Taking advantage of being able to talk to her and share a few memories with her was far more important to him than chasing down some bail jumper. Jenna looked up at him with a warm smile of welcome.

"Is he here?"

She shook her head. "Out on a job."

Steven stopped at her desk to pick up his messages. "Did he notice I wasn't here?"

"Oh yeah."

Just then, a little white ball of fluff came running out from under Jenna's desk and darted beneath Steven's legs, yapping furiously. Steven knelt down in front of the desk. "Hey, killer."

The dog ran back under Jenna's desk. She chuckled. "A real killer, that's him."

"So that's the way it's going to be, eh? You know, you can't hide from every threat, Killer. See, this is a bounty hunter business. We are the biggest, strongest dudes in town. We make bad guys tremble with fear. If you're going to stick around here, you're going to have to show some gumption, little guy."

The dog eased out from under the desk. Steven picked him up. "That's much better. Never show fear." He wrinkled his nose at the mud-matted fur, and distinctly unpleasant odor of wet dog, road kill, and Dumpster diving. He glanced over at Jenna. "Another of Nick's strays?"

"Of course. Found him outside in the bank parking lot. And before I forget, we had a couple of skips come in this morning. They're on Conner's desk. High priority. Nick wanted you to work on tracking them down."

"How long have they been gone?"

"The skips?" She tipped her glasses down and arched a quizzical brow.

"No. Nick."

"Oh. Not long, why?"

"I should have time to call the groomer down the street and see if she can do something with this poor dog," Steven headed down the hall. "He stinks."

Jenna jumped up and started after him. "Steven, Nick is going to be furious if he gets back here and you haven't started on those skips."

"Yeah, and he'll huff and puff, and I'll remind him that I own as much of this company as he does, and that'll be the end of it."

Tuesday, 12:30 p.m.
Downtown Baltimore

Annie cut the engine and pulled the keys out of the ignition. Her hands dropped to her lap. She was so tired she could barely keep her eyes open. Another day in paradise. She grabbed her purse and, using her shoulder, pushed the driver's door open. All she had to do was make it up to her apartment and she could sleep the rest of the day if she had to.

So far, she hadn't found Barbara. But she had found out something that should have been obvious, and if she hadn't been running on emotion, she could have stayed in bed this morning. Women in Barbara's line of work weren't up and around in the morning. They sleep all day.

Which is exactly what Annie felt like doing.

"Hi, Annie!"

Annie was shuffling slowly up the steps of her apartment building when Irene Paige stepped out with her poodle. Time for Chipper's walk. "Hello, Irene. How are you today?"

"Glorious! Just glorious! You're looking a bit under the weather, doll. Coming down with a cold, are you?" Irene was the one who should have been named Chipper. Tall, thin, and always wearing that short, ugly, curly wig, the woman was never without a smile on her face and a kind word for everyone she met.

"Just a few sniffles," Annie said. "I've ordered some medicine from the pharmacy. I'll be fine."

Irene reached out and patted Annie on the arm. "You will indeed. Now I best get Chipper out before he gets an attitude and sulks all day."

Annie mustered up a weak smile and opened the door. As she turned to go in, she spotted a blue car sitting at the curb, engine still running. It looked like the same car that she'd seen at one of the bars she'd gone to.

Nah. Why would anyone be following her? How many little blue cars were there in any given city? One day of looking for Barbara and already she was jumping at shadows.

She headed up the stairs to her apartment. Once inside, she changed into her most comfortable flannel sweats and poured some juice. Within minutes, her sniffles turned into a runny nose and a flurry of sneezes. Groaning as her head began to pound, she curled up on the sofa to wait for the pharmacy delivery.

The phone rang and she ignored it, too miserable to bother getting up.

———⋇⋇⊙⋇⋇———

Tuesday, 1:45 p.m.
Prodigal SUV, en route to Prodigal offices, Baltimore

It had taken about fifteen minutes to pull Angela over. It had taken her that long to figure out that Nick wasn't the loan shark she was avoiding. But talking to Angela had been one giant dead end. She hadn't heard from Richie in nearly two years and apparently didn't want to. She gave Nick and the guys a couple of places to check, and they let her go on her way.

Richie was out there somewhere, and Nick was determined to find him. There were only so many places Richie could hide in the area without someone seeing him. And even if he found some new place to hole up, it was merely a matter of time before he surfaced. Time, however, was not the element Nick wanted to deal with. He wanted to find Richie fast.

When Nick, Conner, and Rafe arrived at the office, Jenna's desk was empty. Nick figured she went out for some lunch. The guys dispersed to their cubicles, and Nick headed down the hall with them toward his brother's cubicle.

Steven was on the phone, jotting down something on a legal pad. As always, Steven's jeans had a crease that could cut steak, and his white button-down shirt and athletic shoes didn't have a mark on them. Nick didn't want to think about how long it had been since he'd bothered to iron a shirt, and he certainly never ironed his jeans. What was the point?

Younger by four years, Steven was as different from Nick as two people could be and still be related. Steven was one of those take-life-as-it-comes people, while Nick had been accused of being intense and single-minded more than once—just one of the many differences between them. Nick didn't think he was all that intense, but he definitely took life more seriously than his goof-off brother.

The two looked completely different from each other too. Steven was two inches shorter, a few pounds lighter, had blondish-brown hair, and had their mom's green eyes rather than their dad's hazel eyes, which Nick had inherited along with their dad's broader nose and thicker neck.

"Thanks," Steven said to the person on the other end of the line. "I appreciate it." He hung up and then scooted back from his desk. "A to Z Bail Bonds sent over a list of skips. They're on your desk."

"Good."

"And one of your snitches called in. I think it was Petey." Steven leaned back and propped his feet up on the corner of his desk. "Said he was following someone you were looking for and would call in again."

"Who is he following?"

"He didn't say."

Not unusual for Petey. He was always afraid someone was going to cheat him out of a possible fifty-spot for turning in a fugitive, so he would only talk to Nick.

"I need to see you in my office if you have time."

Steven lifted an eyebrow. "We're here now. Talk."

"This includes Conner and Rafe. If it's too much effort for you to walk down the hall to meet with us, I'll send you a memo later and let you know what we discussed."

Tamping down his temper, Nick left Steven's cubicle and returned to his office. A few minutes later Conner and Rafe joined him. Steven followed right on their heels wearing a sullen expression guaranteed to be a harbinger of things to come.

"Have a seat, guys." Nick felt the twinges of a headache inching across his temples and tried to rub them away. He reached into his desk and grabbed a bottle of Excedrin Migraine.

The door to the office eased open as Jenna stepped in with a large pizza and set it down on the coffee table along with a stack of napkins. "I'm going to assume none of you stopped for lunch while you were out."

Rafe smiled at Jenna as he reached over and flipped the box open. "If you didn't have us to coddle, you wouldn't be nearly as happy."

"Dream on. And Nick...you have a call on line one. It's Will Gregory. Wants to know if you can get on a skip today."

Nick grabbed a slice of pizza before picking up the phone. "Afternoon, Will." Nick bit into the pizza and nearly groaned with pleasure. He chewed and listened to Will rattle on about a skip. After promising to give it top priority, he hung up the phone.

Suddenly the door to his office flew open, and a flash of red and black appeared in the doorway.

Krystal Shepherd quickly scanned the room. "Hi, everyone."

"Hey, sweetheart." Nick watched as his daughter bounced down on the sofa next to Rafe. He took in the tattered jeans, the shirt that barely covered her midriff, the heavy black liner around her eyes, the bright red lips, and his temper came to a slow boil.

Not today.

Wasn't the day already exhausting enough, without Krystal going in to her rebellious teen act? Swallowing the rebuke on the tip of his tongue, he tried to keep his voice neutral. "Aren't you supposed to be in school?"

Krystal's smile vanished as she gave him a snotty tilt of her head. "There's no school today. Teachers' conference. Mom's at work. She said I could spend the day here with you guys."

"Uh-huh. Well, your mother called and said that you've been skipping school." He glanced down at his watch. "And the school day isn't over. Which means you're skipping now too."

His daughter's shoulders lifted in an exaggerated shrug. "She must have forgot that we have teachers' conferences."

Good news—my daughter has stopped by to see me. Bad news—she's lying.

Nick clenched his pen a little tighter. Just once it'd be nice if she weren't forcing him to come down on her for some misdeed. When was the last time they were able to just spend time together without the conflict?

Lisa's funeral.

And with that thought, the guilt swamped him again.

Rafe leaned down, stared down in the direction of Krystal's feet, and then lifted one eyebrow with a frown. "Uh, Krys, is that a tattoo?"

Nick stiffened as Krystal grinned and kicked her foot up and slammed it down on the coffee table, showing off a black band around her ankle. Nick jerked to his feet, the movement wiping the smile off Krystal's face.

"A tattoo? What possessed you to do such a thing? You know I have already forbidden it. Does your mother know about this?"

Her bottom lip thrust out as she returned his glare. "Mom said I could."

"After I already told you no. That's just great."

Krystal jumped to her feet. "I don't care. You're always telling me no. I can't ever do anything. Why don't you just stick me in some boring private school?"

And he was ready to put that option on the table again. But this was neither the place nor the time, and it had already gone too far. He took a deep, calming breath. "Give me a minute and I'll take you to back to school."

Krystal burst into tears and started for the door.

"Where do you think you're going?"

"Back to school, if you really must know. I can take the bus, thanks very much."

He was tired of arguing with her. "Fine. Take the bus." Then he stopped. The bus. Out on the streets where Richie would have easy access to her. "On second thought, I'm not okay with that. Steven, would you do me a favor and drive your niece to school?"

Steven rolled his eyes. "Sure. No problem, *Boss.*"

"I don't need him to take me," Krystal said.

"And yet he's going to anyway. Wow."

Krystal glared at him before slamming the door behind her. Rafe and Conner followed after her. "We'll keep an eye on her, Boss," Rafe said.

It hadn't escaped Nick's mind that Krystal reminded him of his little sister. He'd even be willing to admit that he projected some of his confusion over Marti onto his daughter. Krystal had barely been two years old when Marti up and disappeared. For a long time, Nick had mourned, thinking his baby sister was dead. But then their father's contacts had hit pay dirt in Nashville. A sighting. Then another confirmed sighting in Brownsville, Texas. Now he knew she was alive. So the search went on.

"Well," Steven interjected with a sharp laugh, "I think that went well, don't you?"

Nick's temper refused to abate with his daughter's departure. "Are you going to take her or not?" He took another deep breath. "I'm sorry. I didn't mean to snap. Thanks for being willing to take her."

Steven just nodded, his face betraying a lingering resentment.

"Listen," Nick said, "there's something else. I know you have these skips to find, but if you have any spare time at all, I'd appreciate what-

ever effort you can put into helping me track down leads on Marti."
He paused. "It's just that finding her is becoming more urgent than
ever."

Steven gestured a salute. "Yes sir. I'll get right on it as soon as I get
back from driving your daughter to school." He snatched up the skip
papers and stalked out of the office.

A moment later, Nick lifted his head to see Jenna standing in the
doorway, her hands on her hips, her head tilted. "What?"

"She's just trying to get your attention."

"Oh, well, she's certainly got it." Nick reached for his slice of pizza
and took a bite. It was cold. He tossed it down on his desk. "A tattoo.
Unbelievable."

"I wouldn't be surprised if Jessica was just as furious to find out that
you'd supposedly allowed Krystal to get a tattoo."

"I never—"

Jenna threw her hand up, cutting Nick off. "Of course you didn't,
but Krystal has, like most children from broken homes, learned how to
play one parent against the other. If you and Jessica could put aside your
own agendas long enough to discuss your daughter, you might find that
Krystal is far smarter than you give her credit for."

Leaning back in his chair, Nick reached for a napkin and started
wiping his fingers. "You're probably right." But he didn't want to talk
about Krystal. That only led to thinking about Lisa. "So. How's the dating scene these days?"

Jenna folded her arms across her chest and lowered her chin. "Not
yet, Nick."

"Jenna, it's been six years. Don't you think it's time? You told me
you'd start dating again when Tim went off to college. Speaking
of…Rafe is interested, you know."

She snickered. "Rafe flirts with any woman below the age of seventy. That's not what I'm looking for."

"If you and he got serious, he wouldn't flirt. You know that."

She shrugged. "Maybe. Maybe not. But I'm not looking for a man that will change because I agree to go out with him. Either he is what I want or he's not."

"Maybe you're just scared, Jenna."

"Scared?" She snickered again, but it sounded hollow. "I am not scared." She sank down in the chair. "Okay, maybe a little. But Rafe is going to push me for more than I can give. A man like him? Women always panting after him? I'm not like that, Nick. I take my faith seriously, and having a casual fling with a man is not on my list of things to consider."

"Rafe takes his faith seriously too."

"I'm sure he does. But I'm just not interested in falling for a heartthrob. You think it's easy for me? Working day in and day out with all of you? I *am* a woman, you know, and I've been alone a long time."

He grinned at her, pretending to curl the ends of an imaginary mustache. "Oh yeah? Want some candy?"

Jenna laughed. "Don't flatter yourself. I was talking about Steven. He just rocks my boat."

Nick groaned as he tossed a paper clip at her. "That hurt." Then he leaned back and met Jenna's eyes, held them for a moment. "For what it's worth, you're going to have to risk something if you're ever going to find love again."

The smile was more of a smirk when she lifted an eyebrow and stood up. "Believe that yourself and then we'll talk."

As the door closed behind her, the phone rang. He pushed Jenna's targeted words aside. "Prodigal Recovery."

"Nick?" It was Petey. "Whatja doin?"

"Just tracking down some leads. You got something for me?"

"Yeah. I was down at Jiffy's Bar talking to Bobby Wheeler. Anyway, I saw a girl come in. I swear it's that woman you're looking for. Zeena Bantham. So I followed her. She eventually went into this apartment. I'm sitting out in the parking lot watching."

Nick stood up, tucking the phone under his chin as he pulled open his top drawer and pulled out his holstered gun. "Hold on, Petey. Give Conner the address, and I'm on my way." He pushed a button on the phone. "Conner? I have Petey on line two. He's got Zeena cornered. Get the address from him and then grab your gear. I'll meet you out front."

Nick picked up his Kevlar vest and left his office. Then he stopped, remembered his detour that morning, and looked around the reception area. "Where's the dog?"

Jenna looked up. "Steven took him to a groomer a few hours ago and dropped him off."

"Why? It's a stray. We aren't keeping it. I just didn't want it left out there in the rain."

Jenna tucked a stack of papers into a file folder and tossed them onto a stack to be filed. "I think Steven's already attached. Anyway, the dog stank."

Tuesday, 1:45 p.m.
The Stark Lily, Park Heights, Baltimore

Jon Carver's office was tucked away above the offices and rest rooms of the Stark Lily. The walls were nearly soundproof, so the music could be rattling the windows half a block away and Jon wouldn't be able to hear a thing. The office was decorated more like the corner office of a corporate CEO, but then, Jon was the head of his own empire, so why not? Plush carpets, expensive paintings, polished cherry desk, matching cabinets and shelves that held a wet bar and safe, and a flat screen mounted on the far wall.

Jon tapped his cigar on the edge of a crystal ashtray and spun it slowly as he listened to a business associate on the other end of the line. He braced the phone on his shoulder and reached down to pull open a desk drawer and retrieve his gold-plated pen.

"Ben, Ben, Ben. I promise you, you're going to be thrilled with this shipment. First-rate equipment." The equipment *better* be first rate. He'd paid enough to those supply officers to get the newest pistols and rifles the army had available. It was worth it, of course. For every dollar he spent in bribes and payoffs, he made a hundred with this deal. Not bad for a day's work.

Bored with his buyer, he picked up the remote and turned on the television, keeping the sound off. He picked up his cigar and took a puff. "Thursday night at midnight. Yeah, yeah."

But when he saw his brother's face flash across the TV screen, he nearly dropped the phone. Grabbing the remote, he turned up the sound. "Ben, something just came up. I'll call you back."

He hung up the phone and listened to the reporter give details on the morning's prison escape. He shouldn't have been surprised that it was all over the news. It wasn't that often that two killers successfully escaped and disappeared.

Richie had called him at five that morning to tell him that he was out and hiding with another inmate up at the farm. Jon had a million questions, but as usual, Richie had no answers. Of course, Richie expected to just come waltzing back into the club as if nothing had happened. But it wasn't going to be that easy for him. More times than he could count, Jon regretted promising his mother that he'd look out for his younger brother.

He shook his head.

He had just sold one of the biggest shipments he'd ever brokered, and now Richie's escape would have every cop and Fed knocking on Jon's door. *Perfect.*

On top of that, his laptop with all his recent shipment dates, points of origin, and sales values had been stolen. He needed to get that back before it fell into the wrong hands. The wrong hands being anyone except his own.

It seemed that God wasn't exactly on his side these days.

But if God was going to play dirty, so would he.

Just then another thought hit him. He massaged his temples. With Richie on the run, that bounty hunter Nick Shepherd would be all over this like a Rottweiler on a ham bone. Jon was going to have to try even harder to distract the good Mr. Shepherd and his team until those guns were safely in the hands of his buyer and the money was deposited in his offshore account. So far, every effort he'd made to bribe Shepherd had failed, but no one was totally incorruptible.

<hr />

Tuesday, 2:15 p.m.
Prodigal SUV, en route to northern Baltimore

After piling into Nick's vehicle, Conner read over Zeena's bail skip information one more time.

"Zeena Bantham. Single, thirty-four, five foot six, red hair, green eyes, one hundred and four pounds. Priors include six for prostitution, two for possession of a controlled substance, and two unpaid parking tickets. Four DWIs. This last arrest was for assault with a deadly weapon." Conner turned the sheet to look at the one below it. "She attacked her john with a knife." He dropped the sheet and went back to her record. "Driver's license revoked in '01. Currently on probation for prostitution and possession. Failure to appear on the twenty-second on the assault charge. Failure to report to parole officer on the twenty-fourth."

Nick navigated the SUV off 695 and into a residential neighborhood. He was a little surprised at the area. Not the usual home base for a street girl.

He made a left off Reisterstown Road onto a narrow side street, and Conner pointed to a red brick, three-story apartment building. "That's it right there: 509. And there's Petey."

Nick spotted Petey's blue Camry sitting near the entrance of the parking lot and pulled in, parking next to it. He, Rafe, and Conner climbed out of the SUV and opened the rear hatch. Nick shrugged out of his jacket and grabbed his Kevlar vest. "What do we have, Petey?"

Petey danced from one foot to the other, his eyes wide with excitement as he held out his hand. Nick pulled out the fifty and put it in Petey's hand. It disappeared faster than a fifty at the grocery store. "She hasn't come back out yet. I talked to this lady that came out a few minutes ago, and she said the broad is a tenant. Apartment 2-E, though she said the broad goes by a different name."

Conner folded his arms across his chest and looked at the cars in the parking lot. "Ford, Chevrolet, Saturn, Volkswagen. Nothing more than nine or ten years old. Not typical of a tweeker's usual economic stratum."

Turning back to Petey, Nick asked, "And the lady said she was a tenant?"

"Sure did. Yep. Said she'd been here about two years."

"Odd." Nick mused. "Okay, Petey. Thanks."

Petey jumped into his car and sped off. Probably heading straight to the nearest bar to spend the money.

"Rafe, check the back. Make sure there's only one door in and out."

Rafe nodded and jogged off behind the building.

Nick zipped up his jacket, dropped the hatch, and headed across the parking lot to the front of the building. Inside the lobby, he checked the mailboxes to confirm the apartment number.

"Half of these have no names." Conner cracked a smile. "No one likes to make our job easy, do they?"

"It isn't personal, I'm sure." Nick replied dryly as they headed up the stairs. Conner already had his gun out, in hand, and hanging at his side.

On the second floor, they cautiously made their way down to apartment 2-E. Without a word from Nick, Conner slipped past him to take a position on the other side of the door. A slight noise had Nick looking over his shoulder. Rafe joined them and whispered, "Covered."

Easing his gun out, Nick nodded and then knocked twice on the apartment door. Immediately, a woman's voice, low and soft, responded. "Just a minute!"

Conner stepped back behind Nick.

The door swung open to reveal a redhead wrapped in a flowered bathrobe. "You made good time," she said, holding out her hand.

The woman in their picture had shoulder-length hair, and the woman in the doorway had spiky short hair, but other than that, there was no doubt that this was Zeena. Thin and gaunt to the point of skeletal, she had dark circles under her bloodshot eyes, her skin was pale, and she was sniffling.

Suddenly her green eyes opened wide as Nick and Conner stepped forward, crowding her back into the apartment. Conner stopped just inside the doorway, gun held with both hands, pointed at her face, while Rafe swept the apartment, covering Nick in case anyone else was there. "Sorry to disappoint you, but I'm not your next john."

"What?"

Nick grabbed her right wrist and quickly turned her around as he reholstered his gun and pulled out his handcuffs. "Zeena Bantham, you are under arrest for failure to appear."

"Failure? What? Wait! I'm not Zeena! I'm Annie. Annie McNamara. You're making a mistake!"

Nick snapped the cuffs. "Nice try, lady. Wanna know how many times I've heard that one?"

She turned and stared up at him, tears forming in defiant eyes. "I'm serious! You're obviously looking for my twin sister. Let me show you my ID. I have ID to prove I'm who I say I am."

Laughing, Nick looked over at Conner. "You ever hear that one before?"

"A million times, more or less. But who's counting?"

"Lady, you were seen at the bar a couple hours ago. And it's the same one Zeena works out of on occasion. What a coincidence."

"I went there looking for my sister. I heard she sometimes hangs out there. That's all. I'm trying to find her."

Conner held a picture in front of her. "Funny. You look exactly like the woman in this picture. Coincidence? I think not."

The woman took a deep breath. "Look in my purse. Everything is there. I am not Zeena Bantham. Believe me."

Conner looked over at Nick for direction. Nick nodded. "Check it out."

Opening the black leather hobo bag on the table, Conner pulled out a wallet and flipped it wide. "Ann Marie McNamara." He looked over at Nick with a frown. "Same birth date as our girl." Then he went back to flipping through the social security card, credit cards, library card, and work identification. "She's a chef at LaRose Catering. And here's what looks like an old picture of her and a twin." Conner held it up. "Looks like she's telling the truth."

Nick took a second to process and then unlocked the handcuffs. "So if I call this LaRose Catering, they'll verify you are who you say you are?"

"They'll tell you I'm out on medical leave, but yes, they will confirm who I am." She rubbed her wrists, and he looked away when he saw a tear dribble down out of the corner of her eye. "Why are you looking for my sister?"

"She jumped bail, Ms. McNamara," Conner replied as he stuffed her wallet back into her purse. "Sorry for the mistake, but we didn't know she had a twin."

"That doesn't surprise me," she said, clutching her robe at her throat as if just realizing she was standing in front of three men in her pajamas and robe.

"You wouldn't happen to know where she is, would you?" Nick said. She shook her head. "No, I told you. I'm trying to find her too."

Nick's phone rang. He pulled it off his belt and saw that the call was from Jenna. "Hey."

"I just got a call from Linc."

"Hold on." Nick nodded to Conner. "Give her our card." He looked over at the woman. "If you see her, please call us."

Then he turned his attention back to Jenna as he walked out of the apartment. "What's up?"

"You need to get down to the station. Krystal's been picked up for shoplifting."

5

Tuesday, 2:45 p.m.
Downtown Baltimore

She was going to die after all. Her sister, Barbara, or the woman they knew as Zeena, was running from the law and would end up captured and put in jail. There was no way she could get Barbara's help if she were behind bars.

Annie sat down on the sofa. She stared at the bounty hunter's business card. *Prodigal Fugitive Recovery Agency. They can run, but they can't hide.*

Now they were out chasing her sister down like—

As she tapped the card against her palm, thoughts formed. Okay, when they found Barbara, they would take her straight to jail. She just couldn't let that happen. The bottom line was simple—she had to find Barbara first.

But between her and the bottom line was a long list of obstacles. She'd love to be able to use those bounty hunters to her advantage. Especially that alpha male, Nick. Attractive, strong.

But how could she get him to help her?

She returned to the sofa, tossing the business card to the coffee table. Then she reached for a tissue and wiped her nose.

There had to be a way. She just had to figure out a plan.

Tuesday, 3:20 p.m.
Baltimore County Lockup

Her dark brown hair looked as if it had been in a windstorm, and her big brown eyes were red from crying. Nick's heart immediately went out to her, but he steeled himself not to show any emotion at all. Ignoring her, he reached out to his old partner, Linc, and shook his hand. "I appreciate the favor."

The officer returned the handshake. "First offense. Not that big a favor. But I won't forget when the time comes I need something from you."

Nick laughed. "I figured that." Then he turned to his daughter. "Let's go."

"Why? So you can yell at me?"

The sarcasm cut right across his last nerve and vibrated right to his temples. She had done nothing but fling sarcasm and bitterness at him since he walked through the door. No gratitude for Linc dismissing the charges. No appreciation for his efforts. "I don't want to hear one more word out of you, young lady."

She lifted her head and headed for the door. "I'm surprised you even bothered coming down here. You usually like to hand your problems off for someone else."

"Krystal, not another word. You've pushed me far enough today."

He unlocked the SUV and opened the door for her. She glared at him as she climbed in and reached for her seat belt. "Since we're so close to home, why don't you just drop me off there?"

"Because I can't trust that you'll stay put. Just relax. We're about to spend some real quality time together."

Folding her arms across her chest, Krystal slammed back against the seat with a pout.

Whipping the steering wheel, he pulled up to the curb and put the SUV in park. Then he shifted in his seat to look at his daughter. "What exactly is your problem with me? You've been like this ever since—" He stopped, emitted a heavy sigh, and ran one hand down his face.

"Can't say it, can you?" She lifted her chin as tears began to spill. "Lisa's funeral."

"Yes," he whispered. "Since Lisa's funeral."

"Well. Are you surprised? You let her die. All because catching some criminal was more important than Lisa was. It's always been more important than me or Mom or anything. Even Lisa."

"No, honey, you're wrong. I did everything I could to save her."

"Oh yeah? Well, if it was so important to you, why didn't you even care enough to show up on time for her funeral? You didn't even get there until it was nearly over. Why? Because you were out chasing another criminal."

It hit him out of the blue, and he stared at her for a long moment, trying to weigh the idea, determine the validity of such a thought. On the surface, it was ridiculous. Then again, he was dealing with a teenager. "Krystal? Is all this rebellion, shoplifting, lying—is all this because you figure acting like some criminal will get my attention?"

She looked out the window and then slowly turned to look at him again, and when she did, he saw the little self-satisfied smirk on her lips. "Well, let's see. My dance recital? You didn't show up. My soccer finals? You didn't show up. The school play I was in? You didn't show. I get arrested for shoplifting and *bam*. You're there so fast they didn't have time to fingerprint me. So you tell me, Dad."

⚬

Tuesday, 3:50 p.m.
White Marsh, North Baltimore

Jessica Shepherd wasn't sure whether she wanted to scream or just cry. "Look. You promised delivery of those leather sofas for January first. Then it was mid-January. Then February. We are now at the end of March, and my client is understandably fed up and so am I. Now, if you ever want my firm to place an order with you again in the future, you will have those sofas delivered, as ordered, to the Chambers home by Friday."

As the man started to sputter, she repeated, "Friday. By five. Or the next call you receive will be from our attorneys." She slammed the phone down.

"You tell 'em."

Jessica nearly jumped out of her chair. She looked over at the doorway to see her boss, Grace Harmon, leaning against the door frame, arms folded. "Was I too loud?"

Grace pushed off the door frame and walked over, easing down into the visitor's chair across from Jessica's desk. Grace Harmon was a legend from the sitting rooms of DC to the parlors of Philadelphia.

"I think the Nelsons heard you from their home in Annapolis." Then Grace waved a hand. "No big deal. That's not what I came in here for. Heaven knows I've had my fair share of screaming matches with suppliers. Allie left a note on my desk that you wanted to talk to me about the Winston House restoration."

The Winston House was one of the oldest mansions in Frederick County. Built in the mid-1800s by Byron Winston, it had reigned as the finest hotel in Northern Maryland. It once attracted only the wealthiest visitors traveling from Washington to Gettysburg, but around the 1950s, it began a downward spiral and had been empty ever since.

But the town council had recently decided its history was worth preserving. So they hired Grace Designs to handle the restoration. It was, without a doubt, the largest and most lucrative project in terms of money and publicity that Grace Designs had ever handled. The pressure was on, and everyone was feeling it.

"The Winston House restoration." Jessica mused as she reached over and rifled through a stack of files, pulling one out. She flipped it open. "The centerpiece of the lobby back in the late 1800s was a red velvet circular sofa placed directly under a magnificent chandelier. I sent pictures of the original chandelier out to every supplier I could think of, and one of them hit pay dirt."

Jessica pulled an eight-by-ten color photograph out of the file folder and handed it over to Grace. "Check this out."

Grace lifted her glasses and perched them on the end of her nose and then looked at the photograph. "It's perfect. It looks exactly like the original."

"Better. It *is* the original."

Grace dropped her glasses. "You're kidding me."

"Serious."

"Wow," Grace said as she leaned back and crossed her legs. "Good find, Jessica."

"Thanks." Jessica took the compliment and bathed in it for a moment. It wasn't often Grace gave anyone a pat on the back, much less

a word of praise. Still, it was far more often than Nick ever compli-
mented her. Or showed any appreciation for the little things she did for
him. And praise? The man didn't know the meaning of the word.

Just as Grace disappeared through the door, Jessica's assistant, Allie,
slipped in. She waved a stack of pink slips and then set them down in
front of Jessica. "Messages. One of them is urgent. I put it on top."

Jessica thanked her and picked up the first message. Then she
groaned. Krystal had been arrested.

Tuesday, 3:55 p.m.
Park Heights, Baltimore

The wind had picked up, whipping through the streets of Baltimore as
if on a mission to send everyone inside. Zeena looked around the block,
hoping to find a place where she could sit and be sheltered from the
wind. Ahead, she saw a couple of old men sitting on the stoop of a row
house passing a paper bag between them. At least they had something
to help ward off the chill. Zeena shifted her backpack and huddled
down in her thin jacket as she darted across the street.

"Zeena?"

Stifling a scream, Zeena whirled around. It was two of Jon's goons
and two of the last people she wanted to see. "I'm not working right
now."

One of the men grabbed Zeena by the arm. "Mr. Carver wants to
talk to you."

"About what? I don't owe him anything." She forced herself not to
fall to her feet and beg for her life. She knew this was about that laptop

that Danny Sloop stole from Jon Carver. If she didn't get away, she'd be dead.

"Danny said he gave you something that belonged to Mr. Carver." He squeezed her arm a little tighter. She winced and tried to pull away.

"Danny is lying to you, Lester."

"Mr. Carver doesn't think so. And he would very much like to get his property back."

"Then get it from Danny," she snapped. She knew Danny was probably dead, but it didn't serve any purpose for her to acknowledge that. Even now, she could see the doubt growing in the man's eyes. "Look. I haven't seen Danny in weeks, and Carver knows I'd never betray him. If Danny had given me something that belongs to him, I would have brought it to him."

The grip on her arm eased up. She decided to press her luck. "Look, call Jon. Get him on the phone. He knows me better than this."

The two men glanced at each other. The lock on her arm eased completely. She took a deep breath and yanked her arm free. Then she spun on her heels and ran, darting around a car, then around a Dumpster.

A bullet hit the concrete wall next to her, and a piece flew off and hit her across the cheek. She didn't bother to check it. A nick was better than dead. Hey, even a deep gouge would be better than dead.

Another bullet hit near her, and she sped up, whipping around the building and darting into a secondhand clothing store. They wouldn't dare come running in here with guns blazing. Too many customers. Too many witnesses.

"My ex-boyfriend," she screamed. "He's trying to kill me! Tell him I went out the back!" She dove under a rack of clothes and curled up, wrapping her arms around her calves, trying to be as small as possible.

She heard the front doors open and a flurry of feet. Then she heard a woman speak up. "If you're looking for that dirty redhead, she went out the back."

Zeena felt like crying with relief as the heavy boots thudded past her and then the sound faded. She eased out, looking carefully around to make sure they were gone.

"You can come out now," a woman with a baby in her arms said. "Hurry out the front."

Zeena scrambled to her feet, secured her backpack, and rushed out the front door, sprinting across the street and into a nearby alley. Only after she was a good block away did she realize that she hadn't even thanked those women for helping her. Oh, well.

Then she heard a gunshot and saw that it hit less than a foot away from her. They'd found her. She willed her feet to run faster. Looking over her shoulder as she turned a corner, she only saw the one man following her. Where was Lester?

She slammed into something. And then hands gripped her tight. "Hello, Zeena. Going somewhere?"

6

Tuesday, 4:20 p.m.
Prodigal offices, Baltimore

Nick drove back to the Prodigal offices in a silence broken only by his futile attempts to get Krystal to talk to him.

Once at the office, Nick dropped his vest inside the door and walked over to Jenna's desk to pick up his messages. One said that his gas credit cards would be temporarily suspended if he didn't send a payment within forty-eight hours. Nick dropped both hands to the edge of Jenna's desk and leaned in, bowing his head. "Could this day get any worse?"

"It could," Jenna replied. "Let's pray that it doesn't. Where's Krystal?"

"Taking her sweet time, of course."

Sure enough, the front door opened, and Krystal came dragging through the door, carrying the rest of Nick's gear and looking none too happy about being a pack mule.

Jenna smiled. "Hi, Krystal."

"Hi, Jenna." Then the girl disappeared through Nick's office door.

Jenna tucked her pencil behind her ear. "Nick, you know, Harvey owes us nearly three thousand dollars for skips."

"Yeah. He's always slow to pay. Stay on him. Remind him that we've consistently taken good care of him."

The front door flew open, sending a blast of cold, damp March weather through the reception area. Jessica swept in, clutching her red wool coat at her throat. He resented the punch to his heart when he saw her. How stupid was it to be in love with a woman who hated him? The woman was an iceberg, but she still had his heart in the palm of her slender little hands. He just wasn't stupid enough to let her know it.

He took a deep breath and braced himself for the next battle of the day. "I thought you were at work."

"I was. Then I get a message from my assistant that my daughter has been arrested. I called the police department only to learn that her father had already picked her up. Not that you would think to call me and let me know."

"Let me get this straight, Jess. First you scream for me to handle her. Then when I do, you gripe because I did. Why don't you make up your mind?"

She pointed a manicured finger at him. Red, probably to match her coat. And probably the suit beneath it. "Did it ever cross your mind that I might be concerned about her safety?"

"Linc said they couldn't reach you. They called me, and I picked her up. I haven't had a chance to call you. I've been a little busy."

The phone rang, but before Nick could use it as an excuse to get away from Jessica, the ringing stopped. Jenna must have picked it up from somewhere else in the building. The traitor.

"Where is Krystal now?"

"In my office."

Jessica looked beyond him toward his office door. "Krystal Marie Shepherd! Out here. Now."

Krystal appeared in the doorway with a belligerent look plastered on her face. "Don't bother giving me a hard time. Dad has already ripped me apart more than once."

"Good for him. Now it's my turn. Out in the car. Now."

With an exaggerated sigh, Krystal shuffled out of the office without a word to either of her parents.

Jessica looked from her retreating daughter to Nick. "If you don't step in and do something with her, Nick, she's going to end up in jail for life."

"Last time I checked, I'm the one that had to go face my friend on the force to get this dropped. I dealt with it."

"I meant that you need to deal with *her*. All her life, she was your little princess. Every time she acted up, you made excuses for her, and now look what you've created." Jessica turned on her heel and stormed out of the building.

Jenna quietly reappeared and handed him a slip of paper. "Harvey called to ask if we found the Bantham woman. I explained about the mix-up, but he swears the woman denied having any relatives when he bonded her out."

Nick just nodded, stalked into his office, threw his keys on his desk, and sank down on the sofa. He didn't know whether to scream or just wave a white flag.

After several long moments of silence, he grabbed his keys and strode out through the lobby. "I'll be at the dojang if anyone needs me."

———※———

Tuesday, 4:45 p.m.
En route to White Marsh, Maryland

Krystal ignored her mother on the drive home. It wasn't all that hard. It wasn't like her mom was doing much talking either. At least not until they got home. Then she apparently decided that Krystal was grounded.

"Two weeks? You're grounding me for two weeks?" Krystal slammed her backpack down on the kitchen table. "You can't!"

"I beg to differ with you, young lady. I warned you that if you got into trouble one more time, I was going to ground you." Jessica slipped her coat off and draped it over her arm. "I think this latest little stunt of yours justifies my case."

Krystal wanted to scream. This was all so unfair! "You just hate me, that's all. I remind you of the biggest mistake of your life!"

"And what mistake was that, exactly?" Jessica opened the coat closet and pulled out a hanger.

Krystal stood in the archway and screamed down the hall as her mother hung up her coat. "Marrying Daddy! You hate him, and you hate me because I remind you of him."

"That is ridiculous." She closed the closet door and returned to the kitchen. Krystal stepped out of the way to let her pass. "I don't hate your father. He and I have some issues, but that doesn't change my love for you." Her mother hesitated. "Or his."

"Whatever. I know you hate him." She picked up her backpack and slung it over her shoulder. "I heard you tell Grandmother that I reminded you of him; stubborn, selfish, and incapable of considering others."

Her mother blushed and started making a pot of coffee. "I'm sorry you heard that. I really am. I shouldn't have said it. But I do love you. And I do not want to stand by and watch you ruin your life. I refuse to let you turn to shoplifting or drugs or drinking or anything else just to lash out at me or your father."

"Why not? You hate me just like you hate Dad. You probably wish I was the one that died instead of Lisa."

Jessica gasped. "Krystal! What a horrible thing to say. I *love* you and would never wish you or Lisa dead. How could you even think such a thing? I know you miss Lisa—"

"You don't know anything, and I don't care what you say. Lorianne is having the party of the year this Friday night, and I plan to be there."

Her mother opened a cabinet and took down a coffee cup and saucer. "Why don't we sit down. Talk about Lisa."

"No. Lisa is gone."

"Suit yourself, Krys. But still, you'll have to send your regrets to Lorianne because you will be spending Friday evening, and the rest of the next two weeks, in your room with your schoolbooks."

"You can't make me." She turned and headed upstairs to her bedroom. "I *am* going out on Friday."

Her mother appeared at the bottom of the stairs. "Don't push me."

Krystal turned at the top of the stairs and stared down at her mother. "Or what, Mom? Maybe you should tell Daddy to put his foot down." She opened her bedroom door, then slammed it so hard the window rattled.

Dropping her backpack to the floor, she flopped down across her bed. She hated her life. Hated feeling pushed and pulled between her parents. Hated the comparisons.

For what felt like the millionth time, Krystal cried, wondering why God hated her so much that he gave her a mom and dad who hated her and then took her best friend away. No one had ever understood Krystal the way Lisa had. If Lisa were here, being grounded wouldn't be so bad.

Well, come Friday night, her mother was going to find out just what Krystal thought of being grounded. How could they expect her to actually accept any kind of punishment? The only time they acted like parents was when she got into trouble.

<hr />

Tuesday, 5:30 p.m.
Lu-Kay Martial Arts Dojang, Baltimore

The dojang was pleasantly quiet when Nick arrived. The afternoon kids' classes were done, and the evening adult classes wouldn't start until seven. Nick changed in the locker room and then headed out to the studio. Dark blue mats covered the tile floor, and one wall had a mirror from floor to ceiling. Other than a few posters advertising upcoming competitions, the walls were bare. As soon as Nick stepped onto the mats, soft jazz floated out of the speakers. Nick smiled to himself. Luke never missed a trick.

During his rookie year as a cop, Nick had been forced to shoot a man in self-defense. While he understood that sometimes he was going to have to use his gun, he began to look for other ways to take a man down without having to kill him in the process. He settled on hapkido, a martial arts discipline that stressed gaining advantage through footwork and body position for leverage rather than the use of strength against strength. Luke was, at that time, just the son of the owner, but when his father retired, Luke took over as the owner and master teacher. Through it all, the two men remained friends.

Nick stood in the middle of the mat, his weight balanced on his left foot as he held his right foot straight out in front of him. He held it there—three minutes. Four. Sweat broke out across his forehead, but he held the pose. Muscles tightened and protested, but still he held it there.

He became aware of someone standing behind him, breathing quietly. "You just going to stand there and watch or what?" he asked.

"Forcing something to obey never works as well as quiet coercion." Luke strolled soundlessly around to face Nick. His Asian roots were obvious in some of the facial features, but he owed his height and name to his American father. "You have been absent for nearly two weeks. It shows."

"I've been busy," Nick slowly lowered his leg. When he finally had both feet back on the mat, he bowed formally.

Luke bowed in return. "You have been missed."

"My apologies. I should have made time to be here."

Luke tilted his head. "You are stressed."

"To the max, old friend."

"Perhaps it would be best if we stretch a little first. Clear our heads. Then I will proceed to show you how badly you needed to be here."

Nick laughed. "Just because I haven't been here doesn't mean you can defeat me."

Nick could sense that Luke was about to move even though his teacher hadn't so much as flexed a muscle. Flipping back, he felt the air swoosh past his ear as Luke's foot nearly clipped him. Spinning and then bouncing up to his feet, he blocked a hand strike, then spun around for a roundhouse kick. It didn't land. Luke had ducked, spinning on the balls of his feet, and then shot out in a sweeping kick that Nick evaded by jumping up and over it.

Their mock battle went on for nearly twenty minutes. A few punches and kicks made contact, but very few. The two men were equally matched and had practiced too many times over the years to be taken by surprise. By the time Nick bowed to Luke, sweat was pouring off both men.

They sank down on the mat. "I can't ever let two weeks go by again. That just about killed me."

Luke merely grinned as he stretched. "How about dinner?"

Nick shook his head. "I'd like to, but I really need to hit a couple of bars tonight."

Luke lifted one eyebrow.

"Business, Luke. Business."

———◦———

Tuesday, 8:00 p.m.
Downtown Baltimore

After sleeping most of the afternoon away, Annie woke up around six thirty. She tried to convince herself that she felt too weak and miserable to go back out looking for her sister, but common sense won out. She didn't have time to be sick.

But common sense reared up and changed its mind when she pulled into Jiffy's. The parking lot was only half full, but it still felt like she was stepping into no man's land. It looked far worse and far more dangerous after dark than it had in the morning. Neon lights advertising four different kinds of beer flashed and flickered in the blacked-out windows. The building itself, a small brick storefront sitting in the middle of a gravel parking lot, had seen better days. She was in over her head. But she could not turn back.

Squaring her shoulders, she tightened her grip on her shoulder bag and headed inside.

The loud music nearly knocked her back through the doors. The bass was heavy enough to pound through her chest with every beat.

Eyes turned to look at her, and then some slid away while others swept down the length of her and then back up to meet her eyes with a question she had no intention of answering. She made her way over to the bar. Sure enough, there were two bartenders on duty, and neither of them was the same one she'd talked to that morning.

"Hey, Zeena. Where you been hiding yourself, woman? And don't you look all prim and proper."

Annie shook her head at the blond bartender as he set a drink down in front of her with a big smile. "I'm not Zeena."

"What?"

"I'm not Zeena," she yelled a little louder. "She's my sister. Have you seen her today?"

The bartender squinted and leaned in close to her. "You're what?"

"I'm her sister, Annie. I'm trying to find Zeena. Have you seen her?"

He backed away, shaking his head. "Not in a few weeks."

"Any idea where I could look?"

He shrugged and held up a hand as someone yelled for his attention. "She usually works this neighborhood, and if she ain't out there on the streets, she's usually in here or over at the Rusty Bucket. See if you can find Delilah. She's the girl with the long, long black hair. Tends to work over on Tripp Street. She sometimes hangs with Zeena. Best I can tell you." He moved away to wait on another customer.

Annie turned to head out and found herself slamming into the chest of a man in a torn T-shirt and a few days' growth of beard. "Zeena, baby. I got a few bucks and an hour to kill. Let's go party somewhere."

"I'm not Zeena." She tried to slide sideways to get around him, but he moved with her, keeping her blocked.

"Ah, come on, Zeena. Don't play hard to get tonight. I ain't in the mood. I'll get a dime bag if you want."

Annie shook her head. "I'm *really* not Zeena. You have the wrong girl. Now, please let me go."

He grabbed her arm. "Okay, half an hour. Let's go."

She tried to pull away, digging the heels of her boots into the slippery floor. "Let me go!"

Suddenly, another hand reached out and took hold of the man's hand. She saw the look of pain that flashed across his face before he suddenly released his hold on her arm. "The lady said you made a mistake. Be nice and go away."

Annie looked up and nearly slumped to the floor in relief. It was that bounty hunter, Nick Sheffer or Shepherd or something. She moved closer to him.

"I got here first, buddy," the man growled, rubbing his hand. "You can have her when I'm done."

"You're not doing anything with her, *buddy*. She's with me. Get your hands off her." He reached down inside his coat and pulled out his badge, flashed it, and then tucked it back inside his coat. "You really don't want to mess with me."

The scruffy man threw both hands up in the air and backed away. "Sorry for the mistake, Officer."

As soon as he left, Annie looked up at Nick. "Thanks. I appreciate the rescue."

"You shouldn't be here."

Annie ignored his comment as she moved past him and out the door. He stayed right behind her. "I know you're looking for her."

Spinning around, Annie dug for her car keys. "And I'm going to find her before you do."

"Ann."

"It's Annie." She pulled out her keys and headed for her car, her boots crunching across the gravel.

"Annie, you can't do this alone. What if I hadn't been here tonight?"

He was right and she knew it, but she also knew that if he found Barbara first, Barbara would be in jail and Annie would have no hope. She couldn't let that happen. But tonight had been enough to scare the red right out of her hair. When that man had grabbed her and she realized that she couldn't escape, images of rape and murder had played through her head so fast she could barely catch her breath.

She turned around to face him again and took a deep breath. If she didn't fight for her life, who would? "Help me find her."

"What?" He took a step back and folded his arms across his chest. "Let me explain how this works. I am hired to find fugitives and return them to jail. I am not a family-reunion specialist."

"But I *need* to find my sister." She threw a hand up to keep him from speaking until she was finished. "I know you have a job to do, and I appreciate that. But I'm willing to cut a deal with you. We find her together, and you can take her to jail and collect your blasted bounty. But first she has to go to the hospital…and see my mom."

He tilted his head, staring at her. She shifted her weight from one foot to the other.

"Why does she have to go see your mom?"

Annie forced herself not to fidget, not to look away, not to do any of the little things that people do when they're lying. It was bad enough that she didn't want his pity, but to have him brand her a liar on top of it would be worse. "Because…my mother is dying and she wants to see Barbara before she goes. That's all she wants. To see Barbara. And she doesn't have much time."

He stood there for a long moment until Annie finally realized she was toying with her keys. She stopped. Then he unfolded his arms and shoved his hands in the pockets of his leather jacket.

"What's wrong with your mother?"

"I don't see the relevance."

"Maybe not, but I do."

Then a thought popped up from out of nowhere, and she grabbed at it. "Help me or I'll sue you."

He laughed. "You can't sue me."

She lifted her chin. "Wrong, Mr. Sheffer."

"Shepherd."

"Whatever. I *will* sue you. And I'll make sure that not only does my attorney find every charge he can possibly dig up—like assault, battery, breaking and entering."

"There was no assault. Or battery. Or breaking and entering. Bounty hunters have the right to enter the premises to pursue a fugitive. But it was a nice try."

"First of all, I wasn't a fugitive you were pursuing. I believe the law states that you may enter the premises of the fugitive, but not some innocent bystander. See? I watch *Dog the Bounty Hunter*. And…" She pulled up the sleeve of her jacket and held up her arm, showing a tiny little bruise around her wrist. "Bruises. I'll say it was assault." She pushed down her sleeve. "And then I'm going to call the newspapers and tell them how you burst through my door, refused to check my identification, threw me up against a wall—"

"You can't be serious."

"Oh, I'm very serious, Mr. Shebber."

"Shepherd…Nick."

"So either we work together, or all of Baltimore will see you brought up on charges that I'm sure will put your entire company in a very bad light."

His eyes narrowed. "You're bluffing."

"Nope." She turned on her heel and headed for her car.

He didn't move. He was calling her bluff. She had one last card to play. Frustrated, she turned around. "Okay, fine. What's your fee for finding my sister?"

His arms were folded across his chest. "Why?"

"Whatever they're paying you"—she closed the distance between them, slowly coming to a stop a few feet in front of him—"I'll double it."

Silence. Then—

"Fine. Go home. I'll find her."

Annie shook her head again, reaching out to place her hand on his arm. "No. I'm going with you. I don't know if I can trust you."

"Why not? You've just doubled my fee."

He had a point. "I've got information, and I'm not going to share it with you unless you agree to my terms."

"This is ridiculous."

"It's not that complicated, Mr. Shepherd. You and I team up and find my sister, and you collect two paychecks for one person. Sounds reasonable to me."

"We find her," he repeated. "And I take her—handcuffed—to your mom and then straight to jail."

"Yes."

"Fine. What did the bartender tell you?"

"We have a deal?"

"We have a deal. What did he tell you?"

"He said to look for a woman named Delilah. She works here in the area. And he also said that Zeena hangs out at a place called the Rusty Bucket."

Nick pulled out his keys. "Sorry to tell you this, but that's not new information, Annie. Seeing Delilah was my next stop after Jiffy's. She's usually a pretty good source. And my partner Rafe is at the Rusty Bucket as we speak." Nick groaned. "Let's go."

Annie followed Nick over to his SUV and waited while he unlocked her door and pulled it open for her, then moved to the driver's side.

She buckled her seat belt and wrinkled her nose. A mix of wet dog, old food, mold, and gym socks assaulted her. When was the last time he had cleaned his car? High school?

They drove over to Tripp Street, just a few blocks away. It was lined with pawn shops, liquor stores, small used car lots, bars, and car repair shops with a few independent grocery and drugstores thrown in. Most of the shops were locked, boarded, or chained down for the night. The few people on the street were here for a reason, and it was usually illegal.

After circling the area three times, Nick pointed to a woman getting out of a Camaro. "There she is."

She was a tiny little thing, Asian, wearing a short red skirt and long black leather coat. As soon as the car sped away, he pulled the SUV up to the curb and hit the button to lower Annie's window. "Hey, Li!"

Delilah strolled over and, folding her arms on the edge of the window, leaned in and smiled at Nick. "Hey, Bounty Hunter. Who you hunting now?" Then she cut her gaze over at Annie. "Hey, Zee."

"Not Zeena," Nick said. "This is her sister. But we're looking for Zeena. Have you seen her around lately?"

Delilah shook her head. "Haven't seen her in…maybe two weeks.

Maybe longer." She looked back at Annie. "Twins?"

"Yes," Annie said, feeling completely out of place.

"Any idea where she might be?" Nick interjected.

Delilah shook her head. "Last time I saw her, she looked *bad*. She was looking for a party. Said she was going to look up Danny, but I don't know if she did or not. Danny has his own troubles."

"Yeah? What's up with him?"

She shrugged. "Word is he stole from some bad people and they're looking for him. That's all I know."

Nick opened the console, pulled out a twenty-dollar bill, and handed it to Delilah. "I appreciate the help, Li. You hear anything, let me know."

"Sure, Bounty Hunter." She stuck the money down her shirt, tapped the vehicle with her hand, and then strolled away.

"She's a prostitute?" Annie watched Delilah stroll over to another car and lean in with a big smile.

"No, a shoe salesman."

"Sarcasm is not necessary. So let me get this straight. You are an officer of the law, and you're not going to arrest her?"

Nick put the SUV in drive and pulled away from the curb. "It's not my job. If she gets arrested, bails out, and then jumps bail, it becomes my business. Until then, she's another pair of eyes on the ground for us. Plus, unless she's caught in the act, even the cops can't arrest her. We keep an eye out and, in the meantime, take advantage of the girl's street knowledge."

It all seemed so tawdry and miserable. How could Barbara live like this?

Nick's cell rang. He set the phone on a hands-free holster on the dashboard.

"Rafe. What's up?"

Rafe's voice crackled from the speaker. "Got a tip. Don't know yet how solid it is. Guy here says he saw Zeena with Danny Sloop. Says no one has seen her since."

"We heard the same thing."

"We?"

"Annie McNamara is with me. Long story." He glanced over at her. She looked back, trying to mask her overwhelmed feelings. "I'll explain later. Any idea where Sloop is hiding out?"

"Guy says he's dealing out of Green Gardens."

Nick nodded even though he knew Rafe couldn't see it. "Meet me there."

"I'll be there in ten."

Nick reached over and disconnected the call. "When we get there, I want you to stay in the car with the doors locked."

—————

Tuesday, 8:45 p.m.
Green Gardens Hotel, Baltimore

When Nick and Rafe got to the Green Gardens, they strapped on their guns, Mace canisters, Tasers, and handcuffs, then put on their Kevlar vests beneath their coats. Leaving Annie in Nick's SUV with the motor running and the doors locked, they headed for the front of the building.

Green Gardens wasn't green, and it definitely wasn't a garden. It was a run-down hotel too far on the wrong side of town to attract anything but squatters, parolees, prostitutes, and drug addicts looking for a place to crash for a few days. The brick building was eight stories high, cheap-looking, and dirty. Worse, it seemed infested with hopelessness.

Three teenage boys were lounging around near the street. Rafe approached them and talked to them for a few minutes. Then he slipped one of them a few dollars. Nothing came free anymore.

Rafe rejoined Nick at the front door of the building. "They said he's been dealing out of 507. But no one has seen him in over a week."

The elevator was boarded off, so they climbed the metal stairs to the fifth floor. The carpet held smells even Nick didn't care to identify, and the walls were stained, peeling, and cracked. Someone should have torn the place down decades ago.

Nick stopped at the door of room 507 and knocked. No answer. He knocked again. "Danny? Open up. We need to talk to you."

Nick began to detect a faint but familiar odor—the rotten-egg stink of a body dissolving itself. He looked over at Rafe, who nodded. "I smell it."

Nick pulled a pair of latex gloves out of his coat pocket and put them on. Then he turned the knob. It wasn't locked. He pushed it open and stepped back when the smell hit him square in the face.

He pulled out his cell phone and called 911. "I need to report a murder."

7

Tuesday, 10:00 p.m.
White Marsh, Maryland

Jessica was curled up on the sofa with a lap blanket tucked around her. Soft blues drifted out from her stereo, competing with something thumping off Krystal's stereo from her bedroom upstairs. Jessica was trying to focus on work, the current decision being whether to go with a cream stripe or an ochre plaid for the Nelsons' sofa. Both would bring out character in their living room. She had been trying for the better part of an hour to ignore the musical conflict, but it was futile.

Tossing the swatches to the coffee table, she closed her eyes and rubbed her temples. What was the point? She tried so hard to create beautiful homes for people, homes filled with color and character, life and love. But how could she, when her own home was a colorless, lifeless place since she and Nick had split up? As for love, he'd taken that with him as well.

When she'd married Nick, she had been walking on air. For the first time in her life she felt loved and cherished and safe. She had become a part of a family—the famous Shepherd family—complete with parents and siblings and cousins and family dinners and big holidays and a hallway lined with pictures of the children growing up. But it didn't take long for the truth behind the facade to show through. The Shepherd siblings sparred, even resented each other, not to mention their parents. Except for Nick, of course. He may have had issues with his siblings, but he loved his father with an unconditional, even blind affection.

But too soon into their marriage, Jessica's so-called knight in shining armor—the man supposedly devoted to family and family values—had turned into someone she didn't know, spending every waking hour with his father, "running the streets," chasing down criminals. And ignoring his wife and child. So many family vacations had been cancelled that she'd stopped planning them. So many candlelight dinners had dried out in the oven that she'd stopped making them.

So many nights she slept alone.

She tried to make Nick see what he was doing to the family, but he wouldn't listen. So she decided to abandon tears and pleas and move to threats. But it had backfired in her face. When she asked for a divorce, he gave it to her without a whimper.

And everything fell apart.

The bass in Krystal's music was starting to thump inside her head, making her headache worse. She'd try one more time to talk to her daughter, and if that didn't work, she just might pull the plug on the girl's music, cell phone, and television. It was about time *someone* put her foot down with that child.

She knocked on Krystal's bedroom door, but with the music blasting, it was no wonder the girl couldn't hear anything.

Jessica eased the door open. "Krystal?"

Still there was no answer.

Stepping into the room, she looked around at the clothes all over the floor and the schoolbooks scattered across the bed. Stepping over a stuffed animal, she reached over and turned the bone-vibrating stereo off. The silence was like a punch to her system, and it took a minute for her ears to adjust.

"Krys?"

She stuck her head in the bathroom, turned on the light, and looked around. Where was that girl?

As she turned from the bathroom door, she saw the curtains fluttering.

Krystal was gone.

———— ✦ ————

Wednesday, 12:46 a.m.
Timonium, Maryland

"You'll be fine here, Killer. Now go to sleep." Steven shut the door to his kitchen and strolled back into the living room to shut off the lights. Just as he bent down to hit the switch, the phone rang. He glanced at the clock. Nearly one in the morning. A little late for someone to be calling about time-shares. He picked it up. "Hello?"

"Stevie?"

His breath went out of him. "Marti?"

"Who else calls you Stevie?"

"Where are you? How are you? What— I…wow."

There was a little laugh, but it sounded heavy. "Yeah, I know. How are you?"

"I'm fine." He reached over and straightened a photo frame he'd knocked askew when he grabbed the phone. "We've been trying to find you."

"A family of bounty hunters, and I can't be found? I'm proud of myself. Listen, I need you to do me a favor."

"Anything. But—"

"Hush and listen. I don't have much time. I need you to wire me some money. Can you do that? Just a few hundred to tide me over."

He smoothed the fabric on the arm of his chair, picking at a tiny bit of lint. "Of course. But—"

"I need you to send it Western Union. You have pen and paper?"

He walked over to his desk. Sitting down in the chair, he flipped open his day planner. "Go ahead."

She gave him the address of a Western Union in Ohio. "Can you do it first thing in the morning?"

"Listen to me. It's been a long time…" He paused. "Dad's gone, Marti."

There was a moment of heavy silence. "As in…"

"As in, he died three years ago. We've been trying to find you. You need to come home."

More silence.

"Marti?"

"I'm here," she whispered. "How?"

"Heart attack. He was out tracking a fugitive and just dropped on the street. Doctors said he was gone before he hit the ground."

"How's Mom taking it?"

"She's in a nursing home." Steven closed his day planner and set his pen down.

"What? Why would you do that to her?"

"I'm pretty sure I could ask you the same question, Marti. And anyway, we had to. She's in bad shape. Please. You need to come home."

"There's nothing I can do for her."

"You can give her a little peace before she doesn't know who you are anymore."

"Give her peace. Geesh, Stevie. Lay it on, will you?"

"I'm not laying it on, Marti. I'm serious. I'll leave now and drive out to pick you up. We can be back here tomorrow night. Please."

He waited for seconds that seemed like hours. "No. Can you send me the money or not?"

He stood and walked across the living room to stare out the front window. "Marti, if you don't come back, Prodigal is history. We're in a lot of trouble…business is just not what it used to be. And you inherited one-third. We can't do anything to save the business without your signature."

"I don't care about Prodigal, Stevie. Don't you get that?"

"Believe me, Marti, I get it. You've made that very clear. But *I* care about Prodigal, and so does Nick. The business pays for Mom's care and the upkeep on her house. Not to mention payroll for the employees. Nick is practically killing himself to keep the business going. It destroyed his marriage."

"Like Jessica was a big loss," she snorted. "I never understood why he married her in the first place."

"Marti…please think about it."

"There's nothing to think about, Stevie."

Steven sighed heavily. Marti always was the most stubborn of the three. "Fine. I'll wire the money in the morning. Give me a number so I can call you when the money's sent."

"No. I'll let you know if something goes wrong. And Stevie?"

"Yeah?"

"I'll stay in touch."

"Okay. Hey."

"What?"

"Love you."

"Same here."

Steven slowly set the phone down. Then he shut off the light and headed for his bedroom. He'd done his best. If he and Nick were going to save Prodigal, it would have to be without Marti. But for the life of him, he couldn't figure out how.

———❈———

Wednesday, 12:55 a.m.
Towson, Maryland

Nick bypassed the front door to enter through the garage. He shrugged out of his coat and glanced at the clock. Almost one. He tossed his coat on the floor.

Good news—I'm finally home. Bad news—I smell like death and decay.

Danny's corpse had been rotting on the floor for at least a week. Maybe more.

Shaking his head, Nick tried to dislodge the sight from his mind. What he needed was a hot shower and a long night's sleep. With any luck, Danny wouldn't haunt his dreams.

He peeled off his shirt, tossing it in the corner of the bedroom with a grimace. Thank goodness Annie hadn't seen it. Hearing about it had been bad enough. When he told her, she buried her face in her hands and trembled like a poodle facing down a Doberman. She hadn't said a word all the way back to the bar where she picked up her car and drove home. Nick had followed her, just to make sure she got home okay. She gave a half wave and ran inside her building.

He should call her and just make sure she was okay. It wasn't every day a woman like Annie had to deal with the smell of death in the air. Nick's thoughts moved to their deal. Why had she lied to him? Her mother wasn't in the hospital. But what then? And her threats? Bluffs. But again, why? What was she hiding, and why was it so important that she find Zeena? Was it just sisterly love or something more serious?

Nick turned on the shower, his thoughts shifting back to Danny. Word on the streets was that Danny had crossed the wrong people. Who? He was a small-time dealer, pushing low quantities of cocaine, crack, or meth, so chances were good that he had ripped off another dealer. It didn't add up though. From what he saw in the apartment, Danny had been tortured before he was whacked. As if he had known something and, even if he'd given up all the information he had, his killer wanted to make sure he wasn't holding anything back.

What if Zeena had been with him? The last anyone saw or heard of her, she was with Danny. Had she walked in on the killers? Maybe, but if she had, wouldn't they have just left her body there with Danny's? Likely. So chances were, if she did see, she got away, and that might be why no one could find her. She'd go as far underground as she could go.

After showering, he changed into a pair of sweats and went into the foyer to pick up the mail off the floor. Bills. Bills. Advertising material. More bills. And a white business envelope with his name typed on the front. No stamp. No address. Just his name.

He ripped it open and unfolded the letter.

Mind your own business and stick to bail jumpers, or something very bad could happen. How is your daughter, by the way?

His mind went hot white with fury. He marched back into the kitchen and tossed the letter down on the counter. It was time to let the police know about these threats. He'd call Linc and—

The answering machine on the counter was blinking. Eighteen messages. What in the world? *Oh yeah.* He had turned his cell phone off when he was talking to the police about Sloop and had forgotten to turn it back on.

He pressed the Play button. "Nick, this is Jess. Krystal's missing. Call me!"

Taking a step back, he felt the fury drain, only to be replaced with panic. "Nick. Me again. Where are you! I'm so scared, Nick. Help, please."

Nick didn't bother listening to any more of the messages. He put on his shoes and ran out the door.

⸺⸺✦⸺⸺

Wednesday, 1:00 a.m.
Park Heights Industrial Park, Baltimore

The old factory was cold and damp, but at least it gave Zeena some protection from the wind. And from Jon Carver's thugs.

"They're out there, aren't they? Waiting for us to show ourselves?"

While Charlie might have been talking about Vietnam, he was still correct. Killers were out there, and they were looking for her. "Yes, Charlie. We have to be very quiet."

Charlie was a crazy but harmless old man who lived on the streets—most of the time, in the corner of this abandoned building. He came home from Vietnam back in the late sixties. His mind didn't.

Charlie had once told Zeena that he liked the old factory because he could see anything—or anyone—coming from a long distance away. She knew he liked her. She didn't know whether he thought she was his sister or his girlfriend, but he had never touched her, never hassled her, and always let her crawl into that small space between him and the wall. He would even share his small stash of food, alcohol, and drugs with her when he had some.

But he didn't have any right now, and she was starving for them all.

"I'll take first watch," Charlie said as Zeena curled up tighter next to him.

"Okay." Zeena shivered under a thin blanket.

She needed a fix, and she needed it now, but at least she was far away from Jon and his goons. When Lester had grabbed her on the street, she thought her life was over. But someone in the store had called the police, and they showed up just as Lester was dragging her to his car. As soon as the police chirped the siren, he'd released her. While he was being frisked by the police and arrested for having a weapon on him, she had made a run for it.

She still felt like she was running—her heart wouldn't stop racing.

She couldn't believe she actually agreed to help Danny sell Jon's laptop back to Jon. What kind of a plan was that? Stupid, stupid, stupid. They must have been insane. No one messes with the Carvers. She had been around Richie long enough to know that.

Danny had called and told Jon that he could have his laptop back in exchange for ten thousand dollars. They'd meet on Reisterstown Road in Park Heights, near a liquor store in town. Carver had immediately agreed to the deal. But Zeena had a bad feeling. Danny brushed off her concerns, confident that they would get their money and be none the worse for it. So Zeena took the laptop and headed down the street to the liquor store where she would wait for Danny to call her and tell her he had the money. Then, as the plan went, she would bring the laptop.

But the call didn't come. And twenty minutes later than scheduled, she saw Carver stalking toward the liquor store. She took off out the back and ran. There was no way Danny would have looked down the barrel of a gun and not told Carver where the laptop was. The next day, the guy at the liquor store told her that Carver and his men had come into the store looking for her. Two weeks later, they were still looking for her.

So now she had to figure out how to get the laptop back to Carver and stay alive afterward. She wasn't sure Carver would be willing to let bygones be bygones if he got his stuff back, but it was better than hiding out the rest of her life. She'd already missed her court date, so now the bounty hunters were probably chasing her too. If she didn't know for a fact that Jon had arms long enough to reach inside the jail and kill her, she'd call the bounty hunters and turn herself in.

In the meantime, there was only one place she felt even remotely safe. And that was with Charlie.

Zeena gripped her backpack—with the laptop safely stowed—and cuddled it close to her body. She didn't know how to get out of the trouble she was in, but one thing was for sure. Losing the laptop wasn't going to help her one bit. It might even make things worse.

"Zeena?"

"Yeah, Charlie?"

"How long are the killers going to hunt you?"

It was one of the few times Charlie gave any indication that he wasn't always in Vietnam. "I don't know, Charlie. Do you want me to leave?"

He shook his shaggy head and stroked his gray beard. "You're my friend. I'll make sure they don't get you."

"Thanks, Charlie."

He stood up and looked down at her. "I'm going to do a little recon. I won't be far."

Wednesday, 1:15 a.m.
Baltimore, Maryland

Jon was not a happy man. He stepped into his condo and slipped out of his cashmere overcoat. "I can't believe it could be this difficult to bring me one drug-addicted prostitute. How does she continue to elude you?"

The two men behind him looked at each other, but it was the tall blond that spoke up, inviting more trouble than he was already in. "Someone called the police, Mr. Carver. I had to let her go. I'll get her. I just need a little more time."

"Put the word out on the street," Jon said in a soft voice that was as strong as steel and as sharp as a shard of glass. "A reward to anyone that brings me information leading to her."

The blond shifted his weight and stepped forward. "You put that word out there, and we're going to have every bag lady and streetwalker in this town lined up in the hall, all trying to convince you that they just saw her down at the local Food Lion."

"Did I ask you for an opinion?"

Ignoring the flash of temper in the blond's eyes, he walked over to his wet bar and poured himself a drink. He didn't offer the hired help any. "I want that laptop back in my hands, and I won't tolerate anyone standing in the way of that. Am I understood?"

"Understood," the blond replied tightly.

"Then I suggest you get back out there and find our little Zeena. There aren't that many places she can hide."

In less than one week, he was going to be moving the largest shipment he'd ever handled, and the last thing he needed was some loose end bringing it all crashing down on his head. And Zeena was a loose end.

Glancing at his Rolex, Jon turned to his two men. "Get out."

The two men nodded and left.

With drink in hand, he settled down on the sofa. If they'd gone a little slower and hadn't killed Danny as soon as they did, he'd have the laptop by now. Why Danny had thought he could steal from Jon Carver and get away with it was a mystery, but one that cost Danny his life.

When his phone rang, he frowned and unclipped it from his belt. "Yel-lo."

"It's me."

Jon sat up straighter. *Richie.* "You okay?"

"I'm great. My new friend and I are just relaxing."

He took a swig from his drink as he let that stew for a moment. In spite of the light, almost-too-casual tone in Richie's voice, Jon knew Richie had been getting himself into trouble. "What did you do?"

"Me? Nothing."

"Talk, Richie."

"Nothing. Really. Just sent the bounty hunter a few little reminders. A promise I made to him."

"Fool! I got business going down and you're provoking him? You trying to ruin me?" Jon ambled to his feet. Began pacing. Richie had his moments where he was worth his weight in gold. This wasn't one of them. The man had a temper and love of grudges. The combination had been getting Richie into tight corners all his life. Of course, he was such a dirty fighter that he usually got himself out of those corners with barely a scratch, but Nick Shepherd wasn't the type to let Richie walk away without some serious damage. If he let Richie walk away at all.

"Chill, Jon. Ain't nuthin I can't handle. It's me he needs to watch out for."

"I want you to stop for now. Give me a week or so to finish up my business. Then you want to bring all hell down on your head, be my guest."

"Hey, hey. Don't go all bad on me. I reminded him of a promise, that's all."

"That better be all. I'm serious. This is important."

"Yeah, I got it. Hey, I got nothing going for me, ya know?"

"I hear ya. I'll send someone soon."

"Okay. Soon."

"Soon."

Jon hung up the phone, grabbed his drink, and headed for his bedroom. He had to get Richie some clothes and bring him in.

And make sure he stayed away from a certain bounty hunter for a while.

———❖———

Wednesday, 1:45 a.m.
White Marsh, Maryland

Nick whipped his SUV into Jessica's driveway, parked, then jumped out. Running across the yard, he cleared the three steps to the porch and yanked open the storm door. He pounded on the door. Hit the doorbell. Pounded again.

Jessica opened the front door. "Nick?"

Nick didn't wait for her to invite him in. "When did you find out she was missing? Did she go out and not come back? Did someone take her from her room?"

"Whoa. Slow down." Jessica eased the front door closed. "I told you in the last phone message. She's fine."

"Fine?" Nick slid down the wall to land on the floor with a light thud as relief exploded through him. "I didn't get that message."

"She's upstairs, and I've grounded her for another week." Jessica tied the belt of her robe tight. "Are you okay?"

Nick nodded. "What happened?"

"Seems our daughter decided she didn't like being grounded, so she snuck out. I was absolutely frantic, but Linc found her."

His old partner on the force. Slowly he climbed to his feet. "You called the police?" Why was he surprised? It's what she should have done. But something about having another man save the day for his own family didn't sit well.

Jessica nodded as she yawned. "When I couldn't get through to you, I called Linc. He stopped by. She was hiding out in the backyard, hoping I'd thought she had run away."

Standing there in the foyer of his old home, watching his wife yawn, listening to the grandfather clock chime out the quarter hour, brought back a rush of memories. He choked out a laugh. "Our drama queen. Remember when she used to hold her breath until we promised to give her what she wanted?"

"You were the one that always gave in. I had a hard time convincing you that she wouldn't actually die."

Nick laughed. "Oh, I knew she wouldn't die, but she went to so much effort to get something out of us that I couldn't help but reward it."

Jessica smiled. "And now look at this teenage monster we have created."

"She'll get over it, won't she?" he asked.

"I hope so." Jessica yawned again. "Sorry. I don't mean to keep yawning."

He watched her for a few minutes, remembering how soft her skin was and how when he held her, she would melt into him like a little kitten, purring with contentment. When he realized he was about two seconds from leaning in and kissing her sweet lips, he stiffened. "Get some sleep. We'll talk about this another time." He pulled open the front door. "Make sure you lock up behind me."

She frowned, holding the door. "Nick? Are you going to tell me what's going on? You're not normally this…frantic."

He stepped onto the porch and turned to look at her. Then he shook his head. He wasn't sure how much he should tell her. No sense sending her into a frenzy over threats that he might be able to handle without a problem.

"I'm just tired. More tired than I thought, I guess. Didn't mean to come barreling in here like a madman."

"Come on, Nick. Don't try and shut me out. Is there something I need to know?"

"No. Really. Everything's fine. Well, it's not fine, but it's nothing I can't handle."

He watched Jessica's expression shift to disappointment as she gently shut the door.

As he pulled out of the driveway, his mind flooded with confusion. As badly as he wanted to bring in Richie Carver, was he willing to risk his daughter? No. Could he allow a criminal to make him jump through hoops? Absolutely not. So how was he going to bring Richie in and keep Krystal safe at the same time?

8

Wednesday, 9:30 a.m.
Prodigal offices, Baltimore

Nick sorted through the mail while Jenna watered the plants in a corner of the front lobby. With only about four hours of sleep, he was moving on nothing more than caffeine and determination. It was also making him a bit touchy, so when he felt the urge to tell Jenna to leave the plants alone and process the mail, he swallowed it.

He was checking his watch when Steven came through the front door and took off his coat. Steven tilted his head. "I know I'm a few minutes late. I had an important errand to run this morning."

"Sounds familiar."

"Not this morning, Nick. I'm not in the mood for it."

In spite of telling himself at least ten times that he wasn't going to get into a fight with his brother, Nick just couldn't seem to keep his temper from spiking. "Are you in the mood to work, or is that pushing it?"

Steven draped his jacket over his arm, walked toward Nick, and stopped just inches away. "You know what, Nick? You aren't the only one that's worried about the business. Maybe I'm trying to save it too."

"It's not your responsibility to save it. It's mine. And I have it under control. All I'm asking from you is that you do your job or go find another one."

Steve tapped Nick's chest with his finger. "I own as much of this company as you do, something you seem to forget. And I have a vested interest in making sure it survives."

Nick gripped Steven's arm. "What could you possibly do that I haven't already done?"

"How about locate Marti? Remember when you asked me to try to find her? Turns out, I do my job, Nick."

"You found Marti? Where is she?"

"She had me send money to a Western Union in Gallipolis, Ohio."

"Why didn't you call me? I could've had people waiting for her."

"She's not a criminal, Nick. She needs to come back on her own terms, not handcuffed and dragged like a fugitive."

Nick wasn't sure whether he wanted to shake Steven or hit him. "How can we convince her to come back, whether on her terms or not, if we don't try—"

"I did try, you jerk! I begged her to come—"

"What did she say?" Nick pointed to his office. "Come tell me everything."

Steven followed Nick into his office, talking the whole way. "Yes, I talked to her. Yes, I told her about Mom and Dad. Yes, I explained why we needed her to come back."

"So she's on her way?"

Steven tossed his coat over one chair and sat down in another. "You aren't listening to me. She isn't coming back. Not yet, anyway. But I'm working on it."

"If she knows about everything, how could she refuse to come home?"

"All I could get out of her was that she didn't want to have anything to do with the family. But she promised me that she would stay in touch. I'll try again another time."

Nick leaned forward. "Steven, we don't have time to wait until a more convenient time for her. If she doesn't come back here and sign the collateral papers, there's not going to be anything to come back to."

Wednesday, 10:00 a.m.
Tri-County Electrical Supply, Baltimore

Annie slowly made her way to her cubicle at her father's office and sat down. She stared at the stacks of accounts receivables and wished once again that she'd called in sick. Every time she thought about that black body bag being hauled out of that building, her stomach shifted and rolled, threatening to send her flying to the bathroom. She didn't know Danny Sloop, but he was dead. And Barbara had been with him. Her stomach flipped again. Was Barbara dead as well? Was her body dumped somewhere?

She'd shown up at work at eight, turned on her calculator, fired up her computer, and tried to concentrate on logging the incoming checks. By the time she'd made four mistakes in five entries, she knew she had to try something else to get her mind off the previous night's events. She tried going to the break room and getting hot tea, but that didn't help either. By 10:30 she hadn't accomplished more than fifteen minutes' worth of work.

"Annie, I'm going across the street to Starbucks." Monica, one of Annie's co-workers from cubicle next door to Annie, stood in the entry, buttoning her coat. "You want me to pick up anything for you? Maybe a muffin?"

With a heavy sigh, Annie pushed away from her desk. "I don't know if I can eat a thing. I still feel so lousy."

"And you look every bit as bad as you feel." Monica hitched her shoulder bag. "Personally, I think you should go home, make a cup of hot tea, curl up on the sofa, and watch *Oprah*. Don't come back to work until you feel better."

"Sounds divine, but I need to get these checks logged in."

"Leave them on my desk and I'll do them. I'm pretty much caught up on orders."

"You sure?"

"I'm sure," Monica insisted with a little bit of laugh. "Go home."

After letting her dad know that Monica was covering for her, she gathered her things and drove back home. But *Oprah* wasn't on her agenda. She called Prodigal and asked to speak to Nick. She was told he was in a meeting and left a message. Then she made the hot tea and curled up on the sofa, but she didn't bother with the television. Instead, she pulled out her cross-stitch project and resumed where she'd left off a few days earlier.

Cross-stitching allowed her mind to wander where she wanted it to go. Where was Barbara, and how could she find her? It was pretty clear now that her original plan wasn't going to work. She wasn't cut out for the streets.

The phone rang, and she almost ignored it, but thinking that it might be Nick, she crawled off the sofa to pick it up. "Hello?"

"Hi, Sis. Looking for me?"

Wednesday, 10:45 a.m.
Prodigal offices, Baltimore

Jenna stepped into the doorway of Nick's office. "Nick?"

"Come on in."

He chucked two Excedrin into his mouth and washed them down with water. "What's wrong?"

She flipped open her steno pad. "I've called the last three surety companies on the list. Only one was even remotely interested in setting you up, but they are going to limit you severely."

"How severely?"

"Twenty thousand, tops."

Nick winced and took another swig from his water bottle. "That's not enough. I don't want to be trapped into only writing low bails. We'd be competing with the little mom-and-pop operations like Kline and Robbins. I don't want to hurt them. They've been good to us."

"Then we're stuck with having to go with property collateral."

"I know." He pushed back from his desk, too concerned to sit still, too frustrated to pace. "Did Steven tell you he talked to Marti last night?"

"I overheard. How did it go?"

"He said he tried to talk her into coming back, but she refused. I don't know how hard he tried, or even if he explained how serious everything is."

"I'm sure he tried his best."

But Nick wasn't so sure how good Steven's best was. Steven had never been much of a go-getter, content to just go his own way at his own pace and let the cards fall where they may.

Jenna picked up the file folders from his desk and left. He reached over, picked up the phone, glanced down at the message from Annie

McNamara on his desk, and dialed. When he heard the answering machine pick up, he set the phone down. Well, he'd try later, or she had his cell phone if it was important.

He grabbed his jacket. As he passed Jenna's desk, he said, "I'm going to hit the streets and see if I can get any leads. Call me if you need me."

———————⋗⋗0⋖⋖———————

Wednesday, 12:25 p.m.
Downtown Baltimore

"Annie?"

It was little more than a harsh whisper, but it was enough to make Annie nearly drop her teacup. "Barbara? Where are you?"

"Never mind that. Why are you looking for me?"

"You heard about that?"

"I have friends on the street, Annie. You may find it hard to believe, but they actually watch out for me. Especially when someone that looks just like me starts asking questions. Now, what do you want?"

Annie closed her eyes for a moment and took a deep breath. "Barbara, I don't know what you're into, but that guy you were with—he's dead. They found his body last night."

"Took 'em long enough." There was a short pause and then a heavy sigh. "I didn't mean that the way it sounds. It's just that once again, the nobodies of this world are just ignored."

The stark disillusionment in Barbara's voice shouldn't have been so much of a surprise, but it pulled at Annie's heart. "Why don't you let me pick you up? I can take you someplace safe."

Barbara's laugh sounded as much bitterness as amusement. "Like you could hide me from these guys. You just don't know what you're trying to get yourself into, Annie. Get out before you get hurt. Please."

"What have you gotten yourself into?"

"Don't worry about it. I'll be fine."

"Barbara, I need to meet with you. It's important."

The silence hung between them so long, Annie wasn't sure Barbara was still there. "Barbara?"

"I'm here. Meet me at Jiffy's at two. If you aren't there by quarter after, I'm sorry, but I'll be gone. These guys have eyes all over the streets, and I can't take a chance on someone seeing me and dropping a dime on me."

Before Annie could say anything else, there was a click. She felt frustrated and scattered. Should she call the bounty hunter and let him know? She weighed the pros and cons while she dressed. If she told him, and he caught Barbara, she had no guarantee that he'd turn Barbara over to her for a while. Could she trust him?

By the time she reached for her car keys, her mind was made up. She'd get Barbara on her own.

———◦———

Wednesday, 1:45 p.m.
Park Heights, Baltimore

Nick pulled into the drive-through at Taco Bell and ordered a couple of double-decker tacos and an extra-large soda. Then he pulled into a parking spot that faced the street to eat his lunch. Glancing up at the gunmetal gray sky through his windshield, he wondered if it was going to rain or sleet. The weatherman hadn't predicted any precipitation at all, but the sky was promising storms.

Since this morning, he'd spoken to just about everyone he knew on the street, and no one had seen anyone he needed to find. Not Tommy Lester. Not Zeena Bantham either, although rumors were flying around about her like flies on a sweaty horse. Something about some items stolen from Jon Carver. If the rumors were true, the woman was on a short ride to the graveyard if Nick didn't find her first.

As he bit into his taco, his cell phone rang.

"Bounty hunter?"

It was one of his street snitches. "Yeah."

"Saw that girl you're looking for. Zee? She's using the pay phone right down from A-One Pawn. You know the place?"

"I know it. Thanks. Catch up with me later."

"'kay."

Now he could only hope the snitch had called him before he called the Carvers. He held the taco in his mouth as he started up the engine and pulled out of the parking lot. He ate as fast as he drove and dialed Conner on his cell. He got his voice mail. Then he tried Rafe, who answered. "I've got a lead on Zeena. Meet me down at A-One Pawn. And find Conner."

"On it."

By the time Nick arrived at A-One Pawn less than ten minutes later, the phone booth was empty. He drove slowly up one street and down the next, hoping to catch sight of her. Who was she calling?

He dialed Annie's number. No answer at her home phone. He tried her cell. She answered quickly and sounded out of breath. "I'm on my way."

"Annie? Where you going?"

"Nick? Didn't he tell you?"

"Who? Tell me what?"

"That Barbara called me. I'm on my way to meet her now."

Nothing was adding up, and the clock was running. "Where are you meeting her?"

"She asked me to meet her at Jiffy's at two."

He did a quick U-turn in the middle of the street, ignoring the taxi that honked at him for it. "I'm on my way. Don't go in there without me."

Pushing the speed limit laws to the edge, he wove through traffic. He dialed his cell phone when he got stuck at a red light. "Rafe? You get ahold of Conner?"

"Yeah, we're on our way to A-One."

"Good. Change of plans. Meet me at Jiffy's as fast as you can."

"What's goin' on?"

"Zeena called Annie." The light turned green, and he pushed down on the accelerator. "They're meeting at Jiffy's. We need to get there and pick her up before she disappears again."

"We're pushing the speed limit."

"Did either you or Conner talk to Annie? Did she tell you that she was going to meet Zeena?"

"No."

So who was it that Annie told? Or was that a lie to cover the fact that she hadn't called him? He'd find out soon enough. "I'm almost there."

"On our wa—"

Just then, Nick spotted Zeena about fifty yards up from Jiffy's. "I see her. She's in the used car lot on Sixth, in the far back, making her way on foot toward the bar. One of you needs to come in from behind her in case she turns back the way she came." Hanging up, he pulled into Gabby's Used Furniture lot and parked. Jiffy's was across the street and down the block about thirty yards. He was going to have to make this fast.

He grabbed his gun, handcuffs, and stun gun from the back, but couldn't see his Kevlar vest. He hoped he wouldn't regret not searching for it. Staying low, he eased out of his vehicle, and staying between parked cars, made his way to the curb. He had to get across the street without Zeena seeing him. If she saw him, she had a far enough lead to disappear before he made it halfway through the car lot. He was dressed in jeans, a leather jacket, and combat boots, which at least would help him blend into Jiffy's crowd. Hopefully she wouldn't look too close at the bulk under his jacket.

Nick spotted her at the end of a row of cars, peering down the street, as if waiting for company but not wanting to be seen. He also noticed a dark blue SUV pull up to the curb a block down from Jiffy's. It was a Navigator—patrons of Jiffy's might have a job washing it, but they didn't have a job good enough to actually own one. Which meant it was one of Jon Carver's.

Just as Nick started across the street, he saw Annie's car pulled up into Jiffy's parking lot. He jogged through the slow-moving traffic. Zeena was on his left. The two men in the SUV were down on his right. And in between them, Annie was getting out of the car.

The two men in the SUV climbed out of their vehicle, their hands hovering at their waists. It was Ira and Scott, two of Jon's enforcers.

Walking quickly down the street, Nick tried to blend in with the local foot traffic while at the same time hoping to draw Annie's attention. But she seemed completely focused on Jiffy's front door.

Good news—I've got Zeena in my sights. Bad news—Jon's goons are standing in my way.

There was no doubt in his mind that the two gunmen were focused entirely on Annie. Of course, they thought that she was Zeena.

Easing his gun out of its holster, then holding it against his thigh, he flipped his cell phone out with his other hand and dialed the police station. Besides the fact that it was law for bounty hunters to call the police when they suspected a possible shooting, there was also no way he wanted to fire his gun without the authority to do so. When he got the dispatcher, he quickly explained the situation and then shoved his cell phone back in his pocket.

Annie was almost at the door when Nick saw Ira slowly draw his gun from under his coat. Nick broke into a run, not sure whether he was going to make it in time.

"Annie! Down! Get down!" he screamed.

Annie stopped and looked around. She saw him and froze.

Out of the corner of his eye he saw the man lift the gun.

No time.

Running, he took a deep breath and dove at her, catching his shoulder in her midsection. She gasped as they made impact, and again when they hit the ground. Nick rolled, standing up between Annie and the gunmen, but he didn't pull out his gun just yet. He revolted against firing—there were innocent people on the street. Someone could get hurt.

Ira kicked him in the chest. He fell backward, pain shooting through him. Rolling, he heard Annie scream and stood up again. He spun out a kick, knocking the man to the ground. Whipping around, he turned his attention to Scott, who was pulling Annie to her feet.

She was kicking and screaming, digging her heels into the ground, trying to get free of his grip on her arms.

Finally, Nick lifted his gun. "Let her go!"

Scott aimed his gun and fired. Three times. Nick felt a shot and flew back.

On the ground, he heard a police siren scream barely a block away. The two men started running for their vehicle. Nick staggered to his feet and ran after Scott. He dove into him, knocking Scott, Annie, and himself to the ground. As he reached out to land a punch, Scott rolled. Nick's knuckles grazed him, but not enough to slow him down. But at least he'd let go of Annie. Scott pulled himself to his feet and kicked out at Nick, who ducked and then delivered a fast kick of his own. The man fell back.

Ira honked the horn, and Scott gave up on Nick and Annie. He jumped into the vehicle and they sped away.

Nick limped over to Annie. She was lying on the sidewalk, a bloody scrape on her cheek. "I told you to wait for me, didn't I?" He helped her to her feet and steadied her. "Are you okay? Is anything broken?" She just shook her head, and he could tell that she had no injuries besides shock. "Go get in your car and stay there. When the police arrive, tell them what happened. I'll be back."

She stared up at him with shock-wide eyes, but he didn't have time to deal with it. He needed to capture Zeena before she got away again. He picked his gun off the ground and took off up the street and around the corner of the building in time to see Zeena disappear behind a van. His shoulder burned like the devil, but he couldn't let her get away.

Weaving through the cars in the used car lot, he splashed through puddles and stumbled on the gravel, trying to keep his eyes on her. She looked back at him once, eyes wide, and then darted behind the neighboring pharmacy.

He came around the pharmacy, caught a glimpse of Zeena running down a side street. He spotted her at the far end of a vacant lot. She scurried over a chain-link fence and hopped-skipped over the railroad tracks. He sped up his pursuit. If she made it to the factory at the far end of the field, she would be gone for good, disappearing into a maze of buildings and levels that would take twenty men more than two hours to search.

Rain began to fall, and it came down with a vengeance, with huge drops of rain that drenched Nick in a matter of minutes.

Nick moved to scramble over the fence, but when he went to climb, his left arm felt numb and his feet slid on the wet metal. He tried again. Only after falling off the fence twice did he realize just how weak he was becoming. Gritting his teeth against the pain, he slowly climbed again, catching one leg of his jeans on the sharp point at the top. He heard it rip, felt the slight drag, but he finally cleared the fence. Breathing hard, he hopped the railroad tracks and kept going.

Zeena ran into a two-story factory.

Keep running, Nick. You can't lose her now. He looked down at his gun and saw the blood running from under his sleeve, dripping onto his Glock. Well, he'd clean it later. He jumped a puddle and jogged through the doorway.

As he entered the building, something hit him square in the chest. *Idiot!* was his last thought before everything went black.

9

Wednesday, 2:15 p.m.
Jiffy's Bar, Garrison Blvd., Baltimore

Annie sat in the back of the police cruiser, hugging herself close, trying to make sense of what had just happened. Never in her life had someone taken a shot at her. Or tried to kill her.

She toyed with the tear in the knee of her jeans. She'd only worn them twice. Her boots were scratched up. Her coat was a muddy mess. She was soaked right down to her skin, and if she looked in a mirror, her mascara was probably nothing more than black streaks down her face at this point.

She looked up to see a police officer kneeling down at the open car door, holding a Styrofoam cup of coffee. "Here you go, miss. Take a sip of this. It won't taste good, but it's hot and it'll help."

"Thank you." Annie reached out and, with trembling hands, took the cup, savoring the warmth.

"Do you know who those men were?"

Annie shook her head. "I never really saw them, to be honest. It all happened so fast. I was on the ground and then I looked up and one of them grabbed me and then they were dragging me down the street and then they started shooting and it was just so—" She shuddered and took a sip of the coffee. She grimaced. It was black and strong. She wanted a cup of hot tea with cream and sugar. She wanted to be as far from Jiffy's Bar as one could get and still be in the state.

She answered the officer's questions as quickly and as succinctly as she could, all the while trying to get warm. At one point, the officer finally noticed that she was shivering and turned the police cruiser's heat up to full blast. It didn't help.

"And you came down here to meet your sister?"

Annie nodded and took another sip of the coffee. "She called and asked me to meet her here."

"What about the bounty hunter that called this in? Nick Shepherd. Were you expecting to meet him here as well?"

"Yes. And thank goodness he was here." She shivered again. "I think he was shot." She lifted her head as the thought morphed into a realization, and stared at the police officer. "Oh my! He was shot! I saw blood when he got up."

He had taken a bullet for her. That brought on guilt, which initiated a whole new level of shakes. She gripped the cup and felt the cup bend beneath her fingers. "You have to find him."

"We'll find him."

Reassured, she sank back in the seat. "I've never had anything like this happen before."

"Okay, so they grabbed you and started to drag you toward their vehicle. And you have no idea why they were trying to abduct you?"

She shook her head. She was about to offer up a suggestion that maybe the guys thought she was her sister, but before she could, his radio chirped and someone said something, but she couldn't make out the words.

"I'll be right back," the officer told her.

When he stepped away, the man whose name she remembered as

Conner leaned in the door. The one Nick called Rafe stood behind him. "Annie, hi. Where is Nick?"

"He took off through that lot over there. After that, I don't know. No one has found him yet?"

Rafe shook his head. "Who's looking for him besides us?"

"He was shot."

Conner stiffened, eyes narrowing. "Shot?"

She nodded, hesitant to say the words again.

Conner turned toward Rafe, his hand resting on the cruiser above Annie's door. "I'll check the lot. You guys look around Jiffy's." Then, without another word, Conner ran off toward the used car lot.

Annie leaned back and took another sip of the coffee. Now that the shock was wearing off, suspicions started rolling. Had Zeena set her up? How had those men known to come at that exact moment? By the time the officer had returned, the shakes were gone.

She handed the officer the cup. "Is there anything else you need from me, or can I go home now?"

"I suppose it would be okay to let you go. If I need anything else, I'll call you."

Annie climbed out of the cruiser. "Thank you."

⎯⎯✦⎯⎯

Wednesday, 2:25 p.m.
Old tire factory complex near Jiffy's Bar, Garrison Blvd., Baltimore

The rain had settled down to a light misty drizzle. Conner pulled his badge from inside his jacket and let it hang where police officers could see it clearly. No sense in getting shot by accident. Or arrested. Kneeling down, he touched a dark spot on the wet grass and lifted his finger to look closely. Blood.

He stood up and looked around the area, wiping the blood off on his jeans. The residential homes were separated from the industrial area by fencing and railroad tracks. *If I were running for my life, which way would I go?*

There was no question. He ran toward the fence.

As he was preparing to jump the fence, he spotted a smear of blood. He was on the right track. Tucking his gun back in his holster, he climbed, then dropped on the other side of the fence with a light thud. He pulled out his gun again and headed over the railroad tracks.

Wednesday, 2:30 p.m.
Prodigal offices, Baltimore

"You bought the dog a collar, a leash, and squeaky toys?" Jenna stuck her pencil behind her ear and shook her head at the collection of goodies that Steven had dumped on her desk.

"Well, he gets bored while I'm at work, so the toys should keep him happy. And how am I supposed to walk him without a collar and leash?"

Jenna stood up and picked up a stack of messages. She headed down the hall. "You were supposed to take him to the pound."

"Yeah, yeah," Steven called out to her.

The phone rang. "Get that!" Jenna called to him from down the hall somewhere.

Steven reached over to pick up the phone. "Prodigal Fugitive Recovery."

"Steven? It's Rafe. Nick's been shot."

"Shot?" He leaned against Jenna's desk and then slowly sank down in her chair. A million thoughts raced through his mind. "Nick's been shot?"

Jenna suddenly reappeared. "Nick was shot? When? How?"

"Wait," Steven whispered to her. "Where is he, Rafe? What hospital are they taking him to?"

"We haven't found him yet. He took off into the neighborhood. Probably chasing Zeena. That's why I'm calling. You might want to get down here and help us find him."

Steven jumped up from the desk. "I'm on my way."

———— ≈0≈ ————

Wednesday, 2:30 p.m.
Old tire factory complex near Jiffy's Bar, Garrison Blvd., Baltimore

More blood. It spurred Conner to move a little faster, a slow jog across the uneven pavement toward the nearest building. There weren't many people in his life that he would call friend, but Nick Shepherd was one of them. He needed to find Nick before the worst happened.

As he ran, images of his and Nick's friendship flashed through Conner's head. Whenever he and Ria would go through a rough patch, Nick never took sides and never divided them. He listened, he advised, he understood. But he never judged. Not that Steven or Marti would ever agree with that assessment.

Sure, there were times when Conner wanted to knock some sense into Nick—like when he gave Steven a hard time—but the man couldn't help being emotionally stunted. He'd lost his father, his marriage, and his mother for the most part. He felt responsible for Steven and Marti, the business, his mother, and his daughter. He dealt with the worst people society had to offer day in and day out. The kind of people who lied to you with a straight face and then tried to kill you. He wanted everyone important in his life taken care of. Sure, Nick didn't know how to say something as simple as "I care," but Conner was inclined to cut his friend some slack. Heaven knew Jessica rarely did.

Carefully, Conner approached one of the buildings, checking through gaping windows and doorways for any movement. The complex had once been a thriving tire factory with manufacturing and storage buildings, docking bays, and large parking lots. But with the revitalization of Baltimore and the expansion in Frederick, the tenants had moved. Now the huge loading doors were gone, leaving gaping holes in the buildings. The parking lot was littered with old newspapers, broken bottles, and trash, and weeds erupted through cracks in the pavement.

Approaching an opening, Conner stopped and listened. Hearing nothing to alarm him, he entered sideways, easing along the broken door frame.

The only light was coming in through the windows, and there was precious little of it. He stayed pressed against the wall, giving his eyes time to adjust to the dark shadows and murky haze inside the building. As he stepped forward, his foot hit something. He looked down.

A body.

Not just any body. Nick's body.

Keeping his weapon drawn and pointed out into the building and his eyes sweeping from one shadow to another, he knelt down and pressed two fingers to Nick's neck. A pulse. Slow. Steady. Good. He whipped out his cell phone and called Rafe.

"I found Nick and he's hurt. Get the EMTs over here. We're in the old tire factory's main building at the south shipping door."

After making sure that no one else was in the building, Conner holstered his weapon and returned to where Nick lay. There was a tear on the right shoulder, and blood was streaking down the front of Nick's jacket.

After unzipping the jacket, Conner peeled back Nick's shirt to examine the wound. It was still bleeding. "You really messed up this time, didn't you, pal?"

Wednesday, 2:45 p.m.
Old tire factory complex near Jiffy's Bar, Garrison Blvd., Baltimore

Nick felt the pain first as it racked across his shoulder. "Quit being such a mother," Nick groaned as he slowly sat up.

"Are you nuts? Nick, you've been shot."

"It's just a flesh wound."

"Just sit tight."

"Conn?" Nick whispered. "Help me up." He shoved back at the pain the way Luke had taught him, concentrating instead on something else. "Zeena got away?"

"Yeah. Do you know who did this to you?"

"A couple of Carter's goons, Scott and Ira." Grimacing, he placed a hand over his wound. He started forward, walking unsteadily out the door of the building.

Rafe was just climbing out of Conner's SUV. "Nick?"

Nick lifted his hand. "I'm not as bad as it looks."

"Well, that's great, because you look like you're one step from keeling over."

He really didn't need all the fuss buzzing around him, but he agreed to sit on the bumper of the ambulance and allow them to clean his wound and bandage it. It wasn't until the EMTs concurred that a bullet had grazed the shoulder, but didn't lodge inside, that Conner showed signs of relaxing.

While the EMTs worked on Nick's shoulder, the police questioned him.

"Did you see the two men?"

"Of course I did. They were standing right in front of me." Nick flinched as the EMT cleaned the wound out with antiseptic.

"Could you describe them to me?" The officer flipped the page in his little notebook and continued writing.

"The driver was about five-ten, five-eleven. Maybe a hundred and forty pounds. Bald with a scar on his chin. He was wearing black jeans, heavy boots, dark shirt, and a navy blue jacket. The shooter was closer to my height, maybe six-two, six-three. Short brown hair, military cut, heavy eyebrows, he was missing an eyetooth, and he had brown eyes. He was wearing jeans, a black pullover, and a brown leather jacket. Button front, not zip-up like mine. The driver's name is Ira. Can't recall his last name. The shooter was Scott Michaels. They're both employed by Jon Carver. Sometimes as his bodyguards, sometimes as his enforcement goons."

The police officer lowered the notebook and grinned at Nick. "Trust you to have everything but their kids' names."

Nick's lips twisted in a hint of smile. "I think Michaels has a kid named after him. Scott Junior."

The officer flipped his notebook closed and shoved it in his shirt pocket. "Any idea why they were shooting at you?"

Nick looked away from the EMT who was taping a bandage over the wound and up at the police officer. "Might have had something to do with the fact that I wasn't going to let them take Miss McNamara."

"And they wanted Miss McNamara because…"

"Because they thought she was Zeena Bantham. What they don't know is that Annie McNamara is Zeena's twin. All I have is rumor and conjecture, but supposedly a dealer named Danny Sloop stole something from Jon Carver and passed it to Zeena, and Jon wants it back. Again, I'm going off street rumor, but I heard it was Jon's laptop and it was stolen out of his car."

Just then, Nick saw Steven's Mustang squeal into the parking lot. Steven jumped out of the vehicle and came running over. "You're okay?"

"I'm fine. Calm down. Do me a favor, would you? Scout around here. See if you can find any trace of Zeena. She went through that old tire factory, but then I lost her. Try to pick up her trail." As Steven started to move away, Nick called out to him. "And be careful. Someone whacked me in the chest with a tire iron or something. And I don't think it was Zeena."

Steven nodded. "Got it."

Nick thanked the EMT who had finished the bandaging job and was packing up. Slipping his jacket tenderly over the wound, Nick stood up. "Any word on Richie?"

The officer just stared at Nick for a long moment. "Don't go there, Nick. We all know about your history with the Carvers."

Nick looked up at the officer. "You arrest them for every crime known to man, and the courts let them out on bail, and then I have to chase them down and bring them back in. Not to mention the fact that the last time you guys let him out on bail, Richie killed a fifteen-year-old girl, who just happened to be my daughter's best friend."

"I understand your frustration, Nick. We all do. But if something goes wrong, it won't look good for you."

"You honestly think I'd just kill him in cold blood? You believe that of me?"

"No, Nick. I know you better. But things go wrong. You know that better than anyone. Let us find Richie and bring him in. Stay away from it."

Nick zipped up his jacket. "What's the story on this other guy? The one that broke out with Richie?"

"Not much I can tell you. He's a heavy hitter out of Jersey. Was arrested making a hit in Baltimore. Sentenced twenty-five to life. Goes by the name of Cutter Thorne."

"Likes the knife, eh?" Nick said as he started walking toward Conner's SUV.

"So I hear. Carves them up pretty good." The officer followed him.

"I'll keep that in mind."

As Nick and Conner were climbing into the SUV, the officer said. "Nick, I'm warning you. Don't get involved in this."

Nick fastened his seat belt. "If you haven't caught him by now, I don't have much confidence that you ever will. When I find him, I'll give you a call."

"Nick…"

Nick grinned at the officer and rolled up his window. "Where's Rafe?"

Conner started the engine and put the SUV in reverse. "I gave him your keys and sent him over to make sure that Annie got home safe."

"Good."

"You think Annie is in danger?"

"They thought Annie was Zeena. Which means they want Zeena bad enough to risk shooting at me in broad daylight. I don't know if Zeena has this rumored laptop or not, but if she does, Carver's not going to give up trying to get it back. And as long as he's looking for Zeena, Annie could be in danger."

As Conner pulled out onto the street, he voiced another thought. "What are the chances that all this about Zeena is a smoke screen to keep us off Richie?"

"I don't think so," Nick replied. "But it is something to consider. The timing would be about right. But I need you to do me a favor."

"Name it."

"I need you to talk to Annie. Find out who she told she was on her way to Jiffy's." Nick looked over at Conner. "She said she told one of us about the meeting. So either you or Conner knew, which I know you didn't, or someone was impersonating us and got the information from her."

"Someone told her they worked for Prodigal?"

"That's the way it sounds."

Conner whistled. "You think it was one of Carver's men?"

"Most likely. It would be a smart thing to do."

"You want me to track down and verify these rumors about a laptop?"

"Doesn't matter. We have a capias warrant for Zeena. So we find Zeena and take her into custody, laptop or no laptop."

Wednesday, 4:10 p.m.
Downtown Baltimore

It took Annie nearly ten minutes to convince Rafe that she was fine and that he could go. But by the time she pushed him through her apartment door, she was breaking out in a cold sweat. As she closed the door behind her, she sank down on the floor, barely able to keep her eyes open. *Okay, I'm not fine, but no way do I want that man to see me like this.*

She was about to crawl to the sofa when she heard the knock on the door. She reached up and turned the knob. Rafe pushed the door open slowly, looked down at her on the floor, and shook his head. "I knew it. Why do women always think they have to be so tough around me? I'm really into damsels in distress. Honest, I am."

He reached down and scooped her up into his arms. She wanted to protest, but by the time her head hit his shoulder, she was unconscious.

Wednesday, 4:30 p.m.
The Stark Lily, Park Heights, Baltimore

Jon's anger was mounting by the second. "You saw her. But she's not here. Why is that, again?"

Scott and Ira didn't blink. Scott was clenching his jaw so hard that Jon wouldn't have been surprised if his teeth broke. "That bounty hunter was there."

Jon picked up a crystal paperweight off his desk and threw it at Scott. Scott ducked. The paperweight hit a picture on the wall and shattered the glass. "I want that girl. Just stay away from that bounty hunter."

"We shot him, Boss. But then the police showed up, so we split."

"Tell me you didn't kill him?"

Scott shook his head. "No."

Jon clenched his fists, then unclenched them slowly. He glared at his men. "Go to the farm and get Richie. Don't make any trouble, and be sure that you aren't followed. And on your way out, send Iris up to me. She'll have to pick up where you idiots left off."

—————⊰0⊱—————

Wednesday, 4:45 p.m.
Prodigal offices, Baltimore

As Steven pulled into the parking lot at Prodigal, Michael's Porsche followed. Michael jumped out of the car and was at Steven's door before Steven had his seat belt loose. "Where's Nick?"

Steven nodded his head toward the building. "In his office. Probably indulging in Jenna's hovering and fretting. You got here fast."

"I got your message, cancelled my meeting, and headed over here. How is he?"

"Refusing to admit that he's in pain. You know how he is." Steven started walking toward the door, and Michael fell into step beside him.

Inside, Michael shrugged out of his cashmere overcoat and draped it over his arm. Jenna was heading toward Nick's office with a can of Mountain Dew. "Hi, Michael."

"Jenna, hi. I was just on my way in to see my boy, but that can wait. I have to flirt with you first. You know how it is."

Jenna laughed as she shook her head. "Yeah, we know. You can't pass a woman without trying to prove that you've still got it." She winked at him. "You lost it in college, but don't worry about it. I won't tell anyone."

Michael groaned and clutched one hand over his chest. "She's brutal, I tell you. Breaks my heart every time."

"Yeah, yeah." Jenna popped the top on Nick's soda and headed into his office.

"The woman is pining away for me," Michael said.

"Jenna? I didn't notice anything," Steven said with a laugh.

Steven's phone rang. He didn't recognize the number, but the area code gave him pause. "Hello?"

"I just wanted to thank you. I got the money."

"You're welcome. I can't talk long. Nick's been shot. Can you call me back a little later? Or give me a number to call you?"

There was a gasp and then silence.

"Hey. You there?"

Finally, he heard her speak again. "I just wanted to say thanks. I'll call later if I have time." Steven heard a click, then he snapped the phone shut.

"Who was that?" Michael said.

"Marti."

"As in your sister? I thought you guys didn't know how to contact her."

"We don't. She calls us. Well, she called me."

"Does she know what's going on here?"

"She knows. But she still refuses to tell us where she is or to come home."

Michael just shook his head and walked into Nick's office. "She always was a spoiled brat."

Steven stared at Michael. Where in the world did *that* come from? Marti was headstrong and independent, but a spoiled brat? He couldn't think of anyone who would describe her that way.

Wednesday, 4:50 p.m.
Prodigal offices, Baltimore

Nick moved from the sofa to his desk when Michael walked in. As strange as it sounded, Nick actually felt uncomfortable looking vulnerable around Michael. He'd been friends with him far longer than he had with Conner, and yet he felt safe around Conner in any form of weakness. But not Michael. Nick could detect some little hint of competition in Michael from time to time. It was nothing overt. Nothing spoken. Just a feeling that kept Nick from wanting Michael to see him wounded.

But when Jessica and Krystal followed behind Michael into his office, he was glad he'd moved to the desk. He didn't want them to see him sprawled out and weak on the couch either. As always, Jessica looked calm and cool as she unbuttoned her coat. "You get shot…and still run right back to work. Typical Nick." A half smile formed on her face, but Nick felt the barb even if it was meant to be lighthearted.

Krystal gave him a quick hug, then pulled out her iPod, stuck in her earbuds, and left the office. Nick felt the burn of her dismissal. Obviously, their little talk about Lisa hadn't helped a bit. Pushing the disappointment aside, he forced himself to smile at Steven. "What did you guys do, inform the whole world I got nicked? Hate to see what all of you would do if I really got shot."

Steven shrugged with a smile.

Jessica nodded at Michael. "Michael. Good to see you."

"Hi, Jessica."

The tension in the room was enough to give Nick a major headache. He eased back down in his chair and opened the desk drawer, pulling out his Excedrin.

Steven held up his hand. "All right, folks. Thank you for coming, but visiting hours are over and the patient needs to get back to work."

"You can't be serious," Jessica said. "He needs to rest."

Nick swallowed two more Excedrin, then looked at his ex-wife. "It's a flesh wound, Jess. It hurts, but it's not going to do much more than aggravate me." If he didn't know better, he'd swear she was actually concerned about him.

Wednesday, 5:10 p.m.
Prodigal offices, Baltimore

Steven watched while everyone slowly filed out. Nick was pale, and if you looked close enough, you could see the pain he was hiding bracketed around his mouth and eyes. But there was something else there, as well.

Steven shut Nick's office door, and Nick moved over to the sofa.

"What's going on? And I don't mean about getting shot," Steven said.

Nick set his can of Dew down on a side table and stretched out, crossing his feet at the ankles. "Am I that transparent?"

"To me you are." Steven sat down on the edge of the coffee table, shoving a stack of files out of his way. "So talk to me."

"I got a threat in the mail yesterday. Threatening Krystal if I don't mind my own business. And Richie made the same threat on the phone to me."

Steven leaned forward, resting his elbows on his knees. "What are they threatening to do?"

"Nothing specific. It was one of those 'mind your own business and oh, how's your daughter?' letters."

"What are you going to do?"

"I'm going to keep Krys safe while I track down Richie and bring him in. I'm close to Richie, Steven. I can feel it. I'm closing in on Zeena, and word on the street about the laptop is growing louder. If I can get that girl, Richie won't be far behind."

Steven bowed his head and then tilted it up to look at his brother. "I have a better idea, Nick. Forget Richie and keep Krystal safe."

10

Wednesday, 7:00 p.m.
Carver Farm, Sykesville, Maryland

Richie Carver didn't know how Cutter could be so calm and quiet. The old farmhouse was driving him crazy. It was *too* quiet, too isolated, too stark. He wanted the comfort of the condo—the bar that was never empty, the soft bed, the hot shower. And what he'd give for a decent meal.

Taking cold showers and sleeping on dusty cots didn't seem to bother Cutter at all. He seemed more than content to listen to the crickets and the birds, and he didn't seem bothered by Richie's pacing from one end of the room to the other.

Where was Jon?

"You said your brother would take care of us, so relax." Cutter lit a cigarette. "You're not accomplishing anything with all this stressing, dude."

Richie was more than a little impressed with Cutter Thorne. He was a good six foot six with the physique of a man who tuned his body as well as any other weapon in his arsenal. He moved with the grace and lightness of a cat, but even in movement, there was a stillness about him that put Richie on edge.

Richie heard a car door slam, and jumped up and ran to the window. "Scott's here."

Standing up, Cutter pulled out his pistol. "Who is Scott?"

"One of our men. Relax." Richie opened the door. "Scott. Where's Jon?"

Scott walked in and handed Richie a duffel bag. "He sent clothes and said to bring you back to the condo." Then Scott noticed Cutter and pulled his gun. Cutter raised his own piece, and the two men eyed each other like two starved pit bulls.

Richie reached up and pulled Scott's hand down. "This is Cutter. He's the one that helped me escape. I owe him."

Slowly, Scott holstered his pistol but didn't take his eyes off Cutter. "As soon as you're dressed, we're out of here. Your brother's waiting."

"Cutter is coming with us," Richie stated.

"Your brother didn't say anything about this guy."

Richie shook out a hooded sweatshirt from the duffel bag and pulled it on. "I did."

Scott didn't move. "No. Your brother didn't say nuthin to me about this guy."

Richie walked over and yanked the gun from Scott's holster and then jammed the barrel under Scott's chin. The man's eyes went wide.

"You work for the Carver *brothers*. I'm telling you to get in that van and do what I say. If you can't do that, I'll kill you here and drive the van myself."

"Okay, Richie, okay. Sorry."

When Richie saw sweat beading on Scott's forehead, he lowered the gun.

Richie grinned at Cutter. "Let's go."

Wednesday, 7:20 p.m.
Carver Farm, Sykesville, Maryland

As content as Cutter was in the Carvers' old farmhouse, he was glad to be on his way to their condo. From what Richie had told him, the place was stocked with better amenities than the Plaza.

Richie Carver was a piece of work, no doubt. No one had ever accused Cutter of being the most stable of men, but he was a brick compared to Richie. The man could go from nervous and tense, to jovial and goofy, to deadly in the blink of an eye. At first glance, you'd dismiss the man as a pawn of his older brother, but stick around long enough and you'd see just how wrong you were.

Cutter resolved at that moment not to underestimate Richie. It might prove deadly.

He followed Richie and his goon out to a dark blue panel van. There was a man in the passenger seat, but since Richie was ignoring him and climbing into the back, Cutter followed suit and sat down on the narrow bench next to Richie.

Richie reached over and lightly punched Cutter on the arm. "It'll be great, you'll see. Mi casa is your casa, pal."

Cutter nodded as he leaned back and kept an eye on Scott. Even though the man was driving and unlikely to try anything during the ride, he wasn't going to trust the man beyond his sight. He didn't appreciate being humiliated in front of someone he didn't trust.

Well, get over it, Scott. With any luck, I'll have your job in a matter of days. Then we'll talk humiliation.

It wasn't that Cutter particularly needed or wanted the job, but the man had ticked him off, and that was enough reason for him to get rid of the guy.

Wednesday, 10:38 p.m.
1428 Larkspur Drive

Marti crept through the backyard, checking for open windows and keeping an eye out for nosy neighbors. Breaking into a house was almost never easy, but breaking into one before the neighborhood was asleep was almost stupid. With any luck, most of the neighbors were too busy watching television or checking their e-mail to care what was outside.

She was cold and hungry and couldn't afford to be choosy. She should have asked Steven for more money. With less than four dollars in her pocket, she couldn't even head over to McDonald's. Her only hope was to find something in this house's kitchen that she could eat quickly.

Bingo!

A small window—probably the bathroom—wasn't locked. Grateful it wasn't on a second floor, she pried the screen out, pushed the window up, and, standing on a lawn mower stowed under the deck, climbed up and through.

She closed the window behind her and took stock of her surroundings. A blue powder room. No bath. Hand towels on the rack, folded neatly.

From there she entered the hall and took a second to get her bearings. To the right were bedrooms. To the left, the living area. And the kitchen. She headed there first.

She hit the jackpot with some leftover baked chicken, a container of cole slaw, and a bottle of soda in the fridge. It would be her first decent meal in weeks. Maybe months. She wolfed it down, standing at the counter, barely taking time to breathe between bites.

When she finished eating, she walked through the house carrying her soda. She sipped and explored.

The living room was small, meticulously neat, but still maintained enough to have a lived-in feel that made her welcome even though she'd broken in and wasn't exactly a guest. She eyed the small enamel box on the fireplace mantel. Could bring a few bucks at a decent pawn shop. A laptop on a small desk in the corner of the room. A vase on the coffee table that turned out to be glass, not crystal, and was dismissed.

In the master bedroom, the bed was made, no clothes tossed around, no dust on the dresser. A gold chain draped over the mirror. A gold and onyx ring in a silver tray on the dresser. A couple hundred dollars in tens and twenties tucked in the nightstand.

She walked over to the bed and sat down. There was a Bible next to the alarm clock. How long had it been since she'd read one of these? The red ribbon marked a section in Psalms. "Hear my prayer, O LORD, and let my cry come unto thee.... For my days are consumed like smoke, and my bones are burned as an hearth. My heart is smitten, and withered like grass; so that I forget to eat my bread."

Or didn't have any money for bread. She closed the Bible and set it down. Too much had happened in the years between the young girl who had skipped to church with a little white leather Bible in her hands and the woman she was now. Far too much.

She checked out the two spare bedrooms. One was little more than storage for a pair of skis, some free weights, a couple of boxes, an old computer, and small television that probably didn't even work, all neatly stacked in a corner. The other room held a twin bed, a single dresser, and nothing hanging in the closet. A guest room, obviously.

She pulled open the dresser drawers anyway. You never knew what treasures could be found in a guest room.

"I suggest that you get your hands up and keep them up. I have a gun, and I will use it."

Marti slowly raised her hands.

"Now who are you, and what are you doing in my house?"

———⊰○⊱———

Wednesday, 11:40 p.m.
Six blocks from the old tire factory complex near Jiffy's Bar,
Garrison Blvd., Baltimore

Grateful that most of the streetlights had been broken out, Zeena slipped through the shadows in the alley. She was probably an idiot to go out looking for a fix, but she was desperate. Some of the dealers usually hung out within a block or two of the Stark Lily. Another block or two and she should come across one of them.

She had trusted her sister, and look what it had brought down on her head. Carver's men and bounty hunters to boot. Why would Annie have done that? If there was one person in the world who she would have bet her life she could trust, it was Annie. Now that was pretty much blown to smithereens.

"Hey, Zee!"

Zeena stifled a scream and turned around. When she saw a street girl she knew, she heaved a sigh of relief. "Hey, Iris. You scared me. What you doing way over here tonight?"

"Had a good night and was looking to party." Iris was a tall, statuesque brunette. Zeena liked her because she was never selfish with her drugs. If she had some, Zeena had some. Iris pulled her faux leopard coat tighter around her neck. "You know someplace we can go? It's cold out here."

"Sure." Zeena waved for her to follow. She couldn't believe her luck. "We can party at the old tire factory."

When they reached Charlie's nest in the factory, Zeena curled up on the mattress and scooted over, making room for Iris. "Charlie's out on patrol."

Iris laughed as she dug through her purse and pulled out her little glass pipe and a baggie. "I expected to see you on the streets tonight, but it's a good thing you weren't. Carver has his men wandering around looking for you."

"Let's hope he doesn't find me." Zeena waited impatiently for Iris to fire up the pipe and do her hit before passing it over.

"I saw that Jerry guy tonight," Iris inhaled, holding it deep in her lungs while she talked through her teeth, passing the pipe to Zeena. "The one that likes you so much? He was looking for you."

"Ugh. Did you take care of him?" She put the pipe to her mouth and took a long inhale.

"Yeah. Told him not to get used to the special treatment, you'd be back soon enough."

Zeena smiled as she gave Iris the pipe to refill. "In your dreams."

———◆———

Wednesday, 11:40 p.m.
1428 Larkspur Drive

"Don't shoot." Marti held her hands out and slowly turned around. "I'm no threat."

Steven gaped at her. "Well, that's a matter of opinion, isn't it, Mart?" He holstered his gun.

Before she could say anything else, Steven swept her up in a bear hug and held on. She had lost a great deal of weight and looked a little worse for the absence. Her brown hair had lost some of its curl and was cut in a straight edge along her shoulders. There was a time when she'd rather be caught dead than be seen without makeup, but he couldn't see a trace of primping on his sister. But it was great to see her. "How did you get in my house?"

"Bathroom window. You should be more careful."

"And Killer didn't bother you?"

Marti stepped back out of his arms and looked him over. "You look wonderful. Who's Killer?"

"My dog."

"Haven't seen any dog."

"Figures. Probably hiding under the bed. I really didn't expect you to come back. I'm so glad you did. Come on. I'll make us some dinner."

Marti shot him a quick grin. "I hope it wasn't the chicken and cole slaw. I pretty much devoured that." Then she frowned. "How's Nick?"

"He's good. The bullet gouged him good, but he's okay."

"Does Mom know?"

Shaking his head, he dropped an arm over her shoulder as they walked back into the kitchen area. "I thought about telling her, but decided that it was doubtful she'd even understand. And if she did, she'd just get upset. No point in going there. Come on, I'll order us some pizza. But first I have to find out how badly you scared my poor dog."

"Some dog. Never even barked."

"Yeah, well, he has some confidence issues."

"You think?" Marti laughed as she pulled out a kitchen chair and sat down at the table. "I like your place, by the way. I was snooping."

"You haven't changed a bit." He opened a cabinet under the sink and pulled out a small bag of dog kibble. "So what did you find?"

"You're still a neat freak. Mom would be proud. You always leave a couple hundred bucks in a nightstand where it can be found so easily?"

"Guilty. Then again, I wasn't expecting someone to break into my house."

"You never know when someone is going to break in. And you left a window unlocked. Bad, Steven."

He picked up a bowl from behind the trash can. "Killer!" he yelled. "Dinner!"

A quick succession of yips came in response to Steven's command. "Where is he?"

Marti shrugged and stood up. "Sounds like the rear of the house."

They searched each room, Steven calling out to the dog and following the sound. They finally found him in Steven's master bathroom. In the bathtub. Somehow, he'd hopped in and couldn't get himself back out. Steven picked him up. "Oh, that was brilliant, Killer. You realize, though, that while you were playing in the bathtub, this woman invaded the house and could have made off with your kibble."

The dog merely licked Steven's face, wagging his tail.

Marti laughed. "Oh, tough canine. I can see why you leave him here to protect unlocked windows."

"I didn't realize the window was unlocked." Steven handed her the dog. "Here. Go feed him. I'm going to change clothes."

When Steven rejoined her, she was sitting on the living room floor, playing tug of war with Killer. He stood there for a moment and studied his little sister. She had changed and yet only in ways that made him wonder what had gone so wrong in her life. The spark was missing, as if something inside her had died. She was thin almost to the point of emaciation, and dark circles ringed her eyes.

"Where have you been, Marti?" he asked without realizing he was going to.

She shrugged and wiggled the string toy to provoke Killer a little more. "Here, there, and everywhere. Memphis, Nashville, New Orleans, Vegas, San Francisco, Chicago."

Steven walked over and sat down on the coffee table, sliding the glass vase out of his way. "I don't want to pry."

"Then please don't. I don't want to talk about any of it, okay? Maybe someday. But not tonight. You wanted me to come back, and I did. Just don't tell anyone that I'm here. Okay?"

"What about Nick?"

She shook her head. "Not yet. I'm not quite ready to see him."

"Why?"

"I'm really not ready to go into it. Just order the pizza. Oh, and some buffalo wings. I'm really tired and will probably just go straight to bed as soon as we eat."

"Do you still keep your promises?"

Laughing, she let go of the toy and, placing both hands behind her, locked her elbows and leaned back. "Heaven forbid a Shepherd not keep a promise. What do you want?"

"Don't just sneak out without saying good-bye."

She stared at him a moment and then nodded. "Okay. I won't leave without letting you know."

"Face to face."

The laugh that slipped out of her almost made her look and sound like the Marti he remembered. "You're still the smartest one in the family. Okay. Face to face."

They talked as they ate, and after the meal, Steven took the dishes into the kitchen. Loading the dishwasher, Steven said, "One question."

"Okay. One. Make it count."

———◦———

Thursday, 12:07 a.m.
Downtown Baltimore

Annie tried reading but gave up when she read the same page four times and still didn't know what was happening. She set the book down on the bedside table and wandered into the living room, trying to find something to occupy her mind. She felt desperate for some sense of normalcy, but she hadn't felt normal in a very long time. It had taken quite a bit of double-talking to get out of the hospital without a battery of tests, but she had finally convinced everyone that stress, fatigue, and lack of food was to blame for her simple fainting spell. She saw a warning in the doctor's eyes, but she ignored it. They all acted as if she wasn't smart enough to know her own body's limitations.

Well, she was.

She knew she was getting weaker. She knew time was running out. No point in shoving it in her face.

When her stomach growled, she made some toast, only to toss it in the trash after one bite. Even the smell turned her stomach. She couldn't stop hearing the sound of gunfire. She couldn't erase the sight of blood on Nick's jacket.

Lost in thought about Nick, it took a few minutes before she realized someone was knocking on the front door. She looked through the security hole and frowned as she unlocked the deadbolt and opened the door. "Yes?"

"Can I come in?"

She stepped back, opening the door wider, allowing Rafe to step into her apartment. "It's a little late, don't you think?"

"Actually, I'll be here all night, parked outside, watching out for you. I just wanted to know if you had any coffee." Rafe held up his thermos. "I'd prefer not to leave the parking lot to go down to Dunkin' Donuts."

"Why are you watching out for me?" She closed the door behind him.

"Because you are a target."

Annie watched Rafe disappear into her kitchen. It took her a second to swallow down the idea that killers would be tracking her. Might even be outside now, planning her murder. She ran into the kitchen. "You really think they those men know who I am?"

Rafe was holding up the coffeepot and frowning at the little bit still left in it. He poured it out in the sink and rinsed out the pot. "Where's the coffee and filters?"

She pointed to the cabinet above the coffee maker, and he set about making coffee. "You told Nick that someone showed up and told you that he worked for Prodigal, and you told him about going to Jiffy's."

"Yes."

"Describe the man to me."

Annie took a deep breath. "He wasn't one of you, was he?"

"No. So what can you tell me about him?"

"I don't know. He was tall, dark hair, nice enough looking. He was coming up the stairs as I was going down. Said that Nick sent him to find out if I'd heard anything from Zeena. So I told him I was on my way to meet her."

"Did he give you a name?" Rafe finished loading the coffee maker with a fresh filter, coffee grounds, and water. He hit the power button and then put the coffee and filters back in the cabinet.

She shook her head. "I never thought to ask and just assumed that I hadn't met everyone that worked at Prodigal."

Rafe folded his arms across his chest and stared at the floor for a moment. "You haven't met Steven, but he has light brown hair and green eyes."

Annie shook her head. "No, this guy had almost black hair and brown eyes."

"So it wasn't Steven. Nick thinks it might have been one of Carver's men."

"But how would this Carver guy know about me?"

"You've been all over the area looking for your sister and leaving phone numbers with bartenders."

Annie inhaled sharply. "I never thought. So they could have run a reverse check on my phone number and gotten my address."

"Pretty much."

"I didn't know that I was going to have killers after me when I went to Jiffy's yesterday."

Rafe cocked an eyebrow at her. "No reason you would have. But what's done is done. Regardless, we have to keep you alive."

As if that were possible, she wanted to say. Instead, she wrapped her arms around her waist and watched Rafe check the coffee as the machine cut off while she tried to sort through her thoughts and emotions. "I didn't mean for anyone to get hurt."

"It wasn't your fault. There was no way for you to know that the man that showed up here wasn't one of us."

"Still, Nick was shot because of me."

Rafe rinsed out his thermos before finally turning to face her. "And I understand how you feel. But it wasn't your fault." He opened the refrigerator. "No cream?"

"I meant to buy some today."

He grabbed the milk. "This'll do."

Annie watched him put sugar and milk in the thermos and then fill it with coffee. "Rafe? Can I ask you a question?"

"Go for it."

He tightened the lid on the thermos and then leaned on the counter, folding his arms with a little tilt of his head, his eyes, dark and brooding.

"Do you think Nick will forgive me? For causing him to get shot?"

"Absolutely. I doubt he'll even expect an apology. At least not for the shooting. Maybe for not being up front and honest with him all along." He zipped up his jacket, grabbed his thermos, and walked toward the door. "Thanks for the coffee."

"Wait. What do you mean I haven't been honest?"

Rafe was at the door before he finally turned around and answered her. "Nick told Conner and me about your little deal with him, and I did some research on you. Your mother is not in a hospital, and she's not dying."

She staggered back a step as his words slapped at her, brutal in their impact. "What exactly did you find out?"

"First of all, you don't think I bought that story about just being tired and hungry, do you? But the truth is, I've known that you're sick for days. Why didn't you just tell Nick the truth?"

She wrapped her arms around herself, stared at him, wanting to lie, to evade, and knowing she couldn't. "Because I don't want to admit the truth. I'm tired of seeing the pity in people's eyes. And I'm trying not to drown in the emotional ramifications of it all."

Rafe nodded, staring at the floor as if he might find some helpful words down there. She knew he wouldn't find them. No one had.

"How much does Nick know?" she asked.

"I haven't told him yet. Right now, it's just between me and Conner."

"Why not? Tell Nick, I mean?"

He leaned one shoulder against the door and looked at the floor again for a moment before lifting his face. "Because I haven't had a chance for one thing. But, honestly, I don't think it's my place to tell him the whole truth. You need to do that." He turned and reached for the door handle, then paused, not turning back to look at her. "How much time do you have?"

She swallowed hard, not wanting to answer, not wanting to put it out there in the air where it would become tangible and real. She closed her eyes and admitted, "Weeks. Months, maybe."

"Never give up, Annie."

She heard the door click and opened her eyes. She was alone.

11

Thursday, 3:20 a.m.
Old tire factory complex near Jiffy's Bar, Garrison Blvd., Baltimore

Zeena?" Charlie poked at her with two fingers, but she didn't move or respond. Not good, not good, not good. He stared at her for a few seconds and finally saw a slight movement in her chest. She was alive. Barely.

Charlie could feel the panic, the confusion. *Call the medic chopper? No. Call. Call. Someone.* Who was he supposed to call? *Wait. No phone.*

"Zeena! You have to wake up."

But Zeena didn't move. Charlie shook his hands as if trying to get water off them while a million thoughts bombarded his mind. *Do something. Do something. Don't let her die. Too many have died. Too many will never go home. One more flag-draped coffin.*

No. Not a soldier. Zeena. It's Zeena. Have to help her.

Charlie reached down and scooped Zeena into his arms. She felt as weightless as a bird. Holding her tight against his chest, he left the building and started walking down the street. From time to time, someone would eye him warily, but no one bothered him. No one stopped him. No one offered to help.

He finally reached the door to the emergency room. He stood there for a moment, wondering if he could go in. No. They would blame him for Zeena's condition.

Gently, he lowered Zeena to the ground. "They'll take care of you, Zeena. I promise."

Sirens rang in the distance. With one final pat on Zeena's cheek, he scurried off into the night.

———※———

Thursday, 4:00 a.m.
Sinai Hospital, Baltimore

Tracie Pinto, an ER nurse, grabbed a gurney and headed for the ER doors. The ambulance with the car accident victim would be pulling up in a matter of minutes, and she had to be out there and waiting.

"Two minutes out," another nurse told her as she ran up and grabbed the other end of the gurney.

Tracie nodded and stopped in her tracks when she stepped through the hospital's automatic doors. A gaunt, sweaty woman lay sprawled on the ground. Tracie knelt beside the woman, feeling for a pulse. Then she recognized her face.

"Call Dr. Burdine," she said to a nearby orderly who was smoking. "Tell him that Ann McNamara is here and she's unconscious. And tell Ben to get out here and bring a gurney."

The orderly rushed off.

Tracie picked up Zeena's hand. "Hold on, Annie. Just hold on."

———※———

A small boy walked down a dirt road, kicking at every stone and rock he came across. Trees, tall and green, towered around him as a cerulean sky shimmered overhead. When he saw a curious-looking black bird, he began to follow it as it moved from tree to tree. Then he saw the man in the distance, walking along, swinging a walking stick as he moved, his feet barely touching the ground. Positive it was his father, the boy began to run, screaming out, "Daddy! Daddy!"

But either the man couldn't hear him or he was ignoring him. The boy ran harder, faster, desperate now to reach his father. No matter how hard he ran or how fast, he couldn't seem to close the distance. As he continued to scream out for his dad, he began to cry. Still, the man never turned around. Never acknowledged him.

The man could feel the boy's anguish. His desperation. His fear of being left alone and abandoned. His breathing became as labored as the boy's. His heart pounded just as hard. Clenching his fists, he fought to run as the boy ran, urging the boy to run faster, yell louder, to not give up. Keep going!

And then the man stopped and cocked his head, as if listening for something. Once again, the boy screamed out, "Daddy! I'm here! Daddy!"

Slowly, the man turned and waited as the boy covered the distance between them. Finally, the boy collapsed at the man's feet, lifting his face to look up at the man through his tears. "Daddy?"

The man looked sad as he gently shook his head. "Alas, I never knew you."

Thursday, 6:10 a.m.
Towson, Maryland

Nick woke with a start, sweat streaming down his face. Or were those tears? Swallowing hard, his heart still pounding, Nick waited while the fear and confusion of his dream lifted. Then he became aware of the pain. It racked his chest. Every breath felt like someone stepping on his lungs. Slowly, he opened his eyes.

His bedroom. His bed. His home.

It slowly came to him. He'd been shot. And Zeena had gotten away.

"Nick?"

He turned his head and looked at Conner. "Hey," he said softly and then licked his dry lips.

"I've got coffee brewing."

Nick nodded as best he could, and then forced his body to obey as he sat up. "Why are you still here?"

"Because if there's one thing I'm intimately familiar with, it's pain. And the day after is always the worst." He nodded toward the night-stand next to the bed. "There's juice and Motrin for you. And if that doesn't help, I have some heavy-duty painkillers in my truck that will help. I'll go grab your coffee." Conner walked out of the room

Nick eased his feet to the floor and closed his eyes. Images flashed through his mind. Running across the street. Jumping toward Annie. A bullet striking him. A sharp, burning pain. An old building. A shadow moving. His ribs cracking, stealing his breath. Running and running and running, stealing his breath.

I never knew you.

I never knew you.

I never knew you.

He opened his eyes. It was just a dream. Didn't mean anything. Just a nightmare.

Still, something about it bothered him. He tried to pinpoint what his dream meant, to understand it. But the more he tried to reach it, the farther away it seemed to be.

Just like God.

How long had he tried to be faithful to God? How long had he been praying for the business? His marriage? His family? And where had God been? Far away, it would seem. He'd been raised to believe that as long as he honored God's laws, as long as he lived the best life he could, as long as he paid his tithes and belonged to a church, he'd be okay. It might have worked for his father, but it wasn't working for him. He may have seemed strong and together to everyone else, but he was nowhere near okay.

So what was the point? The harder he tried to make everything work, the worse things seemed to get. When his father asked him to leave the police department and come to work with him at Prodigal, he'd honored his father's wishes and quit the force. And then what happened? His father dropped dead. He'd taken care of his mom, and what happened? She got Alzheimer's and had to go into a nursing home. He tried to provide for his family, and what happened? His wife wanted a divorce. He tried to take care of the business, and what happened? Bankruptcy loomed. He took a fugitive into custody…and Lisa and her friend were killed.

And when he tried to do the right thing and save a girl's life, he ended up getting shot. Yeah, this God stuff was working out real well.

Thursday, 6:15 a.m.
Sinai Hospital, Baltimore

"Well, you're not Annie McNamara, so I'm going to assume you're the sister she's been looking for. Hello, Barbara. I'm Dr. Burdine, and you're at Sinai. Someone brought you in, but they didn't stick around to tell anyone who you really were."

Zeena blinked against the bright light that the doctor was shining into her eyes. "What happened?"

"You're a lucky woman. Another hour or so and we'd be planning your funeral."

Zeena tried to remember how she got to a hospital. The last thing she remembered was partying with Iris. "How do you know my sister?"

"I'm her doctor. When you were brought in, the nurses thought you were Annie and called me. The problem is, Annie doesn't smoke cocaine, shoot up heroin, or have a rose tattoo."

"No, she was always the good girl." Zeena shifted in the bed and licked her lips. "Look, I've done a lot of drugs in my time, but I've never felt like th—"

"Thirsty?" the doctor asked.

"Yes."

He picked up a cup of ice chips and spooned a few into her mouth. "Well, this is what happens when you overdose on insulin instead of heroin."

"Insulin? No. No way. Iris and me—" She paused, trying to remember if she actually saw Iris shoot up. "That would mean that...Iris tried to kill me?" She shook her head. "No. She's my friend. Maybe. I don't know. She gives me drugs."

"Well, I can't speak to whether it was intentional or not. All I can tell you is that you were lying unconscious outside the hospital doors about three hours ago and that you were in insulin shock."

"Doesn't make sense. I don't do insulin."

Dr. Burdine spooned another spoonful of ice into her mouth. "Well, I'm glad to hear you didn't intend to shoot insulin. I'm not glad that you meant to shoot heroin. You could have died, Barbara. Either way, it's no good for Annie."

"No. For sure, I didn't mean to shoot insulin." But before she could wonder why Iris would try to kill her, she realized the doctor had mentioned her sister. "Wait. What's going on with my sister?"

"We were hoping you'd be able to help her."

Zeena cracked a piece of ice, letting the rest melt and slide down her hot throat. "Help her how?"

"She's dying. Her only chance is a bone marrow transplant. She thought you could be a match, but I didn't realize you were a drug addict. Unfortunately, you're not going to be able to help her, after all."

The shock that she had unknowingly shot insulin was bad enough. But this was much worse. She hadn't been close to her sister in years, but to think of little Annie dying was unbearable. As long as Annie was out there—healthy and successful—it was as if some part of Zeena was out there as well. "Annie? Is dying?"

Dr. Burdine pulled up a chair and sat down. "Yes. I gather you haven't spoken to her."

Zeena shook her head. "No. We were supposed to meet. Things got complicated." She had seen Carver's men and split. She didn't know how they knew she'd be there, but it didn't matter. They were there, and she couldn't stick around to talk to her sister.

"Well, I'll have my nurse call Annie and let her know that you can't help her."

The doctor's words stung. "What about someone else in the family? Can't they help?"

He slipped his glasses off and used the corner of his lab coat to wipe them. "Everyone else has been tested. No one is a match. You being her twin was her last hope."

Annie. Dying. It just didn't seem possible. "Why is she dying? Why does she need a bone marrow transplant?"

"Annie had cancer. She went through chemo. Sometimes, in rare cases, it causes a condition called aplastic anemia. Annie is one of those rare cases, I'm sorry to say."

She didn't know. Her sister had been going through hell and she didn't know. Why had she thought that time had been frozen with her parents and Annie? That things were exactly the same as the last time she had seen them? Nothing at home was ever supposed to change. No one grew older. No one developed cancer. No one became one of those rare cases. No one died.

"How long does she have?"

"Not long. A month. Maybe a couple of weeks."

A month. A couple of weeks. While she was out hiding from her pain, her sister was facing hers and worse. It was time to step up for the first time in a very long time. It was time to do something she hadn't done since she and Annie were just innocent kids with their whole lives in front of them. It was time to help Annie again. One last time.

"Excuse me, Doctor? Could you make a call for me?"

"I can do that. Who would you like me to call?" He pulled out a pen and a small notepad.

"Their names are Paul and Marian Lansing."

"Okay. And who are these people?"

"They're the couple raising my son."

12

Thursday, 6:30 a.m.
1428 Larkspur Drive, Timonium, Maryland

Steven glanced over at the closed guest room door where his sister had spent the night. They'd stayed up late talking; much later than either of them had expected. He wanted to know more about her life, but she refused to answer, which only made the questions multiply in his mind. But he knew that Marti would reveal only what she wanted and in her own good time. Still, he'd enjoyed the time and had to force himself to let her off the hook and go to bed.

Running his hands through his still-wet hair, he made his way into the kitchen.

"Coffee's made."

Marti was sitting on the kitchen counter, dressed in a pair of his sweats that were way too big for her, her bare feet swinging, her hands wrapped around a coffee mug.

"You're up early."

"I usually don't sleep more than two or three hours," she said and then sipped some of her coffee.

"You still have dark circles under your eyes." Steven opened the back door. "Go on, Killer. Do your thing and hurry back for some breakfast." He opened the door for Killer, then looked toward Marti. "Hungry?"

She shook her head. "Don't usually eat first thing. My stomach never could seem to handle it."

"Oh yeah. How could I forget the million and one battles between you and Mom—her insisting that breakfast was important and you only nibbling on a piece of toast."

"A memory I've tried to forget. So, tell me about this case that got Nick shot."

He filled the dog's food and water bowls. "We don't have all the details yet, but rumor has it that a street girl named Zeena—a skip we're after—was involved with a guy named Danny, who made the mistake of ticking off the wrong people. And somehow Zeena is in the middle of it. Now they're looking for her and they don't appreciate that we're in the middle of their hunt."

"So you need to find this girl before they do."

Steven nodded and headed for the fridge. Just because Marti didn't want food didn't mean he had to starve. He pulled out some eggs. "Big detail though—we somehow missed the fact that Zeena has a twin sister. Nick almost hauled her in by mistake."

Marti flinched. "Bet that didn't go over well."

Steven chuckled as he found the cheese and then reached for the milk. "To say the least. So the girl is looking for her sister, Zeena, and insists that Nick help her—threatening that if he doesn't she will sue for breaking and entering or some nonsense. Then she sets up a meeting with Zeena, so by the time he finds out and arrives on scene, he steps into a hornet's nest and gets shot."

"So did he get Zeena?"

Steven cracked some eggs into a bowl, added some grated cheese and milk, and set a frying pan on the stove to heat up. "Nope. She got away."

Killer scratched at the back door, and when Steven didn't appear, he started barking. Steven laughed as he reached over and opened the door. "Impatient little fella, isn't he?"

Marti just offered up a vacant smile as Killer headed for the food bowl. "So now what?"

"We have to find this Zeena."

"Talk to me, Steven."

Steven shrugged. "I'm not very good at working the streets the way the other guys are. I do better on the computer, researching people, tracking down families and friends and that sort of thing."

Marti fell quiet while Steven cooked his omelet. When he finally set it on a plate and grabbed a fork, she reached over and picked up the coffeepot. "I think you're selling yourself short. But then, you always did."

"It doesn't matter. I'll do whatever I have to do. Krystal's life is at risk."

Marti set the pot down hard. "*What?*"

"The main reason we're trying so hard to find Zeena is that she is closely linked to a man named Richie Carver. Richie and his brother, Jon, are infamous around town, and every enforcement agency in Baltimore's been trying to bring them in for tons of suspected crimes. But they've flown under the radar every time.

"About four days ago, Richie escaped from prison. And he's promised to kill Krystal. We know that if we find Zeena, Richie will follow, and we'll kill two birds with one stone."

"Richie is threatening Krys because Nick put him away?"

"You got it."

"And now that's he on the run, you guys think he'll stop and take time to go after her?"

Steven set his juice glass next to his plate. "He called within hours of breaking out and reminded Nick of his promise. Then he sent a letter to Nick's house just in case Nick didn't take him seriously the first time."

Marti sat there, shaking her head in tiny, quick movements. "Well, he's not going to touch my niece, that's for sure." She leaned forward, folding her arms on the table. "I want to help, Steven. But you can't tell anyone about it."

"Tell me how that's supposed to work exactly."

"I know the streets, Steven. I *am* the streets. I can go undercover and search for her in ways that you or Nick or any of the team can't. It'll be simple. I find her. I call you. You come pick her up. No one has to know I was ever involved. Nick sees you as a hero and gets off your back. And don't deny he's giving you a hard time for not being the devoted bounty hunter he is. I know him too well for that."

He thought about it as he nursed his coffee. Finally he set his cup down. "Marti, I appreciate the offer, but Zeena worked the streets. There are some very unsavory people out there, and if you don't understand that world, they'll hurt you."

"I know that, Steven. And I venture to say I understand that world better than you do."

He stared at her a minute. "Tell me you never worked as a prostitute. Please."

She shook her head. "No, but pretty close. Still, I know my way around."

"I don't think so, Sis. But thanks for the offer. I can't let you go out there. You could get hurt."

She laughed, and the bitterness in it stunned him. "Trust me. I've already been hurt."

He looked over at her, studied her once again, wishing he could find answers in those dull eyes. "What happened to you, Marti?"

"Life." The pain in her eyes broke his heart. She stood up and set her mug in the sink. "Now, I better get dressed. I was going to wash my clothes today, but if I'm going undercover, clean clothes is the opposite effect I'm going for."

—⊷⊙⊷—

Thursday, 7:25 a.m.
1428 Larkspur Drive, Timonium, Maryland

After Steven left for work, Marti sat down on the floor and pulled Steven's photo album off the shelf. She slowly paged through it. So much had changed while she'd been gone. Her father had gone gray and brittle; her mother had shrunk. Early pictures of Jessica reflected a smiling woman, but the last pictures of her in the album portrayed someone with sad eyes. But the biggest changes that the album documented had been in Krystal. The tiny infant that Marti had held only twice had gone from precocious toddler to a gap-toothed little girl who morphed into a beautiful young girl, and then into a confused teenager.

Marti felt as if she could reach out to the rebellious part of Krystal and say, "I understand. Been there. Felt that." But Marti wondered what exactly had hurt Krystal so deeply. What had made her eyes reveal a wounded soul? Reaching out, Marti touched a picture of Krystal taken the previous Christmas. The girl was slumped down in a chair, arms folded across her chest. She had clearly closed everyone out, but Marti could see the hunger in her eyes for someone to reach beyond the self-imposed barrier and rescue her.

Or maybe Marti was just projecting her own lingering resentment. She shut the album and slipped it back on the shelf. Projecting or not,

Marti was not going to let some killer terrorize her niece, much less kill her. If she had to hunt the man down all on her own, she wouldn't let Krystal suffer. She had seen enough women suffering in this family.

Thursday, 8:10 a.m.
Prodigal offices, Baltimore

Conner rubbed his red eyes and stared at his fifth cup of coffee since waking Nick that morning. Jenna tried to convince them both to go back home and get a few more hours of sleep, but Nick refused, so Conner did too. He had to keep an eye on Nick and make sure he didn't push himself into the hospital.

In the meantime, while Nick was in his office chasing down leads, he had his own work to follow up on.

Conner leaned back and propped his feet on the corner of his desk, crossing them at the ankle, thinking through all the balls he'd been juggling this week.

First things first. He needed to listen to his voice mail.

"I'm calling for Jack Conroy. This is Ralph Henning over at the Lily. You applied for a job as a bouncer. If you're still interested you can stop by tomorrow at six and we'll get you started."

He hurried through the front door and headed into Nick's office. Nick was on his computer and looked up. "Jack Conroy got the job as a bouncer at the Stark Lily."

Nick grinned. "Jack Conroy, eh? Isn't that your wild-haired biker dude persona? That wig has to be worn out by now."

"Got a new one for this. Much better than the old one. Black with white streaks. Hangs down to the middle of my back. It's so cool."

Nick eased back in the chair, not even bothering to hide the pain. "You miss those days in the ring, huh?"

Conner shrugged. "I don't miss the life, but I miss the fun."

"I hear ya." Nick grimaced as he reached for his can of soda. "It hasn't been much fun around here lately."

"Things will turn around, Nick. They will. If I thought for one minute that this business was going under, I'd be out looking for another job." That was a lie, and maybe even Nick knew it, but he truly did believe that Prodigal was going to turn around. He couldn't have said why he felt so confident, but he did. "Anyway, I'll be working at the nightclub at least four nights a week, so I don't know how many hours I can put in at the office during the day."

"Tell Rafe to cover for you."

"He's playing bodyguard for Miss McNamara in his spare time."

"Oh, right. Well, see if she'll go home to her parents for a few days. She probably needs to visit her mother anyway."

Conner blew out a heavy breath and stood up, strolling over to the window. "That's fine, but I think you should know that there's nothing wrong with her mother."

"I know," Nick said.

"I should have known you'd be one step ahead of me." Conner turned around and leaned back against the window ledge. "Look, considering the fact that she's been playing us, maybe we should just cut her loose. She's not our responsibility, Nick. She brought this on herself."

Nick shook his head. "No. I made a deal with her. I'm going to live up to my end of the bargain whether she does or not."

"The deal was to find Zeena, not play bodyguard."

"And if she's dead, I can't collect my extra bounty on Zeena now, can I?"

Rafe stuck his head in the door. "Anyone available to help me go pick up a skip? I got a bead on him."

Conner nodded. "I'll be right there." Then he turned to Nick. "You going to be okay until Jenna gets here?"

"Dude. I'm not an invalid. Get out there and earn me some money."

Conner just grinned as he left.

———❦———

Thursday, 8:30 a.m.
Prodigal offices, Baltimore

Not five minutes after everyone left the office, Nick was running though phone logs from the prison when he heard the front door open. He had begun to stand up when two men in dark suits came through the door into his office. He couldn't recall ever seeing either one of them before, but they had that familiar air of arrogance tinted with malice that marked them as bullies. One was tall and broad-shouldered with long brown hair pulled back in a ponytail. The other was a few inches shorter but just as broad and just as hard-looking with light hair slicked back and probably held in place with gun oil. "What can I do for you?"

"That's what we're here to discuss with you. Our employer has an offer for you. He's heard about your financial troubles and would like to help you out."

Good news—Jenna isn't in the office. Bad news—no one else is either.

The two men split up, Ponytail walking over to stand in front of Nick's desk, Slick Man moving behind Nick. He swiveled his chair to keep both men in sight. "I'm not sure how you can help me. I'm not looking for any business partners."

Ponytail smiled, but it was as cold as an arctic breeze. "Oh, this isn't that kind of deal, Mr. Shepherd. Our employer would like you to keep doing exactly what you've been doing, but if you help him out on one small thing, he's willing to offer you a substantial bounty. Far more than you would get from the bail bondsman."

"And just what fugitive is Jon talking about? As if I didn't already know."

Ponytail laughed as he pulled the visitor's chair a little closer and sat down. "Oh, you misunderstand, Mr. Shepherd. We don't work for the Carvers. On the contrary, we would very much like the same thing you would—to put Carver out of business. Permanently."

Which meant they were Carver's competition. And there were only two main players in the area other than Carver. Derrick Jamal and his crew, and Ken Benedict. Since Jamal tended to surround himself with boys from the hood, these two must be Benedict's employees. And didn't this just complicate things even more? Benedict hid behind the facade of a real estate developer, rubbing elbows with politicians and criminals alike, with a smooth charm and a bevy of high-priced lawyers that kept him out of jail. Whether Nick liked it or not, he had stepped into the middle of a turf war.

"I see. And what is it that Mr. Benedict wants from me?"

Ponytail gave him a smile that didn't quite reach his eyes. "We were told not to underestimate that good-ol'-boy act of yours." He tipped his head. "So I'm sure you can understand that we're not at liberty to discuss the identity of our employer, but we can tell you that if you bring us Carver's laptop, our employer will reward you with a bounty of a quarter million dollars. That would help you save your business, would it not?"

Nick swallowed hard at the prospect of a quarter million dollars, but the idea of helping these men left a bitter taste in his mouth. "I'll tell you the same thing I told Carver. *No.* I wouldn't turn a rabid dog over to you or to him."

"I know you're a very intelligent man." The spokesman leaned forward, easing his suit coat back to reveal a gun resting in a shoulder holster. "So perhaps you require some additional time to think over the offer. You are, after all, recovering from a very painful accident. The laptop is merely an item that has no bearing on your ability to collect your bounty on the hooker. It would be quite unfortunate if you were to refuse this offer. Your business could end up in bankruptcy court in a matter of days." He moved back, letting his coat drop back into place. "To show our good faith, I'd like to warn you about your daughter."

Every muscle in Nick's body went rigid as he jerked. "Touch my daughter and it will be the last thing you feel before you die."

The man smiled again, but his eyes remained as dead as a two-day-old corpse. And just as creepy. "You misunderstand, Mr. Shepherd. We are not in the business of hurting children. I am merely offering you a goodwill gesture to show you that we are far more civilized than Jon Carver. Your daughter—a delightfully rebellious little thing, but aren't they all at that age—has been known to frequent certain clubs with a fake ID and hang with a somewhat unsavory group of people. We only seek to warn you that it would be most unfortunate if she were to get hurt while on one of her little escapades."

After setting a crisp white business card down on the desk in front of him, the man stared hard at Nick for another moment. "We'll be in touch, Mr. Shepherd." Then he jerked his head at his companion and left the room.

It took several minutes before Nick could breathe normally. All he could see was Krystal sneaking into dangerous clubs and falling into the hands of men like Scott, Ira, or Richie Carver.

———◦———

Thursday, 9:15 a.m.
Prodigal offices, Baltimore

Rafe unzipped his coat as he came through the front door of Prodigal, smiling at Jenna. As always, she was giving him a stern look that he wasn't sure he'd earned. She was so obvious about her disapproval for him that he'd given up on any hope of winning her heart. But dang, he was crazy about the woman. She was intelligent, sweet, feminine, and yet could hold her own around a bunch of macho, alpha-male adrenaline junkies. She was perfect. "Conner here?"

Jenna opened the bottom drawer of her desk and set her purse inside. "I just got here two minutes ahead of you. Doughnuts are in the kitchen."

"Have you seen Nick?"

"He's in his office," she replied as she dropped a file folder and reached down to pick it up.

Rafe was about to say something sharp and witty when everything exploded in a rush of pain. And shattered glass. Everywhere. The last thing he heard was Jenna's ear-piercing scream.

———◦———

Thursday, 9:15 a.m.
Downtown Baltimore

Annie picked up her purse to retrieve her meds. As she unloaded a fistful of bottles, her cell phone vibrated. She flipped the phone open and realized that she'd missed three calls. All of them had come from Dr. Burdine.

She called him back and waited a few minutes while a nurse paged him. "Dr. Burdine? It's Annie. I'm sorry. I just got your messages. Well, actually, I haven't listened to the—"

"Annie, your sister is down here at the hospital. How soon can you get here?"

"Barbara is there?" She felt something surge inside her, and she wasn't sure if it was hope or trepidation.

"Yes. She was brought in predawn. Drug overdose. She's fine. How soon can you get here?"

Annie glanced up at the clock on the wall. She'd promised Rafe she wouldn't go out, but this was too important for any promise. "Give me half an hour."

She hung up and ran into her bedroom to change from sweats to jeans and a plain cotton shirt. She quickly combed out her hair, touched up her eyes with some mascara, and grabbed her car keys.

Barbara was at the hospital. She would see her sister in just a few minutes.

———

Thursday, 9:18 a.m.
Prodigal offices, Baltimore

Nick heard the explosion, and for a split second, his mind argued that he was mistaken. But when he ran out into the reception area, there was no mistake. The entire front window was gone, shattered into a million pieces all over the rug. Rafe was sprawled out on the glass, and Jenna was kneeling next to him, screaming, "Rafe, you get up, you hear me? Don't you dare die on me!"

Nick hurried over and knelt next to Jenna. Rafe had a deep gash at the base of his skull, and it was bleeding profusely.

He gently touched Jenna's arm. "Jenna, call for an ambulance."

She didn't seem to hear him as tears ran down her face, streaking her mascara. "Rafe! I swear I will seriously hurt you if you die on me! Get up. Get up!"

Nick applied a little more pressure, pulling her away from Rafe. "Jenna! I need you to call for an ambulance."

She blinked up at him. "He's hurt. Rafe is hurt. The window just exploded. Something hit the back of his head."

Nick looked closer at Rafe and spotted a brick, half buried under Rafe's outstretched arm.

When Jenna stood up, he noticed the blood on her knees. "Jenna? Did it hit you?"

She shook her head no as she ran through the glass and grabbed the phone.

Nick reached down and pressed his fingers to Rafe's neck. Steady, strong pulse. Knocked out, but other than that, it didn't look to be too serious. Carefully, Nick eased Rafe over onto his side. Sure enough, there were a few cuts on his face, but that appeared to be the extent of his injuries. Grabbing the box of tissues off Jenna's desk, Nick applied a thick wad of them to the wound on Rafe's skull and pressed firmly, hoping to stop the bleeding.

Then Jenna was back. She picked up Rafe's hand and stroked it, looking at Rafe's face with an angelic expression. "He'll be fine," Nick assured her. "Just a knock on the head, and we both know how hard-headed Rafe is."

Jenna hitched back a sob as she curled her fingers around Rafe's. "One minute he was standing there talking to me, and the next thing I knew, it was like the world just exploded. Why would someone want to hurt Rafe?"

In that moment, Nick saw it clearly for the first time. The woman was head over heels *gone* for Rafe. She'd done a great job of hiding it from everyone.

"You're in love with him."

He hadn't intended to say the words, but he saw the response he expected in her eyes. She closed them, took a deep breath, and then nodded slowly. She opened her eyes and narrowed them at him. "And if you ever tell him I will make your life worse than you could imagine."

"Don't worry. Your secret is safe with me."

Just then, Conner appeared in the front of the building, hands on his hips, staring at the broken window. "What happened?" Then he saw Rafe on the floor and jumped through the opening, his feet sliding a little on the glass fragments. "What is going on?"

"I think it's a concussion. Ambulance is on its way." Sirens were starting to blare. "Conner, listen. Get out on the street. Find out if the Carvers were behind this."

"Who else could it have been?" Conner asked.

"Benedict paid me a little visit this morning." Nick brushed a piece of glass from Rafe's cheek. "I'm just making sure, that's all."

Although he didn't think a brick through a window was Benedict's style, he wouldn't put it past one of his goons to put an exclamation point on the morning's conversation.

The EMTs came rushing through the door and nudged Nick out of the way. Nick stood back and watched. When was the last time he felt in control?

Jenna appeared at his side, buttoning her coat. "I'm going to the hospital with Rafe. I'll call you when I know something. I called someone to fix the glass—he'll be here in an hour. Make sure someone's here to handle that."

Nick just nodded and watched as Jenna walked out of the building alongside the stretcher, holding Rafe's hand.

Thursday, 9:55 a.m.
Sinai Hospital, Baltimore

Zeena lay in her hospital bed, tapping her foot and wringing her hands over and over and over. What if Annie hated her? Maybe she should just get out now. She could leave before Annie got to the hospital. Dr. Burdine could handle everything with Josh. She'd called the foster family, and they gave their consent. Josh said he was willing, and Zeena had given her parental permission.

But then Annie was standing there, looking so pale and so thin it made Zeena's heart slam in her chest. She stood up, grabbing the bars on the bed to support her. Her legs felt like Jell-O. "Annie."

Annie broke into a choked laugh and pulled Zeena up in a limp hug. They were both pathetic. "I've missed you so much," Annie said.

"I've missed you too. I didn't realize how much until now." Zeena stepped back and took a long, appraising look at her older sister. "You look as bad as I feel."

Annie grinned. "Same to you."

"Well, you know how twins are."

Linking her arm in Annie's, Zeena led Annie over to the bed.

"Your doctor has explained everything to me, and I'm sorry I can't be there for you."

Annie looked confused. "You can't? The doctor told me you were here…I thought he meant that we were going to do the proced—"

Zeena shook her head. "All the drugs. I have hepatitis C, Annie. I can't give you bone marrow."

Annie looked like she was about to collapse. Zeena gripped her hand. "Hey, wait. Before you go falling apart on me. There's another way. I have a son."

"What? You do? How come I didn't know about him?"

"He's fifteen, Annie. Think back fifteen, sixteen years."

Annie's expression slowly morphed from confused to understanding. "Oh. So *that's* why Dad told you to leave."

"Yep."

"And that's why we didn't see you for three years."

"On the nose again."

Annie squeezed Zeena's hand. "Why didn't you come talk to me? I would have helped you, Barbara."

Barbara. How long had it been since she'd called herself that name. She'd been Zeena, the prostitute, the tweeker, the loser, for so long that it was hard to think of herself any other way.

"Ancient history." Zeena stopped, a coughing fit cutting her off. After taking a moment to catch her breath, she continued. "I was hurt and angry and felt justified cutting all of you out of my life. But it's all in the past. What matters now is that we get you well. Marian talked to Josh, my son, and he's willing to be tested. With any luck, he'll be a match."

"I can't wait…to meet…"

Then Annie went white, and beads of sweat broke out on her forehead. Zeena grabbed her to keep her from slumping to the floor. "Nurse! Help! Someone help me!"

———◆———

Thursday, 11:45 a.m.
Richie Carver's condo, Baltimore

Cutter Thorne was starting to lose his patience.

Richie had dropped him off at an upscale condominium complex the night before. "My brother lives two floors above me, but my condo is in an alias, so you can relax. No one is going to come crashing through the doors with guns blazing." Richie had given Cutter a two-minute tour of the place and then told him to make himself at home.

"I'll be back later," Richie had said. "Relax. Eat. Sleep. I doubt there's anything in the refrigerator, but there are restaurant numbers on the speed dial. Just order and tell them it's for me. They'll bill me. I always keep a wad of singles in the silver bowl by the front door for tips. Just help yourself to whatever you find."

Cutter had helped himself to plenty last night, but since drugs weren't on his list of vices, he passed on the cocaine in the kitchen drawer and went for the bourbon at a chrome bar off the living room. By eight, he had been starving, so he ordered a steak dinner from one of the restaurants and ate it in front of the television in the den.

By midnight, he had given up on Richie and gone to bed, taking one of the spare bedrooms Richie had shown him. He awoke just after eight this morning, showered, dressed, made a pot of coffee, and parked in front of the television again.

If Richie didn't return soon, he was going to have to change his plans. But before Cutter could decide on his next move, Richie came bouncing through the front door. "Hey! Come on. My brother wants to meet you."

Thursday, 12:30 p.m.
Prodigal offices, Baltimore

Nick paid the window repairman who finally finished replacing the glass in the front window. He tried not to consider how bad that eight hundred just hurt his checkbook.

The man left, and Nick locked the front door. He felt so tired that he could have comfortably napped right there on the carpet, remaining glass shards and all.

He headed back to the bathroom and walked over to the mirror. Opening his shirt, he peeled back the bandage and studied the area around his wound. It was red and angry. He considered having a doctor look at it. It could have been infected. It felt hot, and the pain seemed to radiate across his entire shoulder.

But man, he hated going to doctors. They hemmed and hawed and then wrote prescriptions he couldn't read and charged him hundreds of dollars only to suggest repeating the whole routine in another two weeks.

Medical reform, in his mind, meant teaching doctors how to communicate honestly with their patients. *Yes, this is bad, but I've seen worse. I'm going to make an appointment for you to come back in two weeks, but if it gets better before then, don't come back, just cancel the appointment. If it's not better, we'll try something stronger. But don't worry. This isn't going to kill you. It's just going to aggravate you for a while.*

He snorted. Like that was ever going to happen. He resecured the bandage and washed his face. If this wasn't better in a week, well…he'd give it another week.

Shoulder throbbing, he exited the bathroom, only to find Krystal knocking at the front door, peering through the glass. He unlocked the door and let her in, and before he could greet her, she stumbled at the threshold and slammed into him, her head plowing right into his shoulder.

"Ouch."

"Sorry."

Gritting his teeth against the pain, he waited until she stepped out of his way and then headed for his office. Time for more Excedrin. "Why aren't you in school?"

"Because Mom decided I should visit with you for a little while." She plopped down on the sofa in the corner and pulled out her iPod. So much for visiting.

"She could have waited until school let out. Where is she?"

"She dropped me off. She had some errands to run."

Good news—my daughter is here and safe. Bad news—my ex-wife thinks I'm a baby-sitter.

Easing down into his chair, he pulled out the Excedrin and shook three into his hand. Then he popped them into his mouth and chased them with some Mountain Dew. He turned on his computer while he considered the right way to handle the fake ID problem. "Could you turn the music off for a minute? We need to talk."

He looked straight at her, and something in his face must have clued her in to his concern, because she hunched down as she pulled the earbuds out and let them dangle. "Krystal, I need to ask you a question and it's very important that you are totally honest with me, okay? You're not going to get into trouble. I promise. But I need you to be honest with me."

"What?"

"Have you been using a fake ID and visiting clubs?"

She shook her head, rubbing her palms along her thighs. "I don't do that."

"Someone told me that you did. That you've been seen at the clubs. I need to know that you won't do that again. *Ever.* There's a danger out there that I don't want you to fall prey to. It's really, really important, Krystal. Can you promise me that you won't go to any bars?"

She nodded with a wild-eyed look that told him his information was dead-on. Which meant that Benedict's men weren't just toying with him.

"I understand the lure of sneaking into clubs. I do. I did the same thing a few times when I was your age. But right now there's something going on that makes bars especially dangerous places for you. Please promise me that until I say otherwise, you won't go to any clubs."

Licking her lips, she nodded again. "Promise." She jumped to her feet. "I need to use the bathroom."

⋙═══◆═══⋘

Thursday, 2:30 p.m.
The Stark Lily, Park Heights, Baltimore

Cutter slumped down in a leather booth at the Stark Lily, one hand wrapped around a cold bottle of beer, the other stretched across the back of the seat. His eyes were never still. He was taking in everything. He knew how many tables were in the room and how many booths. How many stools at the bar, how many feet it was to the hall that led to the bathrooms, and how many people were sitting around, drinks in hand, chatting away with someone. He knew who was drunk and who was sober, who was clean and who was hiding something. He could see it all.

Including the number of video cameras overhead.

Richie had left him at the booth with a drink, a smile, and a promise not to be long. That was nearly two hours ago. Cutter waited, making sure that the cameras showed nothing more than a man casually waiting and enjoying his drink.

Jon Carver was trying to make him sweat. Make him nervous. Antsy. He wouldn't give him the satisfaction. The Carvers weren't dealing with a lightweight.

Finally, Cutter knew it was time to make his move. He glanced at his watch, frowned. He picked up his bottle and finished it off. Put the bottle down. Stood up and fished into his pockets for a couple of singles. Tossed them on the table. By the time he got to the front door, Richie was running up to him.

"Sorry. Business. You know how it is. Come on up."

Cutter stared at him for a moment. Then he tipped his head in a signal for Richie to lead on. They wound back through the bar and down a long hall. When they reached a locked door marked Janitorial Supplies, Richie pulled his hand out of his pocket, held up the card key, and unlocked the door with a grin. "Keeps people from poking in where they don't belong."

Once through the door, they climbed a steep staircase and then proceeded through another door, entering a whole different world. The hallway alone featured plush carpet, expensive wood trim, and pricey art on the walls. They went through three other doors before stepping into Jon Carver's office.

More expensive art, more lavish woodwork, and a wall-sized window—complete with highly tinted glass—that looked down over the bar. He chided himself for missing the hidden window from below.

Jon sat behind a massive oak desk as if he were the emperor of a kingdom. He was dressed in a navy blue pinstripe suit with a crisp white shirt and pale blue tie. Leaning back in his chair, a cigar in hand, he looked amused. So he'd been enjoying watching Cutter wait. *However the man gets his jollies.*

"Mr. Cutter."

"Thorne. Cutter Thorne." Cutter didn't wait to be invited to sit down. He picked a chair that he assumed Richie probably used and dropped down into it with a heavy sigh and an attitude of someone vastly annoyed and put out. "Business must be good." Cutter glanced over at his watch again. Then he looked over at Jon with a steely bored look.

Jon's amusement faded. "Sorry to have kept you waiting. Had I known you had important business somewhere, I'd have worked you in a little sooner."

"Let's cut to the chase. I'm here because your boy was in that transport van. He begged me to help him escape, so I did. In exchange, he offered me a safe hiding place and a job." He spread his arms out with a touch of belligerence. "I'm always open to a lucrative proposition. Otherwise, I know where to find what I need."

The amusement returned to Jon's eyes. "Well said, Mr. Thorne.

Richie tells me that you have a reputation for getting things done. Your escape from prison was very well executed, so I believe him."

Cutter shrugged. "I'm not a complicated man, Carver. I'm in my line of work because I like it. And I like the lifestyle it provides. So if I'm not working, I'm not happy. And prison prevented me from working. That had to change, so I changed it. Simple enough."

"Things are not so simple around here right now." Jon set his cigar in his ashtray and scooted forward, putting his elbows on his desk and steepling his hands under his chin. "Perhaps you can simplify them for me."

Cutter shrugged nonchalantly as he looked around the office. "Looks like you have everything well in hand to me."

"Looks can be deceiving."

Bull's-eye.

"So what do you need from me?" Cutter asked, keeping his expression steeled.

"I have a large shipment of sensitive material arriving late tonight. I'd like you to oversee the off-loading of the shipment. I have some warehouse space a few blocks from the harbor. I need you to see to it that the shipment arrives at that warehouse safe and sound. And that it stays that way."

Cutter wasn't surprised at Jon's so-called offer. All he was doing was putting the disposable guy on the front lines. If the harbor police or ATF don't show up, the shipment goes to the warehouse. But if the shipment is busted, and Cutter gets arrested, Jon is free from any charges. Plausible deniability.

———⋖⋗0⋖⋗———

Thursday, 4:10 p.m.
Whispers Bar, Baltimore

It was just after four when Marti slid onto a barstool and gazed around the room. It was midafternoon, and the place was nearly deserted. A man and woman occupied a corner booth, having a late lunch, and a couple of men sat at the bar drinking beer and watching the sports channel.

"Whatcha have?" the bartender asked Marti as he wiped down the spot in front of her.

"Stoli, straight up."

He nodded and moved off, returning a few moments later with her drink. As he set it down, she smiled up at him. "You know most of the working girls around the hood, right?"

He shrugged. "Some," he replied warily.

"Just looking for an old friend of mine. She and I used to work together. Had each other's back, ya know?"

"Name?"

"Zeena." She picked up her drink and smiled at him again over the edge of the glass. "She probably hits the streets after you go home. But thought I'd check."

"They don't hang here the way they do down at the Stark Lily." He gave her the once-over. "If you know her and you know these streets, then you know Charlie. That's all I need to say."

Flashing him another smile, she tossed back the drink and set the empty glass on the bar. Reaching for the bills in her pocket, she stood up. "Thanks. I appreciate the help. If you see her before I do, just let her know Candy was asking for her."

She strolled out. Throwing out the name Candy would be a dead end. There was always someone on the street named Candy, so it would sound legit to the bartender and wouldn't raise any suspicions in Zeena.

"Well?" Steven asked when she got in the car.

"The Stark Lily and someone named Charlie. That's all I got so far."

"The Stark Lily we know—Zeena works out of there, and the Carvers own it—but I don't even want to think how many Charlies there are in this town."

"Well, take me to another place these girls frequent. Let me see what else I can find out."

Steven glanced at his watch. "The Stark Lily doesn't really start moving until about six. Why don't we go get an early dinner first?"

"Sounds good to me. And I want Italian."

"Mama Rosa's."

Marti smiled. "They're still in business?"

"They are. And as good as ever."

Thursday, 4:45 p.m.
Sinai Hospital, Baltimore

Jenna held the car door open while Rafe climbed in. "I still think you should have stayed in the hospital so they could keep an eye on you."

"It's just a concussion, Jenna. I'm not dying." Grumbling under his breath, he said more, but she couldn't make out what it was. So she slammed his door with a little more force than she intended and thanked the nurse who had insisted on wheeling Rafe out to the curb. "He's a man. Need I say more?"

The nurse laughed. "I'm used to it."

"So am I, unfortunately. I have four more of them back at the office."

"Are they all as cute as he is?"

Jenna shrugged. "Each in his own way."

"Well, it's obvious he's crazy about you, so toss the others and keep this one."

Jenna was about to correct the nurse, but she had already turned and was heading back through the doors. Oh, well.

After she climbed in the car and hooked her seat belt, Rafe said, "It's about time. Did you two exchange phone numbers?"

Jenna shifted to look at him. "Listen. I know you're hurting. I know you don't like doctors, and I know you don't like feeling weak in front of women, but you listen to me, Rafael Constanza. I'm sorry you got hurt, but I am not going to let you take it out on me. I've spent the entire day sitting around just so I could make sure that you're fine. So I won't put up with your childish tantrums. Just get your attitude adjusted real quick or you can walk home."

Rafe stared at her as if he couldn't believe she was yelling at him. Then ever so slowly, a smile crept up. "You are so incredible when you're mad."

Just how was she to stay mad when he talked like that? Twisting her keys with a little bit of attitude, she started the car and then pulled away from the curb.

"I figured it out, ya know," Rafe said.

She didn't even look at him as she slowed down for an upcoming red light. "What's that?"

"You're in love with me."

She snorted. "In your dreams."

"You are. You didn't go to the hospital last year when Conner had that accident. Or three years ago when Steven was rushed to the hospital with his appendix."

"Conner's wife was with him, and Nick took Steven to the hospital. You didn't have anyone. I just felt sorry for you, that's all."

Rafe doubled over. "Oh, no… Man… Ow…"

His pain was so obvious that Jenna swung to the curb and shifted the car into park. Unhooking her seat belt, she half climbed over the console to reach him. "Rafe? What's wrong? What hurts?"

Rafe swung back, grabbed her face, and pulled her in. He stared into her eyes and held her face for a long moment. "My heart. It hurts." And then, before she could pull away, he kissed her.

She started to pull back, but her mind scrambled. Her only coherent thought was *Heavens to Betsy.*

———◦———

Thursday, 5:00 p.m.
Mama Rosa's Restaurant, Timonium, Maryland

Marti watched as the waitress moved away, and leaned back in her chair. "I can't believe this place looks exactly the same. I figured there'd be a McDonald's here by now, or maybe a Domino's."

Steven folded his hands on the table and looked around at the murals of Italian scenes on the wall, the jars of oils and wines on a shelf along the ceiling, and the vines crawling down booth dividers. "Mom and Dad used to bring us here once a month. How many birthdays did we spend here?"

"I lost count. I think my seventh and tenth were here. I remember that if it was our birthday, we could order anything we wanted. I always wanted shrimp fettuccine."

"I think I ordered…wow. I don't remember."

"That's because you never ordered the same thing twice."

"Ah, true. And Nick—" Steven smiled.

"Always ordered whatever Dad was ordering." They both laughed at the memory. Marti shook her head. "He was always mimicking Dad. Whatever Dad did, he had to do. Whatever Dad ate, he had to eat. He never could just be himself."

"In a way, I felt sorry for him."

Marti was bothered by the sadness she saw in her brother's eyes. "Why? He chose to be that way."

"I don't think so. Dad was always this larger-than-life character. The hero. He knew martial arts and chased down criminals for a living. Nick was the firstborn son, the heir to the kingdom. Dad expected Nick to follow in his footsteps—be a cop and then a bounty hunter. I'm not so sure Nick ever had a chance to stop and consider whether it's what he really wanted to do."

Marti picked up her water. "I don't know, Steven. Nick is incredibly intelligent, and he's amazing at his job. He could have done anything he wanted. But he idolized Dad and chose to be just like him."

Steven started to say something and then paused as the waitress set bread and butter down on the table and scurried away. "I think Nick wanted to feel secure, and he thought the only way was to know that he was following the rules. Dad's rules. He wanted to be the perfect son."

Marti buttered a slice of hot Italian bread and handed it over to Steven. "Perfection is overrated."

"Easy for you to say. You were the darling little princess. Daddy's girl. You could do no wrong."

"Don't even go there," Marti snapped. Bitterness welled up that she hadn't felt in years.

"I'm sorry. I didn't mean anything by that."

She swallowed some water, unable to meet Steven's eyes. She offered a conciliatory wave. "No. Forget it. My bad. I'm too sensitive sometimes."

"Marti, what happened to you? Why did you leave like that? One minute, I thought everything was fine, and then suddenly you're gone and no one will talk about it."

"I gave you your one question, so stop asking. There's nothing to talk about. Let's go back to roasting Nick. That was more fun."

But the moment was lost. The food arrived, and they ate mostly in silence. Steven paid the bill, and they headed out. She kept her hands tucked deep in the pockets of her jacket to keep Steven from seeing how badly they were shaking. She had to get away. Run. She'd find this woman for Steven and then disappear again.

And this time, she wouldn't ever come back.

Thursday, 5:55 p.m.
The Stark Lily, Park Heights, Baltimore

Conner double-checked his wig and the fake tattoo his wife had drawn up the side of his neck and around his biceps. He enjoyed the kick she got out of seeing him in a sleeveless vest and boots with metal heels.

"You look like The Rock at a biker bar for rodeo fans," she told him with a laugh.

"With long hair."

"With long hair," she'd agreed. "But you don't have his tan."

Conner rolled his shoulders, erasing the smile from his face as he walked into the Lily. The club featured dark wood, dark floors, and minimal lighting. Music was blaring. The mood was just heavy enough to make Conner wonder why anyone would want to spend time in such a place. Granted, he'd spent more than his fair share of nights in bars much like this, grateful for the dim lights that kept his sin in the shadows, but it was hard to remember now why he'd enjoyed it as much as he had.

He walked over to the bar and introduced himself. The bartender shook his hand. "Lenny. Good to meet you. You need anything, you let me know. In the meantime, the boss is in the office, so just go on back."

Walking down a hall, passing the rest rooms and one door marked storage, Conner found another small hallway that led to an office. He walked in.

Ralph Henning was a short, thin man with an almost elfin appearance. Conner towered over him, but it didn't seem to bother Ralph at all.

"Come in, come in. Take a seat. You're giving my neck a crick."

A likable guy, Conner thought.

Conner dropped down in the chair across from Henning's desk. "Appreciate the work, Mr. Henning."

The little man waved his hand as if swatting away Conner's words. "Just do a decent job for me and that'll be thanks enough. Just wanted to go over some of the rules with you before I send you out there. No drinking on the job."

Conner nodded. "Not a problem. I don't drink anyway."

Henning eyed him warily. "No?"

"Was an alcoholic once upon a time. Nearly destroyed my life. Did a stint with AA and never looked back. I'd prefer to keep a pot of coffee on hand."

The look in Henning's eyes changed from wariness to approval. "Good. I don't hold with drugs either. I catch you using, you're gone. No hitting on the waitresses while you're working. You find someone interesting, talk to them before or after your shift."

"I'm married, and I don't cheat. The wife doesn't take kindly to sharing me, and she isn't afraid to hurt me if I ever consider it."

Henning slapped the table and stood up. "Then let me show you around."

After a quick tour of the employee area, the bar, the kitchen, and the dancing area, Henning left Conner at the bar. Conner ordered a coffee, black, and took a stool closest to the front door.

He watched the people filing through the door.

Most of them were young, seemed lonely, and were definitely looking for a good time. Some of them had obviously already started partying before they arrived, and some would probably slip out to the parking lot later in the evening for a little boost. But it was only Thursday night, so he didn't expect it to get too out of control. Tomorrow night would be a different story.

13

Friday, 10:30 a.m.
Prodigal offices, Baltimore

Friday morning brought a cold March rain that threatened to stay all day and maybe spend the night. It chilled Jessica to the bone and threatened to sap her energy. But she was too anxious for anything to calm her down.

She had just met with the Nelsons and got the final design approved and the contract signed. *One to-do item down, eight million to go.* She headed for Prodigal's offices.

Yesterday, Krystal had returned from visiting her dad with a long face and slumped shoulders. All Jessica could get out of her on the drive home was that Nick had jumped on her for leaving school early. The insensitive, selfish boor. Never mind that his daughter had been fretting herself sick worrying about him.

Well, he was going to get a lesson on parenting this morning.

She marched into his office ready to tear him apart limb from limb, only to find Jenna going through the files on his desk, Steven sitting on the sofa, Rafe on his cell, pacing by the window, and Nick also on the phone.

Stand in line, Jessica. Hasn't it always been that way with Nick?

She took the moment to study the man she had once been married to. When had he started to go gray? Granted, he was forty-two, but somehow she'd hadn't noticed it before. And the little lines around his eyes. Were those new? Or had she missed them through her haze of resentment?

She slipped out of her coat and folded it over her arm, which got Steven's attention. He sprang up from the sofa. "Hey, Jessica. Didn't see you come in. Here, take a chair."

"Thanks, Steven." She eased into the seat. "How have you been?"

"Good as can be expected," he said above the room's clatter. "You?"

"Busy."

He nodded and then turned to face Nick, who was finishing up his call. "Okay, Conn. Thanks. Keep me posted."

Nick eyed her warily as he hung up the phone. "What's wrong? Is it Krystal?"

"Yes, something is wrong, and yes, it's Krystal." She turned to Steven. "Can you all give us a moment?"

Jenna, Rafe, and Steven took the cue and left the room.

"Is she missing?" Nick asked, shifting position, nearly coming up out of his chair.

"Of course not. She's at home. But thanks to you, she ended up crying herself to sleep last night. She was so tired this morning, I let her stay home from school."

Nick actually had the audacity to look relieved as he sank back in his chair. "Don't scare me like that."

"Scare you? I just told you that you devastated your daughter yesterday, sent her home to cry for hours, and that's all I get?" She jerked to her feet. "You never cease to amaze me."

"Exactly what upset her? That I made her promise not to sneak into nightclubs and bars with her fake ID?"

The breath went out of her. She sank back into the chair. "She's been sneaking into clubs?"

"Yes, Jessica. She denied it, but she was lying. Someone saw her and told me about it." He picked up his soda, took a swig, and then set it down. "I begged her to never do it again."

It was more than Jessica could handle. She buried her face in her hands. "I didn't know."

"What is wrong with that child?" Nick said.

"She's a teenager. She thinks that she's invincible. And of course, she knows better than we do." Jessica dug through her purse and found a tissue. She wiped her cheeks and dabbed at her eyes. "I honestly don't know how to handle her anymore, Nick."

"Me neither. I threatened her with private school when I found out about the tattoo."

"What tattoo?"

"The one around her ankle."

Jessica felt a smile drifting upward like a released balloon. "That's not a real tattoo. It'll wash off. She didn't tell you that, did she?"

He stared at her. "Wash off. It'll wash off." The he laughed. "She had me. Hook, line, and sinker, she totally had me."

Then Nick's look of amusement fled. "Listen, Jessica. You have to make sure she doesn't sneak out. I don't care if you have to sit on her. She's not to go out. Anywhere."

"She's grounded, Nick." Jessica looked at her watch and then stood up. "I have to run. I'll talk to you later."

"I'm serious, Jessica. Make sure she stays home. Just for a while."

"Oh, believe me, she's staying home. For a long, long while."

Friday, 11:00 a.m.
Prodigal offices, Baltimore

Nick watched Jessica leave, wondering if he should have told her exactly how much danger their daughter was in. The future would judge whether he'd been right in keeping it from her, but it hadn't been an easy decision.

Steven walked in. "Looks like you pulled her claws. That's a first."

"Krystal lied to her, and I'm not in the mood to hear you rip at Jess. So what did you really need to see me about?"

Steven stood there a second, looking as if Nick had just turned green. "I went over the books last night. Today is payday. We don't have enough money to make payroll."

"And why exactly were you going over the books? That's my responsibility."

Steven's eyes narrowed a bit, a clear indication that he was getting into another one of his snits. "I own a third of this company, remember? I have a right to look at the books if I want to." He sighed heavily. "Look, I have some ideas about the finances, and I wanted to run them by you. If we take some of the income and invest it, we can—"

"Invest it? Are you suggesting we use that stock market program you got last year? Steven, we can't afford to be playing around right now. This is serious."

"I'm not playing around. And I am serious. Look, I've been following a couple of companies, doing some research, and I think—"

"So all these times when I catch you playing on the computer, this is what you're doing? Researching stocks instead of finding skips? Why does this not surprise me?"

"You're not going to listen to me, are you?"

"Nope." Nick reached for his Excedrin. "Did Kline pay us?"

"No. Not yet. But if you'd listen to me—"

"Steven, enough. I'm not going to let you take what little money we have and gamble it away on some stock market long shot. Now can we get back to business, please?"

"Fine. But even with what Kline owes us, we're not going to make it all." Steven sat down in the chair, a hint of temper flaring in his eyes. "The best I can do is to try to collect from Kline today. If I get him to pay us, you'll have something to live on. Without him, you can pay Jenna and the guys, but you are going to be begging people to invite you for dinner."

"The electric bill is due at the house, and so is Mom's nursing home bill." Nick took a quick drink and then set his can aside. "And what about you? You need money, don't you?"

Steven shrugged. "That stock market *game* has made me a few bucks, so I can handle Mom's nursing home bill this month."

Nick had been dreading this day for months. They couldn't pay their own bills, let alone the business's. "Well, pay for Mom's nursing. Worse comes to worst, I can stay with you until I pay the electric bill."

Steven's expression twisted.

"What?" Nick said. "You not okay with me staying with you?"

"Of course I am. It's just that…well, it's just a bad time. I have someone staying with me right now."

"Who?"

Steven dropped his face and began to pick at imaginary lint on his jeans. "None of your business, Nick."

"Steven, is there a woman living with you?"

"I never said it was a woman, and don't get the wrong idea. I do not have a girlfriend living with me."

"You better not."

Steven jumped to his feet. "Look, you are not my mother or my father. You have no say in my private life. If I ever decided to live with someone, it would be my decision."

Nick lifted his hand to pacify Steven's confusing overreaction, but by then, Steven had turned and stormed out of the room.

Nick rubbed at his temples, trying to ease the headache. He expected a fight with Jessica and didn't get one. He expected a pleasant talk with his brother and ended up in a fight. What was wrong with that picture?

Thoughts of money troubles intruded, and he felt his heart sink. He thought of Benedict's offer. He could make a quarter of a million dollars. Or he could not pay salaries, the electric bill, or his mother's nursing expenses. The scales were tipped, and the only thing holding them steady was his own belief that if he turned Zeena over to Carver, he was signing her—and maybe Krystal's—death warrant.

Rafe stuck his head in the door. "Annie's not answering her cell phone or her home phone. I went by her place, and her car is missing."

"Maybe she's out running errands." Nick didn't have the energy to worry about every move Annie made. "Did you check the hospital?"

"No. If she got sick, I don't think she'd drive herself down there." He slapped the door frame lightly. "But I'll check on it. She has to be somewhere."

Nick spun his chair around and stared out the window, returning to his earlier train of thought. If only Michael had been able to get the bank to approve a loan. Then he wouldn't be sitting here actually thinking about how much a gangster's money would help.

"You look like a man with the weight of the world on his shoulders."

Nick turned to face the door. "Michael. Hey. What brings you here on a workday?"

"I had a meeting nearby and decided to slide in for a few minutes and see how you're doing." He lifted his pant legs a fraction as he sat down, then adjusted his suit coat. "You look better than the last time I saw you."

"Getting there."

"Good to see you improving. How's all the financial stuff going?"

"Same old. Steven was just in here a bit ago to inform me that we can't make payroll today."

Michael winced. "Ouch. It's even worse than I thought."

"Yeah."

"What are you going to do?"

Nick fiddled with one of the pens on his desk, unable to meet his friend's eyes. Hard enough to be a failure to your family. Even harder to be seen as a failure in your best friend's eyes. "I'll think of something. I always do. Of course, having someone throw a brick through the front window yesterday didn't help. I can't believe how expensive that was."

Michael shifted in his chair. "A brick through the window? Who? Carver?"

"That's the way it looks." Nick leaned back in his chair with a half smile. "You remember when we were kids and you threw that baseball through Old Man Johnson's front window?"

Michael reached up and rubbed his chin. "Did I do that?"

"Yep, you did. At the time, I thought it was brave and outrageous. Now all I can think is how much it must have cost Johnson to replace that huge window." Nick reached back and rubbed his neck. "Anyway, whatever. All this is just bad timing because Conner took a night job, so he's not going to be hunting down as many fugitives."

"A night job? What for?"

Nick looked back over at Michael. "Undercover at the Lily. As a bouncer. Trying to get some leads on one of our fugitives. Oh, and get this. I had a visit yesterday from two goons, who I think were from Ken Benedict."

"Oh…never heard of him."

"Just a higher class of criminal. So I have Carver threatening my daughter and demanding I turn this hooker over to him, and this Benedict rides in like some savior promising to help me if I help him bring down Carver."

"Did you turn him down?"

"Of course I did. I am not going into business with a criminal, high class or not. And if I deal with Carver, that woman will be dead in a matter of minutes. You think I want that on my conscience?"

"But if you don't deal with Carver, they'll go after Krystal. Can you live with that? You can't honestly say that a woman you don't even know is worth more than your own daughter. Are you nuts?"

Nick shifted in his chair, searching for the words to help Michael understand. "I have no intention of putting my daughter at risk."

"I can't tell you what to do, Nick. But if I were you, I'd find the skip and hand her in, since she's dead either way. I love that kid of yours. If anything were to happen to her, I don't want to spend the rest of my life looking at my best friend and knowing you were the reason she was dead."

"That's a little harsh, don't you think?"

"Is it?"

"I can protect Krystal and get this woman turned over to the courts. And every one of Baltimore's mobsters can eat my dust."

Michael's expression was skeptical. "What are you going to do, handcuff Krystal to your side for the rest of her life?"

"Michael, do you understand what Carver is doing? If I accept his deal, he owns me. He'll always hold Krystal's life over my head. Could *you* live like that?"

Michael slowly rose to his feet, using one hand to button his suit coat. "I can't make this decision for you. Do what you have to."

With those words, Michael left the room, leaving Nick feeling as though he were trapped in a pit of snakes, wondering which one was going to bite him first.

14

Friday, 11:30 a.m.
White Marsh, Maryland

Krystal!" Jessica slammed the front door behind her, then jogged up the stairs to Krystal's bedroom.

"Krystal Marie!" She knocked on the bedroom door, but there was no answer. She opened it and looked in.

The bed wasn't made, clothes were tossed over chairs, the desk, and hanging out of open drawers. Shoes were scattered from the closet to the bed, and there were more clothes hanging over the closet door than were in the closet.

Krystal opened her bathroom door a crack and peered out. "What?"

"You need to clean this room. It's disgusting."

Krystal rolled her eyes and went to shut the bathroom door.

"Wait! That's not what I came in here for."

The door edged open just enough for Jessica to see Krystal's face while the rest of her daughter was hidden behind the door. "I want you to give me your fake ID."

Krystal deadpanned a look at her. "I told Daddy that I don't have one. How many times do I have to go over this?"

"Well, excuse me if we don't believe you."

"I told him the truth, and I told you the truth. Don't believe me, then go ahead and search everything I own. I don't care." She slammed the door shut, and Jessica heard the water come on in the shower. She walked over and sank down on the edge of the bed. That was way too easy. If she had a fake ID, wouldn't she have fought harder?

So, the fact that she wasn't fighting this must mean that there really was no fake ID, right?

Feeling older than dirt, Jessica rose and headed down to the kitchen. Why did it have to be so hard to raise a child?

How did you wade through the peer pressure, the lies, and the raging hormones to reach the child who once looked at you as though you created the stars just for her? Where did the hero worship go?

Jessica couldn't remember ever not wanting her mom's approval and love. She had been an only child raised by an ambitious, career-driven woman who decided against traditional marriage. Jessica had been the product of a sperm donation. She had no idea who her father was, and since her mother had never married, Jessica had grown up without any male role model in her life at all. She spent most of her childhood either alone in her room playing while her mother worked or attending an all-girls school. She dreamed of having a daddy and brothers and sisters, but it had only been make-believe.

Was it any wonder that Nick and his family had drawn her like a puppy to a fluffy slipper? She couldn't say for sure if she had fallen in love with Nick first or his family.

⚬

Friday, 11:30 a.m.
Golden Valley Nursing Home, Ellicott City, Maryland

"I'm not sure about this, Steven." Marti climbed out of the car and stared at the low brick building that housed the Golden Valley Nursing Home. "I don't think I'm ready."

"You'll be fine, Marti. If you don't see her now, you may regret it." Steven pocketed his keys and took her arm, propelling her forward. "Just be prepared for the fact that she may not recognize you. In fact, she probably won't."

Her doubts didn't diminish as Steven led her down a long hallway. They passed people in wheelchairs and walkers, smiling staff, and the smell of antiseptic, air freshener, old age, and disease.

Steven took her hand when she began to lag behind him, pulling her into a room.

The room was nicer than she'd imagined. Big windows welcomed lots of sunlight to bounce off pale yellow walls and light oak furniture. There was a hospital bed, but it was covered in a quilt of blue, yellow, and green. There was a small table holding a bright bouquet of flowers and two green and yellow striped sofa chairs flanking the table in front of the window.

Marti almost didn't recognize the woman sitting in a sofa chair near the window. Her mother's dark brown hair was now completely white, cut shorter than she'd ever known her mother to wear it, and she was dressed in a velour jogging suit. Her mom would have eaten nails before she'd have worn pants.

But that wasn't the worst of it.

It was seeing her mother sitting there mumbling, her hands moving endlessly, as though knitting, but there was nothing in her hands.

"Mom?" Steven walked over, leaned down, and kissed their mother on the cheek. The woman looked up at him with a blank face.

"Do I know you?"

"Yes, Mom. I'm Steven. Your son. And I brought someone to see you." He drew Marti over and held on to her as if he knew she would flee if given half a chance and wanted to make sure she didn't. "This is Marti."

"What a pretty young woman," her mother replied pleasantly. It brought tears to Marti's eyes. "So nice of you to visit. I have a daughter, you know. Her name is Marti as well. Actually, it's Martina, but she's such a little tomboy. She's ten years old." She went back to her pretend knitting. "She'll be home from school soon."

It sucked all the air out of her body and left her wobbling on rubber knees. She reached over to the bed and supported herself until she could sink down on it.

"I have two boys as well. Both good boys." She smiled up at Marti. "Do you have any children? I have three."

Marti started shaking as she watched a woman she thought she knew so well, now a complete stranger.

"Sweet girl like you. You should find yourself a nice young man and have a few babies. I love babies. I'd have had more than three, but Ros put his foot down." She giggled like a young girl. "He wants to start his own company and doesn't want to make the family suffer while he devotes his time to building the business." She lifted her eyes, her hands went still, and a soft expression moved across her face. It was the look of young love. "He's a bounty hunter."

Steven knelt down in front of their mother. "How are you feeling today?"

Suzanna Shepherd tilted her head and stared down at Steven. Then she reached out and gently stroked his cheek. "Ros. I didn't see you come in. I should start dinner. The kids are outside playing."

Steven grasped her hands to keep her from trying to rise. "No need. I had a late lunch. I'm fine. You just go on with your knitting."

She relaxed and her fingers went back to flying through intricate patterns that meant nothing to anyone but her. "How was work today?"

"It was fine."

Then the hands went still, dropping into her lap. She stared at her hands for a couple of minutes and then lifted her face. "I can't remember, Steven."

"You can't remember what, Mom?"

"I can't remember my life. Did I make breakfast this morning? Did I kiss your daddy good-bye when he left for work? I can't remember." She started to cry quietly, clasping her hands, twisting her fingers.

Steven gripped her hands and brought them to his lips. "You're fine, Mom. I promised to remember everything for you, okay? You don't need to worry about a thing."

Suzanna looked over at Marti, her eyes wide. She gasped, reaching out. "Martina! Oh, my sweet girl." Staring at her mother's outstretched arms, she had no choice but to leave the safety of the bed and walk over, lean down, and give her mother a hug. When she felt her mother's arms go around her, she felt a fissure splitting open the wall she'd built to block her family. She could almost see it, like a crack slowly working across cement.

As Marti moved back, her mother gripped her face with her hands and smiled up at her. "I've missed you. I am so sorry I didn't fight harder for you. It was just all so confusing, and I wasn't sure what the right answer was for you. Your father was so—"

Marti placed her fingertips across her mother's lips. "Shh. Don't. Let's not talk about that, okay?"

And then, in a blink, Marti saw the light go out of her mother's eyes, and the stranger was back. Suzanna looked up at Marti as though she couldn't quite understand why Marti's fingers were on her face. Marti pulled back nervously. "You had a smudge there. But it's all perfect again."

———————

Friday, 12:45 p.m.
Prodigal offices, Baltimore

Nick felt as if he were tied to his desk. He had spent hours calling his clients, pushing to get paid the money they owed him. Combing his fingers through his hair, he moved back from his desk and stood up. He needed some air. And some food.

"Jenna," he called out when he stepped out of his office and realized she wasn't at her desk.

She stuck her head out of the file room. "What do you need?"

"Nothing. I just wanted to let you know that I'm going out for a little bit. I won't be long."

"I can go get whatever you need."

"Thanks, but I need to get out."

She frowned at him, but he could see the understanding in her eyes. "Just be careful."

"Yes, Mother."

He heard Jenna gasp and then turned around. Before he could respond, he was shoved up against the wall.

"Good afternoon, Mr. Shepherd."

Nick took in the three men—all Carter's punks, all carrying guns.

"Hi, Ira. Scott. What's up, guys?" Nick concentrated on the two men that had him pinned against the wall but kept an eye on Jenna at the same time. The third thug had grabbed her. The man looked vaguely familiar, but Nick couldn't place him. But Nick didn't like his look at all.

Ira took the lead. "Our employer sent us to make sure you are on his side. He certainly hopes you have weighed all the pros and cons of this offer and have decided to accept."

He looked at Ira. "Tell Carver that if he goes anywhere near my daughter, he will regret ever *thinking* about her."

The threat didn't seem to faze either man. Ira, with his gaze fixed on Nick's steady eyes, slid his hand up Nick's arm and rested it on Nick's bad shoulder. Then he squeezed, driving his thumb deep into Nick's gunshot wound. Pain shot down through Nick's body, punching the air right out of his lungs.

"I'm sorry. Did that hurt?" Ira said. He released his hold on Nick and stepped back just as Nick reached out to hit him. "I will inform my employer that you have turned down this opportunity. He will be disappointed, I'm sure."

Nick was bent over, his breathing labored. "It just breaks...my heart. I'll...send him a card. Or maybe...some flowers."

"You are a stubborn and argumentative sucker, Shepherd."

Nick mustered a grin. "Actually, this is me...being nice. Stubborn is when...I track you down. Argumentative is when I...pull the trigger... and end your worthless life."

The men turned and headed for the front door. Nick slowly lifted his head until it came to rest on the wall behind him. Then he slowly locked his knees to keep from sliding down the wall.

"Oh, and fellas? Tell Jon...that I'm coming after Richie."

Ira and Scott ignored the comment, but it was the newest member of Jon's team that made Nick take note. He looked uncomfortable. Nick made eye contact with him and held the man's icy pale eyes until the man finally looked away, following his comrades out the door.

Gritting his teeth against the pain, he slowly looked over at Jenna. She was still rooted to the floor, staring at the front door.

"You okay?" he asked.

She nodded and then started toward him. "But what about you? They hurt you."

"I'm fine."

"You're bleeding again. Let me get you to the hospital."

It was the fluttering of her hands and the halting movements that made him reach out and touch her arm. "Jenna," he said softly.

She turned to look at him, and he saw the fire and fury in her face. "I wanted to hurt them. For the first time in my life, I really wanted to hurt a person."

Then he saw the tears spilling over. He pushed off the wall and hunched over to her, wrapping his arm around her and pulling her close. "It's okay."

She buried her face in his good shoulder. "No, it's not. All I could think was that it was men like those that killed my husband. How can people have a soul and still be so cold-blooded?"

"I don't know."

She eased out of his embrace and walked over to her desk. She opened a bottom drawer and pulled out a box of tissues. Her movements were stiff and awkward. Dabbing her eyes, she slowly sat down in her chair. "I'm sorry. I don't know why I'm falling apart now."

"Lots of people do, Jenna. You've just come face to face with violence, and it's bound to have an effect."

"All this time, I thought that somewhere, a man was regretting building that bomb. Killing so many innocent people. He didn't even know my husband. But he killed him. But you know what?"

"What?"

"He's doesn't regret anything. Carver's men laughed at your pain. They don't care. Neither did the guy who killed my husband. He probably celebrated when he heard how many people he killed. It's sickening."

"It is. I'm sorry, Jenna."

"All these years, I've tried not to hate him. I thought that if I forgave him, prayed for him, it would mean that Mark hadn't died in vain. But I do hate my husband's murderer. I want him to suffer the way my family has suffered. I want him to pay for what he did." She took a deep, shuddering breath. "I guess that makes me a terrible person."

"No," Nick replied softly. "It makes you human."

"Would you mind very much if I took the rest of the day off?"

"Not at all, Jen. Go. And if you need tomorrow, take that as well."

She reached down and pulled her purse out of the desk drawer and stood up. She stood there for a moment, then raised her eyes to his. "Rafe kissed me yesterday. When I took him home from the hospital."

"Yeah?" Nick wanted to smile and say something sarcastic like "about time," but he didn't think she was much in the mood for it at the moment.

"At first, I was scared because I felt something when he kissed me. Then I was angry that he made me feel anything at all. Now I'm afraid that my feelings for Rafe are going to push Mark's memory away."

"Mark wouldn't expect you to live alone the rest of your life. He loved you too much for that. You can love Rafe and still preserve your love for Mark."

She pushed the door open and stood there a second. Then she shook her head. "I'm not so sure."

———◦○◦———

Friday, 12:50 p.m.
Sinai Hospital, Baltimore

"She's so frail." Zeena folded her arms around her waist and stared at her sister, who was now hooked up to an IV and monitors.

"She is frail," Dr. Burdine admitted as he wrote on Annie's chart. "I'm just glad you were here when she collapsed. Hopefully we can keep her stable. She is deteriorating too quickly."

"She's always been the sicker one," Zeena said, feeling dazed. She scratched her arms; her track marks itched incessantly. She needed a fix, but *oh* how she wanted to quit. "When we were born, I weighed almost two pounds more than Annie. I was always the crazier one. The loud one who always played with fire and never got burned. But not Annie. She would get sick if she even *heard* the word *virus.*" Zeena curled her fingers around Annie's hand.

"You sound like you feel responsible for that," Dr. Burdine said. Zeena thought he was the nicest doctor she had ever met. That wasn't saying much, though. She hadn't met a lot of doctors, but the ones she knew had operated outside the law, and without any manners.

"I guess I do a little. Like somehow I took something from her in the womb and left her with very little."

"You didn't take anything from her, Barbara. I've seen twins who weighed within ounces of each other, and one will be more susceptible to illness than the other. It's just the way it works."

Barbara felt Annie's hand tighten on hers. Suddenly, a memory came to her that shot a jolt of affection for her sister right through her. Their secret language. Zeena spoke, hoping that Annie would hear the words and remember their code. "Eh, jadda be lona del wey." The words that were once so familiar came rushing back to Zeena, but they felt rough, awkward on her tongue.

Zeena felt the tears spill over as Annie replied with a whispered, strained laugh. "Kay tonna nay."

"The two of you had your own language?" Burdine scratched his chin. "I've read about that before as something common with twins. What's she saying?"

"She wants to know if I set her up."

"What?"

Zeena shook her head. "Never mind." She leaned down over Annie. "No. Oumba Kay tonna nay. Never. I'm so sorry you got caught in the middle of that."

Annie licked her lips but didn't open her eyes, as if speaking alone was more than she could find the strength for. "Nick. Hest nu pay wayla. Ni pok wessle."

"Someone named Nick." It took a minute for it to make any sense at all to Zeena. "The bounty hunter."

"What?"

"There's a bounty hunter named Nick. Nick Shepherd. He's paid me for information from time to time. Years ago."

"Lo tey rem pa wend," Annie whispered.

"Key horna buy." Zeena bowed her head. "I can't remember."

"What?" Dr. Burdine asked.

"The word I'm looking for. It's been years since she and I spoke like this. I can't remember all the words." She leaned down. "Annie. Why do you have to call him?"

"Shem nonna jot klin weff toy."

Zeena inhaled sharply.

15

Friday, 5:30 p.m.
White Marsh, Maryland

Jessica turned the heat down under the broccoli and checked the fish fillets in the oven. Satisfied that they were nearly done, she called to Krystal and then started setting the table. By the time she was putting the brown rice into a bowl, Krystal had dropped down at the table, her iPod earbuds still in her ears, her shoulders shaking in time to the music she was listening to.

Jessica put the rice on the table and pulled out one of Krystal's earbuds. "You can turn that off during dinner."

Out came the bottom lip, forming her trademark pout. Jessica ignored it as she put the rest of dinner on the table.

"I can't believe you're making me miss this party tonight."

Jessica raised an eyebrow. "I believe we've already discussed this topic, and it is now closed. Perhaps you would like me to extend your punishment?"

Krystal smoked her with a look so angry and hot it could have burned her name in concrete. And knowing how upset her daughter was, Jessica figured that Krystal would prefer the concrete to be in the shape of a tombstone. And it wouldn't say "Beloved Mother," either.

The phone rang. Jessica took the receiver from the wall. "Hello?"

It was Grace. "You're not going to believe this."

"What's that?" Jessica forked up a bit of fish and slid it into her mouth.

"I just got a call from Mrs. Nelson. She wants to make some critical changes and needs to meet with you and me immediately. As in tonight, right now, not tomorrow."

"You're kidding." Jessica set her fork down.

"Nope. I'll pick you up in twenty minutes. Be ready for anything."

Jessica stood up, replaced the phone in the receiver, and carried her plate over to the sink, managing two more bites before she set the plate down. "I have to go to work for a couple hours. When you finish dinner, put the dishes in the sink, put away the leftovers, and if I'm not back before you go to bed, remember that I love you, and sleep tight."

"But it's Friday night," Krystal whined.

"And you are grounded." Jessica hated leaving Krystal home alone on a Friday night. Besides the fact that she was actually looking forward to some mother-daughter time with her, she wasn't blind to her daughter's penchant for rebellion. But her job was resting on this Nelson account. And she couldn't say no to Grace. "Krystal, if I learn that you stepped out of our house even to get the mail, I will ground you for another month. Okay?"

"Fine. Whatever."

"There's ice cream in the freezer. Help yourself, honey. I love you."

"Uh-huh."

Jessica ran upstairs and quickly changed into a blue pantsuit, chose a silk scarf instead of trying to worry through jewelry choices, and slipped into a pair of flats. She grabbed her portfolio and ran downstairs, arriving at the coat closet just as Grace was pulling her Lexus into the driveway. She pulled out a beige overcoat, yelled to Krystal that she was leaving, and ran out to the car.

Friday, 6:00 p.m.
White Marsh, Maryland

Krystal heard the front door shut and peeked around the corner. Her mom was gone. She put the dishes in the sink and ran to the front window. Grace's car was gone. Perfect. Her mom could threaten Krystal all she wanted, but she couldn't tie her to the house.

Krystal ran upstairs and grabbed her cell phone. Sitting down on the edge of the bed, she called her friend Hannah. "Hey, I can go. Can you guys pick me up?"

"Yeah. Awesome! Guess what?"

"What?"

"Do you remember my cousin, Marcus? The cute one with the blue eyes?"

Krystal smiled softly. "Like I could forget."

"Well, his band is playing at a club downtown tonight. The Stark Lily. We're going to go there instead of Lorianne's party. You up for it?"

"Sure. Sounds great." She was going to see Marcus again! That was worth all the trouble she was going to be in tomorrow.

Friday, 6:20 p.m.
Tent City, Baltimore

Marti had been in an emotional tailspin ever since seeing her mother, and it was making it very hard for her to concentrate on her current task.

She wandered through Baltimore's Tent City, trying to focus on the homeless people bunkered all around her. Tent City was a small strip of wooded land near the overpass to the interstate. It was used by transients and the homeless as a base for cardboard boxes and ragtag tents. Small fires were burning around the area. Men and women huddled around in small groups, watching Marti with wary eyes filled with desperation and pain.

She stopped and asked about Zeena and Charlie a couple of times but only got the shake of a head and the turn of a shoulder. She was an outsider. They would give her nothing.

Marti finally looked around and picked out two old men who looked like they could be easy marks. She walked over and knelt down in front of them, putting her hands out to their little fire. "I'm trying to find my friend Zeena. She's with Charlie. Have you seen them around?"

They looked at each other, one scratching at his beard. Finally, one of them leaned forward. "He's hiding."

Bingo. This had to be the right Charlie. Now, to reel them in gently. "I know, but he's so good at hiding, I can't even find him to give him the money I owe him."

"I could give it to him," the other man piped up eagerly.

Marti shook her head. "Nice try. You know I can't do that. But if you help me find him, I'll tell him that, and I bet he'll give you a little reward."

One of the men, sporting a long gray beard, licked his hair-covered lips. Obviously the only reward he wanted came in a bottle. "He's out at the railroad yard. Down behind the storage units. One of them don't have no lock on it."

Marti gave them each five dollars. "Thank you, gentlemen. I appreciate it."

"You ain't gonna hurt him none, are ya?" one of the men said, holding on to his five-dollar bill with both hands.

"No," she assured them. "I promise you. I need to talk to Zeena, that's all." As she went to stand up, one of the men reached out both his hands to the fire, and she saw the flicker of metal on his wrist. She eased back down. "Wow, that's a really nice watch."

The old man covered it with his other hand. "It's mine."

"Oh, I know it's yours. I just really like it. It's very pretty."

The old man took his hand away and pushed his sleeve back a little more to show it off with a toothless grin. "It's mine."

"And it's a very good watch. Have you had it long?"

The old man's friend glared. "Some fancy-pants movie star gave it to him. Came through here a couple days ago wantin' us to do work for him."

"Really? A movie star. Wow. That must have been exciting. Was it one of those stars I'd know?"

The man with the watch shrugged. "Looked like a movie star."

"What did he want you to do?"

"Burn down a building. Didn't do it. But I took the watch anyway."

The other man leaned forward conspiratorially. "Come down here acting like we're just dirty old criminals willing to do anything for a few bucks. We showed him." He laughed into a coughing fit.

The old man with the watch didn't look amused, though. He looked worried. "He might come back. Cuz we didn't burn the building down. He might come back."

"He might." Marti agreed. She reached into her pocket and pulled out a few twenty dollar bills. "Tell you what. I'll buy the watch from you for what I have here. Eighty bucks. And you can tell him that you paid me to take care of it, okay?"

The men looked at each other again and one nodded to the other. The watch was slowly removed and handed over to Marti, and her money disappeared.

"What building?" She turned the Rolex watch over and looked at the inscription, then shook her head. She knew from the moment that she'd seen it on the old man's arm that she had seen this watch before.

"Some place down on the corner of Second and Market. A lawyer's office."

Yeah. It was a law office. It was also the Prodigal building. "Thanks, guys. I appreciate this." She reached into her pocket, pulled out another twenty, and gave it to them. "You earned it."

With a parting smile, she stood up and walked away, sticking the watch into her pocket.

A few minutes later, she climbed into Steven's SUV.

"Did you find out anything?"

"Yep." She gave him the description of the railroad yard. "You know where they're talking about?"

"CSX." Steven started the engine. "I know exactly where it is."

She stuck her hand in her pocket and toyed with the watch. She'd have to keep it to herself until the right time. "Listen, Steven. I made you a promise, and I'm going to keep it. I think I'm going to be leaving soon."

Steven turned his head to look at her. "How soon?"

"Tomorrow."

"Why, Marti? Can't you tell me why?"

"It's all too painful, Steven. I'm not ready to talk about it, but being back here, seeing Mom... I just can't do this again. I need to go."

"Will you at least see Nick before you go?"

"No."

"Well, consider this. Please sign the papers before you leave. I promise I'll put your share into a bank, and if you call me, I'll send you a bank card so that you can access the funds when you need to. We need to use our properties as collateral, Marti. Things are getting worse by the day."

Marti stared out the windshield. "That would mean staying until Monday."

"Yes. Just a couple more days, Marti. And then if you still need to leave, you can go with my blessing."

She turned and glared at him. "I don't need your blessing, Steven."

He reached out and touched her arm lightly. She jerked it away. "I just meant, stay and sign the papers, and if you want to go, I won't try and talk you out of it."

She hated herself for being this way with him, but she couldn't get a handle on the whirlwind inside her mind. She only knew one way to handle it. Run. Even though she'd never before been able to outrun the pain or the disappointment—or the resentment.

Finally, she looked over at Steven. "Under one condition. Nick doesn't see me. He doesn't know I've been here until I'm gone. I can sign the papers and then leave. Then you can take them and do whatever it is you guys have to do to keep the business going."

———◦◦◦———

Friday, 9:15 p.m.
The Manchester Room Steak House, Baltimore

Jon Carver pushed his plate to the side and sat back. He wiped his mouth and then tossed the napkin onto the table. "So, our holier-than-thou bounty hunter refuses to cooperate. That is regrettable, but it's his loss. I can't allow him to put my entire operation at risk. I've seen his men watching my home, and I have it from a reliable source that he's put a man undercover at the Stark Lily. It's time to hit this man where it hurts.

"Scott, take out this new bouncer at the club. Give him a clear message to take back to his boss."

Richie picked up his glass. "I want the girl."

Jon gave Richie a hard stare. "We threatened the girl only to get the man to comply. It didn't work. We touch her now, and he'll be all over us, along with the police and most likely the Feds. I can't afford to do that right now, Richie. If you want the girl, take her after I move this shipment."

Richie continued. "Ira, take Lester. Go get the girl. And keep your masks on. I don't want her to be able to describe you."

"And if the kid's not home?" Ira asked.

"Richie, can't this wait?" Jon interrupted.

Richie ignored Jon's question as he continued to give Ira instructions. "Then wait for her to come home, and take her before she can get back in the house. Her mother will just assume she ran away from home, which would work better for me anyway."

Ira toyed with his steak knife. "Whatcha want me to do to the girl?"

"I'll have Cutter watch her until Jon and I bring her father to her. Then both of them can go for a long swim." Richie smiled.

"Cutter is watching over my shipment." Jon reached for the cream and poured it into his coffee.

"And if we take the girl there to the harbor warehouse, Cutter can watch her and the shipment at the same time."

Jon threw up his hands. "You better not mess this up, Richie. I mean it."

"Relax, Jon. This'll be great. You'll see."

Jon watched Richie pour another drink. At least Richie wasn't going to try to retrieve the girl himself. He turned to Ira. "Have you heard from Iris?"

Ira nodded. "Yeah. She didn't find the laptop, but Zeena is history."

"Tell her to keep looking. Zeena wouldn't have hidden it far from her nest. Make sure Iris knows there's a big bonus in it for her."

Lester came in and hurried over to Jon, leaned down, and whispered in Jon's ear. Then when Jon nodded, he hurried from the room.

"You're in luck, Richie. It seems your girl is already out and about tonight. She's at the Lily."

Richie lifted his glass. "Ira. Go get her."

———◆———

Friday, 10:30 p.m.
The Stark Lily, Park Heights, Baltimore

Conner rolled his shoulders and lifted his mug for the bartender to fill. The bartender walked over, grabbing the coffeepot on his way. "I hate the nights when they have a live band," he yelled at Conner.

"My ears will never be the same," Conner yelled back. He put his back to the wall and sipped, watching the room. So far, he'd only had to escort two men out. One was so drunk that Conner wasn't sure he even knew he was being taken out, and the other wanted to beat up someone for looking at "his woman."

The band, a group of young foppish men that had drawn a large group of women to the club, were up on stage, banging out something they called music. It gave Conner a headache. Girls were dancing, laughing, hanging around the stage, and men in the crowd were working hard to draw the women's attention away from the band.

Then the group parted and Conner saw her. He felt a surge of panic and anger. *Krystal?* In this place? What was she thinking?

Setting his mug down on the bar, he wove his way through the crowd, shoving people out of his way to get to her. She didn't see him coming. He saw her lift a beer mug and take a drink. Had he been closer, he'd have slapped the thing out of her hands.

By the time he got to her, she had turned back to the stage and was dancing in place. He put his hand on her shoulder. She turned around. And turned white.

"Conner."

"Krystal. What are you doing here?"

"I came with friends to see the band." Then she lifted her chin. "I'm not doing anything wrong."

"First of all, you have to be eighteen to get in this club, which means you used a fake ID. That's wrong. Second, I saw you drinking beer, and you are underage. Wrong again."

"Just leave me alone, Conner. I just want to hear the band and then I'll go home. I won't drink anymore, if that's your problem. I only had a sip."

"No can do, Krys. It's my job to keep minors out, and you are a minor. You are leaving. Now." He reached down, picked up her purse, and handed it to her. "I'll drive you home or I'll call your mom to come pick you up. Pick one."

Krystal turned red, sheepishly eying her friends, who were staring at her. Conner didn't care if she was embarrassed or not. She was leaving.

"Fine. But Mom is out, so call my dad. But first I have to go to the bathroom." Before Conner could grab her, she skirted around him through the crowd.

Conner began to follow, only to have a young girl step in front of him. "Don't do this, mister. My cousin is in the band, and we just came here to listen."

"She's under eighteen, and I'm sure that if I look hard enough, so are you."

His glare got the desired effect. She backed off.

Conner wove through the room, making his way to the back. What in the world was that girl thinking? Nick would have a heart attack if he found out she was here.

There was a short line to the bathrooms, but Krystal wasn't in it. He looked around but didn't see her. Then he heard her call his name from the end of the hall. He walked down and turned left toward Henning's office.

He stopped in his tracks.

Ira had Krystal, his arm wrapped around her waist, holding her close to him, a gun pressed to her temple.

"Let her go, buddy."

The man smiled like a wolf licking his chops. "I don't think so. She's coming with me. Your job will be to tell your boss that no was the wrong answer."

"I don't know what you're talking about." Conner was shocked. Who blew his cover? Conner steeled himself not to act panicked or reveal his shock.

"I have to admit, the wig had us fooled. When Jon found out who you were, he near busted a gut."

"Look, buddy. I don't know what this is all about, but you need to let the girl go."

"I don't think so, Mr. Bounty Hunter."

Then Conner felt something slam into the back of his head. Everything went black.

———◆———

Friday, 11:30 p.m.
Someplace near the Stark Lily, Park Heights, Baltimore

Krystal had fought as hard as she could after seeing Conner knocked out, but she got too tired and couldn't get away. The two men had tied her hands and feet and gagged her. And they tossed her into the back of a van.

Her dad had warned her, but she didn't listen. She thought he was being so typically parental, but she realized that he really had been trying to keep her safe. She felt so stupid. And now Conner was hurt really, really bad, and maybe even dead. She was in trouble and her dad didn't know and he might never know and they were probably going to kill her. All because she'd snuck out of the house. If she lived through this, her dad was probably going to ground her for life, send her to a private school, and never let her go anywhere ever again without Rafe or Conner going along as an escort to make sure she didn't sneak off someplace.

If she lived though this.

She had no idea who these men were or what they wanted, and it was not knowing that was really, really making her scared. Would they shoot her? Probably. They had guns. Then they'd probably throw her body out in a field or something. Then the wild animals would find her.

She started to whimper as her mind took her down a path that was more terrifying than being tied up in the back of the van with two very mean-looking men. Now she was alive. On that path down the road, she was dead. She had to think of a way to escape.

A short time later, they had parked the van. At that point, she thought for sure she was going to die. So when they opened the back of the van, she was poised and ready to fight. When one of the men tried to pick her up, she kicked out with her feet, catching him in the chin. Cursing, he grabbed her flailing legs and hauled her out of the van. She hit the ground, and the pain jarred up her spine, stunning her into compliance long enough for the man to pick her up and toss her over his shoulder. They went through the back door of a building and into a small, closet-sized room.

Then she was tossed down on some kind of blanket. It was a bit scratchy and looked like maybe it was used for shipping stuff.

"One more bit of trouble out of you, kid, and you won't live long enough for your daddy to know you're even missing. You get my drift?"

Glaring up at him, she just lay there, wishing she had a gun. Or a knife. But mostly, she really, really wished her dad would come storming through the door, guns blazing, and rescue her. But then she remembered that he hadn't saved Lisa. So maybe he couldn't save her either.

Her life was over. Curling up in a ball, she let the tears come and with them, the sobs, the self-pity, and the fear.

16

Saturday, 3:48 a.m.
An alley near the Stark Lily, Park Heights, Baltimore

Conner groaned. It took a few moments for him get beyond the drumming of the headache and think. And remember the incident in the club's hall.

He rolled to his side and groaned again. Blinking, he could see that it was still dark and that he was in an alley somewhere. It took every ounce of his strength to get to a sitting position. He gingerly touched the back of his head, and his fingers came away sticky with blood.

The pain sent a flash of memory through his mind: his famous barbed wire battle with The Rock at Madison Square Garden. The Rock went to hit him with a chair, and as Conner slipped on a drop of sweat on the floor, the chair came down at the base of his skull, drawing blood and giving him a headache to end all headaches.

Wiping the blood off on his jeans, he looked around. It looked like he was in the alley behind the shoe repair store, which meant he was just a block away from the Stark Lily. And his truck.

He felt his pockets and was reassured that his keys and wallet were still there. As he put his hand out to steady himself to stand, it landed on something soft. He picked it up. It was his leather jacket. And his wig. He almost felt a laugh bubbling up. Nice of them to remember that. Not that it had done any good.

He slowly eased the jacket on and then got to his feet.

Staggering like a drunk, he used the wall to steady himself and make his way out of the alley. Yep, there was the pharmacy. He was right. He limped up the street. He found his truck right where he'd left it. But the parking lot was empty. He glanced down at his watch, angling it into the light from a streetlamp and saw that it was almost four in the morning.

He'd been passed out for almost six hours. God only knew what had happened in that time. He had to get to Nick.

He climbed into his SUV and rested his forehead on the steering wheel for a second, then pulled the door closed.

He lifted the console and pulled out his cell phone. He dialed Steven. As soon as Steven answered, Conner gave him the short version of the story and told him to call Rafe.

"Where are you?" Steven asked.

"On my way to Nick's."

<hr />

Saturday, 4:00 a.m.
Timonium, Maryland

Steven jumped out of bed and raced to his closet. He pulled out a pair of black jeans, a black pullover, and his black boots. As he headed back to toss the clothes on the bed, there was a knock at the door.

"Yeah?"

Marti opened the door and stuck her head in. "What's going on?"

"Krystal's been taken by Carver. Conner has been hurt. He's on his way to Nick's. We have to get Krystal back."

Her eyes narrowed. "I'll be dressed and ready to go in a second."

She went to close the door.

"Wait. Marti?"

She stuck her head back in the door. "What?"

"You sure you want to do this?"

She stared at him for a long moment and then lifted her chin. She looked like a warrior arming for battle. "What do you think?"

———⊙———

Saturday, 4:20 a.m.
Towson, Maryland

The drive to Nick's was the longest fifteen minutes of Conner's life. It seemed as though he had hit every red light, but he finally pulled into the driveway and parked next to Nick's SUV.

He probably should have just called, but there was no way he could give news like this to his boss and friend over the phone. When he got to the door, he knocked and then hit the doorbell a couple of times.

When he started feeling lightheaded, he leaned his forehead against the doorjamb, trying hard not to pass out. "Come on, Nick. Answer the door." He hit the doorbell again, jabbing it three times in a row.

The door opened and Conner shoved his way in, nearly knocking Nick out of the way. He sank down in the nearest chair.

Nick closed the door. "What's going on?" Then he stared at Conner. "What happened to you?"

"They have Krystal."

"What? How?"

"Someone made me at the club. They took Krystal. Told me to tell you that no was the wrong answer."

Nick went pale as he started to pace. "I expressly forbade her from going to a club and told Jessica to confiscate that ID."

"Well, she was there. I'm sorry, Nick. I never saw it coming. I had no idea that they knew who I was and that it was all a setup."

"It's not your fault." Nick picked up the cordless phone from the side table and dialed. "Steven. Get the team together. Meet me at the office."

When Nick looked over at him, Conner shrugged. "I already called them."

"Yeah. See you in a few." Nick hung up. "I should have realized you'd have notified everyone. Give me a minute to change." Then he stopped and looked back at Conner. "Are you sure you're okay? Do you need to go to the hospital?"

"I'll be okay. Looks worse than it is." He took a deep breath when another shaft of pain pierced his brain. "I'm sorry, Nick. I feel like I've let you down."

"You didn't. I should have told Jessica about Carver, and I didn't. It's my mistake, not yours."

Conner cradled his aching head in his hands while Nick rushed off to get dressed. He'd blown it, and nothing Nick said was going to change that fact.

Saturday, 4:25 a.m.
Towson, Maryland

When Nick came back out to the living room, Conner had been joined by two police officers. One of the officers was Paul Vizeo, a man Nick had once served with on the force. But he was a stickler for the rules, and Nick was too angry to care about red tape.

"Your brother called us. Tell us what happened." Paul said.

Nick sat down in a chair and started lacing his combat boots, going over everything as quickly as he could. "So now Carver has my daughter, and that's one mistake he never should have made."

He stood up, tucking his black pullover down into the waist of his pants. "If you want to help, go tell Carver he's a dead man."

Vizeo stepped toward Nick, tucking his notebook in his shirt pocket. "I'm really sorry about this, Nick. We'll do all we can, but you know we have no direct proof that Jon Robinson Carver took your daughter, or that his brother Richie did, even though we don't doubt your word or your instincts."

"I know." Nick pulled on his shoulder holster.

"We'll go talk to Carver. See what we can find out. In the meantime—"

"Look, I have paper on one of Carver's men, Tommy Lester. That gives me authority to go in there looking for him. If I happen to find my daughter while I'm at it, well and good. You get my drift?" Nick opened the closet and pulled out his jacket. "You can tell everyone to keep an eye out for Krystal. Leave Carver to me."

"Don't do anything stupid, Shepherd. You know what I mean."

"Don't worry. Just stay available."

"We can do that."

Nick and Conner drove to Prodigal's offices in silence. When they arrived, they climbed out of the SUV and headed toward the office. "We look like the walking dead," Nick said.

"I know I feel like it," Conner replied as he pulled the door open.

The reception area was empty, but someone had made coffee. The smell hit Nick at the door and drew him in.

Conner sniffed. "I'll go get you a Dew."

"Can't fool me. You're headed for that coffeepot."

"You know it. I can almost hear it calling to me."

Nick stepped into his office. Rafe was on the sofa. Steven was sitting on the edge of Nick's desk, feet swinging.

And…

Nick dropped his keys. "Marti."

She rose from his desk chair, a wary expression on her face. "Yeah. I heard my niece was in a bit of trouble. Thought I'd ride to the rescue."

"Marti," Nick whispered again, trying to figure out if he was just imagining it. "You're here."

"Glad to see you haven't lost your keen observation skills." A sad smile twisted her lips.

He walked over. Stared at her a second, registering the little things like how thin she was. She must have known that he was seeing more than she wanted because she dropped her head, shielding herself from any further investigation. He reached out with his good arm and pulled her into a hug. "It's so good to see you. You're too skinny, but it's still good to see you."

Marti choked out a little laugh and stepped back out of his embrace. "Yeah, well."

"When did you get here?"

She shrugged. "Couple days ago."

He turned and frowned at Steven, who had retreated to the far corner.

"I wanted to tell you, but she made me promise." Steven shot a look over at Marti as if begging for help.

Marti reached out and tapped Nick's arm. "Don't go after him. It was my decision. I had my reasons. They don't matter right now. We have a bigger problem to deal with."

"Yes, we do. But then I'm going to have a long talk with both of you."

"He hasn't lost his poppa bear attitude, either," Steven quipped.

Nick reached over and fired up his computer. "Shall we make our plans?"

Saturday, 5:07 a.m.
White Marsh, Maryland

Jessica opened her eyes and stared up at the ceiling. She'd been tossing and turning for hours and couldn't sleep. Giving up, she rolled out of bed and grabbed her robe, slipping it on as she headed down to make a cup of tea. As she passed Krystal's bedroom door, she eased it open to peek in on her.

She walked over and turned on the lamp next to Krystal's bed and looked down.

A doll with brown hair was tucked where Krystal should have lain.

"Krystal, I'm going to ground you until you're twenty-one." But then Jessica looked at the clock and realized that it was just after five in the morning. No way would Krystal still be out at this hour. She would have snuck in hours ago.

Panic. Not again.

Jessica ran back into her room and picked up the phone. She called Nick's house, but after four rings, it went to the answering machine. "Nick, wake up. Krystal is missing. Call me."

Jessica slammed the phone down as she sank to the bed. This couldn't be happening. She picked up the phone again and dialed Nick's cell. No answer. Her hands were shaking so hard that she could barely dial Steven's cell.

"Hello?"

"Steven, Jessica. Do you know where Nick is? Krystal's gone. She snuck out again." She couldn't help the fact that her voice came out part scream and part screech.

"Hold on. I'll let you talk to Nick." She could hear all the voices in the background. Nick already knew.

Jumping to her feet, Jessica began to pace, growing angrier by the minute as she waited for her ex-husband to come to the phone. Finally, he picked up. "Jessica. I was about to call you."

"Yeah. I've heard that before. Where is she, Nick?"

"I believe she is in the hands of two brothers named Jon and Richie Carver."

Jessica gasped and then broke out sobbing. "Why would they have our daughter?"

"It's a long story, but they wanted something from me and threatened that if I didn't comply, they'd hurt Krystal."

Her knees gave out and she sank to the carpet. "And you didn't think I should know that our daughter was in that kind of danger? I can't believe this!"

"Jessica, I'm sorry. I was wrong. I take full responsibility. I should have told you."

She listened to him rattle off the platitudes as fast as he could, but it made no impact on her. She doubled over, rocking into the depths of the pain. "You find my daughter, Nick Shepherd. And you bring her home now!"

She slammed the phone down. Then picked it up, screaming, and threw it against the wall. Curling up in a tight ball on the floor, she began to rock from the pain that was ripping through her. "God, please, don't let this be happening. Bring my daughter home. Please. Don't let them hurt my baby."

———⬦———

Saturday, 5:10 a.m.
Sinai Hospital, Baltimore

Annie opened her eyes and blinked a couple of times, trying to see if her sister would disappear between blinks. Nope. She hadn't dreamed it after all. She licked her dry lips. "Barb?"

It took a second for Barbara to slowly open her eyes, but when she did, she smiled. "Hey, Sis. You're awake."

"I thought maybe I dreamed you."

Barb picked up a glass of water with trembling hands, putting the straw to Annie's mouth. "Drink first."

Annie drank gratefully, letting the cool water soothe her dry throat. "Thanks," she whispered when she was finished. "So what happened?"

"Dr. Burdine is really worried about you."

Annie pushed herself back so that she could sit up a little. "My body is weakening."

Barbara was scratching her arms, which were bright red. She ran her fingers though her greasy hair. "Well, it'll be a few days before we know whether my son is a match or not. So for now, we stay positive, okay?"

"I need to call Nick."

Barb picked up her hand. "And you need to rest."

"Please, can you give me my cell phone?" Annie raised the bed so that she could sit up.

"Annie, please don't."

She just looked at her sister, the pleading in her eyes. "Don't what?"

"You said earlier that you had to call Nick. That you promised him that you would let him know where I was. You don't understand. If you call him, he'll take me straight to jail and Carver will have me dead in a matter of hours. Please. I can't let you call."

"No. You don't understand. He won't. He knows I need you right now. But I made him a promise. I have to keep it."

Slowly, Barb handed her the phone.

Rafe answered on the second ring, and Annie quickly explained where she was, but before she could tell him about her sister, Rafe told her about Krystal. "Oh no. What is Nick going to do?"

"We're working out plans right now."

"I'll let you get back to it then."

"Stay in touch, Annie."

"Will do." Annie closed her phone and tossed it down on the blanket covering her lap.

"What's going on?" Barb asked.

Annie told her all about Nick and Krystal and Jon and Richie Carver.

"They'll kill her," Barb stated flatly. "They're like that. Lives mean nothing to the Carvers."

She walked over to the window, stared out for a minute, and then turned around. "He wants the laptop. In order for Nick to get Krystal back, Nick has to turn over that laptop."

Annie leaned back against the pillow and closed her eyes.

"He might still attempt to kill Nick and Krystal, but without the laptop, they don't stand a chance."

"You need to give Nick that laptop."

"So you want me to turn myself in."

The sudden shift in Barb's tone—the lack of emotion her words conveyed—had Annie opening her eyes and looking over at her sister. "I didn't get a chance to tell them you're here. I'm not asking you to do anything. I just mentioned the laptop in hopes that maybe we can give it to Nick. Not you. Just the laptop."

Barb slowly sat down in the chair, dropping her eyes to the floor. "It won't stop Jon. He wants me."

"But without the laptop, Nick and his daughter don't stand a chance. If the only way to save them is to deliver you and the laptop to Jon… I'll take your place. My life is over anyway."

"Annie, no. That's insane."

Annie reached over and hit the nurse call button. "No, it's not. An innocent young girl's life is on the line, and mine is over anyway. Seems like a logical choice to me." She swung her feet over the edge of the bed. "Will you give me the laptop?"

Barb studied her as a nurse came in and Annie told her to call Dr. Burdine, that she wanted to be released. As the nurse left, Barb reached out and took Annie's hand. "Okay, if you're determined to do this, I'll get the laptop."

———◦———

Saturday, 5:45 a.m.
Jon Carver's condo, Baltimore

Nick brushed his hand over his gun and then pounded on the door to Jon Carver's condo. Conner and Rafe stood behind him.

"Who is it?"

"Open up. We have a warrant for Tommy Lester."

The door cracked open, and just as Nick had anticipated, Ira was still half-asleep. "Lester? He doesn't live here. What's this about, Shepherd? You wake Mr. Carver up, and he's going to be calling his lawyers before you have time to apologize."

Nick pushed through the door, shoving Ira aside. "We have reason to believe that Lester is hiding out here." Nick waved Conner forward while Rafe maintained a stance behind Nick, gun drawn and pointed at Ira. "Check every room, under every bed. If Lester's here, I want him in cuffs."

"Who do you think you are, Shepherd?" Jon Carver came into the room, tying the belt to his robe. "You can't come barging in here like this."

"Sure I can." Nick waved papers in front of Jon's face. "I have every right. So, while we're waiting, why don't you tell me where my daughter's hidden? I'd hate for Rafe to accidentally shoot you before you had a chance to come clean."

Jon narrowed his eyes. "You're going to pay for this, Shepherd."

"I doubt it could be worse than what I've already paid. You crossed the line, Carver. And it's a step you're going to regret for a very long time."

While Rafe held Jon and Ira at gunpoint, Nick went through the kitchen, the dining room, the library, and the home gym. It didn't look like Jon ever used any of the equipment, but it was good for show, at least. Probably stood around drinking while he forced his goons to work out every day.

He finally made the circle back to the living room.

Conner stepped back into the living room. "Bedrooms are clear."

Nick nodded and turned back to Jon. "Tell Lester we'll be back and we'll keep coming back until we have him back in custody. You'll tell him that for us, won't you?"

"I have no idea where he is."

Nick smiled. "I'm sure you'll think of something. After all, you won't want me barging in every few hours. That would be so inconvenient, don't you think? One last chance, Jon. Where is my daughter?"

"I don't know what you're talking about."

"I see. Well, I guess that means I'll be sending that laptop to the FBI. You have a nice day."

"Although, Boss," Conner stepped in a little closer to Nick. "Didn't Benedict offer you half a million dollars for that laptop? Why don't we just sell it to him?"

"Shepherd." Jon stepped forward, tightening the belt on his blue velvet robe. "That would be the very last mistake you ever made."

"My daughter was your biggest mistake," Nick said, leaning in close to Jon's face for emphasis. "I want her back."

Jon tucked his hands in his pockets and gave Nick one of those smarmy smiles Nick hated. "I'll ask around. I'm sure I can find out who has her."

"Uh-huh," Nick replied. "You'll ask around. I'm sure you won't have to search very far for answers. I'll be expecting your call, Carver.

And don't make me wait too long. Benedict's offer is looking better all the time."

"You turn that laptop over to him, and your daughter is dead."

Nick grabbed Jon by the lapels and slammed him up against the wall. "If anything, and I mean any single thing happens to her, you will be dead within a matter of hours. Do you hear me?"

"And you'll go to jail, bounty hunter," Jon said through clenched teeth. "Can you live with that?"

"I can claim self-defense, and you'll be dead. I can live with that." Nick gave Jon one last shake and then released him. Jon staggered but managed to stay on his feet. "Like I said, Jon. Have a nice day."

Saturday, 6:05 a.m.
Jon Carver's condo, Baltimore

As soon as the bounty hunters left, Jon grabbed the phone and called Richie. "I warned you not to take the girl. Thanks to your insolence, Shepherd just showed up at my front door."

"Jon? What? I'm sleeping. Can this wait?"

Jon paced while he talked. "I don't care if you just fell asleep fifteen minutes ago. I warned you not to mess with her until I was done with this deal, but oh no…now that bounty hunter's making threats, holding my laptop for ransom. Brilliant, Richie. Great work, you moron."

"Relax. He's just trying to push you into making a mistake. I'm going back to bed."

When Jon heard Richie hang up, he slammed the phone down.

17

Saturday, 9:30 a.m.
Prodigal offices, Baltimore

Nick let the silence in his office give him space to think, even though his thoughts were far from peaceful. They bombarded him as he sat, his head and arms resting on his desk, the door to his office shut.

He had ruined his marriage. He had alienated his daughter. He'd given everything for a business that now threatened to end Krystal's life. It was his own pride and arrogance that had led to Krystal's abduction. He had taunted Richie, knowing that Richie would have to react. Nick had trusted his own ability to outwit the Carvers without accepting that he could be beaten.

He'd been wrong. And now he might never see his daughter alive again.

Let's hear it for Father of the Year.

He ran his hand over his face. He didn't have time for regrets and self-flagellation right now. He had to find Krystal. He had to do for her what he wasn't able to do for Lisa.

"Okay, people. Let's—" Nick's thoughts were interrupted when a petite redhead stepped into the doorway. "Annie. I thought you were in the hospital."

"I'm okay. I just need to sit down."

Steven pushed a chair toward her. She sank down into it, setting her backpack beside the chair. "I'm sorry."

Rafe continued to hover. "Are you okay? I thought you were in the hospital."

"I was. But I'm fine. " She looked up at Nick. "Call Jon Carver. Tell him that his attempt to kill Zeena failed. That you have her in custody and you have his laptop too."

She reached down, picked up the backpack, and lifted it toward him. Nick reached out and took it from her. He set it on the desk, opened it, and pulled out the laptop. "This is Jon's laptop?"

"Yes. Barbara gave it to me. Tell Jon that you'll trade the laptop for your daughter."

Nick handed the laptop to Rafe. "See what's on this thing that has Jon so concerned."

"On it, Boss."

Nick turned back to Annie. "I already told Jon I had it. A little bluff to push him into giving me my daughter. In the meantime, you just let Zeena go? I thought we had a deal?"

Annie blushed. "You can still arrest her when all this is over."

It all sounded perfect, but there were still details that bothered Nick. "Jon is going to want to see Zeena."

"And he will."

Marti walked into Nick's office, twisting the top of a bottle of water and handing it to Annie. "You look as tired as we all feel, so I thought you could use this."

Annie cracked a hint of a smile and thanked her. "I don't think we've met. I'm Annie McNamara."

"Marti Shepherd."

"Sister? You look a lot like Nick."

"So I'm told."

"Nice to meet you," Annie replied before turning back to Nick. "You can't trust him. That's what Zeena told me anyway. She said that he rarely keeps his word."

Nick rubbed his hands over his face. "Okay. Let's do it." He picked up the phone and called the offices at the Stark Lily. There was no answer, so he left a message. "Jon? It's Nick Shepherd. Zeena says you're not to be trusted. Is she right? Because if she is, maybe talking to you is a waste of time."

He hung up the phone and turned to Annie. "If we can convince him to trade the laptop for Krystal, we might be able to keep you out of this."

Annie shook her head. "Barbara says he wants her dead. He won't settle for anything less than her alive and in the flesh so that he can kill her."

Nick heard the front door open. Rafe eased his weapon out of his holster while Conner picked his up from the coffee table and walked out, holding it down along his thigh. As soon as he reached the office door, he backed up.

Jessica swept into the room, her red eyes and lack of makeup stunning everyone into silence. "Where is Krystal?"

Nick stood up and stepped out from behind the desk. Words failed him as he absorbed the pain that radiated off her in waves.

Jessica launched herself at him, clawing and scratching, pounding him in the chest with her fists. "Why did they take her? Why aren't you out there getting her back? Don't you care? I want my daughter!"

Nick allowed her to slam at him, ignoring every time one of her blows came close to his bullet wound. In a way, he almost felt better for it, as if she were better at punishing him than he was at punishing himself. And he knew he deserved it. As she started to slow down, he wrapped his good arm around her.

"It's going to be okay, Jess. I'll get her back."

"I want my little girl." Jessica muffled her sobs against his chest.

He glanced up and gave a look that sent everyone out of the room. Conner closed the office door behind them.

"Jessica." He stepped away from her, letting his hand slide down to rest on her upper arm. "I promise you, I'm going to bring our little girl home. Okay?"

"She's probably scared out of her mind, Nick. I know I am."

"So am I." He rubbed her arm. "Listen to me. I need you to just give me one minute to say something I should have told you a long time ago." He took a deep breath. "I let you down. In our marriage. And I'm sorry for that. I can't go back and change what I did. I didn't even realize I was doing it at the time. But I won't let you down now. I'll find her for you. For us."

Jessica finally lifted her face, her eyes wide with fear and panic, skin flushed. He knew that he would move heaven and earth to see her smile again.

"What makes you so sure she's still alive, Nick?"

"He's not going to hurt Krystal as long as I bring him what he wants."

She reached up and brushed her hair back out of her face, tucking it behind her ears. "What does he want?"

My soul. He stepped back and rolled his shoulder, trying to ease the throbbing. "I'm going to get Krystal back safe and sound. That's all you need to concentrate on."

She studied his face for a moment. He wasn't sure what she was looking for, but he hoped she found it. Finally, she nodded and leaned into his arms again. "Just bring her home, Nick. Just bring my baby home."

"I will."

The phone rang once and stopped, giving Nick the impression that someone out in the reception area had answered it. Sure enough, there was a light tap on the door.

"Yeah?" Nick called out.

The door opened, and Marti stuck her head in. "Jon Carver on line one."

Nick rubbed Jessica's arms. "Let me deal with him."

"He's the one that has our daughter, right?"

"Yes."

"Then go get him, Nick Shepherd. You don't stop until he's dirt beneath your feet."

Nick smiled. "Tell the gang to get in here. I may need Annie's help again."

He sat down behind his desk, took a deep breath, and then picked up the phone. "Prodigal Recovery Agency. Who would you like us to hunt down like a dog?"

"Funny guy," Jon replied. "Let's see how funny you are when I get through with you."

As everyone filed back into the room, Nick pointed at Annie and then at the chair in front of his desk. As soon as she sat down, he put the phone on speaker.

"Jon. Jon. You still don't get it, do you? You and Richie poked a stick at the wrong dog. And trust me, my bite is far worse than my bark."

"So you call me up and leave lies on my answering machine?"

"And what lie would that be?"

"I know for a fact that Zeena is dead, bounty hunter. You don't have her, and you don't have my laptop. So if you want your daughter back, you're going to have to go back to my original offer. I tell you to back off my men, and you back off. You got that?"

Nick pointed to Annie, praying she could carry it off. Annie leaned forward. "Jon? What gave you the crazy idea that I was dead? Because you sent Iris with some insulin? Please. Do you know how much resistance I've built up over the years doing every drug known to man?"

Nick heard a little gasp, and then Jon whispered, "Zeena? But how?"

"In the flesh, Jon. And I have your laptop. But since you killed Danny and then tried to hurt some people I care about, I think it's time I turned it over to the Feds."

"Don't do it, Zeena. I know about your sister. You wouldn't want me to hurt her, now would you?"

"You can't hurt her, Jon. I made sure she was far away from your reach when I turned myself in. You won't find her."

Nick leaned forward, running a finger across his throat at Annie to cue her to stop. Then he took over the conversation. "You should have remembered, Jon. I never lie. Now, you have my daughter. I have your laptop."

"I want my laptop, and I want Zeena."

"I want my daughter and Richie and Lester."

"I don't have her."

"Liar. Have it your way. Hey, Conn! Would you take this laptop to Benedict? Special deliv—"

"Wait. Okay. I think we can deal. I have a lead on your daughter. We'll make the trade."

"And your brother and Lester."

"No deal."

Nick rubbed his hand over his face. In spite of what Jon planned, Richie was going to be part of the deal. One way or another. But this was not the time to discuss it. "Fine. I'll hand over your laptop after my daughter is returned safe and sound."

"Deal. I'll call you with the details. And Nicky-boy?"

"What?"

"Tell Zeena that she and the laptop are a package deal. Otherwise your daughter may not be in one piece the next time you see her."

Before Nick could respond, Jon hung up.

Nick took a deep breath and set the phone down.

Rafe was staring at Annie. "That was good, Annie. For a minute, I almost thought you really were Zeena."

Annie laughed, but it sounded weary and weak. "Barbara gave me a few tips."

"I'll say." Nick reached for his Dew as he stood up. "If I didn't know you, I'd have been fooled completely."

Nick's office door opened, and two men stepped in. "Mr. Shepherd?"

Instinctively, Nick stepped in front of Jessica. "Yes?"

One of them held up a badge. "Harrows. ATF. We're going to have to ask you to stand down."

"Stand down? What do you mean, *stand down?*"

The other agent stepped forward. "It means that you won't be going after your daughter."

———◦———

Saturday, 10:15 a.m.
The Stark Lily, Park Heights, Baltimore

Jon slammed the flat of his hand down on his desk. "What do you mean you can't wait until Sunday? We had all this set."

"We are in town now and ready to take possession of our shipment. I don't see what the problem is, Mr. Carver. Let's just say I'm a cautious buyer."

"So what? You thought I was going to double-cross you? I wouldn't stay in business very long if I did that to my buyers."

"Like I said, consider me cautious. It's how I stay in business. Now, can we do business today or not?"

Jon glanced at the clock. Of all times for his buyer to arrive early. The girl was at the warehouse. The bounty hunter would be coming in soon with Zeena. He wanted them dead and gone before his buyer arrived.

Richie walked into the office and headed straight for the bar. Jon signaled him to pour him one. Richie nodded. "Yeah. Sure. We can do business today. I just need to make a few calls, rearrange my schedule."

"Shall we say noon then?"

Jon rubbed his temple. "No. After dark."

"Ten this evening then."

"Yeah. Ten. That's fine." He slowly hung up the phone.

"What's going on?" Richie asked as he handed him his drink.

"Barlow decided to come in town early. He wants the shipment tonight."

Richie sat down, stretched out his legs, and crossed them at the ankle. "So what's the problem?"

"The problem, little brother, is that your personal vendetta is now interfering with my business. In case you've forgotten, you have that kid stashed there. And her father bringing me my laptop. And Zeena. And I wanted them all dead and disposed of before Barlow arrived in town."

"So, call the bounty hunter and tell him you'll meet him tomorrow. Or better yet, at midnight tonight. By then, Barlow will be long gone"—his grin spread—"and I'll have all the time in the world to make that bounty hunter suffer."

"What in the world makes you think I can put Shepherd off that long? He has Benedict breathing down his neck. How long do you think it will be before Benedict convinces him that it's in his best interests to join forces against me?"

Richie stared down at his drink. "We can pull it off."

———⊷═◦═⊶———

Saturday, 10:20 a.m.
Prodigal Recovery offices, Baltimore

Nick couldn't believe what he was hearing. "You expect me to allow my daughter to stay in Carver's hands? Are you out of your mind?"

"No, Mr. Shepherd. If you'll let us explain."

Nick threw up a hand. "And how did you know that Carver had my daughter?"

The two men looked at each other, and neither of them was quick to respond. But Nick caught on faster than they probably wanted him to. "You saw it all go down, didn't you? You were at the Lily. You saw them take my daughter, and you did nothing to save her. And you consider yourselves law enforcement. I have a different name for it."

"You have to understand. We have been watching Carver for a long time. His latest dealings are in stolen military weapons, and we've been working overtime to catch him red-handed and arrest him. We can't blow our investigation by your interference."

Jessica practically lunged at the men. "Interference? That's my daughter!" Both of them stepped back, but Nick wrapped his arms around her and held her tight.

"You know where she is? How is she?" he asked.

"She's safe for now. We're going to do everything we can to keep her that way. We have the location under surveillance. I assure you, we will get her out just as soon as we can."

"Why can't you just get her out now? Or maybe an hour ago?"

"Because Carver has men guarding her. If we go in, he'll know we're there."

Nick could feel the anger radiating off Jessica and, combined with his own, knew it could erupt into assault with very little provocation. "I'm going to ask the two of you to step out of my office and shut the door."

"We will be in the lobby, but please don't try anything stupid, Mr. Shepherd," Harrows informed him. "We will be keeping an eye on you."

"Just get out. Or I'll throw you out."

18

Saturday, 11:30 a.m.
Prodigal offices, Baltimore

While the agents hovered, Jessica had fallen asleep on the sofa in Nick's office, so Conner, Nick, Steven, Marti, Annie, and Rafe had gravitated to the kitchen, where they could distance themselves from the ATF agents guarding the front door.

"I don't see how they can force me to stay," Annie stated with fire in her eyes. "I'm just an innocent bystander, right? They can't expect me to go charging off with guns blazing."

"No," Rafe agreed. "They'd probably allow you to go home. You don't have to stay, Annie."

"It's not a matter of not wanting to stay," she told him. "I'm just saying, I *could* go. And I *could* meet someone a block away with a car. You know. In case someone figures out how to sneak out of here."

Nick barely acknowledged the comment. He needed to work out a plan. But one overriding thought—that every minute Krystal was in Carver's hands was one minute too many—made his thoughts foggy and unorganized.

Frustration buzzed through him, keeping him on his feet, pacing the small room. He kept arguing with himself.

Let the ATF do their job.

Are you crazy? Don't trust them with your daughter's life!

"Nick, please sit down. You're making me dizzy." Marti reached out and touched his arm as he passed her.

He sat down at the small kitchen table and glanced up at the clock. Eleven thirty. If he was going to do this, he needed to get started. He pulled out his cell phone, and ignoring the questioning looks of everyone in the room, he dialed. "Luke. Sorry to wake you. I need a favor."

"Name it."

"Don't ask for details."

"No problem. Details I can get anytime. What do you need?"

Nick glanced at the door. "I have a couple of Feds in my lobby. I need them, shall we say, otherwise occupied."

"What do you have in mind?"

Smiling, Nick explained, then hung up. Next, he pulled out the business card Benedict's men had given him and dialed. "I have the laptop and I'll turn it over to you. With conditions."

"I'm listening," Benedict replied.

<hr />

Saturday, 12:10 p.m.
Prodigal offices, Baltimore

Jessica stared down at the coffee in her hand, not quite sure how it got there. She was going through the motions. She couldn't imagine feeling anything until her daughter was back. She reached over and set her coffee down on the table in Nick's office.

"Hey." Nick sat down on the sofa next to her. He stared at her, his hazel eyes full of pain. They mirrored her own. "How are you holding up?"

Jessica stared down at her hands, clenched in her lap. "Numb. I'm just numb. I keep praying and trying to trust God, but it's not easy. So many kids die each year. What if our daughter ends up being one of them?"

Nick stayed silent for a long moment. She felt a palpable tension between them that she couldn't deny. She wanted to curl up in his arms and find comfort, hope, peace. She wanted him to make it all better, but she knew from experience that she wasn't likely to find any of those things in his arms.

He reached out and took her hand. He squeezed it. "I won't let that happen, Jess. I won't."

"How can you make that promise?"

"I just can. Trust me."

Primed by fatigue, stress, and downright fear, she began to speak. She couldn't hide behind her emotional walls any longer. "Once again, I'm exhausted by how you expect to control everything. You expect that people are just supposed to line up behind you and do things the way you want."

"It's just the way I am, Jess."

"I know. And while your heart is in the right place, your methods have always left a lot to be desired. Steven, Marti, me, Krystal. We aren't always going to live our lives the way you see fit. We each have the right to do what we think is right for our lives."

Nick sank back in the sofa, stretching out his legs, but she could see the hint of temper in his eyes. "You wanted the divorce. I let you do what you thought was right for you."

"I never wanted a divorce, Nick. I wanted a husband. I wanted you to spend time with me. I wanted you to talk to me. I wanted to feel more important than everyone and everything else."

Nick looked over at her as if he'd never seen her before. "Why didn't you tell me that?"

"I did. Several times. You weren't listening. I thought if I threatened divorce, it would force you to listen. The joke was on me."

Nick dropped his eyes and stared at the floor for a few minutes. Jessica didn't know whether she wanted to take the words back or not, but she was feeling so vulnerable and raw. Maybe it was time he knew how much he hurt the people who loved him. Then again, maybe it wouldn't make any difference at all.

"Maybe I should have tried harder," she admitted, "but you were always finding some excuse to be away or to cancel vacations and family outings. I lost count of the excuses. I finally just stopped making any plans at all that included you."

Nick leaned his head back and closed his eyes. No longer able to read his expression, she waited in silence.

"You're right," he said softly. "I always put work first. I counted on you and Krystal to be there waiting when I got home, but I couldn't count on a fugitive to sit around and wait for me to show up. That was my rationale, and it was wrong. I was wrong. There's always another day, another fugitive, another chase." He looked over at her, and for the first time, she realized that this had cost him as much as it had cost her and their daughter.

"So Krystal does everything she can to act out, thinking that being bad will make me pay attention to her."

"Oh yeah. And then some. She feels that neither of us love her. I'm afraid I'm as much to blame for that as you are. I didn't make any secret of how angry I was at you, and she took the brunt of that."

"Same here."

"So she rebels. She argues. She does whatever she can to make us react, because I guess any reaction is better than none at all."

Nick groaned. "Jenna tried to tell me the same thing, but I didn't realize how deep this went."

"It runs deep, Nick. And now she's in the hands of someone who may very well kill her."

"No." Nick slapped his thighs and sat forward. "I'm going to get her back, safe and sound, and then I'm going to make sure she knows how much I love her, even if I have to take a month off from work to make sure she gets the message."

Jessica smiled, but deep in her traitorous heart, she wished he had included her in that effort. But what did she expect? She had left the marriage, divorced him, and then made sure he knew the black side of her temper every day since. She couldn't really blame him for not loving her anymore.

"First, I need to bring her home," Nick said. "Then I'll worry about the rest." With another pat on her hand, he stood up.

She reached out for his hand. "Nick."

"What?"

She stared at him a moment and then shook her head. "Nothing."

He stepped back. "Okay. I've got to go get our daughter back." And then he quickly left the office.

Jess swung her feet up on the sofa and stretched out. Curling her hand under her cheek, she realized her face was wet. She wiped away the tears.

Saturday, 12:30 p.m.
Prodigal offices, Baltimore

Nick stepped into the bathroom and locked the door. Bracing his hands on the sink, he bowed his head and let the tears fall. Within seconds, something broke and the quiet tears were joined by a heaving pain in his chest. He locked his elbows to keep from sinking to the floor, only to flinch when pain shot through his right shoulder.

He could come up with a hundred things Jess had done to hurt him while they were married. A thousand things she had done to aggravate him. A million things she had done to annoy him. But he knew that if he added them all up, it wasn't enough to justify never being there for his wife except to wear the clothes she washed for him, sleep in the bed she made for him, use the shaving cream she bought for him, eat the meals she cooked for him. No wonder she'd thrown him out.

He'd been so busy looking for excuses for why Krystal was the way she was when all he had to do was look in a mirror to see the cause for her rebellion. He was the one who had been ignoring his family and letting his daughter grow up thinking that her daddy didn't love her.

What kind of man would do that?

And no wonder God didn't answer his prayers anymore. He'd done the same thing with God. He'd just lived his life his way and expected God to be there to handle things he didn't want to deal with. Never listened to God. Never considered God's opinions. God, do this. God, do that.

He could make a million excuses, and they'd all be good ones—his father had died, he took over the business, the company had financial problems, his mother was ill, he'd gone through a divorce, he had to move back into his parents' home because he couldn't afford a place of his own.

Excuses. Excuses for not being a good husband. Or a good father. Or a good son. He was too busy. Too stressed. Too consumed with doing things the way he expected them to be done.

"Nick?" Conner's voice was followed by a series of hard raps on the door. "You okay?"

Nick straightened and then turned on the cold water. "Fine. I'll be right out."

He washed his face, ran his fingers through his hair, and squared his shoulders. There was nothing he could do about his red eyes. It was what it was. He was beyond caring what anyone thought. He took a deep, cleansing breath. Regardless of past mistakes, regrets, and recriminations, his daughter was out there waiting for him to ride in on a white horse and save her. This time, he wasn't going to let her down.

Yanking the door open, he strode out, passing Conner, who was still there waiting on him. "Grab me a Dew, will you?"

When Nick stepped into his office, Marti was sitting at his desk, Jon's laptop open in front of her. The rest of his team was scattered around his office, talking, reading, and doing research on their own laptops. "What are you doing?"

"Making an insurance policy for you." She pointed to a flash drive sticking out the side. "I'm making a copy of everything on this thing. If Carver doesn't agree to let Krystal go, you make sure you tell him that I have this and if I don't hear from you in a reasonable amount of time, I'll give this to the Feds."

Nick smiled. "My little sister. The warrior."

"You have no idea," she muttered, keeping her eyes on the laptop screen as if it were the most interesting thing she'd ever seen. "The problem is, the good stuff is encrypted and I can't break it." She stood up. "I'll be back."

Nick eased a hip onto the corner of his desk and took the can of Mountain Dew Conner handed him. "Does everyone understand what's going on?"

There were nods all around, except from Jessica, who just stared at him with a vacant expression that hit him hard once again. He took one last sweep of the room, not meeting her eyes. Two of the most important women in his life were in this building, and he wasn't sure he really knew either of them. If he made it through tonight, he was going to make sure all that changed.

If he made it out alive. Nick glanced at his watch. "None of you are obligated to go with me. In fact, I'd prefer if you didn't. I got myself into this. I pushed Carver, and it's come back to slap me in the face."

Rafe made a big show of rolling his eyes. "Can we just get this part over with?"

Conner leaned forward. "I need to speak my piece, Boss."

"Go for it."

"I'm not comfortable with you taking this deal from Benedict. I know you think you have to in order to get Krys back, but there has to be another way. You can't get in bed with these guys or you'll never be free of them."

"Do you trust me, Conn?"

"Yeah."

Nick put his hand out and touched Conner's arm. "Then prove it. Trust me. I believe that I'm making the right decision. I've looked at every angle I can think of. This is my daughter's life at stake. I'm not going to mess it up."

"And you think Benedict is the right decision?"

"I'm ninety-nine percent sure I have this worked out to the last detail."

Conner nodded. "Okay. We'll meet you at the parking garage at Camden Yards, but if you don't call by the time I think you should, I'll show up at Benedict's office with guns blazing."

Nick laughed. "Duly noted."

"Anybody home?" Michael O'Shea's voice boomed through the office from the reception area. Then he appeared in the doorway. "What are you doing here?"

"Krystal's been taken by Carver," Nick said, not missing the wince on Jessica's face.

Michael tossed his jacket down over the arm of a chair. "I figured as much. Nick, I warned you—"

"Shut up, O'Shea. This isn't the time." Conner glared at Michael.

Michael threw both hands in the air. "Sorry. I'm just upset." He turned to Nick as he dropped down in a chair. "What's the plan?"

"Keep your voice down. Those two men out there are with the ATF. They don't want me to leave the office."

"Why not?"

"It's a long story."

Michael glanced from the doorway to Nick. "You doing something illegal?"

"No. Just something they don't like. But right now, I'm more concerned with getting Krystal back."

Michael stepped forward. "Give Jon Carver whatever he wants. Tell him you'll take his money. That'll you'll agree to look the other way once in a while." Michael slumped down. "I'm just afraid that if you don't take his money, he'll hurt Krys."

"Yeah, take the easy way out," Marti said stiffly, reentering the room. "You were always good at that, weren't you?"

"Marti?" Michael's jaw dropped as his eyes widened. "I…didn't know you were here."

She whirled, pointing her finger at him. "You don't see me. You don't talk to me. I pretend I don't see you. Got it?"

"Oh, come on, Marti. That was what, fourteen, fifteen years ago? Don't you get over anything?"

Marti picked up Conner's gun, slipped it out of the holster, and then pointed it at Michael, taking a step toward him.

Michael dived out of the chair and hid behind the desk. "Marti! Are you nuts?"

Shaking his head, Conner took his gun out of Marti's hands. "Play nice."

"I am." Marti said with a smirk, then walked over and sat back down behind the desk. "If I hadn't, I'd have loaded the gun first."

"You haven't changed a bit," Michael griped, red-faced as he stood up, brushing off his slacks.

Nick hid his smile behind his hand. Marti and Michael had never gotten along. It would appear that Marti's absence hadn't changed any of those feelings. "Go home, Michael." He looked over at Marti. "You almost done there?"

"Yeah," she said without looking up. "Yeah, I wanted to give one more try at breaking the encryption on Carver's files, but it's over my head."

Michael stood up. "You have Carver's laptop? And you're looking in it? Do you have a death wish?"

Marti glanced up at him. "Did I hear a mouse squeak in here? You need to call an exterminator, Nick. Mice carry diseases."

"Cut it out, you two." Nick stepped away from the laptop. "I don't have the patience to deal with this right now. It was amusing when you were teenagers. It's not now."

Michael slapped both hands down on the desk. "Nick, I'm serious. You are playing with fire here. If Carver finds out that you've gone through his personal information, there's no way he'll let you live."

"Oh, cool out, O'Shea." Marti turned off the laptop and closed the lid. "All I did was read a few e-mails."

Ignoring her, Michael kept his attention on Nick. "You can't just give Carver that laptop and expect him to just let you and Krys walk out of there. Take the money, Nick."

Nick picked up his soda can and gulped from it. *Lord, help me out here.*

Marti came out from behind the desk, picked up Annie's water bottle, then flung the water in Michael's face. "Go home and dry off, dude. You're dripping on the floor."

Michael came to his feet, sputtering. "What did you do that for?"

"Because this is hard enough for Nick without you whining like a baby about the danger he and Krystal are in. Nick's a pro. He's faced more danger in one week than you have in your whole life. Now get out."

Nick set his can down and then looked his friend in the face. "Michael. I need you to leave now."

"But—"

"Now."

"Look, Nick—"

"Conner, please escort Michael to the front door and make sure he doesn't come back in."

———◦———

Saturday, 12:40 p.m.
Prodigal offices, Baltimore

Marti locked the bathroom door, closing herself and Annie inside.

Annie rubbed her arms. "Okay, why are we locking ourselves in the bathroom with a potted fern?"

Marti laughed. "Because you're supposed to look like you've been living in a drain pipe for weeks." She pointed to the dirt in the flowerpot. "Dirt. Rub your hands into it, girl. Get into the spirit of this. Then rub your hands down your jeans and across your shirt." Marti picked up a handful and began to streak Annie's face.

"You don't like your brother's friend, do you?" Annie asked as she smeared dirt on her clothes.

"I can't imagine where you got that idea." Marti almost flinched but tried to stay neutral, so she gave Annie a little smile.

"It's cool if you don't want to talk about it."

Marti started smearing dirt in Annie's hair. "Smart woman." She stepped back and gave Annie a once-over. "Good enough. Maybe we need to cut those jeans a little. Make them look older."

Annie grabbed Marti's arm. "Tell me the truth. Do you really think Nick can get us all out alive?"

Marti saw the fear in Annie's eyes and knew that platitudes weren't going to work. As much as she wanted to wipe the fear away for this innocent young woman, she knew that sometimes life was hard and dangerous and there were no guarantees. You had to take every day for what it was worth. Good or bad.

"Annie, I can't promise you anything. But let me say this. I know my brother. He's always been something of a cowboy. But he's very smart, and what has always made him good at what he does, whether it was back when he was a cop or now as a bounty hunter, is that he can think fast on his feet and he's fearless. He has a strong sense of right and wrong, and that is unshakable in him. If anyone can get you and Krystal out alive, it's my brother. Is that good enough?"

Annie snorted out something like a weak laugh. "I'd have preferred hearing he's done this exact thing a hundred times before and never failed."

"If you don't want to do this, don't. No one is going to blame you."

Annie shook her head. "I need to do this. I can't let your niece die because I'm afraid."

"And because you need to face death on your terms, not a doctor's… Nick told me about your disease."

Annie slowly dropped her head. "Maybe that too, yeah."

"I understand. Maybe better than you realize. But that doesn't mean you're going to die tonight. You have a great chance of walking out of this alive. And you have a great chance that someone will pop up on the donor list and you could walk out of that to live a long, happy life."

"Maybe."

"Maybe," Marti agreed with a little squeeze to Annie's hand. "I gave up on God a long time ago, but there have been so many times in my life when I should have ended up dead, and I'm still here. And every single time I walked away from a situation, I had this nagging little feeling that God was keeping me alive for some reason. As if he were just blocking death until I came to my senses and came home to him."

"And you haven't?"

Marti shook her head. "No. I can't. There's no point in asking God to forgive me if I can't forgive myself."

"But—"

"Stop. Let's get down to business, okay? Now remember, to Jon, you are a broken-down drug addict, a prostitute. All you're interested in is your next fix. Nothing else matters. You can't show concern for Nick or Krystal. You can't show any interest in what's happening."

Annie wrapped her arms around herself and nodded. "Sounds like you understand an addict's life."

"You could say that." Marti unlocked the door. "Oh, and don't make eye contact. Keep your head down. Try to look distracted."

"Okay. Hey, Marti."

Marti turned. "Yes?"

"Just in case something happens to me, I want you to promise me something."

"Okay…I'm not sure—"

"Just promise me."

"I promise."

"If I don't come back, I want you to tell my sister that I love her. That I've always loved her. Tell her to live long and be happy." Annie reached out and clasped Marti's hand. "You'll tell her that for me, won't you?"

"I promise."

Saturday, 1:05 p.m.
Prodigal offices, Baltimore

Nick glanced at his watch and then looked over at Conner and Rafe. "Time to rock and roll, gang."

Squaring his shoulders, Nick walked out into the lobby. Both agents were sitting in visitors' chairs near the front door. Harrows had his head tilted back, eyes closed, and the other was reading a magazine. "Any chance we can get one of you guys to run out for some lunch?"

The one agent lowered his magazine as Harrows opened his eyes.

"We're hungry, and we need some food."

Harrows shrugged. "Call for delivery."

"You guys are just two of the most cooperative fellows I've ever known. It wouldn't hurt you to remember that we're on the same team."

"At the moment, my team is making sure your team doesn't step on my team's plans. I don't think that puts us on the same team."

Nick threw his hands up. "Fine. But when you get hungry, you can order your own."

He walked back into his office and slammed the door closed. "Twenty minutes and counting?"

"We're ready," Conner told him.

Marti spoke up. "Give me a key to the equipment room."

"Why?" Nick asked as he pulled his keys out of his pocket, found the key she wanted, and handed it to her.

"Because I need a gun, a badge, and a vest."

"You aren't going, Marti." He tried to pull the key back, but she pulled it out of his hand.

"Yes. I am. I'm going to bring up the rear and handle the GPS logistics. That way Rafe and Conner are free to do what they do best."

"Then I want you to stay way back out of the line of fire."

"Yeah, yeah." She headed out of the office.

He shook his head and then glanced down at his watch. "Fifteen minutes and counting."

Everyone in the room stared at their watches. When the time finally passed, Nick stood up and walked out into the lobby.

"Now what do you want?" Harrows asked.

"Food should be here anytime now."

He grunted and went back to reading. Nick leaned against Jenna's desk, folding his arms across his chest, looking as bored as those two agents probably felt.

Good news—they will never see it coming. Bad news—I'll probably go to jail.

"Just for the record, guys. No hard feelings."

Harrows grunted and turned the page.

The front door opened, and both agents glanced up at the man with all the bags and Styrofoam cartons and went back to their reading. The man walked over to Harrows and set everything down in his lap.

"Hey!" Harrows started to object.

In one swift move, the man clipped Harrows under the chin and then caught him as he started to slide out of the chair. The other agent was reaching for his gun when Nick grabbed his wrist, twisted him back, and then held him while the other man hit two pressure points on the agent's throat, and it was lights out.

"You're good," Nick said as the agent sagged to the floor.

"This is why I kept telling you to perfect these techniques," Luke stated soberly.

"I know them just fine, but it's hard to take care of two of them by myself."

"True. The other would have shot you."

Conner stuck his head out the door. "We good?"

"We're good. Cuff and lock them in the equipment room."

While Rafe and Conner locked up the agents, Nick, Steve, and Marti loaded gear bags and stashed them in the vehicles. Nick saw Luke sit next to Jessica. He hoped Luke's presence would comfort her.

When everything was ready, Nick reached for his Kevlar vest and slid a knife in the sheath inside. Both would more than likely be confiscated by Carver's men, but he was hoping to hold on to them as long as possible. He zipped his jacket over the Kevlar and pulled out his keys and then looked back over at Marti. "Look, if something happens—"

"It won't."

"But if it does, I need you to look after Steven."

She all but rolled her eyes. "When are you going to take those blinders off and realize that Steven is a mature, capable, intelligent man? He's not a kid anymore, Nick. He doesn't need anyone to look out for him."

"Well, be that as it may, I'm just asking you—"

"Yeah, yeah. This is one of those *if I should die* speeches you don't need to give. Now let's go get your daughter and bring her home."

Marti walked out of the office, and Nick turned toward Annie, who was standing near Jenna's desk. Sure enough, she was trembling like an aspen on a windy day. Jessica stood up and walked over in front of him. They locked eyes, and he knew there was only one thing he could say. "I'll be back soon. Why don't you wait at home? I'll bring her straight to you."

"I'll wait here. Don't take too long. She's probably hungry, and you know how snippy she can get when she's hungry." She wiped at the tears that were spilling over.

He pulled her into a quick hug and then nodded at Annie. "Let's go get this done."

As he pulled onto the highway, Nick called Michael. "I need you to do me a favor."

"Name it."

"I'm going in after Krystal in a couple of hours. But if I don't come back, take care of Jessica. Okay?"

"Nick. Don't do it."

"Just promise me, Michael. I need to know that I can count on you."

There was a pause and then a heavy sigh. "You can count on me."

⚬

Sometime Saturday
A warehouse building near the water

The walls were metal, the floor was concrete, the door was one of those roll-up things that looked like it belonged on a garage, and there were stacks of wooden boxes lined along one wall. It didn't tell Krystal anything except that she was alone with two men and she was more afraid than she'd ever been in her life. She thought she heard the blast of a ship's horn, so she was pretty sure she was near the harbor. Her dad had brought her here once to see some famous ship from, like, the Civil War or something, and she remembered those big freighters blowing their horns as they went past.

Whatever drug that man Richie had given her had worn off, but she still felt spacey. Krystal looked at the white-haired man who had been staring at her. His ice-cold eyes gave her the creeps, but she tried not to let him know how scared she was. Sitting on the concrete floor with her hands tied, she felt the cold spreading through her clothes and settling into her bones. He must have noticed, because he finally spoke.

"You cold?"

She wasn't about to give him the satisfaction of an answer, so she gave him a look as belligerent as anything she'd ever thrown at her mom or dad. His mouth just quirked up in a smile as cold as his eyes and just as emotionless. "That might work on your friends, but I've seen worse, so it doesn't intimidate me at all."

Lifting her chin, she fought with everything she could not to curl into a ball, wail and cry and beg him not to kill her. But she was a Shepherd. Shepherds were tough. They were strong. They didn't give up. Her dad would find her. He would. Uncle Steven always said that her dad was the most relentless man he'd ever known. Dad would come for her. And then this man would find out he'd made the mistake of his life. He'd messed with the wrong girl.

"Stubborn, aren't you?"

Slowly, he rose to his feet, and tucking his gun into his jacket, he walked over to the regular door next to the big roll-up door.

"Where you going?" the other man asked.

The white-haired man just cut him with a look sharp enough to draw blood. "If I wanted you to know, I'd give you a map." The man left and then returned a few minutes later carrying a wool blanket. He spread the blanket on the floor and picked Krystal up. He set her down on the blanket. Krystal could feel herself shivering despite herself.

"What you worried about her for?" The other man asked. "Not like she's going to live long enough to get pneumonia."

The white-haired man just glared at him. "You want to live long enough to see your boss again?"

"You think jus' 'cause you did Richie a favor that makes you somethin' important?"

The white-haired man stood up tall, and the other man backed up. "It doesn't matter what I think. I'll kill you either way." He paused a moment, then said, "I'm going to grab some lunch. You think you can keep one little girl from running away until I get back?"

"Look, Cutter, I was working for Jon long before you. If he trusts anyone, it's me."

"I won't be long."

⚬

Saturday, 2:00 p.m.
Orleans Street, Baltimore

Nick slowed down as approached the front of the office building, looking for a parking place. "Okay, Conner. I'm coming up on Benedict's building. Everyone's at the Camden Yards?"

"Affirmative."

"I'll call you when I'm out."

"I'll be waiting."

Nick hung up and stuck his phone down in his shirt pocket.

He saw a black Town Car pull away from the curb right in front, so he quickly pulled in. He saw Benedict's two goons standing at the curb waving him in.

One of the men opened the door for Nick. "Follow me, Mr. Shepherd."

The building was a bit of a surprise. Where Jon liked to exploit his wealth, Benedict's building declared him to be far more moderate. The white walls were mostly bare, with basic prints scattered here and there, an industrial-strength blue carpet, and recessed lighting. There was a reception desk, which was hosted by a man. A receptionist? More likely a security guard covering the reception desk.

They took the elevator to the tenth floor and stepped off into an area just barely more showy than the lobby. His guide never said a word as he led Nick down one long hallway and then down another until they reached—surprise—a corner office. The man tapped twice on the door and then opened it for Nick to pass through.

The office wasn't nearly as big as he thought it was going to be. The office featured a simple oak desk, a conference table, and some visitor chairs. And behind the desk was Benedict.

Nick hadn't been sure how to picture Benedict, but this wasn't it. He was much older than Nick had assumed, his hair entirely white, and when he stood, he leaned heavily on a cane. But the eyes told the rest of the story. Benedict's gaze portrayed intelligence, power, and control. When he reached out his hand, Nick shook it and found his grip firm.

"Please, have a seat, Nick. May I call you Nick?" Benedict eased back down in his chair, leaning his cane against the desk.

"Be my guest."

Just then the door opened, and another man joined them. Nick expected it to be another bodyguard, but he was no such thing. He stood maybe five-seven. He was rail thin, with dreadlocks down to the middle of his back, diamond studs in both ears. He was wearing ripped jeans, sneakers, and a T-shirt that said *Every Woman's Dream, Every Mother's Nightmare*.

"Ju called, sir?"

Latin. Cuban, maybe. Nick watched the man walk lightly across the room, as if balanced on the balls of his feet.

"Yes, Ramon."

The man stopped near Nick and held out his hands. "Ju have deh laptop?"

Benedict nodded, and Nick reached down and pulled it out of the backpack. He handed it over and Ramon smiled widely. "Dis won't take me lung."

He sat down at the conference table and opened the laptop. "The files are encrypted," Nick offered.

The man merely nodded. "I set thees up for Jon Carver. Designed the seestem myself."

Benedict folded his hands across his stomach and leaned back in his chair. "Ramon used to work for Carver. And then after he set up all Carver's offshore accounts and software and encrypted his files, Jon tried to kill him. He came to me, and I have kept him safe from Jon Carver ever since."

"Handy."

Benedict smiled with the ease of a man well used to soothing over troubled waters. "Jon doesn't have a very good memory. And he's too paranoid to write anything down, so he wanted a computer that he could put everything in—his properties, his clubs, the names of those who run drugs or girls for him, shipments in, shipments out, names, addresses, phone numbers, and of course, bank accounts, passwords, and financial statements."

"So you're going to just move all his money and destroy him."

Benedict merely shrugged. "I can't say what I'm going to do precisely, but I do abhor violence. I prefer to act without bloodshed whenever possible."

Nick found himself liking Benedict in spite of himself. He had all the charm of a friendly old grandpa but the sharp edge of a keen intelligence. When Nick had planned on setting Benedict up, it seemed easy in his mind. Lay out a few clues, manipulate the conversation, give the man enough rope to hang himself. But something was telling him that if anyone was controlling the situation, it was Benedict.

Nick looked over at the conference table where Ramon was grinning as he plugged in an external data drive and began to transfer the contents of the laptop. He started to feel a little more comfortable that Benedict was going to keep his word and give the laptop back to him. Why keep it if you have all its contents?

"It will only be a few more minutes, Nick. Can we offer you something to drink while we wait?"

Nick shook his head. "I'm fine, thanks."

"I truly am sorry about your daughter. To be in the hands of men like the Carvers—a terrifying experience, to say the least." Benedict raised a hand at the man who had brought Nick up to the office. "Have Mona bring me tea, please."

The man slipped out of the room, and the only sound was of keyboard keys tapping away.

"I sincerely hope you get your daughter out alive."

"I will." Nick crossed one leg over his knee and rested his hands over his ankle. "As soon as you tell me where the Carvers are holding her, I'm going in."

"Alone?"

"Alone," Nick replied casually. He hated lying, but this wasn't the time or place for worrying about such niceties. "I'm not going to risk my team on a personal vendetta."

"Very noble of you, but unwise. You'll need backup. Perhaps I might offer a couple of my men."

Nick shook his head. "I appreciate the offer, but I'll be fine."

As a fortyish-looking woman with glasses and a friendly face came in with a tray, Ramon was plugging a printer into the laptop. As she poured tea for Benedict, the printer whirred away. And when she retreated from the room, Ramon pulled the papers from the printer and walked over to hand them to Nick. "All of Carver's property holdings, as promised. He'll be holding your daughter in one of them."

Nick glanced down at the list of addresses and property descriptions. "I thought you were going to tell me her exact location."

"We don't know that," Benedict said. "I'm afraid I'm going to have to leave that bit of detective work for you."

Ramon returned the laptop to Nick. "All done. Thank you." He handed Nick the laptop and turned to Benedict. "You want me to start?"

His boss nodded. "Just let me know before you start transferring all Carver's funds."

"Will do." And Ramon left the office.

Nick stared at the papers for several moments, then stood up. "There are two properties that seem obvious. A farmhouse in Carroll County and a warehouse down at the harbor."

But Benedict sipped his tea as if Nick no longer existed. Nick took the hint. The deal was done. "Appreciate the list."

As he reached the door, Benedict's guide reached out to open the door for him.

"Nick," Benedict called out to him.

Nick turned around, tensed, waiting for some worst-case scenario to play out.

"If you need anything, do not hesitate to call me. I can have men down there to help you in a matter of minutes."

Nick nodded and left.

———⋯⊙⊱——

Saturday, 2:45 p.m.
Orleans Street, Baltimore

Benedict sipped his tea and waited. When he was sure Nick was gone, he pressed the button to open the hidden door behind the bar. Cutter stepped into the office. Benedict looked over at him. "You heard?"

"Every word." Cutter dropped down in a chair and stretched out his legs. "He's going to find a welcoming party he isn't expecting. But why didn't you just tell him the warehouse?"

"Because Nick Shepherd is a shrewd man. If I'd made it too easy, he'd be wondering how I knew so much and why I was being so cooperative. Make him work for it a little bit, and it'll ease his suspicions." Benedict set his cup down and leaned back in chair. "The girl is alive?"

"As ordered."

Opening a desk drawer, Benedict pulled out a small box and slid it across the desk. Cutter reached out and picked it up, then opened it. A syringe, fully loaded, was nestled inside. He shut the box and slipped it into his pocket. "And this will do the job?"

"Give her the full dose and it will be lights out, bye-bye, gone before she knows what hit her." Benedict narrowed his eyes. "But Thorne, hear me well. I want this done before either of the Carvers, but especially Richie, can touch her. I won't have her tortured or raped by either of those men."

"I hear ya."

"I'm serious, Thorne. I'm not playing here."

"I know, I know." Cutter stood up. "Any other last-minute orders?"

"The weapons are all there in the warehouse?"

"Thirty-six crates. Military-issue fully automatic assault rifles."

"Then let's get this done. Now, get back there before you're missed."

—=≈=≈⊙≈=≈=—

Saturday, 2:45 p.m.
En route to a parking lot near Camden Yards, Baltimore

Benedict and Jon Carver were as different as two men could get. Benedict didn't shove, he didn't yell. There were no thugs standing in the shadows ready to beat you up or shoot you if you didn't agree with him. Class. That's the word Nick was searching for. If it weren't for the many criminal activities Benedict was rumored to be involved in, Nick could easily see him in the boardroom of a law office or a government building. The man was a bureaucrat.

Nick reached out and hit the speed dial on his phone. "Rafe. I'm on my way. Tell Conner and Steven there's a warehouse at the Dundalk Marine Terminal." He gave Rafe the exact address. "Have him scour the area. See how easily we can access it."

"Will do."

Nick hung up. Half an hour later, he pulled into a parking lot a block away from Camden Yards where his team—minus Conner—was waiting for him. Rafe handed him a bag of tacos. "Just thought you might be hungry."

"Thanks." Nick took the bag and pulled out a taco. "Okay, let's go over everything one more time."

Rafe leaned against his vehicle. "You really think someone is going to call Carver and let him know you're going in there now?"

"Yep. I sure do." Nick chewed a bite of food. What he didn't know one hundred percent was *who* was calling Carver and cluing him in to Nick's plans, but he was ninety-nine percent sure. And he'd deal with that after he got Krystal out of that warehouse.

19

Saturday, 3:35 p.m.
En route to Dundalk Marine Terminal, Baltimore

Marti's fingers tapped out an impatient tune on the steering wheel of Jessica's car as she watched Carver's Mercedes and the Navigator following him turn at the light and head east. Next to her, Jessica sat in the passenger seat with her hands clutching the laptop computer. Ignoring her ex-sister-in-law, Marti concentrated on the drive. After a few turns, they drove onto Key Highway. "Looks like we're headed for the harbor."

Marti watched as the SUVs split off at the next intersection; the Navigator was going straight, the Mercedes turning southeast. She followed the Mercedes.

Jessica took a deep breath and then looked over at Marti. "I'm glad you talked me into this."

"I didn't. I just asked to use your car. You're the one that insisted on coming along."

"You don't like me very much, do you?"

Marti kept her eyes on the road, concentrating on staying far enough back that the Carvers wouldn't see the tail, but close enough not to lose them. "You don't want to get into ancient history now, do you?"

"Might as well. It'll keep my mind off what we're doing."

"Then no, I don't like you very much. I'm sure you are a very nice person, but you and Nick didn't work. You were so needy and clingy. Desperate for attention. Nick had enough on his plate without killing himself to reassure you every five minutes that he loved you." Marti glanced over at her for a quick second and then went back to watching the road. "But I guess he stopped reassuring you every five minutes because you divorced him."

"Wow," Jessica said. "Brutal."

"Honest."

"That too. And you were right. I was needy. And I did demand too much of him. Took me two years to finally figure out I wasn't any happier being divorced and another year to figure out why."

Marti slowed down as the Mercedes moved into the left-turn lane at the intersection to wait out the red light. "You telling me you're all grown up now?"

"I wish I could say I was, but I can say that I'm working on it."

The light changed, and the Mercedes made his turn. She followed him. Then she noticed the Lincoln Town Car behind her with windows tinted dark. Far darker than was legal in the state of Maryland.

"Call Rafe."

"What?"

"Call Rafe. Tell him there's a Town Car tailing us. Blacked-out windows."

⟡

Saturday, 4:02 p.m.
Dundalk Marine Terminal warehouse, Baltimore

Cutter was back in the warehouse, watching the girl and Ira. He felt his phone vibrate. He pulled it out and read a text message. Then he slipped it back in his pocket and stood up. "Get out."

"What?" Ira said.

"Get out." Cutter started unbuttoning his shirt.

Ira shifted his weight, as if getting ready to attack or be attacked, and then a slow, evil grin slid across his face. "Oh, I get it. Like 'em young, do you?"

"I'm not going to tell you again."

"You do this and Richie will kill you."

Saturday, late afternoonish
A warehouse near the docks

As the two men stared each other down, Krystal began to figure out what they were talking about. No. No. No. As she started to scoot backward, the white-haired man grabbed her arm so hard she thought it might come off.

The other man laughed and, with a casual shrug, headed for the door.

Shivering with fear, Krystal tried to twist herself out of his grip. It was like wrestling with a wall. As soon as the door closed behind the other man, the white-haired man pulled her close. "Do you want to live?"

She could survive this, right? She just had to hold on. Survive.

God, please help me get through this. Please, help me.

"I asked you a question, girl. Do you want to live?"

Biting her lip, she nodded as tears stung her eyes.

"I'm going to tell you exactly what I want you to do, and you're going to do it. You got me?"

Swallowing hard, she nodded again.

"It's going to hurt a little. But you're a tough girl, aren't you?"

20

Saturday, 4:10 p.m.
Dundalk Marine Terminal, Baltimore

Nick parked half a block from the warehouse. He turned to Annie as he unbuckled his seat belt. "You ready?"

"Yeah. But I'm scared."

"You'll be okay, I know you will. Now let's go take this creep down."

"I love it when you talk tough." Annie opened her door and slid out.

An odd time for flirtation…but then, some women used humor when they were afraid, others froze up, and some made inappropriate comments. Apparently, Annie flirted.

Nick locked the SUV, pocketed his keys, and took a deep breath. Annie circled the vehicle and sidled up next to him. "Tell me again you're going to have these guys begging for mercy."

"No more than half an hour, tops."

As they approached the warehouse, Annie slowed down, staying almost completely behind Nick. He stopped and eyed a door next to the bay.

"How are we supposed to get in?"

"Jon will let us in."

One of Jon's men was standing in front of the traffic door, looking a little put out. Just then, the Mercedes that Nick had noticed following them pulled up to the curb and the Carver brothers climbed out. When the man at the door saw Jon, he stiffened but stayed where he was.

"Richie!" Nick smiled and threw his arms open wide. "You're turning yourself in. Wonderful."

Jon folded his arms across his chest as he ignored the man at the door and concentrated on Nick. "Right on time." Then he smirked. "Hi, Zeena, baby. Where's my laptop?"

Nick cut in. "Where's my daughter?"

"Ah, we have what they used to call a Mexican standoff." Jon jerked his head toward the car. Scott and Lester climbed out.

"Lester. Hey, buddy," Nick said. "I've been looking for you. I'm afraid I'm going to have to take you in. You and Richie in one day. I have to say, I'm a lucky man."

Lester laughed. "Funny."

"Check the backpack," Jon instructed Lester.

Lester pulled the backpack off Annie and unzipped it. Then he pulled the laptop out and handed it to Jon.

Scott pulled out a gun and pressed it to Nick's temple. He searched Nick, finding the gun in Nick's ankle holster and tossing it to Richie. "He's wearing a vest."

"And I'm not taking it off," Nick said.

"If I need to kill you, I'll just shoot you in the head," Jon said.

"As for you, Zeena. You should never have taken my property. Unfortunately, you can consider that the biggest mistake you ever made." Then he snapped his fingers. "Inside."

Nick jerked his arm away from Scott. "Where is my daughter?"

A black panel van pulled up to the curb, and the driver leaned out the window. "We found the bounty hunter's men. You want us to secure them?"

"Absolutely," Richie replied.

In spite of all his plans, Nick was starting to have a bad feeling.

Suddenly he saw Scott's fist heading toward his face. It connected with his chin and brought him up short as black dots danced across his vision.

Nick's arms were yanked behind his back and cuffed, and the pressure on his shoulder felt like a hot blade through the wound.

The man at the door nodded at Jon. "Hey, Boss."

"What are you doing out here?" Jon asked him. "I thought I ordered you to stay inside."

"Cutter wanted a little time alone with the girl." The man winked. "If you know what I mean."

In a blind rage, Nick lunged forward. He was brought up short by Scott yanking on his cuffs. The pain in his shoulder drove him to his knees.

Suddenly there was a shout from inside the building. "Ow! That hurt, you little witch! I warned you!" And then a gunshot echoed out of the building.

Nick's heart stilled in his chest as he stumbled to his feet. "No. *No!*"

Jon shoved open the door, and everyone ran into the warehouse behind him. Nick half ran, half hobbled while Scott dragged him along.

When they walked in, Nick saw Krystal, crumpled on the floor, her shirt torn, her pants unbuckled. Blood seeped slowly out from under her head. It took about an hour for the next few minutes to go by. Nick struggled to stay on his feet as his knees became liquid and his heart twisted, jumped.

She was so still. Limp. And there was so much blood. It was in her hair, on her shirt, crawling across the floor. The only sign of life in her, slowly draining away. He couldn't breathe. It hurt too much.

Cutter tossed a blanket over Krystal, and just that quickly, the devastation was hidden from view. Nick couldn't tear his eyes away. His feisty, beautiful daughter was dead.

"What did you do?" demanded Richie. "I told you that I wanted him to see it. Why didn't you wait?"

"Close enough," Cutter said lazily as he buttoned his shirt.

Nick lifted his eyes from Krystal to the man who had so casually attacked and murdered her. It felt like there was nothing left in him but cold. "I will kill you."

"I doubt it," Cutter said lightly as he tucked his shirt back down in his jeans. Then he turned his attention back to Jon. "We ready or not?"

"She was just a baby!" Nick screamed.

"Grown up enough for me," Cutter replied. "And sweet enough in spite of that nasty temper of hers." He twisted his wrist, looked at it with a frown. "Little witch bit me."

"Too bad she didn't have rabies," Nick told him.

Cutter pulled out his weapon, a 9mm, and looked over at Jon again. "I grow weary of this man. Are we ready or not?"

"We have other business first." Jon replied and nodded at Richie.

Grinning, Richie walked over to Nick and slowly began to circle him. "I've waited a long time for this, bounty hunter. Every day, in that cell, I thought of you."

"Oh yeah? I didn't give you a thought."

Richie grinned at him as he continued his stroll. "Well, I thought about how I'd make you suffer."

"That's always been your problem, Richie. You always thought small."

Richie pulled his arm back and then punched Nick in the stomach. Nick doubled over.

"Did that feel small? Huh, bounty hunter?"

Nick slowly straightened. "Does it make you feel big and tough to beat on a man in handcuffs? Yeah, big man."

Richie looked over at Scott. "Take off his cuffs."

Scott looked over at Jon, but Richie yelled at him, drawing his attention back. "I didn't tell you to ask my brother for permission. Do what I say!"

As soon as Nick's handcuffs were removed, Richie hit him again. Nick knew Richie was just trying to get an edge, but it was a waste of effort. How could Richie lose when he was surrounded by four armed men and his brother? And why would Nick care at this point? His daughter was dead. Whether he won this fight or lost it, he'd still lost this war.

As Richie came in for another punch, Nick swept low, avoiding the hit. He came up on Richie's left and elbowed Richie in the ear. When Richie staggered sideways, Nick shifted his balance to send out a side kick that caught Richie in the ribs. Before he could recover, Nick came in close with four rapid blows in succession. Richie folded to the ground. Nick was about to strike again when something struck him on the back of the head.

Staggering, he went down to his knees.

"I can't let you kill him, Shepherd." Jon jerked his head toward two of his men.

Lester and Cutter lifted Richie up and moved him over to a crate and set him down. Nick couldn't help the whimper that escaped his mouth.

"Well, I must say, this is enjoyable. You really are suffering, aren't you?"

Nick slowly forced himself to look back over at Jon. "You will pay for this."

Jon laughed. "You are amusing. I think I may even miss you." His cell phone rang. He turned and walked a few feet away, answering it.

Nick tuned Jon out as he looked over once again at his daughter's crumpled form. What was he going to tell Jessica? How was he going to live with himself? He felt something touch his hand and then realized that Annie was squeezing it. Whether it was sympathy or fear, he didn't know. It didn't matter. He owed it to her to at least get her out alive. He'd already failed Krystal and her mother.

Annie squeezed his hand again, and he suddenly realized that Jon was talking to him.

"You should have taken me up on my offer, bounty hunter. We could have avoided all of this."

"We could have avoided all this if you weren't a criminal."

Jon laughed as he poked a finger at Nick's wounded shoulder. "I may be a criminal, but you're a dead man."

Nick felt the pain but used it to gain an advantage. He pretended to stagger back from the pain, then came up on the ball of his left foot and spun around, kicking out with his right foot, catching Jon in his chest. Jon's feet came up off the ground by an inch or so as he flew backward and hit the ground. Nick moved forward to deliver another blow. Scott stepped in front of him, pointing his gun into Nick's face. "Don't do it, bounty hunter."

"Why, Scott? Isn't your boss man enough to fight his own battles?"

Jon climbed to his feet, his face red, mouth tight. He pushed Scott out of the way and, drawing back, punched Nick in his wound. This time, it was no act as Nick stepped back, doubling over as he fought not to black out.

Brushing off his suit, Jon stood. "Cutter, kill them all. Then after midnight, dump the bodies in the harbor."

There was a pounding on the door. Jon nodded toward Lester. "Find out who it is."

Lester hurried over and inched the door open. Then he turned to Jon. "Your buyers are here."

"Now?" Jon looked at his watch, then shook his head.

Lester stepped back as four men brushed in, pushing him aside. "Mr. Carver. I'm sorry for this intrusion, but my other business finished early. My trucks are here. Shall we just get this over with?"

"Barlow. I wasn't expecting you until later tonight."

The man shrugged as he handed Jon a briefcase. "Like I said, I finished up early and decided to get my shipment and leave town."

"You were afraid of a setup. I told you to trust me, Barlow."

The man smiled. "Like I said, I'm a very cautious man, Mr. Carver. It's kept me alive a very long time. Shall we proceed?"

Jon seemed to think it over a moment and then nodded. "Fine." Barlow set the briefcase down on a crate and opened it. Jon looked inside, then pulled out several bundles of hundred-dollar bills. Jon flipped through them and then closed them inside the briefcase. "Your merchandise is in those crates. I presume you'd like to check them out before we conclude?"

"You presume correctly."

Nick watched as one of Barlow's men opened several crates. Finally he nodded at Barlow.

Just then, Annie stepped back a few steps and started babbling. Carver looked at her as if she were crazy.

What is she doing?

Barlow raised an eyebrow and then turned to Jon. "If you'll be so kind as to open those bay doors, Mr. Carver, my men will load the crates in my truck and we'll be on our way."

Jon instructed Ira to open the doors, then turned to Cutter. "Take our guests to the back and hold them there until we're finished with our business."

Cutter nodded. "Done."

Cutter motioned for Nick and Annie to move to the back of the room.

Nick slowly made as if trying to stand up, reaching down inside his vest. He eased the knife out of the sheath and stood. Then he reached back and threw the knife toward its target.

Jon's eyes widened in surprise. He grabbed Scott, trying to put the man in front of the knife, but there was no time. The knife caught Jon in the shoulder.

Richie began to come after Nick, but before he could reach him, the warehouse erupted in chaos. Nick looked up to see Conner, Rafe, Steven, and Marti streaming in through the open bay doors. Scott rushed forward and was just as quickly flying backward, hitting the ground after a blow from Conner and sliding a full five feet before stopping. He didn't move.

Nick saw Marti spin around to deliver a roundhouse kick to Richie, who was about to tackle Rafe. Steven came running, plowing into Jon. Barlow headed for the door, only to find Marti aiming a gun at his head, demanding that he hit his knees. He stopped and went down on his knees with his hands behind his head.

Cutter started to move, and Nick headed him off with a blow to his throat. Gagging, Cutter staggered backward a few steps and then came charging back. Nick threw a punch, but Cutter blocked it and hit Nick in the stomach. Hard. Nick stumbled backward into Annie and knocked her down.

"Get behind those crates and stay down," Nick said.

Annie nodded and ran.

Nick moved forward. He and Cutter circled each other. Finally, Nick launched a roundhouse kick that clipped Cutter on the side of the head and sent him spinning backward to the ground. Nick didn't wait. He slammed Cutter with another kick to the side of the head and then one to the ribs. Cutter groaned and rolled over, curling up in a ball. Nick kicked him again, feeling no mercy for the murdering pig.

Conner appeared at Nick's side. "We have them all in cuffs. You want me to call in the authorities?"

Nick shook his head as he wiped blood from his mouth. "They'll be here any minute now. When they come, just raise your hands and make sure your badges are showing."

"Annie?" Nick called out. "You okay?"

"I'm fine," she replied as she stepped out from behind the crates.

"You've done well," he told her.

She nodded absent-mindedly and walked over to Jon. Then Nick saw her pick up a gun and point it at Jon.

"Don't do it, Zeena," Nick said.

"He killed Danny," she replied stiffly. "He killed your daughter. And he tried to kill my sister."

"Because he thought she was you."

Zeena looked up at him, searching his face. Finally her shoulders sagged and her arm dropped. "How did you know?"

"Because Annie has never flirted with me. And she would never pick up a gun," he replied with a smile. "She called the cops when you started jabbering at her, right?"

She nodded.

"Where is she?"

"At the hospital." Zeena pushed her hair back and took off her Bluetooth earpiece, handing it to him.

Nick stuck it up to his ear. "Annie? Good job, girl."

"How did you know?" Zeena asked when he handed her back the Bluetooth.

"I saw the little Bluetooth in your ear. Nice move. Of course, it hurts that you didn't trust me enough to tell me."

She choked out a laugh. "Just figured a little extra insurance wouldn't hurt."

"One more question while I have you here. Who hit me in the warehouse?"

Zeena flinched. "Sorry. That was Charlie. He tends to look out for me."

Suddenly, men in black SWAT gear were swarming in, armed to the teeth.

"Hands up!"

"Don't move. Drop your guns. On the ground. Now!"

Nick shifted, moving in front of Zeena, and raised his hands. "Fugitive recovery agents here! Don't shoot!"

The men nodded at Nick and began arresting the Carvers and their men. Not two minutes later, Baltimore police arrived on the scene and were informed the scene was secured. They looked happy enough to leave everything to the ATF.

Then Nick noticed Cutter walking toward the back of the warehouse, and no one seemed to notice. "Get him. He killed my daughter. He's an escaped convict!"

One of the SWAT men looked over at Nick, ignoring his words as he ripped open crates and began to lift out assault rifles.

Cutter turned and walked back over to Nick, holstering his gun. "Peter Chamberland, ATF."

"You...you killed my little girl. You raped her and then you killed her."

"No sir. I did not. Your daughter is fine." He looked around. "Where is she?"

Zeena pointed to the door. "Marti carried her out of here."

Nick ran out of the building with Chamberland and Zeena on his heels. He found Marti outside in the parking lot, kneeling on the ground with Krystal in her arms.

Marti looked up at them. "She's not dead. What did you give her?"

"Diazepam," Chamberland said. "Not much. Just enough to put her out for a little while."

Chamberland knelt down. "Krystal. Honey? Can you hear me? You can wake up now. Your daddy's here to take you home."

No response. Chamberland tapped her cheek lightly. "Krystal? Wake up now."

Nick almost tripped over his feet to get to his daughter's side. "Wh-what happened? Are you crazy?"

Chamberland didn't even look up at him. "The blood's not real, Mr. Shepherd. I had to convince Richie she was already dead because he wanted me to kill her in front of you. I couldn't let it go that far, and I couldn't take the chance that if I hesitated, he might kill her himself just to torment you." He looked up and met Nick's eyes. "My men were going to come storming in here. I wanted your daughter out of the line of fire. Do you understand?

"Krystal knew what I was doing. I explained it all to her. How she had to play this. That I was going to fire the gun but not hit her. We squirted this bottle of fake blood under her neck."

"Then why isn't she responding? What's wrong with her?" Nick was still finding it hard to believe this guy was telling the truth.

"Relax, bro," Marti interjected. "She's going to be okay."

"I gave her a little knockout drug. Harmless. She understood that I couldn't take a chance on her suddenly getting an itch or a twitch and someone seeing her moving." He tapped Krystal's cheek again. "Krystal?"

And then Nick saw Krystal's eyelashes flutter, and emotion hit him hard enough to hurt. "Krys? Sweetheart? It's Daddy." He reached up and swiped at the tears that spilled down his cheeks. When her lips twitched, he knelt down and pulled her into his arms, grimacing as the effort pulled at his shoulder wound.

Chamberland leaned over his shoulder. "Give her another minute and then try to wake her again. I have some stolen weapons to check on."

Nick saw that Krystal's eyes were open and that she was flexing her fingers. He put his arms around his daughter. "Krystal? Hey, honey."

"D-Daddy?"

"Yeah, baby." He brushed back the hair from her face, gently caressing her forehead. "It's all over."

"Did I do good?"

Nick couldn't stop the little laugh that bubbled up out of him. "Yeah, baby. You did great."

Her lips curved in a little smile. "Can we go home now? I'm hungry."

Nick pulled her up into a hug. "Sure." Then, still holding on to her, he pulled out his cell phone.

"Who are you calling?" Marti asked.

"Jessica."

"She's down the street. In the car."

"What? She was with you?" Nick gave Marti a look of disapproval, then dialed Jessica's number. "Honey? It's over. Yeah. Krystal's fine. Anxious to see you." He handed the phone to Krystal. "Here, talk to your mom for a few minutes." He couldn't believe he had called her "honey," but what was done was done. He just couldn't hide his emotions at this point.

While Krystal talked to her mother, Nick walked over to Chamberland. "Let me get this straight. You broke Richie out of jail, right?"

"Yes. It was the only way we could get close enough to Jon to get to these weapons. I had to make sure Carver never suspected I was anything except a hired hit man. We've been working on getting close to him for two years, trying to get a handle on his operations. When all this came down, it was too important."

"And the two guards that were supposedly killed?"

Chamberland nodded toward two men who were hauling crates. "Alive and well."

"And the buyer, Barlow?"

"One of ours."

Nick shoved his hands in his pockets. "For what it's worth, thank you for taking care of my daughter."

Chamberland nodded, folding his arms across his chest. "She's a little spitfire, that's for sure. More guts than sense. Until she found out who I really was, she was ready to tear me apart." He smiled at the memory. "I'm assuming she gets that from you."

Nick shrugged with a smile. "Feistiness runs in the family. By the way, one of Jon's men—name's Lester—he has a warrant out for his arrest. He's mine."

"I'll make sure that's dealt with." Chamberland looked down at his feet and then back at Nick. "I'm sorry you had to go through this." He put out his hand. "No hard feelings?"

"Now that I know my daughter is fine, no hard feelings." He shook Chamberland's hand. "How soon can I take her home?"

"I'll clear all of you to go. I'm still trying to figure out how your men managed to get through our defenses. My men were all over this area."

Nick shot him a grin. "Professional secret. I could tell you, but then—"

"Yeah, yeah, then you'd have to kill me."

"No, I'd have to hire you."

Chamberland's expression sobered. "We still need to talk about my men. The ones that I assume you have tied up somewhere at your office."

"Oh. Them. Yeah."

"Tonight, take care of your daughter. Tomorrow, we talk about assault on my men."

As Chamberland walked away, a black Town Car pulled up, and the driver opened the rear door. Benedict climbed out, leaning heavily on his cane as he walked over to Nick. "Nicely done, Nick."

"I assume Chamberland is one of yours?"

"He is."

"So you're ATF."

Benedict nodded. "Rumors can occasionally be helpful. The longer people believe I'm a criminal bigwig, the better I can do my job as a federal agent."

"Well, I'm not sure I'm real happy with you using my daughter as bait, but right now, I'd like to concentrate on her."

"We didn't use her as bait, but when Carver brought her in, we couldn't give her back to you without blowing our entire operation. We'd spent too long working on it to blow it this close to the arrest." Benedict looked around, a tiny smile hovering around his mouth. "The Carvers are finally out of business."

"I have one last deal for you, Benedict."

"And what would that be?"

"I won't make noise about the fact that you allowed the abduction of a fifteen-year-old for the sake of an undercover operation. And you won't press charges for the assault and unlawful detainment of two of your men."

Benedict's lips twitched. "Deal."

———— ◦◦◦ ————

Saturday, 5:45 p.m.
Dundalk Marine Terminal, Baltimore

As soon as they were cleared to leave, Nick took Krystal to where Jessica was waiting. His team followed closely behind, leading Lester in cuffs.

Jessica climbed out of the car and ran toward Krystal, sweeping her up into a hug.

Conner pulled out his keys. "Okay, everybody mount up. By the way, Nick, I need to talk to you about something else when we get back to the office."

"No problem." Nick tossed his keys to Marti. "Can you take my SUV back to Prodigal? I'm riding with Jessica and my daughter."

Krystal talked nonstop all the way to Prodigal. By the time they pulled into the parking lot, she had said four times how she and Chamberland had concocted this plan and how important her acting skills had to be. How perfectly she'd played it.

Never mind she'd been asleep through most of it. For some reason, she appeared to have forgotten that little detail.

"Will I see you tomorrow, Dad?" Krystal asked as he climbed out of the car.

Nick leaned over and looked at her in the backseat. "Sure. I'll pick you up around one. How about pizza at Leone's?"

Nick watched the doubt and resignation fill her eyes as she nodded and turned away. She didn't believe him. She figured he'd cancel just as he had a thousand times before.

"Hey, Krys."

She glanced up at him. "Yeah?"

"If I'm not there by ten minutes after one, you have my permission to get a tattoo."

She stared at him and then gave a smile. "See ya tomorrow."

"Yes. You will."

Then he looked over at Jessica. "You're welcome to join us."

She smiled but shook her head. "Not this time. But I'll take a rain check."

"You got it."

21

Saturday, 6:50 p.m.
Prodigal offices, Baltimore

It was nearly seven when Conner finally made it back to the office. Marti was in the kitchen, making a pot of coffee.

"Took you long enough," Marti quipped.

"I dropped Zeena off at the hospital. How long before the coffee is done?"

"Just a couple more minutes," Marti told him. "I thought you were going to turn Zeena in."

"Nick is going to take her in tomorrow with Kline and bail her right back out. She didn't miss her court date because she was trying to avoid it. She was just trying to stay alive."

"Good. I'm glad."

"Where is Nick?"

"He was out of Excedrin, so he and Steven just ran down to the drugstore. They'll be right back. And they're bringing dinner back. Ribs from Smokin' Joe's." She wiggled her eyebrows with obvious delight.

"Sweet." Conner turned and went back to Nick's office to wait for his boss and to think.

He couldn't shake the suspicion that someone tipped Carver off about his job at the bar. And someone questioned Annie, pretending to be one of them. And the brick through the window? Not Carver's style. And Nick said he knew someone was going to be letting Jon know that Nick was on his way to the warehouse. And that meant Carver had an inside source.

When Marti appeared and set a cup of coffee down in front of him, he said, "Thanks. Can we talk?"

"Sure."

Marti curled up in the corner of the sofa as Conner launched into his questions. "Do you get the feeling that Jon Carver knew far more than he should have?"

"I was just asking myself the same questions." Marti's foot started rocking. "Last night, when I was going through the files, I found something. I didn't think much of it at first, but the more I thought about it, the more uncomfortable I got. "

"What was it, Marti?" Conner leaned forward.

"Not yet, Marti." Nick walked in, his arms full of bags and Styrofoam containers. He set them down on his desk. "And I will handle this. Not you."

"No way. We do this together," Marti stated emphatically.

Conner opened one of the containers and inhaled deeply. "Okay, what's going on? Why am I out of this loop?"

Nick ignored the question, and next thing Conner knew, Nick's desk phone was on speaker. While it was dialing, Nick fired up his computer.

Rafe answered. "I'm here."

"Where is he?"

"At the Blue Star Motel on 40."

"Has he made any calls?"

"A couple. The airlines about flights out later tonight and a call to Carver's cell twice, then Carver's office."

"Keep an eye on him. I'm on my way." Nick reached over and disconnected the call.

"Okay, Nick. Give us the juice," Conner said, lifting a rib out of the container and starting to chew into it.

"I had Rafe put a tracker on his car when I started getting suspicious." He quickly wrote an e-mail and then signed off. He grabbed his jacket and stood up. "I'll be back in a bit. Enjoy your dinner, and save some ribs for me."

"We're going with you," Marti said. "I'm not going to miss this."

"Me either," Conner added, lumbering to his feet.

"It just isn't necessary, guys. I don't need this many people to confront one."

"What you need and what you're getting are two different things." Marti linked her arm in his and walked out with him.

Steven was coming through the door with more containers. "Where's everyone going?"

"After a traitor," Marti told him. "Bring the food."

Saturday, 8:20 p.m.
Route 40, Baltimore

Traffic was light, but it still took almost forty minutes to get to the motel. The Blue Star was a leftover from the sixties and didn't look like much had been done to it since. It had once been painted white with hurt-your-eyes blue and pink trim that might pass in Miami but was completely out of place on a commercial strip on the outskirts of Baltimore.

When Nick pulled in, he saw Rafe outside the office, leaning against his car. Nick drove over in Rafe's direction and parked.

"What's going on?" he asked as he climbed out of his SUV.

"He's hiding up in room 203." Rafe touched Nick on the arm. "He is a frightened animal. Be careful."

"I know." Nick glanced up at the room doors and then over at Rafe. "I called for backup. When they get here, send them up."

Rafe looked disappointed that he was being left behind, but he nodded.

Marti ran up the stairs ahead of them. "Let me knock. Please let me."

Nick rolled his eyes. "Fine."

She walked up to the door of 203 and knocked. "It's Marti. Open up. I need to talk to you."

There was only silence. And then the door cracked open. "What are you doing here?"

"Let me in. We need to talk."

"You alone?"

"No." She pushed at the door. "Conner, Steven, and Nick are standing here. Let us in."

The door closed, and they heard the chain rattle. Then the door opened wide. Marti went in first, followed by the men.

The room wasn't in much better shape than the outside. It had dingy walls, faded curtains, cracks in the walls, and a bed that sagged in the middle. Nick saw Conner shut the door and lean against it, his arms folded across his chest.

"How did you know?" Michael said.

"We didn't," Nick admitted. "Not for sure anyway. Until the brick incident. When I ran it past you, you wouldn't meet my eyes. That's when I knew for sure."

"I knew when I bought this." Marti pulled the Rolex watch out of her pocket. "You paid those old men to burn down our building. You are such a lowlife."

Michael stared at the watch and then dropped his eyes, his mouth tight. "I should have known they wouldn't do what they were told to do."

Nick took the watch from Marti, examined it, and then tossed it at his former friend. "So, tell me why, Michael."

Michael let the watch hit the bed and the fall to the floor. He didn't bother to pick it up. "You don't understand, Nick. It wasn't supposed to end up like this, but you get into them for a little bit and before long, they own you." Michael's head dropped. "I needed money. I had been gambling a bit here and there in Atlantic City, and I got in a little too deep. They offered me a deal to make the debts go away. I just had to launder their money through the bank. And to complete the deal with Carver, I needed you to comply with his deal, so…I guess…I tried to scare you into it."

Conner made a disgusted groan, then spoke up from behind Nick. "So what'd you do with Nick's loan papers? Did you bury them?"

Michael slowly lifted his face, wiping at his mouth. "Yeah, I buried them. I had to. They threatened my family if I didn't."

"Oh, the same family you're ready to leave high and dry today? Find a good flight, Michael?" Marti's voice was full of contempt.

Michael's face had gone completely blank, as if he had nothing left inside to muster. "You don't understand. Carver can't let me live. The Feds will tear his operation apart. They'll want me to testify. He'll kill me before he allows that."

"You should have thought of that before," Nick said.

"And Carver's in jail," Conner added.

"Yeah," Michael said. "Until he gets bail. And even if he stays in jail, he'll get the word out."

Nick shoved his hands deep into his pockets to keep from punching Michael. "You have put me and my family through hell. You put my daughter in danger. You risked my life and the lives of my team. All so you can pay your gambling debts? So you can live in that big house and play the big shot?" Nick shook his head. "You come around, acting like my friend, and then run to Carver and tell him every move I'm making."

"He promised he wasn't going to hurt you or Krystal."

"And you believed him?" Conner laughed. "Even after Nick was shot?"

"Please, Nick. We've been best friends for as long as I can remember. You have to believe me. I didn't mean for any of this to happen. I was just desperate."

Marti walked over and opened one of the suitcases. It was full of cash. "Desperate. I can see that."

"That's mine. I earned it."

"You are pitiful, Michael."

"Did you come to arrest me or what?" He was practically whining now. Nick could hardly look at him.

Conner shook his head. "We don't have that authority, and you know it. We just came to get answers."

"Oh, please. I know that the Feds are right behind you!" Michael's tone was frenzied. He jumped up, grabbed Marti, and pulled a gun out of his pocket, holding it to her head. "Drop your guns, both of you."

Nick and Conner pulled out their weapons and dropped them to the floor. "Don't do this," Nick said. "You're only making things worse."

Michael's eyes were darting left and right. But Nick kept looking at Marti, her eyes locked on his, as if she was trying to communicate something.

Conner went on trying to distract Michael. "We can't arrest you, Michael. There's no reason for any of this. You can just walk out of here. You don't have to hurt Marti."

Nick kept watching Marti, trying to figure out what she was telling him with her eyes. She was planning something.

Nick put his arms out. "Michael. We've been friends forever. If the Feds get you, they'll have to do it without my help." He eased forward a step, hoping Michael didn't notice.

Michael choked out a broken laugh. "Mister Justice and Right? You'd be the first one to call them, Nick. No way could you let me walk away free and clear. Wouldn't sit right with those morals of yours." With one arm still wrapped around Marti, Michael waved his gun. "You wouldn't—"

Marti moved so fast that even Nick wasn't ready for it. Whirling around, she brought her hand up, chopping Michael across the throat. His gun dropped as he reached for his throat with both hands. With an upward thrust of her palm, she hit him in the nose. Nick heard the crunch of bone and cartilage.

Howling, Michael doubled over. Marti stepped back, ready to strike again, but Conner had already scooped up his gun and held it with both hands, pointed just two feet from Michael's face.

Nick reached down and picked up his Glock. "Steven? See if Linc is here. If he is, tell him to come get this piece of trash."

22

Four months later

The boy ran faster, desperate now to reach his father. No matter how hard he ran, he couldn't seem to close the distance. As he continued to scream out for his dad, he began to cry. Still, the man never turned around. Never acknowledged him.

The man could feel the boy's anguish. His desperation. His fear of being left alone and abandoned. His breathing became as labored as the boy's. His heart pounded just as hard. Clenching his fists, he fought to run as the boy ran, urging the boy to run faster, yell louder, to not give up, to not give up. *Keep going!*

And then the man stopped and cocked his head, as if listening for something. Once again the boy screamed out, "Daddy! I'm here! Daddy!"

Slowly, the man turned and waited as the boy covered the distance between them. Finally, the boy collapsed at the man's feet, lifting his face to look up at the man through his tears. "Daddy?"

The man looked sad as he gently lifted the child into his arms. "I've missed you, my child."

"I'm sorry, Daddy. I just got lost for a little while."

Saturday, 7:15 a.m.
Towson, Maryland

Nick awoke with a start, sitting straight up in bed. Taking a deep breath, he looked over at the alarm clock, then collapsed back into the pillow. The dream had seemed so real. But the man he called Daddy wasn't the man who raised him.

But he knew who it was.

With a smile, he rolled out of bed. Today, he couldn't be late.

———❧———

Saturday, 10:30 a.m.
Towson, Maryland

Nick straightened his tie and buttoned his suit coat. He hated wearing ties, but today was special. Fingering his hair in place one last time, he nodded in satisfaction, then picked up his keys and walked outside.

A tow truck was just backing up in his driveway with a '75 Corvette on the flatbed. Curious, Nick walked over as the driver emerged from the cab of the truck. "You Mr. Nick Shepherd?"

"Yes. What's going on?"

The driver handed him a padded envelope. "Was just paid to deliver this and the car. Where do you want me to drop it?"

"Right there is fine," Nick replied as he opened the envelope. Inside, he found car keys, the title, and a letter. He opened the letter.

Dear Nick,

I'm sorry I turned you away when you came to check on

me and the children, but all this has been so difficult. I still don't understand how Michael could have done this to any of us. The other Corvette was confiscated, but since I could prove I bought this one for Michael with part of my inheritance from my grandmother, they left it with me. And I want you to have it. By the time you get this, the children and I will have left for New Hampshire. I'm going to stay with my parents until I get back on my feet. You're a good man, Nick. Don't ever change.

    Megan O'Shea

Nick tipped the driver and pocketed the Corvette keys. His heart broke for Megan. Nick looked over at the car. He wasn't sure what he'd do with it. Driving it would feel as though, somehow, Michael was making restitution. But nothing could have been further from the truth.

He glanced at his watch and chided himself. He was going to be late if he didn't hurry.

Half an hour later, he picked up his mother at the nursing home. A male nurse was waiting with her. She was all dressed up in a flowered dress that Marti had bought for her. When he pulled up to the curb, he got out and helped the nurse transfer her from the wheelchair to the SUV. She slapped at their hands. "I can walk, you know."

Nick and the nurse shared a smile and let her fasten her own seat belt.

All the way to the church, she was like a little girl at Christmas, bright-eyed with wonder as she sat in the front seat of his SUV and chatted away, sometimes knowing who he was, sometimes referring to him as Ros. It didn't matter to him at all.

She might not always know that he was her son, but he always knew she was his mother.

When they arrived at the church, he walked slowly with her, letting her lean on his arm. They found Marti, Steven, and Krystal waiting just inside the doors for them.

"You're late," Marti chided. "The service is about to start."

"I'll explain later." And just that quickly, he knew what he was going to do with the Corvette. He knew his sister would love it.

In spite of her constant hints at leaving again, Marti had stayed with them. She signed the papers, although it turned out they didn't need to use their assets. The bank had quickly given Nick a line of credit to satisfy the Department of Criminal Justice. Nick had an idea that Linc had explained what Michael had done, and they wanted to cut off any lawsuits before they got filed. Not that Nick was thinking that way, but the bank wasn't taking any chances.

And that made Nick think of Annie and Zeena. Annie was doing well, back working as a chef, and spending time getting to know her nephew. Zeena had turned herself in to Nick as promised, and he had Kline bail her right back out as promised. As soon as Annie had her surgery, Zeena went into rehab and was determined to turn her life around. Nick wished her well.

While Marti and Steven settled their mother in a pew, Nick made his way down to the front of the church. The pastor met him there.

"You ready?"

"I am now."

With a nod and a smile, the pastor turned and nodded toward the back of the church. Nick barely noticed the organ music when it started. His attention was on his daughter as she made her way down the aisle, dressed in a yellow gown and carrying a bouquet. It was like a punch to his gut to see her like this: so beautiful, so full of promise, so close to being the woman she was meant to be.

Then the music grew more dramatic, and Jessica stepped into view. She looked like something from a dream he had once. He didn't even know the color or shape of her dress. All he could see were her eyes, bright with tears and love, just the way they were the first time he'd married her, but this time, there was something else there as well. The understanding that this wasn't a fairy tale. It was real life, with all the problems, joys, pains, and laughter that real people experience every day.

He wasn't sure how it had happened. Somewhere in the midst of trying to rebuild his relationship with his daughter, he'd found himself building a bridge back to the only woman he'd ever loved.

When she stepped up next to him, Nick reached out and took her hand. She tilted her head to look up at him and then whispered, "I love you."

Good news—I have my family back.

Last Will and Testament
for Roswell Shepherd

— ⋅◦═◦⋅ —

To my firstborn, Nickolas Samuel Shepherd: I leave my
Glock—use it with wisdom and mercy. I leave my grandfather's pocket watch—redeem your time wisely. And I
leave one-third of Prodigal Fugitive Recovery—may you
continue to be the leader you were born to be. I leave in
your care your mother, your younger siblings, and the
family business. I know you'll serve them all to the best
of your ability.

To my son Steven James Shepherd: I leave my Mustang—
you always did feel more comfortable in the fast lane. I
leave my war medal—never forget what really matters in
life: honor, justice, and mercy. And I leave you one-third
of Prodigal Fugitive Recovery Agency—use all your talents
to make the lives around you easier, fuller, and richer. You
have the ability; don't waste it.

Acknowledgments

My heartfelt thanks to my editor, Shannon Hill Marchese, who believed in this project; my agent, Greg Johnson; Nicci Jordan Hubert and the wonderful people at WaterBrook who put as much effort into this book as I did.

A huge thank-you to Melissa Backus of Backus Bail Bonds, Winchester, VA; J.T. Fugitive Recovery Agent, Baltimore, MD; Scott Harrell of CompassPoint Investigations; Aileen Ferguson of Hargett Farms; Author Robin Caroll; and Jennifer Peterson of Ms. MS for their invaluable help.

And to the residents of Baltimore—I hope you'll forgive me for moving a few things around and changing the names of some of the streets for the sake of the story. I'm proud to be your neighbor.

And last, but certainly not least, a special thank-you to all my readers who have waited so patiently for this novel; the incredible family and friends at ChiLibris, ACFW, CCWC; and in particular, my daughter, Jayme.

An Excerpt from

Shepherd's Run

Prodigal Recovery Agency:
Book Two

Prologue

I am not selling stolen guns! This is all a big mistake." Andrea Morrow twisted her hands in her lap, hoping the two men across the scarred table would believe her. The alternative was unthinkable.

"Miss Morrow, you were recorded taking a briefcase full of money from known gun dealers and giving them the keys to a storage unit that contained a large quantity of stolen weapons. Now, what part of that recording is false?"

She looked up at Agent Chamberland, or the Ice Man, as she was starting to think of him, with his white blond hair and cool blue eyes. He never showed any emotion at all—just stared at her with those pale-as-glass eyes as if he could see straight through her.

"All of it," she insisted. "Maybe that's what you see, but there's an explanation. I didn't know what was in that storage unit. I *swear*."

Agent Chamberland strolled over, pulled out a chair, spun it around, and straddled it. She couldn't avoid grimacing at the cop cliché. "You're a kindergarten teacher, is that right?"

"Yes," she said, leaning forward. "At Midway Elementary. I've been there five years."

She a ran a finger over a deep scratch in the Formica tabletop and thought about the small tables, perfect for six-year-olds, in her bright classroom. Would everything she worked for crumble into dust? It made her want to scream. If they'd just check her story out, everything would be okay.

"And your boyfriend called you and asked you to do him a favor?"

She nodded at Chamberland. "We were supposed to have dinner. I was home when he called and said he had to work late." She pushed her hair behind her ears. "Look, I've explained this at least twenty times already. Why don't you just call Paul and have him tell you what happened?"

"We've tried to call him, Miss Morrow." Chamberland scratched his chin with his thumb. "The number you gave us went to a prepaid cell phone. No one is answering it, and we can't trace it. We went to the address you gave as his employment. There is no such company as Forton and Conrad in that building, and no Paul Roush works for *any* company in that building. So let's try this again."

None of that made sense to her. She knew he was there. "Paul asked me to come by his office and pick up a set of keys to give his friend. He met me out in front of the building. Please go ask around again. Maybe you just missed him the first time."

"Do you have a picture of Paul?" the other agent asked.

She thought for a moment. "No. We haven't been dating that long. I can't think of any pictures he'd be in. Maybe one of the people at the party where we met might know him well enough to have a picture."

"That's convenient. Another rabbit trail." Chamberland leaned forward, and if his eyes were cold enough to freeze water before, they could give her frostbite now. "I'm getting a little tired of the dead ends, Miss Morrow. As we can't find any legitimate information on a Paul Roush matching your details, I suggest you start telling us the truth."

Andrea stared at the two agents, and her heart sank. Realization began to emerge through the confusion and the fear. She had only met Paul six weeks ago. How well did she really know him? He said he worked at 4375 North Seventh, and she'd picked him up in front of the building once, when his car broke down. She never questioned the veracity of anything he'd told her. Why would she? He was nice looking, funny, thoughtful in ways a lot of men weren't, and had never pressured her for more than she was willing to give. He claimed he had been swept away the first time he saw her. If he lied about where he worked, what else was a lie? Was it all a lie?

She looked up at Chamberland as the tears welled up in her eyes. "I've been set up, haven't I?"

Prodigal Recovery," Steven Shepherd said, slapping the paperwork for Jimmy Turner down on the counter in front of an officer. "Bringing in a prisoner."

The officer took the paperwork and began to page through it. "Magistrate is running late. I'll have an officer take him down to lockup until we're ready."

Steven wasn't surprised. This was Baltimore, after all. In some counties, he could get a guy turned in and get out in under an hour, but Baltimore was a whole different world. His record for the shortest time handing over a fugitive in Baltimore was a shade over two hours, the longest just shy of four hours. Steven wished he had brought a book. His brother, Nick, would be horrified by the thought of Steven's nose shoved in an economics book while he waited for a skip to be processed. He'd carry on about the agency reputation; what would the cops think about the Prodigal Recovery Agency and those Shepherd boys?

The desk officer stood up and stretched, looking over at the leash Steven held, then down at his dog. "You can't have him in here."

"Know somewhere I can leave him?"

The officer tilted his head in disbelief. Steven shrugged. "I know, I know—but my ride just left and I'm stuck."

"Not my problem, Shepherd. Get the dog out of here."

Steven handed Jimmy over to a guard and walked Killer outside.

"What am I going to do with you?"

If Connor hadn't had to run off to help Nick, Steven wouldn't be in this situation. Killer would have been fine to hang out in the car. Having him around for the ride made chasing a fugitive more palatable.

The dog yipped and jumped up on Steven's leg. Leaning down, Steven picked him up. "Cut that out. No licking. My reputation is taking one already, you being here."

He was mulling over his choices when he heard a familiar voice behind him. "You guys at Prodigal don't have anything better to do than hang around here like it's a dog park?"

Steven turned to face ATF Agent Peter Chamberland. "What are you doing here in the trenches? I figured you'd be briefing the president on your outstanding job with Carver by now."

Chamberland's lips curled in what could only be identified as an amused smile. "Cute." He reached over and scratched the dog behind his ears. "And I'm not surprised Nick demoted you to dogcatcher."

"Seriously, Baltimore is a little out of your usual stomping grounds, isn't it?"

"We go anywhere, anytime." Chamberland glanced around. "Why are you standing out here? I was inside, getting a drink, saw you down the hall, so I followed you out. Haven't talked to you or Nick in a while."

"I just turned in a fugitive, but they made me take Killer here out of the building."

"Killer?" Chamberland smiled with near-warmth as he scratched at the bichon's chin. Then he glanced over at the Expedition parked at the curb and jerked his head. In response, a young man climbed out from behind the wheel and hurried over.

"Sir?"

"Watch this dog. Mr. Shepherd and I need to talk."

The young agent stared up at Chamberland as if he couldn't quite wrap his mind around the fact that he'd just gone from ATF agent to dog-sitter.

"You have a problem following orders, Nebel?"

"No sir."

Steven set the dog down and handed Agent Nebel the leash. "Be careful. He thinks he's a Rottweiler."

The agent shot Steven a look, then walked Killer down the street.

Chamberland led Steven back into the building. "We've been tracking shipments of guns coming in from South America. We know that at least three shipments have come in through the Baltimore ports. If we know of three, there are more."

Steven glanced up as two young men, handcuffed and cursing, were led into the fingerprint room. "What does this have to do with me?"

"We set up a sting today and caught some of those involved."

"But not the ringleader?"

Chamberland frowned and shifted his gaze to look down the hall. "I wish. I think he suspected we were on to him." Chamberland turned back to Steven. "We caught one young woman we think was being used."

"By?"

"We don't know for sure. Either the group leader or one of his men. She claims she was just asked by her boyfriend to drop off keys and got swept up in all this. Thing is—we can't find any trace of this so-called boyfriend."

Steven stopped at the vending machines and fished down in his pockets for a wad of singles. Chamberland waved him off. "It's on me."

"You're making me nervous, being so nice."

Chamberland didn't smile as he fed a couple of singles into the machine and punched his selection, then nodded for Steven to make his choice. "I don't know whether she's an innocent being framed or just a very good actress."

"So what does this have to do with me?" Steven selected a water and dug it out of the shoot.

"My gut tells me she's innocent. If she is, she's going to need some friends on her side. All her family is on the West coast. I just figured you could bail her out. Help her get an attorney. That sort of thing."

Steven tipped his head back and drank some of the water, taking his time while he weighed Chamberland's words. After the way the ATF agent handled Krystal's abduction last spring, Steven wasn't inclined to trust him. "Just playing good Samaritan, is that it?"

"Not exactly, but I don't want to see an innocent kindergarten teacher go to prison simply because she didn't have good taste in men."

Steven studied the man for a few minutes. Those pale blue eyes gave away nothing. Or maybe there was nothing to find. He had a hard time telling the difference. Give him a company's yearly report and he'd have it dissected in minutes, but people weren't nearly as easy to understand as numbers.

"Well, it won't hurt anything to at least talk to her. Where is she?" Steven twisted the cap on his water.

"Follow me."

Chamberland led him to a room where she sat at a table, her hands in her lap, her light brown hair tousled from hours of running her hands through it, her makeup smeared from crying, and her nose red from the rough, low-grade tissues. When she lifted her head and looked Steven in the eyes, he felt a jolt strong enough to make him want to punch Chamberland in the face.

Instead, Steven grabbed the agent by the arm and pulled him out of the interrogation room. "This is a joke, right?"

"What are you talking about?"

"That woman is as involved in criminal activities as I am!"

Chamberland looked amused as he folded his arms across his chest. "And you know that from what? Two seconds of evaluation? Wow, Shepherd…I want you on my team. We could cut interrogations down to minutes instead of hours."

"How could you even arrest her?" Steven wanted to step back into that room, wrap his arms around her, and assure her it was all over, that it would be okay. He didn't have much respect for Chamberland before. He had even less now.

"We have the evidence. Cut the hero act or help her out."

"If you know she was framed, why are you even bothering to charge her? Why not just cut her loose?"

"I repeat, I have the evidence. But I asked you to help her, didn't I? I could have just tossed her into the system and let it eat her alive."

"Yeah, yeah. You're just a peach of a guy." For once, Steven wished Nick were around to handle this. While Steven knew something didn't feel right, Nick would have known exactly how to cut through Chamberland's apparent benevolence and get to the truth. But Nick wasn't there, and it was up to Steven to deal for now and pray Chamberland wasn't setting him up down the road. He pulled out his cell phone, scrolled through the address book, and dialed a number. "Liz? I need a favor."